THE SILVER HORN ECHOES

A Song of Roland

Michael Eging
and
Steve Arnold

THE SILVER HORN ECHOES
A SONG OF ROLAND

iUniverse books may be ordered through booksellers or by contacting:

iUniverse
1663 Liberty Drive
Bloomington, IN 47403
www.iuniverse.com
1-800-Authors (1-800-288-4677)

Because of the dynamic nature of the Internet, any web addresses or links contained in
this book may have changed since publication and may no longer be valid. The views
expressed in this work are solely those of the author and do not necessarily reflect the
views of the publisher, and the publisher hereby disclaims any responsibility for them.

ISBN: 978-1-5320-2020-9 (sc)
ISBN: 978-1-5320-2021-6 (hc)
ISBN: 978-1-5320-2022-3 (e)

Library of Congress Control Number: 2017908429

Print information available on the last page.

iUniverse rev. date: 07/22/2017

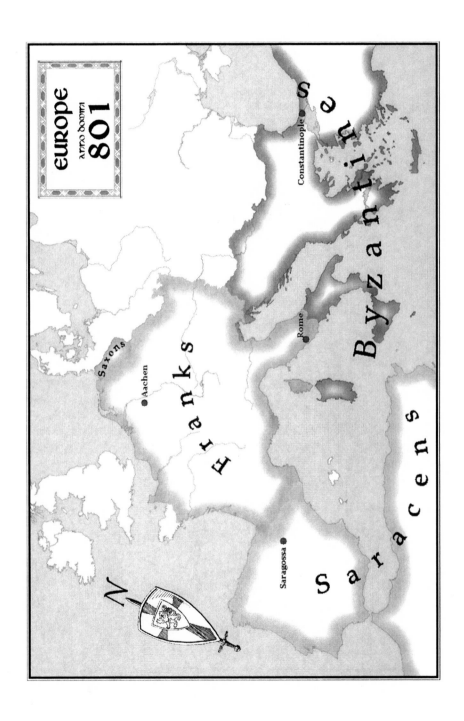

europe
ANNO DOMINI
801

Saxons

Franks

• Aachen

Byzantine

S

• Constantinople

• Rome

Saracens

• Saragossa

N

P R O L O G U E

The Bastard of Normandy

Southern Coast of Britain
October 1066

Single-masted ships crowded the gray waters of Pevensey Bay, spilling the implements of war from their bellies onto the beach in a steady stream. Under the leaden sky, men, horses, and equipment surged through the swells of waves to track up the muddied rise onto the plain. William, duke of Normandy, known best to these men as their Young Bastard, scanned the flow of men and material to the blossoming camp with fierce gray eyes. Among the Normans, he was a tall man who stood with a confident martial bearing and yet bore an unpretentious appearance, clad in the worn and proven harness of a soldier—mail coat, plain helm, and a utilitarian sword belted to his side. His mud-colored hair was, like the meanest of his troops, trimmed tightly, as was the close-cropped beard shadowing his strong jaw. He glanced up at the autumn sky threatening rain and pulled his cloak tighter about his broad shoulders. A curse slipped from his lips. In his many hard-fought years, he had experienced few divine graces to inspire him to proffer words to the God who had cursed him from birth for his father's sins. Such words would never move the heavens anyway, he reckoned. Even now drops of rain fell to the ground, ensuring the army's progress would soon be mired in slop.

A grim smile touched his lips when he turned toward the encampment, which was bristling with steel and sinew. Soldiers struggled under the weight of sharpened logs that they carried from the forest then planted in mounds of earth to form a crude wall—nothing elaborate as the stone ramparts of Normandy, but serviceable enough and quickly made. Others bent their backs to dig a trench before those walls, stiffening the fortifications against the inevitable assault by William's own cousin Harold Godwinson and his Saxon curs, who were even then on their way south from a narrow victory at Stamford Bridge over Harold's brother Tostig and the Hardrada, Tostig's patron and king of the Norse.

Yes, Harold, we will be prepared for your assault, the duke mused. *You will not drive us back to the sea.*

He mingled with the men slogging up the slope. Just behind him, his young squire struggled to bear the ducal banner, occasionally having to use the flagstaff for a walking stick through the slick mud. On the duke's other side stood the gaunt figure of Aimeri, viscount of Thouars, protected from the weather by a thick cloak and trousers. He was a lean and unpredictable killer who carried himself with an air of strained control that motivated the youth to struggle all the more to keep the pennant and his feet moving toward the camp.

"Keep that out of the muck, you whelp!" Aimeri growled, swinging a boot at him and flicking mud across the youth's pockmarked face.

The lad attempted a half bow and nearly slipped.

"No sense scaring the lad witless," William observed. He turned to the boy. "Hurry on there. Stow that in my tent. Then see to the preparations for the council."

A look of relief eased the youth's muddied face. He rolled up the pennant, tucked it under his arm, and, in a squishing walk-run, awkwardly dodged through the traffic toward the center of camp.

"You're too easy on the boy," Aimeri muttered. "One day he'll thank you for a cuff on the ear before battle. He'll be grateful for you toughening him up."

A wolf's grin touched William's lips. "First we finish this scrape. Then we'll talk about toughening him up. I'm sure his father will appreciate if we return his eldest son to him whole."

Aimeri snorted, and a trooper coaxing along a reluctant warhorse glanced their way at the sound. "What are you on about?" Aimeri said curtly, startling the animal. "Git up there and make sure you get that rust off your hauberk. You'll want the sparkle for the Saxons when they arrive!"

William sidestepped the spooked horse, his steps sure from spending his life on campaign. He kicked along a clot of miry earth.

"And when they do arrive," the duke said, "I want to hit them before they have time to breathe. Hardrada softened them up for us, and I don't want to waste the opportunity to take Harold's head."

They made their way through the cantonment as the men pitched tents, stowed gear, and began foraging to keep the army warm against the chill autumn rain. Smoke from sputtering fires drifted through the air, and William took in a deep breath with relish.

This is where men sort out their differences, he thought, *in the field looking the enemy in the eyes. Not behind veils and masks, dressed in fine hose and vests, hoping to conceal their intent by perfumed smiles and droning banter. Yes, Harold, your sweet words of disinterest in the throne will bite you in the arse if I don't take your head from your shoulders first.*

A rider outfitted in the lightweight garb of a forward scout trotted against the tide of men. He sighted the duke, rode closer, dismounted, and came to a knee in the mud.

"Simon. What word?" William asked.

Simon hesitated, and William knew the man's news was not what he wanted to hear.

"Speak, man! I'll have it now, not cosseted away in my tent!"

"My lord, the usurper … his armies approach."

Aimeri raised a hand to cuff the messenger, but William caught his wrist, stopping him short.

"But it's a lie!" Aimeri hissed. "Godwinson couldn't march his men from the north that fast. Not after the mauling they took from the Northmen."

Simon continued. "'Tis no lie, honored lord. I saw their fires with my own eyes. He's come with his host and his personal guard of housecarls at the center."

He pointed past the ridge of hills toward the plain. "There!"

William spun on his heels and called for his horse.

The Saxon camps clung to the muddy hillsides, their distant bustle of rounded helms glimmering in the gray light like steely flies on a manure pile. From a sheltered perch atop a wooded knoll, William gauged the flood of troops streaming up the road.

"Damn. Damn him to hell," he muttered. "How did he march them the length of England so quickly? Fulford is ten days from here!"

Aimeri shook his head. "Possessed devils. We'd heard they were days, if not weeks, behind our landing."

William squinted and began counting men and animals milling about in the enemy camp. The early arrival of Harold's force created a wrinkle in his plans. The battle at Stamford Bridge had pitted two armies in a bitter struggle to see who would face the Normans for final control of Britain. William had heard the Saxons, though victorious, had been forced to lick heavy wounds on the push south to meet him. They should have been days away, and yet here they were. The housecarls, Harold's elite bodyguard, moved about the center of the Saxon camp with a martial efficiency that easily matched that of William's own Norman knights.

"My lord," Aimeri said urgently. "We must move along. Your cousin won't allow us to remain here for long." In fact a squad of Saxon infantry even now peeled from the distant host to approach their position.

William nodded curtly, remounted his horse, and led his companions back to the Norman lines.

Nobles crowded the table in the center of the hastily erected fortifications. An impatient William stalked in and took his place at the table's head. Aimeri dominated the shadows behind him, a wraith of death that silenced the quick-witted among them with a glance, who then in turn hurriedly shushed their less attentive fellows.

William tossed a scrap of carefully lettered vellum that bore bits of Harold Godwinson's wax seal onto the map spread across the table.

"He taunts us, this self-styled king. He taunts us, but that shall soon come to an end!"

"My lord," offered Roger of Mortimer, bushy brows over intelligent eyes framed by short-cropped hair. "Meeting us here, before we can consolidate, is a feat of logistics."

"But can he make them fight if they're dropping from exhaustion?" William placed his hands flat on the map. "Then this plain called Hastings will be the final killing field. This will decide the issue. Once we have beaten Harold, the earls will flock to our banner as we march on London."

"As you say," Roger said, bowing his head. "But if we are to strike, we must make it soon so he cannot rest those troops from their miraculous march."

"Yes," William agreed. "We must grind them now. Then the earls will break."

As the gloomy day deepened into evening, campfires sputtered from sodden fuel. Amid the flickering light and vaporous smoke, knights checked harnesses and weapons, sergeants inspected hauberks and helmets, and squires repaired worn gear. Those who had finished their labors stood in lines for one last hot meal on the eve of battle.

William drifted through the camp, his eyes keen on the tasks and his ears open to the tenor of the men who would soon battle and die in his name. Five paces behind him, close enough to be at hand while distant enough to be innocuous, his young squire trotted in similar plain garb. As he wandered the camp, the duke witnessed the campfires become smoldering hotbeds for gossip of the Saxon usurper Harold and his vaunted housecarls. Rumors of the victory over Tostig and Hardrada, the Norse king, grew with each telling from mouth to ear, from fireside to bedroll, throughout the camp as the men recounted what they knew and embellished what they didn't.

"Possessed," a foot soldier whispered. "The demon Saxon slew the reaver king Hardrada with his own bow—an arrow right through his eye!"

The men around him murmured.

"I remember when he was at court," said a sergeant, looking up from oiling his sword with a rag. "Giant, he was—his arms as thick as my waist. When at sport, he put men down and snapped their backs ..."

A younger man fitting woolen padding to his helmet ventured to speak up. "I hear his housecarls drink the blood of the fallen in some unholy ritual! And they bear Norse axes with runes on them. Marks that ensure if a man is nicked by one—why, he will bleed to death!"

A grizzled veteran grumbled, "Harold is but a man. The Saxon buggers will run sure enough when we sweep the field with horse. They'll run, I bet my own mother on it."

The first soldier, undaunted by the other, whispered conspiratorially. "He used the magic of Albion, I've heard, to transport his army so quickly from the bloody bridge. And I heard that he took Hardrada's head with his own ax and stowed it in a faery bag as payment for the trick!"

The younger soldier nodded in all seriousness. "I reckon he spirited his army on the backs of swamp bats." But pride in his contribution to the conversation was cut short when William stepped from the shadows, pushing back the cowl on his cloak.

"Horse shite," the duke spat. "You'll find them men when you meet on the field. And what are you? A pack of cowering curs?"

The men tumbled to their knees, heads lowered beneath the indignation of their liege lord.

"By God, get off the ground! You look like groveling worms! Norman blood flows in your veins! Don't dishonor it. Let it burn within you!"

Before the men could stammer a reply, William whirled around and stalked away, his cloak lashing at shadows.

Between campfires, the squire ventured close. "My lord," he said, "the whole camp whispers of Harold. The Norse king's blood is barely cold, yet there he stands with his whole Saxon army." His face belied the dismay that he strained to keep from his voice.

William paused, his face consumed by the very shadows that raged through the hearts of his men. "It's not devilry, sorcery, or witchcraft. He is a soldier who demands much of his men. Nothing more!"

"Yes, my lord. But the men see the fires extend from horizon to horizon."

William gritted his teeth. "You speak well beyond your years," he said grimly. "But they can spread from here to Rome for all I care. It changes nothing. But I've a thought. Yes, I've a thought indeed."

Joachim, the lanky minstrel, roared with laughter as the stocky veteran pulled a dagger from his belt and tossed it into the pile of bets. "You'd risk that? Your last kiss if all else fails on the battlefield?" he asked. His blue eyes were keen as he mentally tallied the pile of weapons and heirlooms that rode on one final roll of the dice in his fingers. He shook them. The rattle was reassuring, for luck was on his side.

"I'll take my chances with our Bastard," the soldier said, wiping a sweaty hand on his dirty tunic. "Harold may be a trickster, but his fortunes just hit a Norman wall."

"Then we'll roll on this …" Joachim tossed the knucklebones and watched them bounce before settling.

"And you keep your fine weapon for another day!" The tall dandy laughed and grabbed a wineskin. "Win or lose, when the earls come howling for your head, you'll have her right at your side!"

William stepped forward from behind Joachim. The men around the bard scrambled to take a knee. The duke reached out a hand to the minstrel's shoulder when he rose with a start.

"Lord William," Joachim sputtered. He glanced nervously at the collection of belongings by the fire. "Just keeping their spirits up, my lord, you understand?"

William ignored the game. "We must talk, Joachim. It's time." The minstrel slung his lute over his shoulder and followed him into the fluttering shadows outside the campfires.

William walked in silence. The usually irrepressible Joachim swallowed his words, for he knew the duke to be a man who determined when and where speaking would be done. They stopped at the camp's edge. From there, Joachim became acutely aware of the close proximity of the Saxons, strung out across a low ridge, sentries' torches moving like midsummer fireflies against the starless night.

"There," William said, gesturing across the gap between the armies.

"The reason you've come on this adventure. The very jaws of the Saxon lion prepare for us on the morrow."

"Yes, my lord," Joachim hissed through clenched teeth. "Harold is quite a magicker."

"Forced marches and filling the ranks of the fallen with farm boys and broken old wretches. I intend to rip the sheet from his sorcery. But that's where I need you."

The minstrel bowed his ragged flaxen head with a flourish of his hand.

"Of course, my lord. I knew it would soon be time to sing for my supper."

"Yes, better a song than your head. This is not a recital for a party at court. Every one of my men must be able to hear the song. They must not faint before the morrow's fight."

"You wound me, sire. I've seen men and women swoon from my words. But never fear, for I brought the best with me, my lord. Each fire will hear the song from an accomplished bard. I promise this."

William nodded and turned back toward the camp. Joachim, understanding the audience was at an end, bowed to William's back and unslung his lute, plucking at the strings as he fairly danced in the duke's wake.

Within an hour, a ragged band of minstrels fanned out across the Norman camp. Sergeants gathered the men about their fires. Before a pavilion erected near William's wooden keep, oily braziers and a log-stacked bonfire chased back the night.

Joachim, dressed in colorful motley, strode into the circle of light. The duke, lounging in his campaign chair, signaled for the assembled nobles to take their seats. More common soldiers crowded around the fringe, straining to hear from the grand bard himself rather than the scattered surrogates. Joachim found a perch on a barrel and plucked at the strings of his lute.

Abruptly William launched himself from the chair to the center of the circle, his iron-gray eyes sweeping nobles and commoners alike. In each face illuminated by the blazing fire he saw the imprints of previous ventures on the continent, scrapes and battles that had tested their mettle and found it worthy. His face softened slightly as the brotherhood of arms filled him with pride.

"On the morrow," he said, projecting over the heads of the assembled, "we shall face a Saxon host hurried to battle. They are bloodied and bruised from their dalliance to the north with the Viking king and spent from the rush to meet us. We, however, shall rest tonight so that when we face them we shall stand together, readied for the test."

They cheered with one voice, echoed around campfires throughout the field.

He continued, "Now is the time to seize destiny by the throat! Now, for we are as the great heroes of old! God will strengthen our arms! We will prevail!"

The men cried out in raucous delight to be standing with their beloved Bastard. After a moment, William waved for silence and signaled to Joachim. The minstrel stretched his fingers, stood, and strutted about the campfire, his shadows dancing upon the men before him.

"Well, my boys," he said with a gap-toothed smile. "This song belongs to you ... and to the ages! I have for your pleasure this even ..."

The troops held their breath as one.

"'The Song of Roland!'"

The assembled men, noble and common alike, cheered once more— and with that, the minstrel from far-off Aquitaine began to sing.

> "Charles the King, our Lord and Sovereign,
> Full seven years hath sojourned in distant Spain,
> Conquered the land, and won the western main,
> Not a single fortress against him doth remain,
> No city walls are left for him to gain,
> Save Saragossa, that sits on a high mountain ..."

A Θ I

CHAPTER 1

LORD OF THE MARCH

Neustria
Spring, AD 801

Thick clouds leaked gray mist into the air, chilling the bones of the dour folk laboring to prepare the fields for the season's crops. Thick-sinewed men guided plows drawn by stout Frank horses to turn over last year's rutted furrows before nightfall as their wives and children scattered handfuls of seed in their wake.

A crude track ran through the patchwork, reaching from the distant choppy sea to a motte-and-bailey keep built atop earthen ramparts overlooking the hinterlands. Over the main gate, two pennants dueled in the desultory breeze. The first, a brilliant white banner emblazoned with a crimson wolf, sign of the late William, former count of Breton March, snapped defiantly. The other bore a white lily on a blue field, the personal standard of Ganelon, count of Tournai and, by order of the king, master of the march since William's death.

Within the wooden bastions rose the clang and clatter of freemen training for the call to arms, whether to repel roving sea-wolves in their low-slung wooden longships or renegades who ventured across the ill-defined borders of the Bretons. The men of the march drilled even this late in the day with oval shield and sword, working shield-to-shield in tight formations or training alone with wooden wasters against a battered stump sticking up from the earth.

At the rear of the courtyard, considerably different sounds drifted through the spring air from the optimistically named great hall—a mixture of laughter, clanking mugs, and barking of errant dogs begging for scraps. Smoke poured from the chimney of the adjoining kitchen where serving girls in woolen skirts and jackets crowded the open door to collect skins of dark Frank wine and platters filled with meat. Those waiting their turn warmed hands by the ovens and chattered about the young nobles carousing inside the hall until they could rush back to the celebration laden with the spoils of nobility—steaming joints of venison and boar, local-grown leeks and onions, and chunks of crusty bread.

Once back in the hall's torch-lit interior, the chaotic cacophony broke over them like crashing waves of a turbulent sea. Young men reveled with laughter and tussled one with another to impress both their fellows and the girls refilling their plates and cups. Broken strains of music fought to be heard over the noisome chorus from musicians plucking on well-worn instruments and singing in ragged voices that thumbed their noses at harmony. But no one cared, for the drink flowed and the food steamed from the kitchen. Thus the musicians were left to pursue their obscure tunes from unknown taverns without regard for anyone's standards of artistic merit.

A larger table stood at the center of the hall, crowded with young bravos dressed in their finest peacock and jostling for attention from the vibrant young man who sat at the head. This youth tore at a joint with strong teeth and then washed it down with a draught from his cup. His cheeks were flushed, his strong-jawed face framed in a wild thicket of dirty blond locks. Over his fine linen shirt he wore a wine-stained woolen surcoat bearing the crimson wolf. One after another, the young nobles shouted bawdy jokes, and he lifted a cup in recognition to each in turn, his ready smile breaking into willing laughter. A fresh-faced serving girl feigned outrage at the humor until he turned his keen northern blue eyes on her. She took notice and leaned close so that her bodice opened to view. He pulled her onto his lap. The wineskin in her hands sloshed when she settled against him. She dropped it onto the table and raked her hands playfully through his tousled hair.

In the doorway, a figure outlined in fading sunlight shook out a long cloak. He was a tall youth who bore a sober look that was out of place in the festivities, his face framed by dark hair trimmed short for wear beneath a helmet. His traveling clothes were of a fine cut, but mud clung to them, particularly from his boots to his knees. The serious bearing on his tanned face dissolved when his eyes rested on the young man at the head of the table still playfully tugging at the servant girl amid the chaos.

"Roland!" he shouted. He threw his cloak over a stool and strode across the room, dodging servants and carousing nobles alike.

"Oliver, come in!" the blond youth replied. "Have a drink! Fill your belly!" With a pinch of the girl squirming on his lap, he continued, "You've just arrived?"

"Oh, yes," Oliver said, planting a foot on the adjoining chair. "See? I still wear the mud from the road." He swiped a cleaner stool from under another reveler and swung it next to Roland at the table. "And how is our fair Eleanor today?"

The girl flashed Oliver a smile and pursed her lips flirtatiously.

"I've been missing you, of course," she said, tossing her flaxen locks.

Oliver winked in response. "Of course you have, my dear. It's been too long since I've visited. Do you mind if I take a moment with Roland?"

Eleanor pouted, her lips moist and red, but she wriggled free from Roland and kissed Oliver on the cheek.

"Of course," she said. "Brothers in arms first!"

As she sauntered away, her hips moving to a seductive rhythm with each step, Roland leaned over to Oliver and whispered conspiratorially, "It seems you only attract virtuous kisses, my friend."

"Oh, you're just jealous because she'll be thinking of me long into the night," Oliver replied, reaching across the table to grab a cup and a dripping joint of meat.

Roland slapped Oliver on the back.

"Honestly, I don't care who she's thinking of as long as I'm the one in her bed!"

Oliver tore at the meat with his teeth. "You know," he said around a mouthful of venison, "I've ridden all this way, and you still haven't told me what you're celebrating."

"It's my birthday, of course!" Roland replied.

"It's not your birthday."

"But it will be. Someday."

Oliver pushed Roland in friendly exasperation, unsettling his friend's wobbly stool and making him jostle the arm of another youth. Wine splattered over the other man's gold-trimmed tunic.

"Hey! Have a care!" he growled, shoving back. Then the young man plucked a wineskin off a passing tray and poured the dark liquid into Roland's lap.

"Scoundrel!" Roland cried. "Is that any way to treat your host?"

He launched himself from his chair, toppling the other youth onto the table. They locked into a wrestler's embrace amid the platters of meat and pastries and kicked food on the other revelers as they struggled for advantage. They rolled off the table and into the rushes on the floor. Within moments, others, both human and canine, were joining the fracas in a flailing mass of limbs and tails.

In an open doorway, Gisela, Roland's mother and sister to King Charles, paused in shock, slender hand raised to her mouth. She was elegant and beautiful in a way that being great with child only enhanced, and normally carried herself with unshakable poise—but not now. Color rose to her cheeks, for, even knowing her son's habits, the scene before her was extreme. Ganelon, her husband, stepped from behind her into the doorway, his hawkish eyes quickly taking stock of the room and his thin-lipped mouth tightening in anger. He was a lean man of two score and ten summers, yet the close-cropped beard on his angular and stern face was dark like a much younger man's. A warrior of great renown within the circles of power at Aachen, now brother-in-law to King Charles himself, his marriage had brought him a wayward stepson and the leeching spawn of hedge knights about the region. His cheek twitched with pent-up anger.

In the deeper shadows of the hallway, Ganelon's personal steward of many years, the spidery Father Petras, hovered near his lord's shoulder, a specter in brown clerical homespun.

"Hard coins wasted on debauchery," Petras noted coldly. He rubbed at his bald head and with his other hand sharply traced the cross on his sunken breast. "God have mercy on us all for permitting this."

"Your son will make paupers of us with these incessant drinking binges!" Ganelon spat at Gisela. He wiped his beard with the back of his hand.

"He's just compensating for his loss," Gisela replied with a cautious demeanor. "His father meant the world to him."

"You coddle him too much," Ganelon snorted. "It must stop!"

He stalked into the hall and pulled Roland out of the midst of the scrum of bodies, fists, and feet.

"Enough!" Ganelon shouted above the noise. "Enough already! There will be no more paying for your games!"

Roland wriggled free, straightened, and offered the other youth a hand to his feet.

"You know," Roland muttered to his fellow celebrant, "he pays for nothing here." He grabbed a cup of wine and stepped in a haughty fashion from floor to bench up to the table. He strode the length of the tabletop, placing his feet between upturned plates, scattered cups, and drunken bodies, raising the cup and urging other revelers to do likewise.

"A toast to Ganelon! The lord of the march, by the king's own decree! We owe him thanks for our supper!"

One of the young nobles shouted, "The wolf speaks! Listen to the wolf!"

The other attendees drunkenly got to their feet and toasted Ganelon in a chorus of profanity. Gisela swept through them to her husband.

"I'll not stand for his insults," Ganelon growled, his face darkening.

"Please, have some understanding," Gisela pleaded. "He's my son. Come away, husband. They will sleep it off, and all will be well."

The count grabbed her face in his hands, forcing her to meet his piercing steel eyes. "I need you to stop protecting him!"

Roland, still holding his cup aloft, sauntered back down the table's length toward them, his face set like a reveler's mask. His companions' chatter died as he stopped to stand over his mother and stepfather.

"As you all know," he said unsteadily, "my father lies cold in the grave, God rest his sainted soul. And yet this man keeps my mother very warm. Let us drink to the pleasures of the living, at the expense of the dead!" He drained his cup in a suddenly uncomfortable silence.

Ganelon pushed Gisela roughly against a chair. One of the older kitchen maids cried out and rushed to her aid.

Ganelon ignored them. Instead he drew his sword, the blade glimmering dully in the firelight.

"No!" Gisela begged, grabbing at Ganelon's arm. "Please, he meant no harm!"

"I've had quite enough, son or not!" Kicking a dog aside, he leaped onto the table with a murderous grace.

Roland threw his cup at his stepfather and danced backward across the tabletop. Ganelon advanced through the remains of the feast, knocking scraps to the floor where the hounds eagerly pounced upon them. Roland snatched up a butcher's knife from a tray and lunged, tapping Ganelon's blade aside and driving inward. But he took a drunken misstep and spared Ganelon's throat by a hair's breadth. The count recovered and struck Roland with the back of his free hand, and then the guests scattered to avoid the sudden fury of the swinging sword, the stabbing knife, and the battling fists.

Ganelon lowered his shoulder, driving hard against Roland's midsection. The youth stumbled over the edge of the table to sprawl onto the rush-covered floor. Dogs yowled and scrambled out of the way. Ganelon thrust his sword into the table's planks, leaped down after Roland, and pinned the younger man to the floor, grabbing his face in one hand.

"I've killed wolves before," he hissed breathlessly. "What's another to me?"

Roland's eyes widened. "What did you say?" He struggled under the older man's iron grip.

A shadow loomed over them and blotted out the torchlight. Oliver wrapped his arms around Ganelon, pulling him from Roland, and other guests rushed to intervene.

The count angrily shrugged Oliver off. Glaring at the human rampart assembling between him and his quarry, he straightened his clothes and threw back his shoulders. "We will speak of this later, stepson." He stalked out of the hall with Petras and Gisela in his wake.

"Be careful," Oliver advised Roland as they watched them go. "He speaks on behalf of the Crown."

Roland shook the last drunken cobwebs from his head then grabbed his friend's shoulder.

"No. He speaks only for himself."

As the chilled night blanketed the keep, dreams did not come easily to Roland.

His bedchamber was spartan, more by choice than necessity. Roland preferred the open skies rather than the keep's constricting walls. Only a spilled chalice on the tabletop dripping wine onto the floor marked it as his—that and Eleanor sleeping quietly amidst the tangled covers. But Roland tossed restlessly, even in his dreams unable to find peace.

A shape emerged from the darkness at the end of the bed, a wavering shadow of twisting smoke that resolved into the form of a man with features reminiscent of the boy in the bed—a strong face, with a set jaw that had come from a lifetime of staring down violence and death without flinching. William, once count of Breton March and champion of the realm, obscured the moonlight that streamed through the nearby window, not so much blocking it as absorbing the rays. In a hushed rasp, his lips huffed words as if on a chilled winter wind.

"I've killed wolves before."

Roland awakened with a start, his body shaking and chilled with sweat. Eleanor stirred from her sleep and rolled toward him, wrapping him in her arms.

"Another nightmare?" she ventured in a sleepy whisper, her fingers instinctively caressing his chest.

Roland nodded and set her arms aside. He threw the covers over her lithe body.

"Not right now," he said. "I'm sorry."

He walked over to the window and rested his elbows on the sill. He took in a deep breath of the crisp night air.

7

"Dear God," he whispered, "take my father to thy rest. And leave me to mine."

He snatched his tunic from the floor, and stepped out of the room.

The family chapel, unlike the rest of the fortifications, was built from finely hewn stone chinked with genuine mortar. Inside the cramped space, guttering candles provided only the barest illumination.

In an adjoining room, the parish priest awoke at the opening of the outer door. He scrambled from his bed, gathered his robes about him, and glanced out the window at the westering moon. Through his bleary eyes, he saw Roland standing in the chapel's open doorway, the youth's eyes haunted. The priest rushed to prepare the room, but Roland did not wait. The young knight took a guttering nub from the candle stand near the doorway, carried it around the bustling priest to the altar, and set it onto a wax-covered plate before touching each point of the cross on his person and sinking to his knees. The priest, taking this cue, set down the offering tray in his hands and quietly backed into his bedchamber.

Roland clasped his hands and bowed his head. He took a deep breath. "Heavenly Father, it's been a very long time since I've ventured here to share my thoughts with you. Even now, I don't know where to begin …"

Next to Roland, William's figure gathered substance from the shadows once again. Though dark emotion hardened his face, his features softened when his unfathomable eyes fell upon his son. "And yet to be the sword of your king, you must be conversant with your God, my son."

The familiar voice tore at Roland's heart. The youth raised his eyes and regarded his father's shade. Then he looked down at the floor. "First you haunt my dreams, Father, and now my waking hours as well? Am I to take your place as his champion? That is a hard thing to require."

"Sometimes we are required to do difficult things, my son—to be honorable in the sight of God and your king. I beseech you, take up this task."

"It must first be offered, Father. Surely there are great nobles who are better respected. And the way Ganelon lords it around the march like he's my wet nurse, no one will take me seriously in any case."

William raised a hand, withered and gaunt, not vibrant and firm as Roland remembered from when he had been alive. "You are to be Charles's sword, the champion of God. There is no other choice for Charles to make. It is ordained."

Roland shook his head and rubbed at his eyes. "God could have chosen more wisely. Someone worthy of His call."

William shook his head, a weariness spreading across his features as his form lost substance and dissolved. "He knows what He is doing. Trust in Him and act."

The door creaked open once more, and a gust of air dissipated the last of William's visage. Oliver entered the chapel and paused.

"There you are, my friend," he said, loosening his cloak from about his shoulders and tossing it across a stool. "Who were you talking to?"

Roland smiled wanly.

"No one. I was just having a reading session with your bookish priests."

"In the middle of the night? Why don't I believe that?" Oliver walked to the altar, knelt next to Roland, and crossed himself. "Something is bothering you. Tell me what it is."

Roland sucked a deep breath as he shifted through his father's revelations as well as the hazy memories of the earlier evening. "Ganelon," he said after a pause. "Oh, I know what you're thinking. There's nothing he does that pleases me. But seriously—it's something he said."

"He's said many things," Oliver noted, "on many days. He's an ass."

"This was no joke," Roland said. "I'm sure he murdered my father."

"What? I thought your father was wounded in battle. And died of a fever."

Roland shook his head. "No. I've been thinking—my father's wounds were clean. He was gaining strength. Then, suddenly, he just died. And Ganelon wasted no time in marrying my mother. You remember—my father wasn't even cold in his grave when he petitioned the Crown for control of the march."

Oliver leaned over closer, his voice a bare whisper. "Do you have proof? Or is this all just speculation?"

"You heard him in the great hall," Roland said, his voice flat. "His own words betray him."

A Θ I

The keep's tower was built of rough stone, its walls covered with dead brown ivy not yet ready to bud with the fresh season's growth. It rose from the surrounding earthen fortifications with lines of sight to the west across the Breton frontier, north to the channel and eastward to the nearby town of Le Mans. Gisela looked out from her bedchamber window into the night, her hair loose about her shoulders. She pulled a shawl up against the chill. Ganelon stirred from the nearby bed, rose, and crept up behind her, a blanket about his own shoulders.

"I'm sorry," Gisela said. "I didn't mean to wake you."

"It's not you," Ganelon replied, extending his own gaze through the window across the fields. "It's your son. He accuses me of murder."

"It's just the drink. He doesn't believe that. You see more than what is there."

Ganelon took her by the shoulders, wrenching her around to face him and glaring fiercely into her eyes.

"But he does," he said sternly. "Oh, he certainly does, the drunken fool. Charles was right giving me control over the march. You must watch him and keep him from his wild notions. I won't allow him to stain my family's reputation."

Gisela looked away, shrugging his hands off her.

"He's just a boy, Ganelon."

Ganelon snorted.

"I've told you not to coddle him. He's old enough to be held accountable for his actions." He forced her face to his, pressed his lips hard on hers. "But enough of his foolishness. It's time to think of your husband."

She stiffened beneath his touch, her fingers clenching at her side.

CHAPTER 2

CAMPAIGN SEASON

Sunlight filtered into the room through thin homespun curtains to where Oliver lay in a twisted tangle of blankets, his breathing rhythmic and deep. In the distance, a rooster's crackling crow jangled through the early morning.

The door banged open, and Roland burst into the room, jolting Oliver awake with a start. "Rise and shine, lazy bones!"

"What?" Oliver grumbled, groggily rubbing at his eyes.

Roland laughed with a mischievous smile. "Come along! The day is slipping away!"

"Oh, dear God in heaven," Oliver murmured as he sat up. He fumbled at the bedside table for a cup, which he quickly filled with water from the nearby pitcher and splashed onto his face. He shook the droplets from his eyelids and squinted at Roland. "You're up early for a drinking man. What's the idea?"

Roland flopped onto the bed next to him.

"Well, I figured you might need some time to pray before we get started!"

"Started?" Oliver asked as he poured another cup, drinking this one. "Am I going to need prayers?"

Roland laughed and tossed one of Oliver's boots at him.

"We're all in need of prayers," Roland assured him, suddenly less exuberant. "Pray for me as I take my first steps on the road to Damascus."

Inside the home guard's barracks across the courtyard, shutters remained closed for the men of the Breton March slept off the previous evening's carousing, stretched out on their straw mattresses with their clothes and gear strewn across the floor.

The door slammed open, and Kennick, the master-at-arms, a grizzled soldier with rough tanned skin and a salt-and-pepper beard, stormed into the bay banging on an old pot. Roland and Oliver followed behind, clapping and shouting at the top of their lungs. The groggy men scrambled to their feet protesting loudly.

One man stubbornly pulled a cover over his head. "Out with you!" he groaned. "We spent our strength with you last night!"

Kennick ripped the blanket off of him.

"All right, my sleeping beauties," he shouted. "Up and out! Up and out!"

"Mary Mother of Jesus what is this?" groused a young recruit from a local village. "I left this behind with the shite on my boots from my father's pigs!"

Roland grabbed the youth by the feet, pulling him from the bunk onto the cold floor with a loud *thunk*.

"Come along, Gunter! The spring levies will be called up soon! The marchmen fought many campaigns with my father in years gone by. But are we happy with past glory? Or do we prepare for a new future? A future of our making!"

The marchmen grumbled but rousted from their beds nonetheless.

Later, near the muddy track that was the main road, the marchmen maneuvered in tight rectangular formations of the long-departed legions of Rome. Shoulder to shoulder with shields interlocked, they executed commands bellowed over grunts, curses, and the sucking mud by a priest reading from a worn vellum manual. Roland and Oliver sweated and marched in the center of the company alongside the men.

Along that same road, a rider in the brightly colored livery of the king of the Franks galloped to the gate. His lathered horse blew steam from its flaring nostrils as he pulled the animal to a halt. A guard straightened from where he rested against the wall, salutes were exchanged, and then the rider clattered across the drawbridge over the stagnant moat into the courtyard. He leaped from the saddle and hurried toward the great hall, stripping his cloak and tossing it to a squire who fell in behind him.

Inside the hall, Ganelon ate his midday meal at a long table with his son Gothard, a younger, lankier version of himself with thick, dark hair and the same permanent condescending scowl pressed into his features. The younger man looked up from his food long enough to eye the muddied messenger with disdain, then brushed his unkempt locks back and returned his attention to the meat. Petras, however, emerged from a shadowed corner, drifting purposefully across the floor. He always held a keen interest in the comings and goings of the nobility. Ganelon's ambitions would tolerate nothing less.

The rider strode across the rushes and offered a stiff, restrained bow.

"You may speak," Ganelon barked.

"I bring you greetings from Charles, where he assembles the nobles at Aachen," the messenger replied. "He commands you to gather your levies from Tournai and meet him in Saxony."

He handed Ganelon a rolled vellum message, the scarlet wax seal stamped with the imperial eagle.

"And Roland?" Ganelon asked.

"I have no orders for the son of William."

"Good. Very good." Ganelon waved for a serving boy. "Make sure this man has meat and drink. Hurry now, see to it!"

The boy led the newcomer to the kitchens. Ganelon caught Gothard's eye.

"So we are off to Saxony then. Petras!" He turned to the priest. "I will require you to watch over the march in my absence. Maintain order by whatever means necessary. Oh, and do ensure my wife and stepson are monitored appropriately."

Petras pressed his bony hands together in a show of fealty.

"Of course," he replied. "I will alert you to any undue activities."

Ganelon dismissed him with a wave of his hand, and the cleric slipped from the room without another word.

"He'll demand to come with us, you know," Gothard said in a hushed tone.

"Let him demand." Ganelon reached for a crust of bread, tore it apart, and sopped it into his stew. "I removed William. I will remove Roland, when the time comes."

"You're far too patient, Father."

"Yes, I am." Ganelon smiled, thin lips stretched over strong teeth. "But my patience will be their undoing. Mark my words. I will have the throne. It is my right."

The marchmen straggled into the courtyard covered in sweat and accidentally spattered blood to lay their weapons and shields in rows by the barracks before assembling into ranks. Roland and Oliver emerged from their midst to stand before them.

"You're the pride of the march, boys!" Roland called over the sound of stacking gear.

Kennick, on the other hand, stood sentinel behind them at the barracks steps, the last barrier between the men and their supper. "Time to get your pride cleaned up!" he roared. "The last man to stow his gear gets dog scraps!" He glared at their sagging shoulders. "You heard me, boys! Why are you still standing here?"

He leaped to one side as the abruptly revived men erupted toward the door, jostling to get through.

Roland grinned at Oliver.

"See, finished before your evening prayers."

"And before your evening cups," Oliver replied. "So it's been a good day indeed." Oliver paused as Ganelon strode from the main hall, Gothard jogging at his side.

"Hang on a moment," Roland said as he struck out across the courtyard.

He stopped a dozen paces from Ganelon. "When do we march?"

"'We?'"

"I saw Charles's messenger," Roland observed. "The men are ready for campaign."

"Ah, yes. So they seem." Ganelon looked toward the milling logjam of men at the barracks door. "This season, Charles has different plans for the marchmen, I'm afraid. They will do as their name suggests—they will protect the frontier from land and sea. Breton March will be secure during the summer raiding season."

"Garrison duty?" Color rose to Roland's cheeks. "Garrison duty! But Charles needs his best troops! These have served him faithfully since my father was champion! They have been the backbone of Charles's center in every campaign since he gained the crown!"

Ganelon's jaw muscles clenched. "Those days are gone, stepson." Behind him Gothard crossed his arms and smiled. Ganelon continued, "This is my final word on the matter. While we are on campaign, neither you nor your marchmen will set foot in Saxony."

CHAPTER 3

Imperial Whispers

Saragossa bustled with activity within its sheltering ring of mountains.

From its tangled mass of dusty streets seething with the trade of a continent, a Roman bridge thrust across the blue Ebro River. Its stark functionality formed the sole link between the daily muddle of life of the city's provincials on one end and an opulent palace on the other. That palace was home to the most cosmopolitan court to grace the expanse of Iberia in many generations. Over this grand edifice, a proud banner snapped in the breeze, bearing a scimitar thrust through a crescent moon—the sign of the House of Marsilion, emir of Saragossa. And within those muted pale walls, courtiers bedecked in silken garments hurried through columned hallways in slippered feet that had never felt the rough paving stones of the city whose affairs they oversaw.

Deep in the center of the royal residence, the ornate doors of the throne room formed a final barrier between the emir and his domain. Outside their gilded panels, emissaries from distant lands cooled their heels, whether adorned with bushy beards and northern furs or garbed in linen and sandals, and waited on the pleasure of the man within—all these, in fact, but one. At this particular moment, a single willowy figure confidently advanced to the regal portals, his long black cloak wrapping about his body and whispering across the polished tile floor. With his hood over his head, he seemed like a wraith of exotic origins. A curved saber-sheath protruded from under the fine fabric shrouding his hip.

Two heavily armored guards stood at either side of the doorway.

They moved to stop the man but paused when they saw the flash of an imperial insignia on his shoulder—the golden eagle of Rome, which clutched his robe in its talons and declared his identity more surely than words: he was Honorius, envoy of Eastern Empire. He pushed back his hood to reveal curly dark locks that rolled to his shoulders and a slender face tanned to an olive complexion, his dark eyes darting observantly about his surroundings.

"I will see him now," he announced with a casual air. He unbuckled his blade and handed it to one dumbfounded sentry. The guard glanced at his more seasoned partner, who nodded curtly then pushed open the tall doors. Bright light spilled out, and Honorius strode into the chamber without waiting for invitation or announcement.

At the far end of the arched expanse, near wide windows opening to a panorama of the city, Marsilion sat on a pile of fluffy tasseled cushions while well-groomed scholars laden with documents and bureaucrats in expensive robes hurried back and forth on important errands. While age had crept up on Marsilion, he still had the look of a man barely two score years—a man who had come to the seat of power early in life. The emir distractedly adjusted his silken garments as attendants vied to review stacks of reports and legal instruments with him, but the staccato beat of Honorius's boots on the tiles diverted his always-volatile concentration. He ran his fingers through his peppered beard and eyed the approaching man suspiciously.

General Blancandrin, supreme commander of Marsilion's armies and an imposing presence even without his elaborate armor, disengaged from the emir's side, stepping forward to intercept the emissary. He snarled, exposing flashing teeth amid his dark, close-cropped beard. His black eyes found Honorius's and held them as if with an unspoken challenge.

Honorius paused only long enough to offer the tall champion a stiff nod of acknowledgment before sidestepping him.

"Please let him through, Blancandrin," Marsilion commanded.

Blancandrin bowed dutifully and took a step back, but his eyes never left the newcomer. His hand slipped to the scabbarded blade at his side and toyed with the pommel.

Honorius took a perfunctory knee. "Emir Marsilion, master of Saragossa—I bear the respects of my master, Nicephorus, emperor of the Romans in Constantinople."

"I heard you were coming," noted the emir tartly. He stretched his frame and dismissed the courtiers and their endless documents with a wave. "And this time will you offer any words not drenched in diplomatic doublespeak?"

"My honored emir!" Honorius's tone feigned insult. "My master would cry out from such a deep wound had he heard you speak with his own ears! But fear not, for my message will carry clearly to your ears the intents of the emperor."

The general took a step forward, his jaw clenched. "Intent is proved by more than words, Greek. All the caliphate knows of your double-dealing."

"Direct and insightful, as always, my lord," the messenger replied. "Diplomacy can be a dangerous sport—be warned before entering the Hippodrome, as we say." He alluded to the intense rivalry of the Blues and the Greens, audiences of the vicious chariot races in the great stadium of Constantinople who wielded enormous influence within that city, the same mob that had caused even emperors to pay with life and throne to satisfy their fickle whims. "But today, Emir, I bear you news of an opportunity—an opportunity not likely to be soon repeated."

"I'm listening." Marsilion covered his mouth with the back of his hand as he sucked in a yawn.

Honorius leaned closer and dropped his voice. "My ship just arrived from Saxony, great Emir—by way of Francia. Charles prepares to march north as the weather breaks. He draws troops from the south to engage his Saxon problem."

"Lies," Blancandrin said curtly. "Emir, do not listen to this man. Charles would never deplete his defenses beyond the mountains. To do so would leave all southern Francia exposed."

"Ah, but he does, my dear general," Honorius countered. "Charles swore before the altar of his great cathedral at Aachen that he would finish the Saxons during this campaign season. He believes his alliance with Barcelona keeps him safe, that it shields him from the might of your master, the caliph."

Suddenly Marsilion jolted upright. "Allah be praised!"

Concern creased Blancandrin's brow. "Please, my emir. We're not prepared to launch an assault on the Franks. Barcelona would be at our backs with our supply lines vulnerable."

Marsilion's gaze clouded for a heartbeat. Honorius, sensing him waver, pressed harder. "You can bypass Barcelona easily, Emir. You can be across the mountains and into fresh lands with plentiful forage before he can catch you."

"And then the Franks return from Saxony, and *they* are before us—with Barcelona blocking the return home!" Blancandrin insisted.

"The Franks will be battered and bruised when they return from Saxony, even if they do win. They will be easy pickings, Emir—and it will take them precious time to regroup to mount a defense in any case. You can take control of a port, I'm sure, and so stay within reach of the caliph's ships if need be. Perhaps Carcassonne? Now that would be a feather in your cap to take that city."

Marsilion looked out at the tiled rooftops of Saragossa, spread out behind strong fortifications and graced by elegant towers and minarets. Beautiful Saragossa was proud of its heritage and painfully cognizant of its singular defeat at the hands of the Franks decades before.

"Send to the caliph!" he commanded Blancandrin. "We'll petition him for support. My father's bones lie on the fields of Tours, and Allah has given us an opportunity to seize a prize that has been denied us for a generation! Now is our time—our time to bring sword and cleansing fire to the infidels!"

Blancandrin flashed Honorius a dangerous glance. But the Greek simply rocked back on his heels, a smug grin on his face.

"Tell me, dear Emir," he asked sweetly, "have you yet saddled the magnificent horses I brought on my last visit? You remember them, a gift from my master, the emperor?"

ΑΟΙ

A low-slung ship, better suited to the warm middle sea than the choppy sullen breakers along the west Frankish coast, glided through the waves toward the dock as the crew shipped their oars. An officer called out a hail, first in Greek and then in German, as the ship's flank grated against the pier. Bare feet dropped onto creaking planks, and sun-browned men bent backs to hurriedly tie ropes to iron rings embedded in columns jutting up from the sea.

Demetrius stood upon the foredeck, tanned face turned toward the shore, and he adjusted the imperial cloak that flowed from his shoulders. Beneath a thicket of dark hair, his shadowed eyes scanned the track leading up from the water. No one stood upon either the pathway or along the rough-hewn dock that jutted into the waves. He rubbed absently at his carefully trimmed beard.

The ship scraped one last time against the pylons as mooring lines were drawn taut. With a shrug, Demetrius jumped to the jetty and strode to the muddy track leading to what many in these parts considered a castle. He, however, held a different view, having lived and worked in fortifications from Antioch to Messina to Constantinople herself—each ringed by miles of stone walls and crenelated gatehouses that would put the muddy earthworks and wooden battlements of the Frank keep to shame. Still, it was what it was, and he marched blithely on. A herald hastened up behind him, motioning with each step for porters to follow with Demetrius's trunks. From among the crew, two men dressed in dark garments and cloaks, scarves wrapped about their faces, fell into line as well.

Voices echoed from across a field where a clot of men drilled in time-honored formations of shield and sword. Officers shouted orders, and the men locked shields, all the while maneuvering weapons and marching in well-ordered ranks. Demetrius hiked up his cloak and strode across the rutted ground toward them.

"Well done, men," a tall youth in dirty scale armor yelled above the tromping of the formation. "Well done, indeed!"

The herald stepped forward, placing fine shoes carefully amidst the mud, and announced above the din, "The esteemed Demetrius, legate of the Roman Emperor, requests to speak with the Frank champion!"

The young man called a halt. The ranks rippled to a stop as men heaved in relief. Then the youth turned to face Demetrius directly. He wiped sweat from his begrimed face and managed a sketchy bow. "There is no champion here, good sir. Just men of the march."

Demetrius nodded to the herald to resume his place a few paces behind. "I seek William—William of the Breton March."

"He is dead, sir."

"Dead?" Demetrius could not afford to miss a breath, even though the news surprised him. "That is sad news indeed. Who is lord here?"

"The lord of the March has ridden with Charles to Saxony," Roland replied. "Only the home guard remains to keep watch over the henhouse. But come! Where are my manners? You've traveled far, and we've meat and drink."

Roland playfully booted at a hound that squirmed its way between the men as they entered the great hall. Servants stoked up the fire and began preparations to feed their guests. Demetrius blinked as he stepped into the building, taking a moment for his eyes to adjust to the shadowed interior that smelled of wet dog, smoke, and roasting meat. The Byzantine contingent followed a few paces back, gratefully accepting cups of Frank wine from the servants.

"But why now?" Roland asked, tossing his gear on the tabletop. "The border has been quiet for nearly a generation."

Demetrius took a cup from a serving girl, swirled it gently, gave it a sniff, and finally sipped the contents. "Ahhh, very good! Now where was I? Oh, yes." He took a seat at the long table, shedding his cloak onto a bench. "Marsilion knows that Charles marches to fight deep in Saxony. The emir covets the lands of southern Francia, as did his fathers before him. My lord, the Emperor Nicephorus fears that with such a move, the emir could cut off the empire from its Christian brethren.'"

Roland sat across the table. "You've proof of this? Proof enough to bring to Charles?"

Demetrius raised his cup with a dramatic flourish. "Of course!"

The Greek nodded toward his two shrouded companions standing apart from the others. One man stepped forward quickly and bowed low. The other remained rooted in place, watching with dark, measuring eyes.

"No need for that," Roland said, gesturing for the man before him to rise.

He straightened and lowered the scarf from his face, revealing lean, sun-browned features. He had dark eyebrows, a hawk nose, and a youthful beard that framed a genuine smile. "I am Karim, son of Sulayman, emir of Barcelona," he announced. "My father is an ally of your king. And this—" he waved the other man forward. "This is Saleem, the very son of Marsilion himself. He bears information on his father's court for the ears of Charles."

Roland set his cup down.

"The son of Marsilion himself? Here? Why?"

Saleem shrugged, his slender frame remaining stark straight. He did not make a move to unwrap the scarf. "I am the younger son of an unfavored wife—exiled to seek my own fortune in the world. There's nothing for me in Saragossa, and so, here I am."

Roland nodded. It was a practiced, brief litany that Saleem had clearly had to repeat too often already. "I know what it means to be a captive of your birth." He turned to Demetrius once more. "You have the advantage of me, sir. I am more than intrigued." He finished his drink and called for another. "Now then. Tell me about this plot."

The room was quiet with just enough sunlight coming through the window to allow Gisela to focus on the detail in her needlework. Bright patterns reminded her of the wildflowers of her childhood home in Aachen and usually served to divert her attention from the clattering arms that accompanied her son's incessant drilling of the marchmen beyond the keep's walls. And today she felt she needed the diversion. There were many days like this of late. Indeed her room was decked in tapestries stitched methodically by her own hands over the years, as well as those created by her mother and sisters in days long past. Scenes of warriors mounted on armored horses on hunts through verdant woods were interspersed with more idyllic scenes of gardens and dancing nobles, hanging ready to transport her to distant memories far afield from Breton March. She wrapped herself in these reminisces of another place and time, a lost world as out of reach as the march was from her brother Charles the king, or a separation as final as from her beloved William, Charles's once champion and father to her son.

There was a knock at the door. Gisela looked up.

"Yes, do come in."

Roland cracked open the door. "Am I disturbing you?" he ventured.

"My dear—no, not at all."

He slipped in, closed the door behind him, and took a seat on the stool next to her.

"You have a talent for fine detail," he observed. "You know, I could never do that."

She looked up at him, a smile touching her lips. "When my father and brothers rode to war, I learned to occupy my time. But you didn't come to hear a mother's silly stories, did you?"

"I love your stories, especially of our family," Roland admitted. "They make all this bearable. But you're right—I needed to speak with you. Word has reached me of a danger to the kingdom. I must bear that information to Charles."

Gisela set the needlepoint on the cushion next to her with trembling hands.

"What danger?" she whispered.

"An attack from Iberia, south of the Pyrenees. Saragossa is preparing to wrest Aquitaine from the kingdom. The messenger must reach Charles on the Saxon frontier."

She looked up at him, remembering his face just years before as a young boy—a child with his father's eyes. "But Ganelon ordered you to stay here at the march."

"Please, Mother, don't command me in his name. Not in his name. His creature, the priest, watches my every move."

"And what would you have me say?" she asked in a hushed voice. She stole a reflexive look at the closed door, as if she could hear Petras's breathing on the other side. "I must keep faith. I keep my vows with God. Ganelon entered into this marriage to watch over me, over the march."

Roland leaned forward, his voice urgent. "Taking to himself his dead friend's wife—really, Mother. Father was barely cold."

She clenched her fists, bracing herself. "What are you saying?"

He took her hands in his, the gentle touch of his calloused fingers smoothing out her knotted joints. "What you're afraid to say, Mother. Father's wound was clean—he was on the mend. It's before us all."

She shook her head, tears welling up in her eyes.

"You've no proof of this!"

"Mother," Roland continued. "You are gentle and kind. You seek the best in everyone. I beg you, please set aside your nature. When you arrive at Aachen, look carefully through Father's belongings. Tell me if you find anything amiss."

A pang tightened in her chest, nearly choking the next words that escaped her lips. "What kind of things?"

"I don't know. But there may be something that strikes you as out of place."

She pulled her hands from his, her voice shaking, "I do my duty to my husband, but you tear at my heart!"

Roland's expression softened, and he wrapped her in his arms.

"I'm sorry, Mother," he said. "But I must know the truth. That alone must guide my actions from here on."

Saleem felt drained and ashamed. *Let one more lout ask me the tale,* he thought bitterly. *Are they so thick that they cannot understand why I am here?* He stood in the midst of the fort's yard, watching the comings and goings of the Franks with disdain. He swallowed hard, driving his scorn far down out of sight. Chickens and goats mingled freely with Roland's squires. It was no real surprise, though. These Franks were but human flotsam lapping at the edges of the caliphate—barbarians playing at being civilized.

The question had been posed many ways but remained the same. *"What brings you so far from the court of your father, Marsilion?"* Idiots. So their church forbade multiple wives—that didn't stop them from siring braces of bastards on whatever comely housemaids would lift their skirts. And they knew what fate awaited those accursed offspring. His half brother Farad knew as well, he whose harlot mother Ashifa had gained favor in Marsilion's eyes with her lithe body and flowered words. She whose Arabian family was more highly prized than the allied Visigoths of his own mother Braminunde's royal house. *Farad* had been handed the keys to the kingdom. *Farad* was showered with glory in Saragossa, while Saleem ignored the stink of these beggared Franks' muddy trackless "empire" while plying the only coin he had in this wilderness beyond the Pyrenees—information.

It should be Farad begging for scraps from the Frank table. It should be Ashifa crying in the night for her lost son!

A baby bawled, and a heavy-bosomed woman with field muck caked to her aprons set down a basket of potatoes to nurse it. The infant latched on desperately. *Like a flea*, Saleem thought.

Like me.

He could feel the eyes upon him, this stranger in their midst. Even here, in this backwater armpit of Europa, one could see travelers from far lands—Celts, Turks, Rus, and judging by overheard snatches of conversations, even Ethiopes ventured this far north. But no one had ever seen the likes of Saleem before. Arab by name and by dress, but bearing an odd mix of a Saracen's dark skin and the light hair of a Germanic noble. The alabaster walls of Saragossa were gone for good, exchanged for the rancid grime of the Frankish hinterlands, but the wary distrust was the same. A burly sergeant stalked by, and his eyes swept over Saleem with a flinty hardness. Saleem fingered the jeweled dagger at his waist. Such a look in Saragossa would not openly be tolerated, though even there he had felt such looks at his back.

Karim emerged from the great hall and crossed the muddy ground, a grin upon his face. He thumped Saleem on the shoulder when he drew near.

"Why so glum, my friend?"

"Oh … let's see …" His eyes swept across the yard. "We are consigned to a shit-hole nest of lice-infested Germans. I betray my own blood that has washed their hands of me. How could I not be overwhelmed with joy?"

Karim's smile faded into sudden disquiet.

Now it was Saleem's turn to slap Karim on the back. "'Why are you so glum, my brother'?" he mocked. "We are on a mission to save a barbarian kingdom from the evils of the decadent south. What more could we desire?"

ΑΘΙ

The courtyard surged with the activity of a handful of troopers who saddled their horses and made final preparations for the journey. In that group, Demetrius and his companions—with their brightly colored travel clothes, burnished armor, and exotically furnitured weapons— stood out from the homespun heavy wool of the marchmen. Kennick, at the ready with Roland's great roan, held the spirited beast's head as Roland buckled his shield and sword in place behind the saddle, snugged the girth, then swung up onto her back.

"Sir," he said. "The men will fight for you, as surely as they did for your father."

Roland reached down and squeezed the man's shoulder.

"Ganelon rules here by Charles's command," he said. "I'm willing to risk myself. But I won't ask the men to join me in disobeying his order."

Roland took the reins from Kennick and touched his heels to the steed's flanks. The horse danced away, and the remaining members of the party fell in—Oliver, the Byzantines, the pair of youths from the distant south, and a handful of Frank soldiers as escort. Roland raised a hand in salute to those remaining behind and then urged his horse toward the gate.

"Men of the march!" Kennick roared over the milling soldiers crowding the courtyard. "Will you send your master off in silence?"

The men broke into a raucous cheer as the party rumbled across the drawbridge.

Far above, Gisela stood at the bedroom window casement, thoughtfully rubbing her rounded belly as she watched Roland's company reach the road and break into a gallop. A nursemaid in a simple linen smock took Gisela's hands in hers.

"Come away, my lady," she said. "You'll catch the death of cold."

"Death of cold?" Gisela's eyes remained on the company that now raced between the fields to the forests beyond. "My son leaves me with a heavy burden. Death might be a comfort."

The nursemaid tugged at Gisela's hands.

"Please, my lady. Let's not have such talk. You've a child to be concerned with."

"More than one, Ruth. Though it seems I've already failed the oldest."

Buds dotted the tree limbs with a thin veneer of green as all around the Breton March the forest struggled to emerge from its winter slumber. Along the rutted road, the men rode in silence, now at a brisk walk intended to cover the miles without exhausting their mounts. Roland, his cloak flowing behind him like the wings of a great predatory bird, sat tall in his saddle several yards ahead of the rest. Oliver urged his chestnut steed to catch up and filled his lungs with great draughts of the crisp air, glad to be out of the closeness of the keep once again.

Roland grinned at his friend then squeezed his knees to his horse's ribs. The mare burst willingly into a long gallop. Oliver laughed and with a flick of his reins took up the challenge, chasing after him. The men of the company frantically followed behind as the two youths raced through farm and field before Roland finally slowed his heaving horse to allow Oliver to reach his side once more.

"Is this mission just to get a message to Charles, or were you just chomping at the bit for an excuse to break Ganelon's command?" Oliver laughed.

"It was an order made to be broken," Roland replied with a grin. "Like so many I've seen him issue since he came to stay at the march. Why make pronouncements that no one intends to keep?"

Oliver leaned over and punched Roland in the arm.

"Because in his world, no one would dare defy him."

Roland rolled his shoulder, a mock grimace on his face.

"Well, let's not spoil this fine morning with thoughts of his sour face." He laughed. "Rather, tell me news of the vale. And tell me about your fair sister, Aude. She is, what, sixteen now?"

"My sister? Seventeen. But that's of no matter." Oliver clucked with his tongue to encourage his horse to keep in stride with Roland's.

"No matter?" Roland asked. "She is radiantly dirty, always with mud on her skirts from chasing frogs—frogs that could be the lost princes of the marsh. Unless, of course, she's grown up while I've been away."

Oliver pulled up his horse short.

Roland wheeled his mount's head around and stopped next to him.

Oliver frowned. "Look, you're like a brother to me. No, you truly are more than a brother. But I've seen you tumble more women than I can even remember. You touch—no, you even *think* of my sister, and I'll be forced to demand satisfaction."

Roland's face broke once more into his irrepressible grin.

"No need for anything so drastic, I'm sure!" he said brightly. Then, a little more seriously, "I swear to you, Oliver, we're only passing the time at your expense." He eased his horse's head to face back down the road. "Race you to the Le Mans Bridge!"

With a shake of his head, Oliver spurred his horse after Roland. The rest of the company rounded the bend then, thinking they had finally caught the two, only to find they had to race headlong once more along the muddy track or be left behind.

CHAPTER 4

·OF DAVIÐ AПÐ GOLIATH

The camp stretched along the ridge, a serpent of tents, helmets, and sputtering fires that fought against the morning mists. Frank scouts had already pounded across the countryside, relaying to the pickets news of Roland's approach. Thus they were not surprised when the young knight's party appeared out of the fog making for them at a canter. The duty sergeant stepped out onto the rutted track and raised his hand for a halt. Roland pulled up abreast of him, his mount lathered in muck from the miles of hard riding. After exchanging a few words, the sergeant waved them forward, though not without giving the two Iberian Arabs a suspicious stare as they passed.

The party tramped along the track toward the center of the camp where soldiers directed them to an empty plot of ground. There Roland dismounted at last and ordered the men to set up the tents that would provide them with barest shelter from the bleak Saxon spring. He struck out across the encampment to seek audience with Charles.

Time wore on, and the sun neared midday, finally burning through the mist that clung to a nearby river flowing through thick forest and overgrown fields. Oliver secured the last tent rope and straightened from his task to examine the terrain. In the distance beyond the river, trails of smoke marked the location of the Saxon camp. He tossed his gear onto a camp table and walked a little further beyond his comrades to see the pickets from both armies mirroring each other's movements along the river's banks.

A gaggle of squires passed close by. Oliver called them over, setting them to lend a hand to Demetrius in stowing his diplomatic travel chests. Oliver quietly believed those chests were elbow-deep in gold solidi—the empire's coinage, all of proper weight and purity, of course. The two Moors stood apart from the activity, and Oliver's attention shifted to them with great curiosity, for prior to this venture, he'd never seen an Arab or Muslim before. Upon the road from the march, he had examined their every tic and movement. With what he'd seen thus far, he determined they were much like the princes at Aachen—used to having commands obeyed and to being surrounded by finer things, even on campaign.

The sound of tromping boots broke through his thoughts. He glanced back toward the tent to find Roland returning at last. Even before he gave voice to the question, the look on Roland's face spoke the answer.

"We are not to see Charles?"

Roland walked past him and tossed his cloak into the tent.

Oliver cleared his throat. "I am here, you know."

Roland stopped, shoulders hunched.

"I'm not to see Charles until after he crosses the river!" His voice was sharp with bitterness.

As Roland snatched up the remainder of his gear, Gothard sauntered into their midst.

"When the scouts told me it was you who rode up the road, I could not believe them!" A sneer coiled his thin lips. "I thought even you could not be so stupid! I almost had them flogged! But here I stand corrected. You've now surprised even me." He leaned forward in a mocking half bow.

Straightening from sorting his belongings with a crack of his back, Roland offered his stepbrother a bright, dangerous smile in return. "Go away. I'm not here to suffer your idiocy."

Gothard's hand dropped to the long, wicked dagger slung on his hip. "Suffer me? I'm the least of your worries. You disobeyed a direct order from my father—our father."

"Don't presume to lecture me, or use family to sway me. We're at war. It was a stupid order."

"Mind your tongue!" Gothard snapped. "Your words were overlooked in the march. But they will not be here!"

Roland shrugged.

"I'll remember that. But if you decide to press the point, you'll find me ready."

Gothard's face clouded as his anger rose. He slid the dagger halfway from its scabbard then rammed it back home with a sharp snick. "I'll remember that, brother." He lifted his hand from the weapon, flexing his fingers. Then he spun on his heel, slipping in the wet, matted grass, and stalked off.

"You shouldn't bait him," Oliver warned. "He has many friends at court."

"He may have many friends," Roland replied as he tossed his gear in a heap into their tent, "but he hasn't enough."

Overhead the sun had already passed midday, the rays providing scant warmth to the Frank soldiers crowding along the riverbank. They cheered and groaned with the ebb and flow of the single combat splashing and clanking in the chilled waters before them. A towering Saxon warrior, broad chested beneath a scale mail shirt and with arms like tangled oaks, swung his ax at the smaller, armored Frank who ducked then lunged in return, mud sucking at each of his steps. The Saxon blocked the broad-bladed sword with the ax haft and hammered his own pommel home into the Frank's helmet. The knight stumbled, his guard faltered, and the Saxon lifted the ax into *oberhau* position above his head with both hands. Muscles flexed with the down stroke. The ax bit deep, opening the knight at the hip, spurting crimson clouding the water.

The knight cried out. The Saxon wrenched the ax free then sliced again, catching the Frank under the arm, the keen edge separating iron and bone. He followed with a crushing blow to the knight's face, and the man crumpled to float facedown in the bloody current. The Franks groaned in unison even as the Saxons broke out in a raucous cheer. With a grim laugh, the Saxon champion raised his ax once more then buried it deep in the knight's back.

"Is this all you've got to send to Hengest?" he spat, his accent thick and guttural. "Is this the strength of the Franks?"

Charles stood silently among the crowded nobility, snowy beard framing his lean, pinched face under his heavy crown. His cheeks flushed with anger.

"My lords!" he snarled in a low voice. "Who will meet the Saxon and remove him from the crossing?"

Roland stood bolt upright a few paces away, disbelief spreading across his face. Bertrin, count of Poitiers, a solid man with a horseman's muscled calves and the silver pate of a seasoned veteran, shouldered past him to stand before Charles. Behind him came Geoffrey of Anjou, a middle-aged noble with a close-cropped brown beard and impatient, fiery eyes. Both were veterans of Charles's wars in Italy.

"Let me move up archers to clear the bastard and have done with it, my lord!" demanded Bertrin.

Geoffrey raised a gloved hand to counter his old comrade. "My king! If we did that, what would we have of our honor?"

"By God, Anjou!" Bertrin fumed, "You question my honor?"

"Where is the honor in assaulting him from a distance? What else is the purpose of single combat, if not to prove ourselves better?"

"Well, I for one have had enough of being made a fool like this!"

"And you think we will look less craven if we simply shoot him?"

"Craven! How dare you!"

"Enough!" Charles barked, his voice effectively leashing their exchange. "Tomorrow I will require one of you to stand against him."

The nobles grumbled in assent but only faintly, for this was the third Frank knight to fall beneath the Saxon's butchering ax. Charles swept away from the riverbank back to his camp.

Pepin, Charles's elder son, watched the exchange with keen brown eyes beneath meticulously combed hair. His face was shadowed by the barest of a man's growth, his skin pale from long days sheltered inside the palace at Aachen. The prince limped toward Anjou, his lifelong infirmity clearly visible, and bemusement visible upon his face. He leaned close to the man and whispered, "He doesn't value your honor, Geoffrey, and he never has."

Geoffrey pulled at his beard a moment as he watched soldiers fish the fallen knight's remains from the river. "Indeed. Yet I must honor my oath of fealty, for he is my liege. What would you have me do, were you standing in my stead, my prince?"

Pepin waved his hand casually, affectionately placing his other arm around Geoffrey's shoulder.

"I ask for nothing but your love, Geoffrey. We piss away our strength on these Saxons, while other dangers lurk far to the south in Saracen lands. For your love, I would end this war to protect Aquitaine and Anjou."

"Welcome assurances, my prince," Geoffrey said. "Our lands would be open to an incursion, should the Saracens take a notion to make one."

"I intend to make more than assurances," Pepin said. "When the time comes, I'll remember you, dear Anjou."

Oliver left the quartermaster with a bag of supplies slung over his shoulder. He glanced to one side to see Roland marching mechanically from Charles's enclave in the camp center, ignoring the commotion around him. Oliver hurried through the milling troops to Roland's side.

"If you don't watch what you're doing, you'll end up a blot on the bottom of a wagon wheel," he quipped.

Roland said nothing. Mist steamed from his nostrils like a dragon's exhaust.

"Well," continued Oliver as they approached their tents, "are we to ford the river and take the other bank?"

"No!" Roland threw up his hands. "Another has fallen before this Hengest. Saint Michael's bones, we sit while the Saxon mocks us!"

"But one of our knights will finish this today?"

Roland tugged open the tent flaps and began rummaging through his gear. Oliver stood at the entrance, watching him.

"No, they wait until tomorrow," Roland said. "This whole challenge is a game to our nobles, but there will be hell to pay when the entire Saxon army arrives. They stall us here, bound in our honor, for a reason!"

From deep in his saddlebag, Roland pulled a long dagger. He drew it from the sheath, balanced it in his hand for a moment, and then tucked it into his belt.

"What do you mean to do?" Oliver asked.

Roland crossed himself, lowering his head to mutter a prayer under his breath.

"Come on," Oliver prodded. "I know you better than this. You're dodging the question. Wouldn't our purpose be better served if we just pushed our way into Charles's tent? You are his nephew, after all."

"He won't see me until we cross the river, remember? So—" Roland cracked open his eye and smiled. "I'll race you across!"

"No," Oliver replied. "It's not our place. You're not the shepherd facing Goliath, you know."

"Of course I'm not." Roland laughed, patting the dagger affectionately. "I don't even know how to use a sling."

He slapped Oliver on the back then dashed out of the tent and hurried across the camp toward the river.

The curse of a soldier's existence is to hurry up and wait. In the midst of troops busying themselves with menial tasks to distract their minds from the slowly building Saxon army across the river, a thick-bodied cleric caught sight of the two friends pushing through the soldiers. His merry, round face bristled with a gray-streaked beard, and his tonsured head glistened with sweat, even on this cool day. This particular man of God wore a war kit over the robes of his ecclesiastic calling. And amid the ordered chaos around him, the familiar youths' single-mindedness piqued his interest.

He stepped into their path. "Roland! Oliver! Where are you two going? I'd have thought you'd be joining your company at prayer!"

Roland pulled up short, Oliver a half step behind. "You mean my stepfather's men, dear bishop, not mine."

Turpin wrinkled his nose. "You haven't answered my question. Where to in such haste? Answer me true, lad. You know better than to lie to me."

"I am going across the river," Roland said.

Aghast at Roland's audacity, Turpin took him by the shoulders with hands made more for wielding a sword than a bishop's crooked staff. He peered into the youth's eyes.

"This isn't a game, you know. Besides, suicide is a sin, my son."

"I tried to tell him that," Oliver snorted.

Roland shrugged off Turpin's hands.

"I have no intention of dying today, Father."

He gave the cleric a quick bow and continued his jog through the camp.

Oliver and Turpin followed Roland past the guards and pickets near the river to where the usual collection of nobles and onlookers waited for something—anything—to happen. Charles, for his part, was nowhere to be seen, likely still at prayer himself at this hour.

Moments later, a heavily armored sergeant scratched his head curiously, watching Roland splash into the shallows. He signaled one of the idle troopers nearby to report back to the king. When he looked back, Roland was already halfway across the river, feeling about the bottom with his feet. After a moment, he cupped his hands and yelled toward the enemy camp.

"So, tell me this, are the Saxons ready to fight? Or have they come to shovel pig slop? Is there any Saxon without shite smeared on his breeches?"

The call echoed through the boles of trees back into the Frank camp, and within minutes it erupted into a wave of men rushing toward the river. In their midst flowed the royal colors as Charles and his entourage likewise scrambled to see what was unfolding.

Across the river where he sat by a smoldering fire pit, Hengest unfolded his long limbs and wiped crumbs from his mouth with the back of his hand. He laughed, grabbed his ax and shield, and settled his helmet over his thick locks. Then he swaggered down to the river's edge and roared with mirth when he saw the Frank youth standing in the ford pulling a dagger from his belt.

"You're going to fight me with that pig-sticker?" he growled.

"No, I'm here to join you for breakfast," Roland replied. "Shall we spoon porridge and carve sausages together? Or shall I just cross and take your whole meal?"

The nobles not far off on the Frank side of the river opened their ranks to allow Charles to approach the water's edge. His face was stern, much unlike the surprised ogles of those around him.

Hengest's laughter roared from deep within his barrel chest. When he strode into the water, his body created a bow wave that pushed out before him. His ax swung dangerously with a whisper of a whistle. "Come, little fishy!" he said with a wicked, gap-toothed grin.

He drew up an arm's length from Roland and with a snort cut savagely at him.

The youth dodged in a flurry of water. "You can't cut a pudding like that!" Roland taunted.

"Swinehund!" Hengest attacked again, muscles rippling like coiled snakes. Roland flopped back on the waves, and the ax blade sliced through his shirt. His footing slipped, his arms flailed, and he sank beneath the muddied surface. The Saxon beat at the water, kicking and cursing as he searched.

Roland broke the surface behind him, slinging fistfuls of mud at his back.

"There is shite on you, sir!" he spurted through a mouthful of water.

Hengest snarled and spun around with astonishing speed for a man so large. Roland ducked under the ax's arc, straightened again, and stuck out his tongue. The Saxon's fist followed the weapon, striking Roland's jaw with a crack, throwing him off his feet into deeper water. Hengest wallowed after, teeth gnashing and nostrils flaring. He splashed with his hand, trying to break through the churned cloudy murk that obscured his quarry. Something bit into his leg, and he howled then floundered toward the riverbank.

Roland burst from the water nearby, dagger glistening in his hand, and spat water at the retreating champion.

"I'm over here!"

The Saxons crowding the opposite bank gasped, horrified at the turn of events.

Roland launched his body into Hengest's unsteady bulk, slowed by the water but driven by the momentum of the fight. The Saxon staggered, arms windmilling, and the ax slipped from his fingers. Roland plunged after him, wrapping his arms around Hengest's neck and pulling him under the surface. Limbs and bodies churned up muck. Then crimson blossomed across the rippling surface.

A few heartbeats later, Roland splashed though the surface, heaving Hengest's body off him with a gurgle.

The Saxons broke, fleeing through their camp and, in the rush, leaving behind their equipment. Roland yanked his dagger free from Hengest's throat then waded ashore on the Frank side, dropping to a knee before Charles, who thoughtfully tugged at his beard.

"The crossing is yours, sire," Roland choked breathlessly.

"So it would seem," Charles replied. "I'll see you after we've crossed the river, nephew." Without another word, he stalked away, his astonished entourage straggling after him.

Common soldiers surrounded Roland, clapping him on the back and lifting his arms high.

Within hours, the Frank war machine began to lurch into Saxony.

Nobles streamed in and out of the royal tent that had been hastily carted across the river and pitched on a rise within sight of the sprawling Saxon host. Roland navigated the throng of court bureaucrats— monks, scholars, brilliant liveried squires, and personal servants. He sidestepped pages burdened with scrolls that still dripped scarlet wax, the lads scurrying to find the recipient of each royal dictum. At the flap of the royal tent, Roland ducked his head and found himself in a crowd of northern counts who chatted in a contained courtly manner. Many observed and reacted with measured responses to those who could be potential rivals for royal favor. A squire approached Roland and signaled for him to follow through the milling officials to Charles's private audience chamber, a room of canvas walls and woolen carpets separate from the main body of the tent.

At the far end of that room, Charles waited upon a gold-leafed traveling throne, chin resting on hand. The young knight stopped a respectful distance before the throne and bowed.

"Do stand," Charles said sharply, waving his hand with a familiar agitation. "You've stirred up the nobles, my boy. And not only for this morning's stunt. Just for being here, some want me to send you back to Aachen with the empty supply wagons and lock you away in a tower. Maybe even throw away the key!"

Roland straightened. "I meant no disrespect."

Charles examined the youth's face for a moment with an imperious gaze. Then he chuckled, like cracking flint. "No, of course not. I know in your heart you didn't. Yet here you are, the young bravo—instead of in Breton March where Ganelon left you."

Roland's eyes never left Charles. "I'm here because Demetrius, the emissary from Constantinople, brought news. Important news."

"He did, did he? And this news is?"

Roland felt his heart pulse in his throat. "An invasion by Saragossa."

"Invasion?" Charles leaned back in his chair, tangling his fingers together. "Demetrius has proof of this?"

"Yes," Roland said. "He brought with him the sons of Barcelona *and* Saragossa. The son of Saragossa, this Saleem, has detailed information on the emir's plans."

"Saragossa's own son?" Charles nodded, staring off into space for a moment, then asked, "And you trust Demetrius?"

"He *is* the ambassador, sire."

A frown sagged Charles's face. "That's not what I asked. Ambassadors are men. And more than most men, they cloud the truth."

The youth's eyes never wavered. "My father trusted him, and I trust him."

Charles narrowed his eyes and stood. He paced slowly around the chair, clutching its back until his knuckles whitened. "We must finish our Saxon problem first. Afterward, we'll assemble the court and present your news." His voice dropped to a whisper. "This is serious, indeed."

"Yes, sire. I remind you that if they surprise us, they could drive all the way to the heart of Francia."

"I am well aware of that," Charles replied with ill-concealed annoyance.

"My king, I meant no—"

"No disrespect, I know, nephew. I know. You never do." He seemed to loosen slightly, like a tree bent by a wind that suddenly relents. "You have yet to learn the subtleties appropriate to your station. But then, perhaps diplomacy is not your calling." He motioned Roland closer. "If this is true, this invasion must not happen." Charles's voice remained low and firm. "And you've a role in this. Once this business with the Saxons is done, I want your father's spies activated. I must know more ..."

He trailed off, rubbing his beard, then suddenly turned back to Roland and fixed him with an intense glare. "As for tomorrow, I cannot look to play favorites. You disobeyed an order from my appointed representative in the Breton March. You'll go to battle but in the reserves—under Count Florian's command."

Roland opened his mouth, but before the words could tumble out, Charles raised a hand. Seeing the audience was over, Roland sketched another bow and slowly backed the way he had come. By the time the canvas flap ruffled closed, the king was already at his camp table rifling through documents, muttering beneath his breath.

Night descended on the tense fields, and the two armies congregated about campfires for their final meal before the hostilities of the next day. The smell of wood smoke and burnt meat drifted bucolically across the fields, the same fields that would be sown with blood on the morrow.

Ganelon stalked through the shadows of the Frank camp, his face stony, eyes focused on the steps before him through clusters of troopers readying equipment for the engagement. By the time he finally reached the tents he sought, some simple and some exotically different, the sun had descended below the horizon.

Roland emerged from one tent, shrugging and stretching.

"I thought that had to be you." Roland laughed when he saw Ganelon's darkened face.

"And here you are instead of in the march." The words spit from Ganelon's mouth in a rapid fire staccato. "And what you did today? Disgraceful! You acted like a damn fool! Despite all your birth and blood, it's clear you've no regard for honor or decorum. You're nothing more than a spoilt child playing at war!'"

"I did what any soldier would. I used the ground to my advantage," Roland countered. "Securing victory for Charles is all that matters."

Ganelon stepped closer, expecting to cow the impetuous youth. "Not only dishonorable but arrogant. Today you stole honor from many great lords. Men who have fought and bled to earn the right to stand beside their king."

"You mean the same great lords who leaped forward to take up our cause?" Roland spat back. "Now the Saxons have fled. We have crossed the river, and Charles has his honor."

Ganelon motioned toward the soldiers stitching torn garments, honing edges on weapons, and repairing saddles. "Look around you. While you crow about the king's honor, noble men prepare to die."

"I see them. Yet this morning I saw noble men stare at their boots as the Saxon mocked us!"

"How dare you!" Ganelon snarled as Oliver pulled back the canvas to step out at Roland's side. "Your cavalier attitude disgusts me!"

"Then," Roland said levelly, "perhaps you should have offered to fight the Saxon."

Ganelon's hand fell to his sword hilt. "How dare you? I am not some drunken sot ..." His eyes bored into the younger man's, and his knuckles whitened on his pommel.

"Really, Roland," Oliver quipped. "Baiting him like that. You know better. You'll back him into a corner, and his honor will require that he draw a sword. Oh, what a blood feud that would begin!"

"Stay out of this!" Ganelon spat. But his attention had been broken.

"As you wish, my lord."

By now Ganelon heard a change in the camp sounds behind him, a subtle shift in the character of the creaking leather and chinking metal. His eyes darted around. Several of Roland's companions had risen to their feet. Though no weapons were blatantly readied, each man had a blade, a club, or some other deadly implement close to hand. Ganelon swung his gaze back to Roland, who returned it unflinchingly.

"It occurs to me, Roland," Oliver offered gently, "now is not the time to be disrespectful. We've a battle in the morning. A better use of the time for all might be sleep."

Roland held Ganelon's gaze for just a heartbeat longer. Then suddenly his face broke into a grin.

"Of course, Oliver! My apologies, honored stepfather." He bowed deeply. "It would seem I have spoken out of turn."

Ganelon glanced between the two youths, Roland with his innocent dancing eyes, Oliver with the silent admonition to take the exit offered. His anger burned, but he knew the price of causing a disturbance on the eve of battle.

"Apology accepted."

Ganelon slapped at the leather scabbard and dismissed them with a wave of the hand as he turned and stalked into the night.

ΑΟΙ

Morning broke brisk and cold as the sky turned from shades of black to gray with darker clouds above rolling in that threatened rain. With that first light, the Frank camp became a sea of activity. Soldiers streamed into ranks stretching along the edge of the great forest across the fields to the sea, jostling one another beneath the rough admonitions of their sergeants. Pennants and standards waved bravely, each signifying a noble house taking a place in the line—infantry companies in the center with archers behind, Bertrin's cavalry on the right flank and Ganelon holding hard by the sea on the left.

Before the Frank host stood ranks of Saxon foot soldiers spread along a low ridge near the dark, silent wood, secure behind oval shields and sporting a varied assortment of weapons hefted over their shoulders. Some wore homespun wool and animal skins like their Frank cousins, though most would strip off the encumbering layers before noontime as the grip of battle would soon enough provide sufficient warmth. Massive war-dogs roamed freely among them and barked madly at the Franks.

Horns blared, and the Frank army surged forward, slowly at first as the sergeants strained to keep an orderly advance and conserve energy, then picking up speed until they were charging across the field. Charles rode atop his dappled mare with his personal guards forming the center. Pepin and Louis, Charles's younger son, both resplendent in fine armor and brilliant surcoats, rode at his side.

But outshining even them in the morning rays, a silver horn bounced among Charles's finery on a polished chain. The martial instrument was crafted from a large bull's horn, its milky smoothness chased with silver bands ornately carved with Germanic dragons and triumphant saints. This was the Oliphant, whose pure note in battles past had sounded Charles's victories from the Northern Sea to the banks of the Rubicon, and even from the walls of Rome.

Roland sat upon his horse among the rearguard near Bishop Turpin, stewing in his armor as he watched the advancing troops move off. Fire burned within him, not from the anticipation of battle but rather from watching others fight and die from a distance. He flexed his hand around the reins, tightening his knuckles on the leather straps, fighting the urge to bury his spurs into his horse's flanks. What a glorious race that could be to outstrip Bertrin and his cavalry to the Saxon line! But it was not to be, for near him old Florian of Burgundy leaned forward on his steed, squinting with rheumy eyes through bushy eyebrows. The man's belly pushed against the saddlebow when he wheezed through his mustaches, a thick-jowled bear of a man with a bristly gray beard.

"Hold your place," Florian grumbled.

In the distance, a horn sounded.

The roar of thousands releasing their battle-lust answered. Roland watched, lips pursed, as the Frank center struck and Charles's eagle banner surged forward, the accompanying infantry driving a wedge into the Saxon middle. The two armies locked into a brawl whose winnings would be measured by yards of muddy ground and blood.

Atop his lunging warhorse, Charles leaned low in the saddle and with his sword hewed down a Saxon warrior. The long minutes of the initial collision stretched into an hour of mortal combat where Frank troopers pushed hard against the stiffening Saxon shield wall.

Amid the chaos, a Frank horseman, his surcoat already torn and bloodied, urged his steed toward the royal guard that fought like lions to keep the Saxons at bay. His face exuded nothing but confidence as his mount danced past a thrusting enemy spear.

"Sire!" he shouted over the din. "He's flanked them! Bertrin mauls them on the right!"

Charles gestured nearby troopers forward into a newly opened gap in the Saxon line. He then pulled his horse back from the fray, choking for breath for a moment before he responded. "Ride on to Ganelon. He must hold against the sea!"

The messenger saluted, hauled his horse around, and spurred through the infantry to the left of the Frank line. Charles raised the Oliphant to his dry lips and blew a note that broke across the Frank center, cutting through the din of battle like the cry of an avenging angel, rallying the men in another mighty push to break the Saxons.

With the notes still echoing across the fields, Oliver rode up beside Roland and pointed across the battle to Bertrin's heavy cavalry. The horsemen charged with wicked iron-tipped lances into the Saxons and drove them back but in so doing pulled away from the center and opened a gap between. Before them, the enemy staggered back against their own lines as men bunched together then fell back.

"Look! They buckle! The Saxons will not stand!" Oliver cheered.

But Roland could see the impending danger. His feet twitched in the stirrups.

Florian mumbled, "Hold the line."

Bertrin raced to envelop the Saxons, leading the entire right wing around the enemy flank and widening the gap between him and the Frank center.

Just then northern horns blared from the wood beyond the battle. Roland's blood chilled.

"God, no!"

He spurred his horse forward, heedless of Florian's fumbling, as rank upon rank of Dane warriors emerged from an arm of the forest reaching to the ridgeline. The pale sunlight glinted from their helmets while a ragged cheer broke from the Saxons. Even from this distance, Roland could mark their jarl, ringed by his mailclad bodyguard and bannermen.

The Danes lifted their bows and bent them skyward. Upon a distant command, they released as one, the arrows hissing high and then screaming down to tear into Bertrin's exposed flank. Horses and riders tumbled, churning up muck as steel barbs found chinks in their armor. The Danes let out a raucous cheer then bent their bows once more, releasing a rain of fletched death down on the combatants, Saxon and Frank alike.

"My lord!" Roland shouted urgently to Florian. "They must not be allowed to join with the Saxons! The whole right flank will crumble! We must intervene!"

But as the count turned his wide girth in the saddle to shout commands, something else consumed him. He began suddenly garbling and choking. His eyes desperately darted back and forth as he vainly sought words. With a huff, he sagged into the saddle, his limbs quivering and his faculties unresponsive. Squires rushed to support his violently twitching body.

"Apoplexy!" Turpin exclaimed as the squires struggled under the count's sporadic thrashing and sagging bulk.

"Dear God! Gather the bandon commanders!" Roland shouted, pulling his mount's head around to face the reserves once more. A pair of squires scampered away to gather the nobles commanding the ragtag units that constituted the reserves.

"They must fight!" Roland whispered urgently to Oliver.

"Then you must lead them!" his friend replied.

Roland felt breath chill in his throat with Oliver's words, for this could quickly turn into a slaughter when they reached the gap and faced the full fury of the Northmen. It was one thing for him to rush into the fray with seasoned troops from the march who had fought for his father. But these with him now—these were only a hodgepodge of poorer hedge-knights and peasants who barely knew their place in line, let alone the measured movements of a well-disciplined formation. Regardless, the task had to be done. He spurred his horse's flanks and cantered up the ragged group. Too many faces—there were just too many for him to remember each one that looked to him for guidance and direction. And all too soon they would be trampled under Danish boots to be forgotten even by the realm that was about to throw them into the breach.

He sucked the chilled air between his teeth and prepared to give the order to advance, when from the midst of the reserves, rank upon rank of Breton marchmen pushed to the fore. Kennick's familiar grizzled face strode before them, a grin splitting his salt-and-pepper beard. The marchmen halted and locked their shields, their precise movements a peerless reflection of the moldering texts Roland had drilled into them while slogging through the muddy fields of the march.

"God bless you, Kennick!" Roland reached down to clasp the warrior's arm in his hand. "But what on earth have you done?"

"Well, my lord," the grizzled veteran grumbled, "it seems that in your rush to get off to war, you forgot something." He handed Roland a saddlebag with road mud still on it. "I thought you might be needing this."

Roland reached inside then looked sharply at Kennick. "You know there will be hell to pay for this."

"I always pay my debts, boy."

Roland tugged out the folded banner, shaking it to its full length. A grin broke out across his face—the rampant wolf of Breton March had arrived to lead them to war.

"Squire!"

He handed the banner off to a youth who tied the pennant to the end of a lance. Roland grabbed it back eagerly. The men fell silent as the wolf rose proudly overhead. The sign of the champion had returned to the field.

"Men!" Roland called over the distant clash of battle. "Our king is sorely pressed, and we're honor bound to aid him! You'd follow Florian into battle. Now, I ask that you follow me!" He thrust the banner into the air. "Today, will you live and die with the wolf of the Breton March?"

The men shouted in an incoherent cheer, banging their weapons against their shields. Roland handed the lance to the squire, crossed himself solemnly, then clasped his hands together. He bowed his head, and the anxious men clustered around following his example.

Bishop Turpin dismounted and knelt in their center. "Dear God," he said, "deliver us, your faithful servants, from the hands of the heathen. Amen!"

Roland drew his sword, the long steel flashing in the uncertain light, and wheeled his mount back around to face the battle. A glitter of gold caught his eye when out of the throng Demetrius, Karim, and Saleem trotted forward and settled into the front rank next to him.

"You're here as well?" Roland said. "But this isn't your fight!"

Karim flashed bright teeth. "Our fathers are allies, are they not?"

Demetrius shrugged. "I ride with my friends."

Saleem only grunted and appeared aloof.

Roland nodded. "Your friends welcome you." Then raising his voice, he continued, "Cavalry, with me! Oliver, draw up the infantry and fill the gap. We will strengthen Bertrin's left and cut off the Danes. Strike hard!"

Horns blared and the reserves leaped forward—hedge knights on bony nags and footmen with mismatched armor—with Roland at their head.

In the center of the now struggling Frank line, Charles found himself urgently waving troops forward through a field choked with the dying and the dead. Arrows continued slicing down, finding chinks in armor and bare exposed flesh. His mount suddenly pitched over and crashed to the earth, an arrow through its eye. Guards rushed to his aid, fighting desperately against the surging Saxons driven with wicked abandon as they sniffed victory at hand. The guards cut at Charles's harness, freeing him from the tangle of leather and dead horseflesh. He grabbed a soldier by the arm and staggered to his feet.

"Father!" Pepin yelled from his vantage point atop his steed. "The Danes flank Bertrin! They'll encircle us!"

"Send to Florian! He must commit the reserves to the right. To the right!" Charles stepped into a gap in his own line, thrusting his sword under a Saxon's chin. The man staggered back, clutching at his open throat, to be finished by another Frank who shouldered him off balance and punched a hammer against his temple. Cheers drew Charles's eyes toward the rear of his own army, but he could see nothing afoot.

"What is it?" he demanded.

"The wolf!" Louis shouted, drawing his own horse up near his father. "Breton March rides before the reserves!"

Charles straightened, his bloody sword clenched in his fist. "We must hold! Saint Michael be praised!"

He lifted the Oliphant, pressing the silver horn to his lips, and blew. Its clear, sweet note echoed above the din of battle, and his mind flew for the briefest instant to a time when he had held his first field command and used the same horn to call for help. A knight had ridden to his side that day—a knight named William of Breton March.

Hooves churned through the muck on the rear of Charles's right flank, and the reserve cavalry raced toward the edge of Bertrin's line. Dane arrows voraciously rained upon them, dropping horses and men in headlong flight, but it did not slow their charge. Roland's banner surged to the fore of a wave of iron under the ringing note from the Oliphant, and then the Frank cavalry collided with the Danes, armored knights wreaking havoc among the lightly armed skirmishers, trampling them like so many blades of grass and driving the survivors before them.

A Dane howled a battle cry and drove his spear into the chest of Roland's charging mount, toppling horse, rider, and attacker into the muck. The Dane leapt to his feet first and snatched the butt of his broken weapon from the horse's carcass. He lunged. Roland awkwardly parried the attack even as he struggled to free himself from his own harness.

Oliver raced through the butcherous cacophony, his lathered horse lashing out with iron-shod hooves to those reckless enough to offer challenge. Roland's opponent fell when Oliver struck him above the collar of his hauberk and severed his head in a fountain of blood. Nearby, the squire bearing the wolf bravely fought more Danes, but an ax opened him up at the shoulder, and the standard faltered, dropping from his slackened hands. Oliver leapt from his steed to grab the pennant from the muck and fight back the Danes. Then he hefted it high above the fray. Roland extracted himself at last and rushed to Oliver's side to keep the northern enemy from stripping the marchmen of their standard.

A wave seemed to ripple through the Danish ranks. Not far away,

Kennick and the marchmen, having stabilized the line, now shoved further into the enemy to recover their young lord. Locked shields bore down against the loosely formed Danes who gave way as the Franks stabbed and slashed, each man protecting his comrade to his left.

The reserve cavalry regrouped under Demetrius's direction and advanced as well. Karim and Saleem fought like lions in their midst, deadly Damascan blades carving a path of mayhem.

The tide began to turn.

Otun, broad-shouldered and mail-clad champion of the Danes, had been fighting in his jarl's bodyguard until the battle's confusion had separated him from them. He now roved down the flank with a great murderous ax gripped in both his meaty hands, laying into any contenders within reach. His green eyes, deep-set under bushy red brows, were fixed on the Frank reserves that had stalled his countrymen's advance, and the knight fending off fierce Danish warriors from under a wolf banner.

That standard would be a welcome trophy for the Jarl's great hall, Otun mused as if a whisper from a Valkyrie had placed the thought in his battle-drunken head.

He hefted the ax, spat mud and blood, and with a bellow upon his lips launched into the chaos surrounding this youth. Frank troopers fought back, but he shrugged them off and answered only sparingly with the edge of his weapon. He had no time for such trifles. He was focused on his prize, this young man cutting, thrusting, and barking orders.

Roland pulled his blade from the groin of yet another enemy, the man collapsing in a gush of blood and jumble of flesh. Turpin yelled something that was incoherent in the chaos, and Roland spun in time to see a great red beast of a man, covered in finely made chain and bearing a deadly two-headed ax, breaking through the ring of marchmen around him.

This Dane cut at him with a roar, but Roland deflected the ax with an adroit tilt of his shield. Slightly off balance, the red-bearded giant swung again, driving forward with knotted shoulders, pushing Roland back and splintering the shield. Roland dropped the ruined board, rolled to the side, and threw his blade forward at an angle just as his assailant brought the ax down in a two-handed overhead maneuver. The sword flexed dangerously from the ax head's impact on the flat, but his hand braced the blade and deflected the cut away from his body. He drove the sword and the ax into the ground and smashed the Dane in the face with an armored fist, then hooked his foot around the other's trailing leg as he lunged forward, toppling them both. Roland landed atop the Dane and tugged his dagger free, pressing the edge to the enemy's throat.

"Yield!" Roland demanded.

The Dane sputtered, flailing his arms. He noticed for the first time the young warrior's motley collection of companions, from poor knights and farmers to an exotically armored Byzantine standing near two Saracens. "What manner of man are you?"

"Do you yield?" Roland pressed the dagger down, drawing blood.

The fallen man ceased struggling.

"Who do we yield to?" he rasped.

"I am Roland, son of William, who was count of the Breton March!"

The Dane twisted his head to one side, calling to his struggling comrades. "Jarl Sigursson, is he dead?"

"He is fallen, Otun!" replied a Dane warrior who paused, notched sword still at the ready, and was covered from head to toe with blood and earth.

Otun's red eyebrows knit together. Then he forced the words from his mouth, "We yield to the wolf!"

One by one as the Danes recognized the word of their champion, they disengaged and lowered their weapons.

Oliver thrust his sword skyward to the reserves' ragged cheer, the ripple of which was felt through the entire line of battle—from the forest verge, through the torn fields, to the edge of the sea.

Under the clearing vermillion sky, a brilliant note echoed off the hills. *Victory*, it sang.

Charles lowered the silver horn from his lips, his eyes scanning the wreckage from the day's business. Around him stood the stalwart men

51

who had held the center even as Bertrin recklessly chased after the Saxon feint. The bodies of Danes, Saxons, and Franks lay tangled among dead horses and war-dogs. Crows circled and cawed overhead, anxious to feast amid the cracked armor and torn gambesons.

From the fading light that engulfed the carnage emerged those who had held the left flank through the crisis on the right—Ganelon, who had fought with his back to the sea as the Saxon onslaught consumed the center; Alans, who had rolled over the Saxon king's position and slaughtered his guard to a man; and Gothard, who had stood knee-deep in corpses when the tide turned following the reserve charge. *Good men, all.*

Alans took a knee before Charles. "We shattered them, my king."

Charles laid a hand on his shoulder. "Yes. We did indeed. I pray to God they accept the terms." He scanned the field once more. "And the reserves, what of them? What of Florian's command? I lost them when they hit the Danish host."

A soldier pointed toward the darkened forest. From the shelter of its ancient boughs a disparate group of men in mismatched arms picked their way through the fallen and the broken, pausing here and there to lift another survivor to carry along with them. At their head strode Roland, followed by Kennick, Oliver, and Bishop Turpin.

When they reached the king, Roland dropped to his knees next to Alans and held up a canvas bundle. Charles took it from him, his hands shaking slightly when he unwrapped it.

"What is this?" he breathed, his voice low as he folded back the cloth.

"The sword of the Dane jarl," Roland replied, bowing his head.

Charles drew forth the gleaming blade and lifted it for all to see, its hilt and pommel a scrolling work of art that belied the butcher's intent of the thick blade.

"A prize indeed." He lowered the weapon and examined its workmanship. "We owe you much, young Roland."

Taken by a sudden urge, he lifted the blade again. "With my nobles here assembled," Charles's voice rose with majestic authority, "I make this pronouncement before God and his angels ... Roland of Breton

March, by the authority I hold as anointed ruler of this people, I bestow upon you the rights, privileges, and honors of champion!" He touched Roland on the shoulder with the steel blade. "Arise, son of William! Arise, champion of the realm, and sword of God!"

The Frank soldiers shouted their approval, striking their shields with mailed fists. The rearguard crowed the loudest and the longest.

Gothard leaned to his father's ear. "He now has a champion to protect him once more. Father, you've planned so long!"

Ganelon's face remained a stoic mask. "We are the house of Clovis, blood of the first king. Patience. Always patience. Draw no attention to yourself. Trust me when I say no champion will stand between us and the throne."

CHAPTER 5

CHAMPION BORNE

The stream ran cloudy with mud stirred by clerics wading down into the waters. Still more men of the cloth guided prisoners cut loose by the guards to participate in the sacrament of the Church and satisfy the terms of their parole, terms that had been set to prevent these beaten warriors from fleeing over the forested hills to take up the fight yet again. The captives stretched in a line back toward the ancient trees that at the start of this day had hosted worship to the Germanic gods—one-eyed Wodin and thundering Thor. Standing with their Saxon and Dane charges in the shallows, the priests muttered mechanically in Latin then they pushed the prisoners under the water and pulled them dripping back up, before leading them to the far bank where soldiers awaited them. On the muddy shore, they knelt before Bishop Turpin who recited the words to their oath:

"... And before God and these witnesses do you swear to never again take up arms against Charles and his people ..."

The prisoners, as had the group before them, replied in a single word, "Yes."

The soldiers then dragged them to their feet and goaded them to still more clergymen, who supplied them with simple homespun clothes and hard bread. In the shade of the ancient trees, they were finally allowed respite to tear hungrily into the small loaves and shake the water from their hair. Armed Franks prowled the area to ensure continued compliance as another group was led down into the water.

Otun stood tall among the flowing line of prisoners ambling slowly forward to the river, stripped to the waist, hands bound and feet hobbled. Yet he held his head high, his beard bristling defiantly. Before him, his brothers, cousins, and friends took upon themselves the promises of the Christian god who dwelt in a far-off city and swore to keep faith with the Franks. He strained at the bonds around his wrists, digging the cord deeper into his already raw flesh. From a knot of men nearby, the young knight Roland, his last adversary on the battlefield, watched the proceedings with apparent interest. Otun held his head defiantly higher.

At the lapping edge of the river, a guard shoved him forward.

"Get in. It'll be over soon, and you'll be off to your hovel and your pigs—including your wife!"

The man guffawed at his own wit. Otun balled up his fists and swung, smashing him in the face and sending his helmet flying over the heads of his fellows. Another soldier grabbed at him until a jab from the Dane's powerful elbow knocked the wind from him. The guard reeled into the other prisoners who grappled for his weapons. More soldiers rushed in and beat the prisoners down with fists and pommels.

"Wodin's eye be damned!" Otun roared, facing the naked blade of a Frank with murder in his eyes.

"This is the one," the Frank snarled. "The instigator!"

From out of the mix of brawling Danes and Franks, Roland pushed his way forward. He grabbed the guard's arm, halting the man's sword inches from Otun's bared chest.

"What's going on here?" Roland demanded.

Otun's breath hissed through his teeth.

A cleric, shivering and cold in the stream, piped up helpfully. "This man," he said, pointing at Otun. "This heathen profanes a sacrament of God!"

Otun held his bound fists before Roland. "This is too much to ask! If I do this thing, my soul will be exiled from the halls of Valhalla!"

Roland nodded, but his words held little comfort for the Dane. "Terms of parole, I'm afraid. I can't countermand King Charles's own order. All will be baptized. That is his word."

Otun spat at Roland's feet. "Your god was weak. I've heard your mewling priests tell the tale of him strung up on a tree!"

"Yet it is He who strengthens my arm," Roland countered. "He who is my shield."

"Thor's wrath makes the heavens and earth shake with fear!"

"And yet for all his rumbling," Roland said quietly, "your god didn't grant you victory."

Otun glanced around at the line of prisoners, his own Danish comrades from distant villages of the north. They watched their champion carefully, awaiting his next move. After a heartbeat, his shoulders sagged.

"It is true. I cannot deny it." He lowered his hands. "But I would serve a warrior. I would be an arm of the gods. Not ..." he nodded scathingly at the priest in the river, "not one of *these*."

Abruptly the giant Dane fell to his knees before Roland.

"Your God will grant me strength in battle?" Otun demanded.

"Yes," Roland said warily. Then, with conviction, "Yes, He will. Both in body and in spirit. But only—" he held out a warning hand, "only if you truly give yourself to Him."

Otun considered this. He could feel the eyes of his countrymen on his back. Then, making his decision, he twisted his palms together as a supplicant and reached out to Roland.

"I watched your priests do this with a squire and a knight," he said. "Before I make promises to your God, I swear to you first."

Roland considered this great warrior beast that had laid so many low but a short time ago. "This isn't in the terms. Do you know what it means to be a vassal? To be my sworn man?"

"You are the champion, are you not? I hear your heralds proclaim it. And the Franks are a mighty people, are they not?" From his knees, he straightened his back and puffed out his chest. "I would serve you, Roland, champion of the Franks." From beneath strands of blood-matted hair, his beard cracked into a grin. "Even if it meant feeding that ugly Frank nag of yours!"

Marking the effect of Otun's words on the gaggle of prisoners, Roland clasped the Dane's brutish hands between his own and bowed his head.

"My horse and I are honored. We accept."

Roland drew his dagger and sliced through Otun's ropes. As if a dam burst, other Danish prisoners clambered forward, straining against their own bonds to follow in Otun's footsteps and speak the words binding them to the Frank champion.

The morning sun chased away nightmarish shadows from the battlefield, but the cleansing rays of light could not remove the stench of death. Throughout the night, Franks and Saxons had ranged across the fields to comfort those who struggled for life and take away those who had succumbed. The bodies were separated—the noblemen worthy of transport to their homeland for proper burial were laid aside from the commoners who would be interred in a mass grave where Saxon parolees even now bent their backs to deepen the pit.

Another stone clacked into place as two clerics completed a rough field altar for the service later in the day. They paused and stretched their sore backs as Roland approached. One, the abbot of a local monastery, tonsure as gray as the mist rising from the fields, bowed gratefully and pronounced blessings upon the champion for his service to God's kingdom on earth. The other, a layman in sagging homespun that billowed from the cinch at his waist, likewise bowed and backed away from their crude handiwork.

"Please, only if you're done," Roland said.

The two holy men stammered an inarticulate response and left the knight to his meditations.

Roland sank to his knees, burying his head in his hands.

"I begin here, Lord. I just pray you will guide me along this path."

Weariness bore heavily on his shoulders. He hadn't slept well the night before amid the groans of the wounded and the maimed that drifted through the thin canvas walls of the tent he shared with Oliver. Robbed of sleep, he had crept from the tent to labor with the camp surgeons. The earliest rays of dawn had found him covered in dark stains and still seeking out his men.

Now, with this moment of peace, he recalled a long-ago day when as a lad of nine or ten he'd burst from the stables in a flurry of sobs and tears. A stable boy tending his father's steed had just taunted him about the preparations for the spring campaign to Italy that would leave the youth with the other children. He ran to the courtyard where William directed the marchmen. Roland remembered him a giant standing head and shoulders above those he commanded, exuding boundless energy in his preparations for war. He was Apollo in the sky of his youthful son. It did not matter that he was the right hand of the king and, as champion, the right hand of God himself, for to Roland, William held a much simpler title—that of father.

Seeing the outburst, he caught his son by the arm and knelt down to meet the lad's eye.

"What is it, boy?" William asked, brushing tears from Roland's cheeks.

The lad puffed out his chest and straightened up, a young soldier bucking up under inspection of his commanding officer. But that wasn't all William saw in Roland's eyes.

"You're sending me to the vale to page. And then you leave too. Why must you leave me?"

"Well," said William, a man known for his few words, "it's my duty."

"But it will be such a long time!" Roland sniffled. "Who will take care of Mother?"

William smiled then, no longer the champion but the husband and father. "Sometimes we are asked to do hard things. Even your mother will miss both of us while we are away. But our calling is to serve. And Charles is God's anointed, so we are engaged in a cause for our family, the march, and the kingdom."

Roland clutched his father, burying his face against his chest, arms straining to encompass the whole of the man. "Then take me! Don't send me away. I can fight! Father, tell God I will serve Charles! Just take me with you!"

"This is not your time, son," William said, kissing the lad on the cheek. "Nor is it my place to tell God what He should do. Your chance will come, I promise. You will serve Charles."

Roland pushed away from his father's embrace. "But when? I can use a sword. You know I can!"

William laughed and ruffled the lad's hair. "Yes, I do, and I still have the bruises to prove it. God will show you when it is time. And when that moment comes, you must not just *use* the sword. You must *be* the sword. You must be the sword of God."

"My lord!" The voice broke into Roland's thoughts, and he lifted his head, blinking in the light that had grown since he knelt. A squire panted nearby, waving his hand toward the camp. "My lord, Oliver has sent for you. You must come now. You must hurry back to camp!"

Roland jumped to his feet and rushed through the Frank encampment to the march's enclave, all the way dodging men who stepped in his path to congratulate him on his new office. His breath clouded in the chill morning air, leaving a trail of mist in his wake. When he approached his square of tents, he could see Ganelon flanked by his personal escort. The count of Tournai emphatically gestured with his hands while he stomped back and forth before the assembled troopers. Kennick stood at their head, shoulders back and head high, bearing the harangue in stoic silence. Unoccupied soldiers started to gather at a safe distance to watch.

"You disobeyed your liege lord!" Ganelon's voice rang out.

Oliver placed himself between the grizzled veteran and the red-faced count.

"The heir of the march entered harm's way," Kennick responded evenly. "I knew my lord would want him protected."

"Protected from his own foolishness!" Ganelon fumed. "I commanded that none leave the march!"

Roland pushed through a knot of onlookers to Kennick's side. "What game is this?" he snarled. "This man did both you and the king a great service!"

Ganelon pointed a finger at Kennick then swept that same hand over the marchmen. "And broke his oath, stepson! This man holds rank! He bears trust for all these men. For that there must be account! Do you hear me? He will receive seventy-five lashes and shall consider himself lucky. I pray when you are count in the march they will have learned to not be so surly!"

"You've no cause!" Roland stood his ground. "I gave the order in the face of new information that you couldn't have known about."

"I have every cause," Ganelon snarled back. "I hold Breton March under Charles's own writ. My word is law until I am relieved."

"And not a day too soon!"

"And yet today my will be done!" Ganelon snapped.

Gothard stepped forward, smugly directing Tournai men to take Kennick and drag him to a nearby hitching post. Armed men blocked Roland. Marchmen rumbled with displeasure. A threat of blood hung in the air.

Ganelon's men stripped Kennick to the waist and stretched him on the post. A heavily muscled trooper tugged a knotted whip from his belt and snapped it with a crack.

"Wait!" Roland shouted. He lunged into the cluster of troopers between him and Kennick, dropping one with a blow across the jaw and twisting past the others. Marchmen surged toward Ganelon, but Roland spun back and held up a warning hand. "Hold!" They stumbled to a halt, confusion on their faces.

Roland snapped back to Ganelon once more. "For Christ's sake, if this man is to be punished for coming to my aid, punish me instead!"

Ganelon drew himself up, a shrewd look on his face. "Intriguing— the champion of the realm torn under the lash for a broken vow? No man may strike the champion and go without retribution from the king himself." He tapped his chin thoughtfully. "But this is my right and my justice. Not even Charles can fault the exercise of my duty. This man must bear the weight of his own crime!"

Roland threw his body before the lash, and Ganelon's man pulled the whip short.

"My lord," Kennick growled to Roland, "you must not. My honor requires this. I broke my word. By God, I'd break it a hundred times over to fight by your side. But break it I did. We can choose our actions. But we must accept the consequences."

"Kennick—" Roland began.

"I always pay my debts, boy."

"Father, he stops you from discharging your duty!" Gothard whined. "This cannot be tolerated!"

Roland straightened and snatched the whip from Ganelon's man.

"This man is mine," he shouted. Then he raised his voice above the growing discontent among the marchmen. "This man is mine! Be still, marchmen! I command you to stand down!" Roland lifted the whip and waved it at Ganelon's face. Behind him courtiers and nobles gravitated to the commotion. "This man will be mine when I am confirmed in my inheritance. As such, I demand the right to punish him. No man will exact punishment on any of my men but me!"

The marchmen pounded the ground with their feet, affirmation that they stood with William's son. Ganelon's face darkened, his brows knitting together while the bystanders grew in number and crowded closer.

"Carry out the punishment, and honor is satisfied," he growled.

Roland faced Kennick's back and hefted the whip, the knotted length falling about his feet. By his own hand, the leather lashed across Kennick's flesh, each stroke tearing a raw mark. Gothard loudly barked a grim count with satisfaction. The veteran clenched his jaws as his skin was flayed over and over. In time his knees buckled, but he struggled to regain his feet and to keep his already scarred body erect. His eyes stared ahead at his men, no cry escaping his lips.

Ganelon stood with arms folded and grim, watching with wicked contentment the blood spattering the air. Many of the crowd turned away from the gore before the whip fell for the last time and Roland dropped it to the ground. A breathless groan accompanied Roland when he rushed to cut Kennick loose. The veteran collapsed into his arms, and the marchmen broke ranks, surrounding their own in an iron embrace.

CHAPTER 6

SARAGOSSA'S HEART

In distant Saragossa, preparations for war continued to the rhythm of drums and horns. Beneath the martial staccato, the emir's troops assembled for inspection before the city's dun-colored walls. Marsilion reclined in his typical fashion beneath a silk parasol near the parade grounds, sipping a chilled drink while the sun beat down on the nobles who sweated uncomfortably beside him.

Blancandrin, unwilling to show any sign of discomfort within his dark armor, approached the emir's canvas pavilion from amid the ranks of troops and prostrated himself. Marsilion let him remain in the dust for a moment while he visibly accounted the strength of units passing before him. Finally there was a break between battalions, and he motioned distractedly for the general to stand.

"Speak," Marsilion ordered, sipping his drink and wiping stray liquid from his beard. His eyes darted after a fly racing for the edge of his cup. He swatted it away.

Blancandrin cleared his throat to refocus his lord's attention. "Our scouts have returned from Barcelona," the general reported. "We've sufficient arms to keep Sulayman caged within the city, but we will be hard-pressed north of the Pyrenees. And the caliph ..." his voice trailed to silence.

"What of His Eminence?" the emir eagerly asked. "What aid does he promise us?"

Blancandrin ground his teeth as he glanced to where Honorius stood among the nobles, resplendent in his impeccable armor, decorative eagles glistening in the midday sunlight. His painted-on smile seemed oblivious to the heat.

"The caliph has not committed men," Blancandrin said. He silently prayed for an opportunity to remove the Byzantine's head from his shoulders before the emir led the army, and the entire city, down the road to ruin. "Instead, at the ambassador's request," he nodded deferentially in Honorius's direction, "he's sent us Greek prisoners. Broken men in chains! My emir, what we need are soldiers!"

Marsilion flashed his general a diplomatic smile. "Calm yourself. Our other allies have committed troops. Look—" He gestured across the plumed and armored formations ranged before them. Though pennants hung still on the windless day, only rarely rippling when a rider fidgeted or a foot soldier dared swipe at a fly, they presented an impressive vista of deadly might. "See the splendor of the tribesmen from Morocco! See the Algerian lancers!"

"Yes, my emir," Blancandrin acknowledged. "Enough for Barcelona. But not to hold even a few steps into Francia."

The emir drained his cup and handed it off to a waiting youth. "Nevertheless, we will send war parties to the north. Prepare the army to cross the mountains, once we dispose of Barcelona." He stood and stepped out from under the canvas into the blinding sun, drawing close to his general.

Blancandrin bowed. "As you command, Emir."

"We must have more information on Frank movements, Blancandrin. Perhaps we will find a weakness we can exploit?" Marsilion flashed a genuine smile this time, placing a hand on the other man's shoulder. "Do your best, old friend. I will send to the caliph again. And I'll beg for his support if I must. I've also thought there may yet be some in the east who have interest in our doings. I'll petition them as well. But mark me, ours is the greater glory for redeeming the honor of our dead. Tours will not be forgotten!"

Marsilion returned his attention to the troopers, but his thoughts were far afield, lingering on a bygone defeat at the hands of Charles Martel those many years ago and the grandeur that would be regained by the grandson of him slain on that bloody field deep in the heart of Francia.

CHAPTER 7

REUNIONS

All of Aachen turned out to witness Charles the Great's triumphal return—nobles, merchants, and commoners alike jostled and elbowed for a place along the muddy street. They crowded against armed soldiers for a better look at the processional that squeezed into the narrow lanes. Not since the liberation of Rome from the Lombards had the city turned out in such riotous numbers. Roland rode in a place of honor just behind the royal entourage among a troop of his men. Otun marched on foot alongside him, sporting a fierce grin and bearing high the standard of the crimson wolf rampant on its white field. The banner snapped viciously in advance of the marchmen and blond- and red-bearded Danes that marched in formation in their wake. Rabble and nobles alike roared their approval when Bishop Turpin lifted his war hammer, calling in a raucous voice to young women leaning out of upper windows, spilling cleavage in defiance of the critical glares of their disapproving matrons.

"Good Bishop," Oliver laughed, waving at the same enticing faces framed in tumbled locks, "it seems you've been away too long!"

"Yes, far too long," the cleric mused with a round-cheeked smile. "Now home to warm the flock with plenty of drink and tales of the summer campaign!"

Oliver snatched a flower that drifted from the hand of a bright-faced girl, her bodice revealing spring and promise. "I'm afraid it will take more than ale and stories to warm them!"

Both men laughed, their voices pleasantly lost in the cacophony of the moment.

Far above the celebrations, in a richly appointed room of the palace, Charles's willowy daughter Aldatrude examined bolts of Greek silk from a merchant just returned from the Orient. Her blonde locks fell loose about her lovely pouting face, and a hand rested upon her hip in a nettled pose. Silks and expensive linens clung to her form, accentuating each of her quick movements. Her sister Berta, shorter and darker with round, flushed features, feigned interest and waited for the inevitable outburst of temper and the lash of Aldatrude's sharp tongue.

Forgotten in the deliberations, Aude, Oliver's sister, wandered to the nearby window. Where Roland's companion was dark haired, she bore their mother's golden tresses that framed high cheekbones highlighted with a faint scattering of freckles and features that bore the stamp of ancient, even Celtic blood. Oh, and she was bored with the talk of baubles and trinkets, trinkets and baubles—on and on without end, the women of the court possessing nothing more to fill their chatter or their minds. They had all waited, for hours it seemed, for the army to snake past their window. But there was only one company in all the mass of troops in which she had an interest. She squinted through the spider web of autumn frost covering the glass and rubbed at it with her slender fingers. Out of habit, her other hand brushed back a golden strand of hair and tucked it behind her ear.

At last the procession appeared in the warren of streets below. From her vantage point, she saw resplendent guards clad in crimson and gold turn the corner and march with precise martial dignity. The crowd continued to press closer, and troopers pushed back with spears and shields. Charles's expansive personal retinue followed and flowed toward the palace, brave banners rippling in the crisp late autumn sunlight. She whispered to herself as she recognized each one, from the crimson boar of Aquitaine to the golden stag of Anjou. Above them all floated the great Roman eagle, gold, black, and scarlet, under which rode Charles himself with his sons and heirs, Louis and Pepin.

"They're home," she barely dared breathe, her fingers rising to her lips. "Here they come!"

She threw open the window as the other women, suddenly galvanized by her words, dropped the exotic wares and flocked to the casement. Just then the wolf of Breton March rode into view, and she caught her breath. Next to Roland, Oliver appeared as well, riding with his companion. "Oh, he's changed so much," she whispered as the two princesses crowded her to one side to see their father and brothers.

"Who's changed?" asked Berta, frantically squeezing for a place at the casement and waving for all her audience below. "Oliver?"

Aude lowered her hand. "Oh, yes. My brother has become a man."

Aldatrude's shrewd eyes darted between Aude and the marchmen. She tugged her sister from the window. "Why, indeed he has. As have my own brothers, Pepin and Louis. I almost missed Oliver among that rabble. Are those the marchmen? It looks like they leashed some unruly Danes and Saxons as part of their wolf pack." She examined the troopers more closely. "Look, there's Roland! He rides in a place of honor—I hear he acquitted himself well in the victory over the Saxons." She gathered Aude's hand in hers. "A fine catch for some noble family, don't you think? A kissing cousin to the king's family, so to speak."

Aude lowered her eyes. "Oh, I wouldn't know, my lady. Such things aren't for me to venture."

"Indeed," Aldatrude mused. She leaned out to catch Roland's eye.

Oliver waved to the window where the women of court fluttered hands and handkerchiefs in greeting.

Roland followed his friend's gesture and caught a fleeting glance of Aude before Aldatrude and Berta crowded her completely out.

Ever astute, Pepin reined his steed back a pace to fall in line with Roland, smiling and tossing an occasional coin to bystanders who scrambled for the rare bit of hard currency.

"You've a following at court, cousin," he said, nodding toward the royal welcome above that was blooming into a spectacle of sisters scrapping for attention before the citizenry.

"They squeal and blush for their brave prince returned from the wars," Roland replied. "Not the hedge knight from Breton March."

Pepin chuckled, slapping Roland on the shoulder. "Court's different than you remember when you ran the palace halls as a child. Now you're our champion! You'll attract many at court, friends and foes. From here on you must consider well in whom you place your trust."

Roland ducked his head from a bit of female clothing that fluttered by to be snatched up by a marchman just behind him. "I will. Thank you for the advice, cousin. I'm most grateful."

Pepin offered Roland a dark, humorless smile.

"Yes. I'm sure you are. We shall speak again, cousin."

With that, the prince nudged his mount with his heels, the steed skittering forward to rejoin his father and brother.

Oliver pulled up alongside Roland. "What was that about?" he asked in a low voice.

Roland shrugged. "A bit of brotherly advice, I suppose."

A Θ I

Charles wasted very little time convening a conclave of nobles—the realm's stalwart vassals from Aquitaine, Burgundy, and Languedoc, and even sworn men from territories in northern Italy and along the Alammani frontiers. They descended upon Aachen in pomp and ceremony that extended days before the official gathering, flooding the streets with brightly colored surcoats and young bravos—a noisome, bickering amalgamation of Franks and foreigners who could rarely agree on the time of day let alone the call to war in far-off Spain. Roland spent those days greeting, feasting, and carousing, but behind the cup in his hand, the champion began to piece together the intricate relationships of men, families, and fortunes.

And then came the day the royal heralds trumpeted the first notes that signaled the beginning of the deliberations.

While the council members entered the room and noisily sparred for position, Charles stood at the head of the great table in the center. Its expanse of wood was scarred from many battles—some with these very men, who had been battered and beaten into submission to keep the Frank kingdom united. Covering the head of the table, a large map outlining the entirety of the Frank lands also roughly sketched the realm of the caliph at Cordova south of the Pyrenees Mountains. A dagger pierced the map at the gap through the mountains at Roncevaux.

When all the nobles had finally jostled through the doors, Charles raised his hands for silence. The chatter in the room muted but did not immediately abate. Irritated, Charles thumped the flat of his hand solidly on the table.

"Gentlemen! Brothers in arms! By now you have heard the reports from Karim, the son of Barcelona, and Saleem, the son of Saragossa." He waved a hand to indicate the two men standing apart from the rest. "You now have the same news that we have. I will hear your thoughts on the matter."

Turpin examined the map and slapped a dour Geoffrey of Anjou on the back. It didn't seem to improve the nobleman's humor, as his lands would lie in the path of any invasion force that swept out of Iberia.

"Sire," Turpin said, "I feel the need to remind my noble colleagues that we've beaten Saracens before. With God's strength, we'll crush them again."

Geoffrey leaned forward, his look earnest.

"My king," he implored, "an attack on southern Francia will devastate the region for years to come. I would beg you take heed to these reports and strengthen us in the south."

Bertrin chewed his mustache as he examined the map, his face wrinkled with memories of the fresh campaign in Saxony. "But the Saxons are not wholly beaten. When the snow melts—and it shall—they will swarm the Rhine," he murmured. "This is madness. Instead of drawing our troops over the mountains, we should be bolstering the northern frontier with greater numbers."

Ganelon, ever calculating, folded his arms across his chest. "Sire, you are being manipulated, even though it's well intentioned. We've not suffered an invasion from the south in a generation. The reason is simple—the mountains are formidable."

"Have you not heard from the Saracens' own mouths?" Alans demanded, pointing at Saleem. "It would seem they think differently now!"

"Just talk, Alans," Ganelon replied. He turned away from the young southerners and dropped his voice for those nearest him to hear. "From heathen whelps. Who knows what games they play?"

"Games? Games? Damn you!" snapped Alans, his face the color of beets beneath his bristling beard. "If Saragossa invades, it will be *our* homes that burn!"

A dozen voices erupted at once, each straining to be heard above the others. Charles slammed his fists on the table once more. "Enough! I seek answers, not squabbling! We've enemies enough to spare. The question before us is do we prepare for the Saxons to break faith? Or march across the Pyrenees into Spain?"

Chatter broke out once more, many simply unable to agree.

"Come now!" Charles commanded. "We must have a decision."

Roland stepped forward from his place at Charles's right hand, cutting an imposing figure in a new surcoat resplendent with the wolf embroidered in gold piping. While younger than the other men crowding the table, he'd grown in stature after the incident with Kennick, and Ganelon's tight-lipped smile spoke volumes about the animosity between the two men.

"Majesty," Roland said, "if I may—send a contingent south. Prepare for war there. But leave enough force to garrison along the Rhine." He traced a finger down the winding track of the river, marking where the Saxons were most likely to cross.

"You would have us divide our forces?" Ganelon remarked. "Should we guard two fronts only halfway? This is folly!"

"We can afford to leave a sufficient force behind on the Rhine. There are only so many places to cross, and each is a bottleneck. With proper fortification they can be held. And southward, if the Saracens must indeed be dealt with, Barcelona and our allies in Spain have promised us aid. They can bolster our numbers against Marsilion."

Charles chewed on the champion's words for a moment.

"Yes. If the caliph moves against us, we'll need support from south of the mountains."

"We will," Alans urged, his voice rising above the renewed chatter. "My king, it is time to take action! Aquitaine must not be exposed to attack!"

Geoffrey nodded. "I am agreed, my king. Anjou stands prepared to support the expedition to the south."

Naimon, Charles's most trusted counselor, had been quietly observing the exchange. Despite his aged frame being bent from years of service in the king's name, there was a compelling air about him that could cow even Charles's impulsive vassals. When he spoke with measured deliberateness, all side discussions halted. "You've been given sound advice, sire. In the balance, we must watch and monitor the peace, but sending forces south to gauge Saragossan resolve is critical."

Charles pondered, studying each face in turn.

"We shall send troops to the south," he finally commanded, straightening from the table. "They will prepare for war against Saragossa. Pepin, my son, after Yule I task you to lead the advance party. Select from my knights for this mission." He paused before continuing, his face crinkling with humor. "And don't let your brother fill the ranks with monks and friars."

Pepin rolled his eyes dramatically as he dutifully bowed to his father. But Louis pushed his way through the crowded chamber to Pepin's side.

"Father, this should be a joint command," he said. "We both should lead this effort!"

Pepin laughed and leaned back to take pressure off his halt leg. "There's no room for a divided command—on the battlefield or in our house. Besides, you always drag on my coattails, brother. I won't let you have command. Content yourself with the chanting of your priests."

"You little prig!" Louis growled. He knotted his fists and unleashed a punch across Pepin's jaw, sending his older brother sprawling into the arms of the surrounding nobles. "The command is not yours; it is ours!"

Charles stepped between them, a stern look chiseled into his features as he folded his arms. "Now, boys, there's no need for this."

Louis's head bowed as he lowered his fists. "I'm sorry, Father. But you see how he baits me. It was a natural response."

Pepin spit blood and shrugged off the hands supporting him. He straightened his robes, his eyes never leaving his father.

"It was a brute's response—nothing more than mindless violence. Get him away from me!" He parted the nobles and limped for the door.

The war council had concluded.

Ganelon sauntered out the palace doors. Alans trotted to catch up with their squires shadowing them a few paces behind.

"What do *you* think of our new plan, Ganelon?" Alans ventured as he drew even with Ganelon's elbow. "I suppose I could live with it." He studied his comrade's face, watching to see if he would take the bait. It wasn't that he was necessarily trying to anger Tournai, but the man had been insufferably moody since arriving at the city, even more than after the embarrassment at the whipping post. His foul temper had begun to grate on the old warrior's nerves. It was time for a little jab in return.

Ganelon, however, ignored him. When they reached the limit of the grounds, he took an unexpected turn to the left.

"Where are you going?" Alans stuttered in surprise. "Our quarters are this way—" He pointed onward down the path, but Ganelon tromped away with a deliberate step.

Peeved that his barb had fallen flat, Alans huffed after Ganelon with their equally confused squires in tow.

Ganelon led them around to the southern flank of the palace grounds, where there stood a tall gatehouse of mixed construction, moss-covered Roman near the ground and bare Frankish at the top. Ganelon stopped and stared at its battlements, still taking no notice of his impromptu train.

After a long moment, Alans cleared his throat. Ganelon, in the grip of some strong emotion, growled brokenly.

"What?" He tore his gaze away from the stonework. Alans was stunned to see his eyes, always so hard and calculating, were red-rimmed and wet. "What do you want?" He looked at them as if he had just noticed them. "Why did you follow me?"

"I ... um," Alans was, for once, at a loss for words. "You just walked away!" he finally answered a little too gruffly, caught off guard. "If you didn't want me to come with you, you should have said something!"

Ganelon turned back to the gatehouse, his voice once again a barely restrained growl. "No matter. You can stay if you wish."

Alans stared at him as his eyes bored into the stones. He turned suddenly to the squires. "Go! Back to our quarters! You have duties to attend to there, I am sure. Go!" The young lads, as confused as ever, turned on their heels and ran.

Once they had cleared the corner of the grounds, Alans turned back to his companion. "What are you doing here?" Ganelon's rigid back offered no answers. Alans waved a hand around them. "No one is here but you and I, Ganelon. What is this place? Is this why you have been in such a mood?"

"'Such a mood,' you say?" A flash of the steely cold Ganelon that Alans knew so well reappeared. "'Such a mood'? You know nothing, old man."

"Then tell me." Alans did not much like Ganelon, but the count of Tournai was always steady in a fight, and largely that was because nothing could shake him. This was a new side of the man that disturbed Alans. If he was to stand next to Ganelon in battle, he wanted to know what could possibly get under the man's skin like this—for such a weakness could be a liability in the field. "What was it?"

Ganelon breathed deep. When he spoke, the iron curtain had again descended over his features, and his words were even and measured. "Nothing that concerns you, Alans. Only the death of my mother and my younger brother."

He turned and marched past Alans, who was now twice speechless in one day.

Α Θ Ι

That night the clouds blew away over Aachen, eventually allowing the moon to shine through.

As he walked from the palace, Roland drew a breath and let out a cloud of mist before his eyes. His thoughts were consumed with planning for the coming expedition to the south. As champion, he now found himself sitting through endless meetings from morning to night while nobles wrangled over how many resources each would provide for the venture. Lucky for him, Pepin always presided with a shrewd eye for detail and a fair amount of arm-twisting to stretch the royal resources committed to the campaign and make sure the counts put forth their fair share. Roland rubbed his temples as he moved around an iced-over garden pool in the shadow of the palace.

Above him, Aude leaned out of an open window, watching him walk lost in thought, a hint of a smile touching her full lips.

"I wonder," she mused with a laugh, "if the knight skates better than a squire I once knew in my father's house at the Vale?"

Roland looked up with a start. Recognizing her face, the cobwebs in his brain cleared immediately. He shrugged lightheartedly, testing the ice of the pool with a toe. The surface creaked when he stepped out onto it, but on the second step he lost his footing and fell with a crack.

Aude stifled a laugh with her fingers pressed to her lips and quickly closed the window. She appeared a moment later at the garden door, skipping down the portal steps two at a time in a fashion her matron would generously describe as *unbefitting a lady.*

Roland scrambled to his feet then offered her a gracious bow.

"Have we met before, fair lady?"

Aude gracefully stepped toward him, offering him her hand with an excess of formality.

"Oh," she said, "was I too freckled then, a little girl?"

He took her hand in his, examined her face, then pulled her onward into the moonlight, all formal pretenses fluttering away.

"Aude?" he exclaimed in feigned astonishment. "Is that you?"

She nodded, tugging her hastily shouldered cloak higher about her shoulders. "Three long years, and I feared you wouldn't remember me. Like some long-lost dream of spring, forgotten when your eyes flutter open."

He gave her a more serious look. "If I recall, that lady of the vale drafted the squires and pages to bake mud cakes with her for the faire.

That's not something easily forgotten, my lady. Those are dreams that are meant to be remembered, to be cherished."

Aude brushed his cheek with her hand.

"Oh, you tease me, sir! A champion who draws strength from childhood dreams?" she mused. "How rare! I hear tell from the youngest pages in the palace that the new champion draws strength from the souls of the slain as he wades through fields of blood." Her voice grew bold like a herald relating a heroic saga. "All the while bringing glory to God and his king!" Then her voice dropped to a whisper. "Not from memories of muddy days at the Vale."

Roland smiled as he pressed her hand to his face.

"Do they sing my song already?"

"Oh, yes," Aude replied with a grin. "Like a lullaby to calm a child who refuses to go to bed. Now, let's see—*hush now, child that Saxons fright, be still, be still. For Roland will save you with all his might, be still …*"

"You know," he said, "it's too bad I've been warned to keep my distance now that we're both grown."

She slid her arm into his.

"Oh? I suppose you've been spending too much time with Oliver. Well, my brother isn't the one who waited three years to see you again. It was an eternity to me."

"And I've spent a lifetime looking but only now see for the first time. Aude, you must remember the things Oliver told you about me. They're likely true—or worse."

She placed a finger on his lips, shaking her head slowly.

"They are forgotten. You are here."

He wrapped his arms about her, pulling her close and breathing her in as if for the first time. Then they kissed.

Aachen's populace fled the weather and the encroaching night, hurrying along the ice-crusted streets bound for warmth indoors. Standing above it all, surveying the breadth of the city from his window, stood Ganelon, his distant claim to the throne based on a family bloodline as ancient as the first Merovingian kings. From Clovis through the ill-fated Childeric, they had ruled the land and spawned mythic tales of princes with long locks of gilded hair. These very kings of folklore had been tossed aside, not vanquished in glorious battle against an overwhelming foe but by perfidious dictate of the pope and their own house steward—Charles's father, Pepin the Short.

It was Pepin's brutal purge of the Merovingians that had driven Ganelon's mother, his infant brother in her arms, to leap from the scaffolding where Pepin had been rebuilding the gatehouse rather than let him take her. Clearly she had chosen the place as a clarion signal to the usurper, but it had been Ganelon, barely five summers old, who had found them in a bloody heap while chasing finches.

The center of his world had been ripped from him that day.

It was not until years later that he would finally understand why it had happened—and who had been responsible. He wrapped himself in the cold embrace of his own gall, using the burning shame of it to stoke the fires of his heart. His glance drifted across the buildings where the visiting nobles were quartered, their doorways marked by banners emblazoned with the devices of the noble houses. Breton March stood out among them—the very blood of Charles's family.

"I should have silenced that bastard whelp long ago," Ganelon muttered.

Someone knocked at the door.

"Come in, come in." He pulled the shutters closed and stepped back into the room. The door opened with a clatter, and Gothard entered, anger written across his face.

He slammed the door behind him.

"Something on your mind, boy?" Ganelon asked evenly. He had little room in his heart tonight for anyone else's pain, and the measured tone should have signaled that to Gothard.

But it was not to be. "Father!" Gothard sputtered. "You are the king's brother-in-law—the champion's title and honors should be yours!"

Ganelon's laugh rasped. "What? Not so much as a 'Good even, Father'? Maybe Gisela's brat will have better manners than my eldest."

Gothard growled at the rebuke but was stopped short when Ganelon pounced, grabbing him by the throat and pinning the young man to the wall.

"I hope that was your dinner digesting, son."

"I meant nothing by it," Gothard choked. Ganelon released him, leaving wicked red marks on his throat. "You fought bravely," his son rasped, rubbing at his windpipe. "You kept the Saxons pinned against the sea. We fought with honor!"

Ganelon crossed the room to a chair, flopped into it, and began pulling off his boots. "Our house, the house of Clovis himself, has been eclipsed by rabble from the Breton March and the nursling of a usurping butler. Yes, it seems more than we can bear. But bear it we must, my son. Patience will bring us closer to the throne. We play our parts as dutiful vassals and wrap all our actions in patience. Remember— remain focused on the prize, not the distractions. It matters not to me who is champion."

He tossed the boots to the floor in a heap and leaned back in the chair, propping it against the wall as he continued. "But with a new champion at Charles's side, we'll need to remain vigilant to ensure our plans bear fruit."

"And someone will be dead before spring?" Gothard asked.

Ganelon's lips twitched in a murderous sort of smile.

"Let the great drama unfold. Kings and princes now take the stage. We shall ever be ready when the throne room door opens to us."

Charles's suite was spartan compared to the opulent chambers found elsewhere throughout the palace in areas laid out for public consumption. Except for a few treasured trappings of imperial rank, bestowed on him by the pope or won through hard-fought negotiations with the emperor in Constantinople, little suggested the power of the room's occupant. Charles was not a man for reveling in finery; rather he preferred to spend his time at a simple desk with a manuscript spread before him. This great searching soul, focused on the attainment of ancient knowledge, had himself only recently learned to read. His ability was still unsure. He leaned close to the page in his hand as he traced the words with his finger and spoke haltingly.

"Caesar ... crossed the Rubicon. From that point ... there was no ... turning back."

A latch rattled and squeaked then the door cracked opened. Pepin, in his finely brocaded night robe, thrust his head through the opening.

"There you are," said Charles. "Come in, my son."

Pepin limped across the room.

"Is it chilly in here?" Pepin asked as he tugged his robes more tightly about his waist. "You really must put more wood on the fire, Father."

Charles chuckled, pushing the manuscript aside. "At my age," he said, "every night is chilly. But let's cut to the chase, my boy. You've come to convince me, haven't you? You really should read the Cicero we just translated. He was quite good at this sort of thing."

"Yes," Pepin replied wryly. "Backed the wrong side when Caesar died, if I recall. Ended up a head short."

Charles pulled his fingers through his beard. "Too much wine, I understand."

"Father, this is serious," Pepin said. "Even now we prepare for war with enemies intent on carving up the kingdom. Enemies on two sides, and I'm afraid there are more within us as well. If you were to fall, the entire Frank nation would bleed from uncertainty and disjointed authority. Think of it! All you've worked for—education—reviving ancient learning—the rebuilding of Rome herself—all for naught!" He placed his hands over his father's. "For the welfare of the kingdom, Father, name me as your sole successor!"

"And what of your brother?" Charles asked, shaking his fingers loose and pushing back from the desk to lock eyes with his eldest son. "I can't deny my own blood—*your* own blood. And under Frank law, you both have right to the kingdom. You will both be crowned at my death. The law is clear on this."

Pepin limped closer to his father's side, the malady that pained him more pronounced since the summer campaign.

"The law is antiquated," Pepin said, appealing to his father's sense of reason. "It sows chaos and division of our nation's strength. Name one heir, to ensure stability! I'll care for Louis, father. You have my word."

Charles leaned forward and placed a hand on Pepin's shoulder. For the first time, the younger man noticed the thin skin and blue veins that traced the tired, knotted knuckles.

"*I* will care for him," Charles said, "by doing things my way. You will do as I command in this."

Pepin relented and offered his father a stiff bow.

"I am your dutiful son," he said. "Good night, Father." He pecked a kiss on his father's cheek and left the room.

When the door closed, Aldatrude peered into the room from behind a curtain, her lithe body barely covered by a silky gossamer gown.

"What was that about?" she purred to her father. "The cub snarls at the lion, and I lose my beauty sleep."

Charles drummed his fingers on the side of his desk for a moment. Finally he said, "The cub learns to show his claws. But I must consider all my children."

"Even Augustus had but a single heir and the empire prospered. But, come, let's think of more pleasant things." She curled around him and settled sensually into his lap, pressing her lips to his, but he was not to be deterred.

"So you take his side in this?"

Aldatrude pouted. "You think that?" She curled his beard in her finger. "I take your side in all things, dear." She leaned over and snuffed out the oil lamp on the edge of his desk, plunging the room into darkness.

ᴀ ᴏ ɪ

The following day, a coach rattled over the frozen, rutted road that twisted through the countryside toward Aachen. Across the empty window frames, quilted curtains had been pulled down to keep the biting wind off the passengers. Armored knights, bearing both the sigils of Breton March and the imperial eagle of Charles on their surcoats, rode escort.

Within the gloomy interior, Gisela bounced on a seat wrapped in heavy blankets, a small gurgling bundle nestled in her arms. She leaned over her baby's round face and cooed gently. Across from them, a willowy, hawkish woman hunched over them both—a nursemaid to attend to the needs of the mother and child. Her sharp nose stood out redly from her winter trappings. Next to the nursemaid sat the gaunt figure of Petras, his eyes closed and his head bowed.

Gisela felt a prickle run up the back of her neck every time she glanced over at the man who even in sleep had thin hands clasped together before him as if in prayer. But she knew he wasn't oblivious. The priest absorbed each and every word around him, catching stray utterances like moths in a spider's web. Those same words would later be regurgitated up like a starling feeding its young for his master, her husband.

Outside the carriage, the escort troopers began shouting. "What is that?" Gisela asked the nursemaid. "Do you see anything?"

The woman tugged back one of the curtains and peered into the chill sunlight.

"Riders, my lady!"

The carriage slowed to a halt. Gisela held her breath. These roads had ever been the hunting grounds for bandits; even armed parties traversed them with caution.

A familiar voice carried into the carriage.

"Is she here? Mother!"

Relief swept her. "Roland, is that you?"

With that, the priest's eye twitched and slitted open.

The door flung open, and Roland leaned in, blond hair trailing from beneath his helmet. His wolf-emblazoned surcoat was visible under a cloak spattered with mud from the wheel-rutted track of a road. Behind him trailed a squad of Charles's men, entourage of the new champion. Gisela caught her breath—he looked so much like her beloved William.

She leaned forward in her seat and touched his scruffy cheek with a hand. "Winter has ended now that I've seen you," she said brightly.

Roland noticed the bundle in her arms and frowned.

"Is that his?" he more stated than asked.

"He's your brother Baldwin. My son. As are you."

He turned his eyes from the child to her. "Have you done as I asked, Mother? I do so need your help."

Gisela lowered her eyes, a pained look crossing her features. She glanced across at the priest. Roland's eyes followed hers, and his mouth tightened when he saw Petras.

"Then you betray your true beloved husband," he said. "Thank God he didn't live to see it." He stepped back, leaving the door swinging open, and climbed back into his saddle. He spurred his horse's flanks and continued along the frozen path onward to Aachen, his companions falling into place behind.

The nursemaid leaned forward, pulled the door closed, and rapped on the roof to signal the driver to get underway. As the carriage lurched into motion, Gisela glanced across at Petras and felt her breath freeze in her lungs. He was holding the curtain open, his serpent eyes following Roland and his horsemen as they cantered down the road.

CHAPTER 8

THE METTLE OF MEN

Charles stalked the corridors of the palace trailing a squire behind him, the lad burdened with fluttering sheaves of paper for the king's signature. They passed courtiers, maids, and stewards apparently distracted by a clatter echoing from the courtyard outside. Wondering what they might be gawking at, Charles stopped at an unoccupied window and rubbed at the frosted pane, but the icy surface resisted his attempt to see through. He gestured for the squire to help him open the casement.

"What's this?" he asked, craning his neck to search for the source of the noise.

The yard below was covered in snow trampled by Roland, Oliver, and the marchmen. In their center stood a wooden pell—a wide, smoothed log topped with a thick cross-arm and embellished with a battered helmet. The marchmen attacked it with wooden practice swords while Louis watched the exercises with interest from a perch on a low retaining wall. Otun, just arrived from the kitchens with a warm loaf, stopped in his tracks and roared with mirth at their efforts, spraying breadcrumbs.

"Would Thor practice fighting giants by striking a scarecrow with a butter churn?" he asked. "Let us be about man's work!"

Roland stepped forward, his linen gambeson stained with sweat.

"Look and learn," he replied. "With a wooden waster, we can practice striking like this."

He stepped toward the pell, striking it with fierce intent again and again from different positions and stances, the waster thumping and clacking against the wooden post until the blade cracked. He stepped back and took another from a pile ready nearby. "It keeps our limbs ready to fight in the spring," he panted.

Otun stretched his expansive chest, took up his ax, and hefted it with a warrior's grace. Flashing Roland a skeptical eye, he shouldered past him to where he squared off at the pell like a woodsman. With remarkable quickness, he swung the ax over his head and split the pell, cleaving the helmet and burying the blade deep in the seasoned wood. He turned toward Roland with a mischievous gleam in his eye and was caught off guard when Roland thrust with his waster, striking Otun hard in the chest and knocking the breath from him.

"Eh?" the Dane huffed, rubbing at his breastbone. "What's this?"

"Footwork!" Louis shouted from the wall. "It's all about footwork!"

Again Roland struck Otun square in the chest. The Dane backpedaled and grabbed the ax haft with one hand, fiercely wrenching it up and down to free it from the pell while using the other to deflect Roland's bothersome prods. Roland gracefully sidestepped past Otun's swatting hands with a pivot cut and laid the flat of the weapon alongside Otun's neck. Louis hooted and kicked his heels against the wall.

Undeterred, Otun wrapped his thick arms around Roland, tumbling them both into the muddy snow. Slush flew into the air as arms and legs thrashed while each tried to gain advantage.

Louis jumped from the wall. "My companions!" he shouted. "Our pell is struck, and we must make reply!"

Oliver joined the prince and leaped into the muck with the combatants. Chaos erupted as the rest of the marchmen joined in. Around the outside of the yard, courtiers and bureaucrats timidly peered at the scene from behind pillars and window frames.

From high above the commotion in the yard, Charles chuckled and flicked snow off the windowsill. Beside him the squire stood in silent amazement when the king of the Franks joined his voice to the chaos below.

"Oh—there he goes! Watch there!"

The courtiers looked up to see whose voice cheered the muddied contenders. Charles snickered, watching arms, legs, and bodies collide and slide through the slush below. He remembered his own comrades who had fought mock wars in the very same yard so many years ago, and especially William, the squire from Breton March who would be his friend and champion. Many times William had outfoxed older boys with a martial deftness yet always had a ready smile for those he vanquished.

"My sons," he mused, "care well for these men. These are they who will strengthen the kingdom when you rule. Alas, the blood of my generation grows cold. It grows cold, and the world needs warmth."

An elbow jabbed Roland in the eye. He pushed Otun off, only to have a Frank sergeant replace him with thrashing legs and boots dripping with slush. Roland heaved against bodies until at last he was able to sit up. He rolled to one side, grinning, and watched the fracas over his shoulder. Oliver and the marchmen gave as good as they got, throwing snow and driving other men into the muck. But near the sheltered walkway, members of the court began congregating. Some cheered, and others huddled together whispering. Through the curious gaggle stepped Pepin, his countenance darkening at the sight of the kingdom's elite warriors flopping through the yard like common brawlers. In his wake strode Geoffrey of Anjou, likewise scanning the scene with a critical eye.

Roland regained his feet and gave his cousin a polite bow.

"I see you've taken my advice to heart," Pepin said, his words dripping. "The peers of the realm engaged in a match more suited for a squire who serves a cup at Vale Runer."

The prince's comments rippled through the yard, and the marchmen disengaged and straggled to their feet, looking shamefaced under the royal disapproval. Even Louis, panting, red-faced, and bruised, could not bolster a smile under the scrutiny. Otun, however, lifted his bulk to tower over the rest, a wild grin on his bristly face, his bushy red eyebrows fierce over defiant blue eyes.

"I mean no disrespect, sire," Roland replied. "But the men strain at the bit for the spring campaign. It's but an outlet ..."

"Yes, and as any rider will tell you, if the horse is not performing to satisfaction, the bite of a whip may be needed. Do you have the hand to provide that whip, Champion?"

"As you say, cousin. Some prefer to use the whip. But my father taught me to also to prize the stallion and, on occasion, give the beast its head and hang on tight in awe of the magnificence."

"Pah," Pepin spat. "Such is nonsense when ruling men. You must organize and move the entire herd, Champion—not allow the nags to run wild."

Louis brushed muck from his breeches and stepped to Roland's side. "Never mind him, cousin. My loving brother speaks to me." The prince shook his hands in the air, flinging glop in Pepin's direction. "But I've need of a bath and clean clothes."

Louis stalked off past his brother.

The gawking courtiers collectively released their breath. Pepin glared at Louis's back and, after a moment, spun around and limped back inside. Anjou, however, remained as the marchmen gathered their gear.

"Cocksure and ever the drunk," he said imperiously. "A bit of advice, cousin to the king—leave the cups here when you campaign."

Roland's boots flew across the bedchamber to a skidding muddy heap—quickly followed by his soiled linen gambeson. The young champion stormed across the room, tugging at his trousers before he noticed the page trailing behind him to gather up the heap of garments.

"Leave!" Roland shouted, and as soon as the harsh word left his mouth, he regretted it. But nevertheless the page skittered away fearing a thrashing, or worse.

Roland pounded the stone wall with his fist, leaving red scraped across the gray. On the table near the bed, a flagon of wine remained with an empty cup. He gathered up the Burgundian vintage and heaved it into the fireplace where it sloshed with the cold ash.

He sat down on his father's great oaken chest at the foot the bed and closed his eyes, distant memories washing over him.

The tavern was alive in the waning afternoon when he stepped through the threshold. The ride from the capital had been invigorating.

The young knight waved cheerfully to the revelers, many of whom he would later drink under the table. Yet he wasn't there for them. Across the room, a lithe form rose from a table, blonde locks tumbling beneath the hood of her cloak. Deidra, a merchant's daughter, opened her full lips to call his name. Roland reached for a flagon ...

He remembered very little else of that night, for when he returned to Aachen the next morning, his father lay dead.

He opened his eyes. The fleeing winter sun left the room darkened and chill, made even more so by the familiar figure sitting on the chest next to him and regarding him with a shadowed gaze.

"I've begged God to bring you peace," Roland whispered. "Bring *me* peace. But there is no forgiveness, it seems."

William's shade seemed to draw the darkness to him, and Roland felt a chill in the silence.

"Speak," he begged. "Please. We both know I abandoned you to seek my own pleasure. I never thought it would be for the last time."

The shadows clung to his father's face. His ethereal lips parted. "All we are given is a limited number of breaths, Roland. It is what we do with them that fills the songs sung of us."

"And what song shall they sing of me? That I left my father when he needed me? And now you have returned to—to torment me, to call me to account and demand repayment. I don't want this, Father. I'm afraid of what I will find. What it will do to Mother. Her child is his. If I prove the deed, Baldwin will be fatherless and Mother will be a widow once more." He stood and paced the floor. "Is there a purpose, Father? Justice, of course, but the price ..."

William's ghost was immovable.

A draft from the chimney brushed through from the hearth, filling his senses with the smell of wine and ash. He inhaled deeply until it passed, and when he looked back, his father's shade was gone. He staggered, exhausted, onto the bed, looking up at the dark ceiling, despairing and hopeless.

And then sleep consumed him.

CHAPTER 9

Knight of Swords

Church bells pealed rollicking notes that echoed above the snow-covered city. Nobles and commoners flocked together toward the sound with cloaks pulled up to their ears and their hands buried in woolen mittens. Though some could afford fur-lined boots, many simply covered their feet in worn rags. The swelling crowd poured into the city to celebrate the day the champion Roland would be vested in his patrimony and inherit the lands of his late father William—putting an end to Ganelon's conservatorship. As well, in the grand tradition of the court, Oliver would be confirmed to his own lands and titles in place of his ailing father.

People bottlenecked at the cathedral doors, jostling and stomping to gain access to the interior. From deep within the choir voiced a haunting deep-throated hymn. Beyond the imposing tympanum over the doorway, dominated by Christ and his saints, the vaulted interior stretched to a glorious altar where light from the high clerestory windows illuminated the square-checked masonry designed by Muslim craftsmen as a gift to the great king in Aachen. The altar was draped in Charles's imperial colors, a riot of crimson and gold surrounding the imperial eagle of the Romans and Franks, and upon the altar lay two bared swords alongside scabbards fitted with the finest metalwork Frank armories could turn out. These were the storied blades Durendal and Halteclare—each representing royal favor and, some believed, divine interest.

A hush fell across the crowds when the first of the royal carriages clattered up to the steps outside. Troops pushed through the massive doors to part the straggling masses so the royal family could enter the building. There was a breathless pause as carriage doors opened and closed, leather springs creaked and horses stamped, until finally Charles, followed by his children, appeared in the archway. The crowd drew breath to cheer, but he held up his hand for silence to preserve the solemnity. He then waved reassuringly to the throngs and began his somber procession.

The people knelt before the king as he slowly walked to the altar. Bishop Turpin, in his finest vestments, waited before the altar to greet his monarch. When Charles paused at the first step, the bishop raised his worn shepherd's staff in blessing to all the assembly and addressed them with a commanding voice.

"God grant strength to our noble king, the sword of God upon the earth, even Charles, protector of the realm and the holy church—crowned and ordained at the hands of the bishop of Rome as imperator of the Romans. Brother to Nicephorus, the Roman Augustus in Constantinople. We give thanks for thee and ask God to continue to bless thee with wisdom and grace."

Charles ascended the rest of the steps. His family fanned out behind him, and the spectators rose to their feet for a better view.

Roland and Oliver entered the nave from a side door, clad in armor polished to a high sheen over brilliant white linen gambesons and shining black leather boots, as befitted the occasion. As they marched in step to the altar, Roland allowed himself a quick glance across the celebrants. Near the surcoats of the marchmen, he saw Gisela leaning on her nursemaid. His eyes paused on Aude next to her, her face luminous. Her eyes met his and she smiled across the distance. After a mere heartbeat, he lost sight of her behind the intervening crowds.

He and Oliver approached the altar where Charles stood flanked by his sons. The companions dropped to their knees, Roland before Charles, and Oliver to his friend's right. They bowed their heads and raised their hands, palms pressed together in supplication. Charles placed his hands around Oliver's and then around Roland's accepting their gesture of fealty.

Turpin blessed the act and then spoke to the two young knights.

"Roland son of William of Breton March. Oliver son of Quintus of Vale Runer. Do you take upon yourselves the burdens of the enemies of your king, pledging to uphold his interests and protect the realm?"

The knights bowed their heads in deference to their king and said, in unison, "Yes."

Turpin turned, lifted Durendal from the altar, and handed it to Pepin, who in turn handed it to his father. Charles took the sword by the hilt and touched Roland on the shoulders with the blade.

"Roland. Durendal was the sword of your father, William—a holy weapon. With it, I confer upon you your rights and privileges as his son and name you count of the Breton March, and a peer of the realm. I leave you with this charge, to use the sword to strike hard, as did your father before you, for God and your king."

Roland took the weapon from Charles and the scabbard from Pepin, sheathing the blade quietly. Louis then passed Halteclare to his father's hands. Charles touched Oliver on the shoulders with the blade in a like manner as he had Roland.

"Oliver. This is my sword Halteclare, a symbol of our esteem. With it I confer upon you the rights and privileges of the count of Vale Runer and name you a peer of the realm, as requested by your father, Quintus, in his illness. I leave you with the same charge, to strike hard for God and your king."

Oliver accepted the weapon.

"Arise, Roland, count of Breton March, and Oliver, count of Vale Runer."

From deep in the crowd, Otun raised his fist to the vaulted ceiling. "Roland and Oliver!" he shouted. "The gods fear their names!"

The stalwart men of the Breton March cried out approval of the Dane. Their voices shook the clerestory windows, echoing through the doors and ringing through Aachen's frosty streets.

Charles shook his head and leaned over to Roland with a knowing grin. "Remind that one that he is now a Christian man," he whispered.

Oliver laughed. "Sire, the last time he tried, the Dane nearly bit off his ear!"

In time the many well-wishers satisfied themselves of the need to offer congratulations, sage advice, or both and straggled out of the cathedral doors, leaving Roland and Oliver to wander through the cathedral to a grotto built into the side of the wide nave. There they tossed their brocade surcoats to the cold tile floor and flopped down for a welcome respite. The winter sun broke through the gray clouds and touched the cathedral's interior with angels' fingers of light. In its beams both knights examined their swords, marveling over the craftsmanship, the intricate hilts, and even the balance of the weapons in their hands. For Roland, holding the sword of his father brought a certain tangible comfort that could not be found in the elusive and troubled visions that haunted his sleep.

"Can you believe it?" Oliver said, his voice low. "Today felt like a dream somehow. Why, only yesterday we were at the Vale, just children playing silly games."

Roland nodded absently as he leaned back against the wall and laid Durendal's steel length across his lap. "I don't know," he mused. "I've waited so long for this, wished so intently that it would happen, that now it is finally here—I don't really feel anything." He paused, brow furrowed. "Not as much as I would think, anyway. I mean—it seems a natural thing, not something special like I expected." He shook himself. "Now the silly games are gone, and we're men grown. Soon we'll be off to another war, just as our fathers before us, and our grandfathers before them. When will it end, do you suppose? I wonder if wars will ever end."

Oliver lowered his weapon, his blue eyes fixed on his friend for a moment.

"I suppose it will end for us when we've completed our mission," he said.

Roland nodded and offered Oliver a grim smile.

"I suppose then we'll be laying cold on an altar somewhere."

Oliver scrambled to his knees.

"But if I must fight, I want to fight at your side." He held Halteclare before him as a martial crucifix. "Before God, I swear to you my eternal friendship!"

Roland took a knee facing Oliver and raised Durendal into a mirror of his friend's devotion.

"As do I to you," he whispered.

They clasped hands through the crossing of their swords. When they released their grip, Roland examined Durendal more closely, no longer a lad admiring his father's weapon but rather as a man holding the very tool that would serve him the remainder of his life.

"Such workmanship," he observed. "You know, they say Durendal's blade served Hector, champion of Troy. And see here, in the reliquary?" He turned the pommel to Oliver so his friend could examine it as well. "I'm told that the bones of St. Peter reside there."

"A holy weapon, indeed," Oliver replied. "A weapon that will rally men to its cause and serve its champion well. And bring swift justice."

Roland lowered the sword. "I fear I'm not worthy. Can it really bring swift justice, even when I think murderous thoughts?"

Oliver frowned. "There is no one more worthy of this sword. Why do you doubt yourself so?"

"I wish you could understand," Roland said.

"Why don't you just start with trusting me?" Oliver encouraged.

"My father, he was recovering here in Aachen, you know, surrounded by faithless friends. But I didn't see it—I didn't look hard enough."

"Go on," Oliver coaxed him.

"He was getting better. I—I spent the night drinking. I was addle-headed. I chased after some girl from Burgundy. You know me—I pursued my own pleasure. When he died, he died without me, choking on his own vomit, with only Ganelon at his side. I wish to God I had absolute proof of the man's treachery."

"You know," Oliver noted, "Turpin used to tell us to give our burdens to the Lord. Sometimes it's just not for us to bear."

Roland leaned back against the wall, his eyes rising to the shadows of the grotto.

"I must bear this. I was stupid and thoughtless. But I must avenge my father."

"Trust God," Oliver urged. "He will reveal the truth."

"You sound like my father." Roland laughed.

"Then I am honored indeed." Oliver scrambled to his feet and offered Roland a hand. "Come, there are banquets in our honor—or so I'm told. And I am starving!"

As the night wore on, the street crowds thinned as revelers drifted into the various feasts to sate appetites for food, drink, and companionship, and workers and servants found their way home to their beds in exhaustion. Saleem stepped outside the palace gates onto the empty paving stones and pulled his cloak up about his neck. He wrinkled his nose. Aachen seemed to lay in a perpetual stink from the mix of slops tipped from citizens' windows and cattle dung from beasts carting goods through the streets. He walked carefully to the middle of the way and gave each direction a long look. He'd had enough of meetings in cramped rooms with unwashed illiterates who nodded sagely at written reports they couldn't decipher without the priests who stuck their noses into everything. Now was his time to explore what lay beyond the palace walls.

To his left lay the cathedral, and the merchant quarter beyond. But when he set upon that direction, he saw a familiar figure emerge from the palace. Roland had a determined look upon his young face, which instantly piqued Saleem's curiosity. Despite his simple gray cloak, the champion stood out from the other rustics with his confident step and his wild blond hair tousled about his shoulders. Whatever was on his mind seemed to occupy his entire attention, and he did not appear to notice Saleem falling into step behind him.

Roland strode past the cathedral to the shops further down the street. A few yet remained open, trying to catch the last straggling customers of the early evening, and Roland stopped at one well-appointed establishment. He knocked at the door then stepped inside. Saleem paused for a long moment, adjusting his cloak while he considered his next move. To follow him in would certainly be a breach in propriety. He walked past the door.

He stopped and laughed at his own childishness. There was little else to do tonight, and he was curious. He strode to the merchant's steps then thrust the door open and stepped inside.

Roland and the balding shopkeeper looked up from a table strewn with glinting finery.

"Hello," Saleem said with a hint of habitual condescension. "It was cold outside. I thought I'd found shelter."

Roland's face suggested nothing of his interests here, so Saleem stepped uninvited toward the silken-draped table. Atop the cloth were laid out pieces of jewelry, some the squarish Frank style silver and gold; a few more elaborate things imported from the east, Ravenna or Constantinople; and one necklace in particular displaying a small finely cut ruby surrounded by a delicate silver filigree.

"From Damascus?" Saleem asked, pointing to it.

"Why—why, yes," the shopkeeper replied, surprised.

Roland lifted up the bauble and examined it against the light. "You recognize it?"

"Recognize it?" Saleem laughed. "Jewels, gold, and silver links—maybe even the silk that covers this table? Such things are rarely found on the battlefield as soldiers fleece the pockets of the dead." He offered Roland a knowing wink. "I learned from merchants plying the middle seas from northern Africa to the Levant. This style is exceptional."

Roland cleared his throat and put the necklace down. He examined other adornments until his eyes fell on a pendant of amber set in northern silver on a necklace of spun links.

"You've good taste, my lord," the shopkeeper said. He smiled as he leaned conspiratorially closer to the knight. "Fit for a very noble lady, indeed."

"I don't know." Roland put it back and plucked up the ruby again, holding its gleaming crimson close to the lamp.

"This is for a woman then?" Saleem was surprised. From what he had seen of Roland in their time together, to be this much out of sorts simply for buying a girl a trinket seemed odd. "This woman? She is of good birth, I suppose?"

Roland lowered the necklace, considering it as he spoke. "She is. From one of Francia's noblest houses."

The champion is smitten. Knowing this small secret of Roland's soul gave him an unexpected fragment of peace he had not felt in some time.

While a boy growing up in Marsilion's house, he had been an intimate to the plots and maneuverings of his family. But here, Saleem remained a stranger to their alliances, their motivations, or their desires. "Not that birth matters," he quipped conversationally. "Women of all sorts to warm the bed, far less costly, can be found. And on the battlefield, a soldier's right is far cheaper."

Roland bounced the ruby against his palm. "There is none that compare. Some bonds are forged stronger than those of blood and lust."

"Bonds? Lust?" Saleem chuckled. "Lust is the only bond. Trust me on this, my friend. I stand before you a product of lust and passing fancy. It is that passing fancy that rearranges the order of hearth and home, as well as great kingdoms."

Roland shook his head and clutched the necklace in his hand. When he spoke, his voice was more sure. "I've had my fill of such things."

Saleem slapped Roland on the back, a calculated gesture to regain his footing in the game. "As have I! As have I, my friend!" Feeling expansive, he threw his arm around the shopkeeper's shoulders, smelling the man's foul breath as he leaned closer. "So, let's talk about the price. I'm sure we can make a fair deal."

Later that night, Pepin slipped from the palace with a dark cloak wrapped about his slender frame that couldn't quite mask his limp. The prince made the most of the moon's shadows to remain obscured from prying eyes, of which he was certain there were many. A royal wandering the streets without escort would attract the attention of noble and commoner alike. Since his destination was unfitting to one of his royal station, the prince opted for as much anonymity as he could coax from the night's darkness.

After cutting through alleys and backtracking through closed-up markets, Pepin ended up in a mean section of shops and warehouses, near a ramshackle tavern with a boar stuck on a pike for its emblem. Across from the faded sign was the alley he sought, a dark crevasse between the buildings. His hand dropped to the long, wicked dagger hung from his belt, his fingers nervously clenching the hilt. He carefully stepped into the alley between piles of trash and refuse until the way terminated in an overgrown courtyard within another cluster of equally run-down buildings.

Rats scuttled around his feet. A flutter in the shadows across the open space caught Pepin's eyes.

A man stepped forward, barely into the moonlight, likewise clad in a dark cloak and boots, his hood pulled down past his nose to cover his features. He held up a gloved hand, indicating for the prince to stop where he was.

"I came as Herwig said," he said in a muted voice. "You haven't been followed?"

"Of course not," Pepin stated flatly. "Princes in the kingdom practice walking unseen."

"So you say. But I've seen princes lose body parts for their lack of precautions." He lowered his hand and crossed the yard to stand close by. His voice dropped even lower. "What is it you require of my patrons?"

Pepin peered at the man, hoping to penetrate his identity. But it was useless amid the tenacious shadows. The prince felt off balance— he hated being exposed without knowing with whom he bargained. Especially when bargaining for a throne.

"I wish to put down a beloved family pet."

The man snorted. "Yes. I'm sure you do. I suppose you'll wish for this 'pet' to slumber off into the beyond with no lingering questions."

"Yes," Pepin said. "And do tell your sponsors that they will be richly rewarded for this assistance."

The man bowed slightly. "My prince," he said from the depths of his hood, "if you succeed, you will have their best wishes. But upon payment, you will never hear from nor see us again."

ΑΘΙ

The champion's official chambers lay in the palace complex near the royal quarters. Amid the grandeur, in a side corridor, a single, simple door stood marked with a placard of the rampant wolf above it. Gisela stood before that door, glancing back over her shoulder, her heart in knots. She swallowed hard, hoping the baldpate of Ganelon's priest did not glisten into view. She cautiously pulled a thick iron key from her robes and tried it in the lock. The primitive mechanism sprung with a groan, and the door opened.

She quickly stepped inside and closed the door behind her. There was no one in the anteroom, so she quickly crossed the simple quarters to the bedchamber.

"It's been so long since I've been here, dear departed husband," she whispered, barely daring to speak the words. She paused at the bedroom door. "But our son believes something is amiss."

She hesitantly opened the door and stepped within, her mind lost in memories. A merry child's laugh rang off the stone walls, and, of a sudden, the child slipped past her, brushing her skirts, his blond hair a tangled mess. She stopped in the middle of the room, her limbs refusing to move further.

"Roland?" she whispered.

William, her dear husband, stepped into view from around a corner—tall and broad-shouldered, his face creased with a smile and framed by golden locks similar to his son's. He roared like a lion.

"Where has my dinner run off to?" he snarled with a playful grin.

Gisela took a step back as he nearly collided with her.

But William's shade parroted something already said on that far-distant day. "What is this haunting vision stalking my wood?" he said breathlessly with a smile meant only for her. "Come to steal my supper?" He reached for her face, but his fingers passed through her flesh, and he faded to the sound of a child's laughter.

"Oh, my cherished memories, I should not have come," she whispered. Roland's clothes lay tossed about at random, lying where they had been cast off—so typical of her son. She felt a tightening in her chest knowing that she might only have a few moments before some squire or other arrived to care for the knight's belongings.

She quickly scanned the room. At the end of the bed, she saw the worn and familiar chest where William had often locked away his valuables. She crossed to it, dabbing at the wetness around her eyes. In her hand was another key, this one a slender bit of brass. The catch turned freely, the lid lifted easily, and she bent to search through clothing, bits of jewelry, and scattered papers until she found a cache of medicine bottles. These had been obtained for William when they had brought him back to the city to recover from his wounds. Each bottle bore an apothecary mark stamped into the primitive glass. She examined them one at a time, giving each a little shake, recalling both the marks and the contents—she had fetched most of them for the royal surgeon herself, long ago.

But there was one bottle, plain enough, yet bearing an unfamiliar mark, a Greek letter worked into a floral pattern. She held it up to the light and turned it slowly. The dark liquid trembled inside with each motion. She tugged the cork loose and took a sniff, filling her nostrils with a pungent odor. She stoppered it back, slipping it into the folds of her skirts.

A noise at the door startled her. She smoothed her skirts, rising when a page entered, a small wisp of a lad with wild brown hair that could use a good combing.

"Well," she said. "Where is your lord, Roland?"

The page's eyes widened when he recognized Roland's mother who was sister to the king.

"My lady!" he said, bowing awkwardly. "He's—he's at the stables."

She flashed a sweet smile then brushed past him to the door.

"If you see him, tell him his mother was here to say hello."

The lovers wandered through the royal gardens beneath trees reaching spectral limbs to the clear sky above, branches glimmering frostily in the moonlight. Roland and Aude walked together nearly as one, whispering and leaning into each other to hear what the other had to say. Near a small grove of trees, Roland pulled Aude under the crook of a great oak. She threw her arms around his neck, burying her head in his chest. He brushed loose hair from her face and lifted her chin so that her eyes met his. Tears left a wet trail across his hand.

"What is it that bothers you?" he asked.

She tried to blink away the tears and smile. "Must you go?" she asked. "It breaks my heart even now to think on it, with you still here."

He cupped her face in his hands and kissed her softly, her lips warm and wet against his. "When spring comes," he said, "the campaign will begin. And much needs to be done—gathering supplies, training the troops, reconnaissance of the region. Charles has placed his faith in the information I've been charged to gather."

She frowned, clearly not interested in the minutiae of campaign logistics. "But the last time you left, it was three years before I saw your face! Three years before I could breathe again and dare to claim your heart."

At a loss, Roland fumbled at his belt pouch and drew out the ruby necklace.

"My first wages as champion," he said. "A symbol of my troth."

She laughed then touched his face to smooth away the hurt she saw in his eyes. "It's beautiful. Truly it is. But it's not shiny bits of stone I want."

Roland took her hand in his and pulled her out from under the tree. "Then come with me," he said.

A Θ I

The dimly lit pub bustled with young noblemen carousing and drinking. Weapons clattered, and bravos exchanged heated words over minor offenses—the glance of a comely girl, an ill-spoken barb, or even a reference to questionable parentage. In the corner opposite the fireplace, someone broke into a slurred song, pounding his fist on a table to keep unsteady time.

Shrouded in a dark cloak, the agent entered the inn and glanced about the room. When he pushed back his cowl, the dim light revealed his face, flesh sunken and sallow, eaten with pox and bearing a scar down his left cheek from eye to jaw. His searching gaze skimmed over a far corner where another man sat, this one more handsome and refined—Gothard. The young noble lifted a cup to his lips, but the man noticed that he didn't swallow. *Smart*, he thought. This wasn't the time to indulge and become addled in the head.

The agent loosed the cloak from his shoulders, feeling the heat from the smoky fire in the stone hearth when he passed. He pulled up a stool and sat at a table to Gothard's side.

Gothard sloshed his cup around then raised it once more to his mouth. "You met with the prince?"

"Yes," the agent replied. "There was a request for something subtle. To ease a beloved pet into the eternities."

No emotion registered on Gothard's features. "Well. I know someone who has expertise in such things, a learned man who studied with alchemists in Constantinople. He's served well in the past."

The agent raised his own cup. "It would please our dear prince."

"Yes, it would. To watch the last gasping breath of his beloved, that is."

This time Gothard did take a drink.

CHAPTER 10

Conspiracies

The room was dark, but it was not still. Bishop Turpin lay in a tumble across the simple bed with a homespun blanket pulled up about his ears, and his snoring rattled the cup on the table nearby.

Someone rapped on the door, and he snorted, stuttered, and coughed. He rolled over to bury his head deeper in the thin feather pillow. After a pause, his snores once again resumed their rollicking rhythm.

The knock was repeated, this time more forcefully.

Turpin mumbled unintelligibly. He rolled from the bed, rubbing his eyes and scratching at his woolen nightclothes. Another knock came, rattling the cup more than had his snores.

Turpin shook his head and found his voice. "I'm coming!" He took a drink from the cup and slammed it down. "Can't you give a man a moment to clear the cobwebs?"

The royal chapel was usually quiet at this time of night, save for the occasions when Charles sought the Lord at the candlelit altar. Turpin entered still dressed in his bed robes, searching the shadows for something, anything, to drink.

"Oh, I'm in need, that is certain," he grumbled, tugging on his priestly vestments. Roland and Aude followed him into the chapel, their hands clenched tightly together. Turpin waved them to the altar where they knelt down together.

Aude whispered to Roland, "Our commitment is for God and us.

Please, it would kill my father in his sickbed if he thought he failed to drive a bargain on his daughter's dowry."

Roland squeezed her hand in his. "Of course. But *someone* should be here."

"Someone?" Aude asked.

Oliver stepped into the light then, waving off the page escorting him when he saw what was unfolding at the foot of the altar.

"Hello. What's this?" he said, color rising to his cheeks. He pulled out his dagger as he crossed the floor to them.

Roland raised both hands and spoke quickly. "I wouldn't betray her trust, my friend! Or yours—that's why we're here!" Oliver hesitated for a heartbeat. Roland took the pause as a chance to drive onward. "She knows everything that makes even you blush when I tell it, but still she'd have me. Before God, I love her. I promise to love no other!"

Oliver searched Roland's face for falsehood. "Is this true?" Oliver asked his sister at last. "Do you love him? Will you accept him?"

"Yes," she said with a smile. "I do—with all my heart. I will. And now you'll be together in battle ..."

"And united in our love for you," he finished for her. He tossed the dagger to the floor and placed his hands in hers, and Roland clasped his own hands around theirs.

Turpin dabbed at his eyes with a corner of his nightshirt. Then he opened a worn old vellum Bible, held it up to the candlelight, and squinted at the hand-scrawled print.

"Not much call for this sort of thing on the battlefield," he mumbled. He straightened, tugged at his bishop's accoutrements, and then began.

"We are gathered here in the sight of God and His angels, to see this man and this woman united in holy matrimony ..."

Not all chapels that served the faithful and the sinner in Aachen were adorned in gold leaf and exotic silks. Some could be—only very generously—described as humble.

At one such ramshackle edifice, Pepin crept through the graveyard, stepping carefully past crude markers to a shadowed chapel door. He tugged at the latch and pushed the door open. The inside was shrouded in stygian darkness, forcing Pepin had to feel his way to the broken-down confessional. His heart filled his throat as he opened the door and sat on the stool.

It was one thing to dream of being king and quite another to realize the act of becoming one. He longed to be unbridled from the ancient Frank customs that split households, estates, and entire kingdoms between sons when a father passed on. A quaint tradition for backwater homesteads in a much simpler time, he supposed—but tradition was no way to run a kingdom beset on all sides by enemies. So here he was to firmly take his fate into his own hands. He pulled the curtain closed then leaned close to the fretted wooden panel at his elbow.

"Forgive me, Father," Pepin said dutifully, "for I am about to sin."

The agent, shrouded by his cowl, opened the small door in the panel and passed Pepin an amber bottle. "Yes, well, my master wishes you Godspeed."

"I'm not sure God fills my sails at the moment," Pepin admitted. "When this is over, though, I'll build Him a fine monastery and set my brother to watch over it."

He stood up, pushing open the confessional door, and stalked from the chapel before his sickly knees could buckle. Pulling his cloak tightly about his body, he hurried through the cemetery and quickly rounded the yard to the thoroughfare in front. Stepping out to the street, he nearly collided with Demetrius. But the Greek hopped to the side, allowing the prince to continue on.

"Good evening, my prince!" Demetrius said with a slight bow.

"Yes, my apologies, Ambassador," Pepin said, pulling his hood up.

"It's not safe for you to wander alone on the streets," Demetrius called after him. "Shall I escort you?"

Pepin waved a hand dismissively. "I'm safe enough. Good evening to you."

He continued down the street.

Demetrius glanced at the decrepit chapel. Just then a hooded figure exited by the side door and rushed through the graveyard.

"What's this?" Demetrius muttered under his breath. He fell in a fair distance behind the man and started following him through the dark streets.

Roland and Aude stood facing each other before the simple bed in the champion's chambers, the room bathed in the subtle glow of winter moonlight. They kissed, and in that kiss Roland discovered something in himself.

He pulled back his lips and looked into her eyes as her lips parted invitingly.

"Oh, my beautiful wife," he whispered, fully intoxicated with her. "I will always love you, beyond my last breath and into the eternities."

Aude stretched on her tiptoes to reach his lips once more. "And I you, my husband. The knight of all my dreams ..."

Roland traced her face with his fingers, caressing each curve of her cheekbones. "Are you happy?" he asked. "Even if we didn't have a public spectacle for a wedding?"

She laughed in a throaty manner. "To the depths of my soul. And you?"

Roland began tugging at her bodice. "More than I have ever known."

Their clothes fell in a rumpled heap to the floor as the two tumbled to the bed.

Servants checked the red-hot braziers to ensure the king's room remained warm through the night. One fluffed the royal pillows, another drew the curtains, and still another turned down the blanket and sheets. Through the nightly ritual, Charles sat at his desk, his tired, red-rimmed eyes scanning endless manuscript pages. He scratched out letters in the margins with an ink quill that blotted at annoyingly random intervals.

Naimon stood next to the desk holding another sheaf of vellum documents, an urgent look on his face even though the hour was late. "Sire, these need to be signed as well."

Charles pushed the documents to the side.

"I'm sorry," he said with a yawn. "Writing my name over and over again is so taxing. Call up my wine. I'll finish this in the morning."

Naimon bowed professionally, and quickly gathered up the scattered documents. He hurried from the room with the bundle at arm's length, fearful that still-wet ink would stain his fine robes.

Demetrius hurried to keep up with the cloaked man while remaining unnoticed. It was a task made all the more difficult by the scarcity of people about at this hour, not to mention the man's expert dodging between carriages, back-alley vagrants, and stray dogs. When they crossed into the less savory sections of the city, Demetrius found himself forced further into the shadows.

The Greek suspected that any one of the ruffians and cutpurses lazing about would likely recognize his quarry's face if confronted. Demetrius picked up the pace, closing the distance between them, but the man scurried along faster. Throwing all caution to the wind, he rushed to cut the man off before he could bolt down an alley, but the man dodged again and broke into a loping run. They were sprinting now, hopping over the clutter of trash, crates, and barrels. Then the man looked over his shoulder and tripped on his cloak. With a cry, Demetrius was upon him, bearing him down to the frozen ground.

"I see you have time for me after all, my friend!" the Greek huffed, drawing out his dagger and pressing it hard to the man's throat.

"And I'm in need of drink and a warm bed! Now let me go. Here, take my money. It's not much."

Demetrius grabbed the man's arm—his hand bore a dagger instead of a purse. The Greek smashed the man's knuckles against the ground, over and over again until the weapon clattered away.

"That's an awfully slim 'purse,'" he said. "Now quickly, it's news I require—news of princes and dark deeds!"

The man chewed up dirt as he spoke. "Princes? You think I rub elbows with royalty? You're daft!"

"Am I now?" Demetrius whispered as he drew the dagger's edge along the man's throat, a line of crimson springing up on his skin. "Princes and paupers. I wonder what they do worshiping together. By the time this is through, we'll know who's daft."

He pressed the dagger point under the man's chin.

"Now, you were saying? Quickly, man, before we test the knife's edge yet a little deeper."

The steward, his gray locks a riot of tangles, shuffled down the hall bearing a tray with a precariously teetering cup threatening to tumble with each of his steps. Of course, he wasn't so much worried about the cup spilling—he'd done this nightly for the better part of fifteen years. No, he was much more worried about not getting the wine there quickly enough, for the king dearly loved his drink before his other nocturnal activities. The steward was a religious man, and he shuddered at the thought of the things that went on behind those closed doors. To him the king revealed a paradox of passions and intentions, most of them rightly ordered—others, not so much. He nearly dropped his charge when Pepin stepped from a doorway ahead of him.

"Oh, sire," the steward said, rebalancing the cup with a hand. "My apologies. I could have run you over!"

Pepin raised a hand. "No apologies needed, good man. I'm going to my father's chambers. I'll take that."

"But …" the man stammered. Yet the look in Pepin's eyes would brook no argument. "As you wish, sire." He handed Pepin the tray and hurried back the way he'd come.

Pepin continued down the hallway to the royal chambers. Geoffrey of Anjou waited there, clad in his mail coat with his sword riding at his side in a worn scabbard.

"Is all in place?" Pepin asked.

"At your command, sire" Anjou said with a wolfish gin.

"Very good," Pepin said. "And when this business is done, remind me to purge the serving staff. They could be complicit to murder, you know."

Roland sat up and rubbed his eyes with a balled fist. Something hit the door, and he started. He threw the wool covers over Aude's slender form then slid to the side of the bed, grabbed his trousers, and stepped into them. The stone beneath his feet was cold as he padded across to the door.

He drew back the latch and pushed it open.

"What is the meaning of—?" The words froze in his throat. An armed warrior knelt over the prone form of Roland's squire. His mailed fist dripped red. The soldier looked up and gestured to unseen comrades who with rough hands shoved the door open wide.

Aude sat up and screamed.

Several armed men forced their way in, reaching for Roland. But he danced back into the shadows then leaped across the bed and his wife. He grabbed Durendal and tossed aside the scabbard.

A sergeant, wearing Anjou's colors, stepped into the room behind the others.

"Kill him!" he growled. Three soldiers advanced.

Durendal flashed in the waning moonlight, a wraith in the hands of a shadow. Aude pressed herself against the wall, reaching for her own dagger in an end table as her husband drove headlong into the guards. Men groaned and cursed when the sword bit. One sank to the ground, grasping at his throat. Steel grated against steel, Durendal ever quick in the hands of the champion, sliding from guard to ward to whistling cuts as if possessed, until the blade blurred in the shadows and another soldier fell, the point sprouting from the man's neck.

"Roland!" Aude called. He spared a glance back—one of Anjou's men teetered on the bed, right arm dripping blood from the bite of Aude's dagger.

Roland swung the sword in a mighty arc, and the blade severed the man's head from his neck. Blood sprayed across the sheets as the corpse fell in a tangle. Roland returned his attention to the door. Only the sergeant remained standing.

Roland lunged.

Steel and flesh collided. The sergeant cut at Roland, following with a mailed fist. A grunt escaped Roland's lips when sturdy knuckles connected with his ribs, but he drove the man back into the doorway until he slipped in the pool of the squire's blood. The sergeant was unbalanced for only a heartbeat, but it was one heartbeat too long. Roland wrapped him in his arms and drove him back into the sitting room.

The sergeant tripped backward over a chair and struck the wall behind. His ribs cracked from the impact, and Roland followed by hammering Durendal's pommel up into the man's jaw, shattering bone and teeth. The sergeant gagged and kicked. He fumbled for his belt but instead found Roland's hand clamped about his wrist. With a deft switch of his grip on the sword, the champion rammed the blade up the man's groin under his mail coat. The sergeant sagged, gurgling on broken teeth and blood.

Roland spat on the corpse.

Aude stood nearby, pressed against the wall and covered in blood, eyes wide. Roland pressed a hand to her cheek.

"Don't leave our rooms," he said, more gruffly than he intended. He sucked air through his teeth at a pinch of pain in his ribs. "I'll send someone. I promise."

Aude forced a brave smile. "Go. You must see to the king."

Roland bent and, with a foot on the corpse's chest, yanked Durendal free.

Charles maintained a simple field-altar next to his bed for personal worship. The small crucifix was rough-hewn from olive wood imported from the Holy Land itself, and the tiny beeswax candles surrounding it guttered with the slightest disturbance—this time Pepin pushing open the door bearing the cup of wine in his hands. Charles looked up from where he knelt in his night robes.

"Ah, my son. To what do I owe this visit?"

Pepin set the tray on the desk and lifted the cup in his hands. "Does a son really need a reason to serve his father?"

Charles smiled as he reached for the offered drink. "Words I would expect more from Louis. But I thank you."

"I am nothing if not a dutiful son," Pepin replied with a smile.

Throughout the palace, heavily armed men wearing green surcoats blazoned with the red rose of Anjou rushed to secure positions within the corridors and along the walls. The royal guards mustered out to stop the flood of intruding steel, but many were brutally cut down before they could gather in sufficient strength to resist the interlopers. The coup became a slaughter.

Outside the walls, Demetrius could hear the sounds of struggle as he dragged his ragged prisoner to an alley overlooking the palace gates where a handful of royal guards faced Anjou's overwhelming companies. Behind the Greek came the steady *tromp, tromp,* tromping of boots— this time the marchmen, emerging from the shadows with Oliver, Otun, and Kennick leading them. Their mail coats and weapons flashed in the winter's moonlight.

One of Roland's squires crept from the shadows.

"My lords!" he said. "Roland is already inside the palace!"

"What is this?" Oliver asked sternly. "We came as fast as we could muster out!"

"Pepin has moved against Charles," Demetrius reported. "And Anjou supports his cause."

By the distant gate, they could see Anjou's men butchering the guards, their blood running in dark streams from the entrance. The southerners finished the last of the defenders and started closing the ironbound portal.

"Damn!" Kennick growled. "We'll need more men if we have to force the gates!"

"And Roland is alone in there," Demetrius reminded them.

A wicked smile formed on Otun's lips. "Now's the time for blood!"

Oliver lofted Halteclare over his head. "All right, then. As one!" he commanded. "In tight formation. We'll drive the gate open!"

The marchmen formed up smartly, locking their shields in Roman style. On Oliver's signal, they charged the gate.

Charles lifted the cup from the tray and rose, arthritic knees making him a bit unsteady at first, but he recovered quickly and navigated into a nearby chair.

"Have you thought about my request?" Pepin asked, leaning in close. "I am the eldest. I can hold the realm together. Advance your legacy. Please, Father, God would not want you to go to your rest and allow this, His kingdom, to descend into civil war and chaos!"

"I cannot abandon your brother," Charles murmured with a hint of sadness in his voice. He had argued round and round too often with Pepin on this issue. "I will take care of my children. Frank law and tradition are preeminent in this matter."

"But your entire reign breaks with tradition!" Pepin said, his voice rising. "You war against the encroaching darkness of tradition and ignorance by translating the ancients' law and philosophy. You've instituted higher learning, brought together the finest Christian, Muslim, and Jew scholars. Father, name me your heir. I swear by all that is holy and sacred that I will keep your dream alive. The Frank kingdom will be the light on the hill!"

Charles shook his head, his face drawn and tired. "As with any father, my children are my legacy. My kingdom, on the other hand, is a legacy to all Franks, no matter if each of you governs a piece of the whole. Now please, I am tired, my son."

Pepin bowed deeply. "Of course, Father."

Charles lifted the cup. Before the wine could pass his lips, Roland crashed through the door and stumbled in. In his hand, Durendal dripped blood.

"My king," he said breathlessly with a bow, though still moving forward to close the distance. "Cousin," he nodded at Pepin.

Pepin shuffled to block Roland's approach.

"What is this, Champion?" Pepin snapped. "You've interrupted the only time I've had with my father in days."

Roland bent to his knee and lowered his head to the king.

"Sire, there is a threat to your life!"

Charles leaned forward in his chair, setting the cup on the table beside him.

"Tell me," he said.

"What threat?" Pepin challenged. "How can there be danger to him in his own house?"

Roland pointed at the cup sitting near Charles's hand. He glared unrepentantly at Pepin.

"Would the betrayer dare to take up the cup?" he challenged.

The color drained from Pepin's face. "You're insane! Father, he accuses me!"

Charles leaned forward, his brows knit together. "You tread dangerously, Champion."

Roland took a step toward the cup, his hands spread before him, blade turned away.

"If all is as it should be, then drink," he baited the prince.

"He's mad, Father. Probably murdered your guards to get in!" Pepin snarled. "I'll have him removed. Then we'll get to the bottom of this."

Roland brushed past the prince, lunging for the cup. He grabbed it and lifted it to his mouth. "If you do not drink, then I will! You will stand condemned by my last breath—"

Before Roland could taste the cup, Geoffrey burst through the door. His face was flushed, and blood stained his fine garments.

"Anjou?" Charles stood. "What have you done?"

"You?" Roland spat. "I supported your cause! Charles committed to defend the south for you!"

Anjou laughed. "Why should I trust you? You being champion is an insult to your betters, and Charles was mad to have chosen you!"

Roland set the cup down on a table, hefted Durendal in his hand, and raised the long steel blade to guard.

"You're a traitor!" he said, accusation dripping from his voice.

Geoffrey launched at him, the keen edge of his weapon whistling through the air. Roland sprang forward into the attack, jarring the downward cut to a stop by slamming his own blade into Geoffrey's cross guard, then snatching the stalled weapon and ripping it out of the count's hands. Geoffrey desperately clamped his hands around Roland's throat, but his grip slackened and failed when Roland's blade sprouted bloody from his back. The count of Anjou wheezed and spat blood into Roland's face.

"Go to hell," Roland growled.

Oliver burst into the room, Demetrius on his heels dragging the man he'd captured in his wake. Oliver skidded across the bloody stone to place himself between Pepin and Charles. Demetrius hurled his prisoner to the floor, tossing a few of the man's fingers after him.

"Apologies, Your Majesty," Demetrius said with a bow. "I see we're not too late."

Pepin could not help but glance fearfully at the cup on the table.

Marchmen crowded into the room, many half-dressed and lightly armed. Before they could react, the prisoner lunged for the cup and thrust his face into the drink, draining it. Waving his bloody hands, he fell to the floor cackling madly—but he would spill no more secrets. He expired as the marchmen hauled his corpse to its feet.

CHAPTER 11

CONSEQUENCES

A leaden gray sky cast its pall over the remaining members of Charles's retinue that filed out the palace door. Freezing rain clung to clothes and soaked through to bones, but undeterred they assembled around the battered ancient stump that thrust up in the middle of the confined space. These, the great men of the realm, were accustomed to death and betrayal, yet they were pale and silent, tugging their cloaks and furs further up about their necks. Many fidgeted and stomped chilled extremities.

They didn't have to wait long, for a small portal to one side screeched open on icy hinges. Guards marched from the darkness, stiff, somber, and formal. Behind them, draped in iron manacles and chains, limped Pepin. He was cleanly clad in plain linens and leather shoes. He held his head high even while shuffling through the slush to the executioner's stump. Behind him, Roland followed the procession to the center of the courtyard.

Charles emerged from the palace door flanked by the remainder of his children, Naimon, and a few other close associates. Louis appeared dour, keeping pace with his father. Both Aldatrude and Berta had clearly been crying, and though they marched stiffly with all the gravity required of them, their faces remained red and puffy. Charles's face was set and stern. He stopped before Pepin.

A hush fell across the yard. The tension between father and son was palpable.

"Pepin. My son." He paused for only a moment. "You've been found guilty of murder … of treason."

The prince stared back with venom.

Charles struggled to press on. "Pepin, Pepin … I held you as you took your first breath of life!" The king's voice broke, but his eyes remained flinty. "We laughed together as you took your first steps! Cried when you were sad! Pepin, my son, you've broken my heart!"

Pepin threw back his head and laughed. The nobles stiffened visibly at this blatant display, this stunningly unrepentant rebellion against the very order of God.

"Well, Father, I got my way after all! It seems you will only have one heir now—too bad it's the wrong son!"

Roland whispered to the sergeant next to him. The soldiers took hold of the prince, but he shrugged them off. Silently he stepped forward, sank to his knees, and extended his neck across the block. He gave a sidelong glance at Roland and hissed, "Use this well, Champion."

The executioner stepped forward hefting an ax that glinted sharply in the diluted light. He sighted on the prince's neck, raised the blade high overhead, and swung it down with a huff through his nostrils. Pepin's head sprang from his shoulders in a pulsing spurt of blood.

Tears welled in Charles's eyes, spilling over and tracking down his cheeks. Roland walked across the yard to Charles's side.

The king's voice trembled. "How could he do this—my own flesh?"

Roland shook his head. "You are much wiser than I, sire. But it seems ambition blinds ties of blood."

Charles clenched Roland's shoulder, leaning on him and taking strength from the young champion. They walked back to the open palace doorway. "Promise me you'll never be so blinded," he whispered.

"With my whole heart, my king," Roland replied.

A Θ I

The next morning dawned crisp and cold. Aachen's shutters and doors remained closed—bundled up against the stubbornly resurgent winter. Louis rode from the palace atop his warhorse, bedecked in plates of scale and elaborate arms, as befitting a prince of the realm. His travel cloak was tight about his body to fend off the chill. But his eyes were unfocused and far afield from the martial procession unfolding in his wake, for Louis both hated and grieved for his lost brother.

Behind him rode the troops handpicked for war with Saragossa, a clattering, rattling river of living steel that churned through the morning crust of ice atop the muddy track to the main gate. After Louis, Roland rode next to Oliver atop a spirited black warhorse that tossed his head and bellowed steam from his flared nostrils. The banners of Breton March and Vale Runer streamed behind them, between which Otun rode a bit unsteadily, towering over Kennick and Turpin beside him. Next in line rode the marchmen atop their solid Frank mounts. Behind those stalwart companies rode the Dane and Saxon warriors who had sworn fealty on the distant riverbank in Saxony.

The black warhorse beneath Roland strained at the rein to overtake Louis, its strong teeth chomping against the bit. The knight handled the beast with a strong hand, and though it clearly desired to fly through the countryside at breakneck speed, the great black remained reluctantly apace with the column.

Above the procession, Aude stood in the window of the champion's quarters, the shutters flung wide so that she could watch them go. A brisk cold wind brushed at her cheeks, but she ignored it. Roland's spirited warhorse pranced and lunged beneath her vantage point.

"Carry him with honor, Veillantif," she whispered to the animal, her fingers toying with the gem about her neck. "And bring him safely home to me."

The soldiers and knights rode out through the main gate. There each man passed two long spears standing upright, planted before the spring crops with their grisly fruits for all to see—Pepin's and Geoffrey's severed heads, silently awaiting the crows as they stared across the plaza.

117

CHAPTER 12

COLLATERAL OF WAR

Emerging buds lent a hint of green to the stark branches of the gnarled trees, but the muted color was the only thing marking the return of spring to southern Francia despite the weeks that had passed since the army marched from Aachen. Birds fluttered among ancient trees that had stood sentinel when the Franks' ancestors first appeared in long-ago Roman Gaul. Above the rolling foothills, the dark Pyrenees' snow-capped peaks broke the expanse of sky above the trees' outstretched fingers. A muddy track was worn into those foothills, no more than a footfall wide.

A small patrol astride their Frank mounts picked along that root-broken way. At their head clattered the portly Count Marcellus, clad in a mail coat that hugged his girth and mounted atop a warhorse sprinkled with gray from tail to mane. The count's face, in contrast, sported an unruly bristly blond beard under an iron helmet covered in a dark patina. Oliver and a handful of southern knights followed.

In the distance, shadows thrashed through the underbrush.

"He's on them like a hound!" Marcellus exclaimed, standing up in his stirrups for a better look.

Oliver squinted, trying to track the movement. "Pray we catch the hound before the quarry turns on him!" He spurred his horse and waved the men forward in a canter.

Ahead of them, a Saragossan raiding party plunged through the forest, pursued by a single knight atop a black steed. Roland stretched

MICHAEL EGING AND STEVE ARNOLD

low against Veillantif's neck to dodge branches snatching at his scale mail coat. The raiders broke from the trees and brambles into an open field, racing toward a burned-out manor house still smoldering from the torch. Roland and Veillantif erupted from those same trees in close pursuit, the great black steed stretching into a gallop that chewed up the distance behind the knot of men they pursued.

Within the low walls surrounding the wrecked house, a group of raiders idled themselves by tormenting a clutch of peasant prisoners. The approaching riders yelled for their attention and madly gestured at the lone knight trailing behind as their horses leaped the broken walls. Upon seeing the sudden increase of numbers arrayed against him, Roland reined Veillantif short and tugged Durendal from the saddle's harness. He hefted the weapon in his right hand as his left settled into the leather armbands of his shield.

"Heavenly Father, be my strength," he whispered, his breath rising in a gray chill mist before him. He leaned forward and patted the steed on the neck. "We're to be blooded, my friend. I trust Aude chose you well."

He pressed his knees into the horse's ribs, launching forward—an intractable juggernaut of steel, flesh, and bone. In a heartbeat he was among the raiders, laying about him, deflecting curved sabers and straight Arab blades. One rider's flashing steel skittered off the band of Roland's shield, catching his shoulder and crunching through the mail. A warm stream trickled down his side, but he ignored it and returned the attack with a vicious lateral swipe. Durendal struck the rider just under his helmet brim, and the wound gushed blood and brains as the man toppled from his saddle. Roland jammed his shield edge-wise into another rider's chest then hammered the man's face with Durendal's hilt as he rebounded forward. Bones crunched audibly as the blow struck. The raider tumbled backward into another that pressed forward to get at the knight, throwing him off balance and spoiling his attack.

Veillantif's hooves dug at the soft ground as he bounded into a sprint toward the larger war party in the ruins. The two horsemen raked their heels into their steeds and caught Roland short of the manor walls, thrusting and cutting to halt the headlong charge. Roland plied

120

Durendal wickedly, and the dance began in earnest—the combatants circled each other, probing for advantage as the soldiers within the walls gathered the peasants together.

Roland cut at a raider, but the man grinned when he blocked the blow. The knight quickly riposted, Durendal whistling through the air in a blurred arc, and blood sprayed from the man's neck. Roland pressed his knees against Veillantif's side, and the horse wheeled around, mist streaming from its nostrils and its hide slick with sweat.

The remaining Saragossans moved into a confining cluster around the peasants and prodded them back through a gate toward the far wall. Roland spurred his horse and galloped around the ruins to meet them there.

One of the raiders, marked as their leader by his ornate gold-trimmed mail coat, rode a few paces out of the gate and raised his armored fist. His face was lean, the tanned features sharp and hawkish, accentuated by a close-cropped beard.

"Hold where you are, Christian!" he shouted, spittle flinging from his lips.

Roland skidded Veillantif to a halt. The raider reached down into the huddled mass of farmers and dragged a young woman, kicking and shrieking, up across his saddlebow. Her sobbing daughter desperately reached up for her mother's arms. Ignoring the child, the raider drew his saber and laid it against the woman's neck. She quieted at the touch of steel on her skin.

"Their blood will be upon your hands!" he threatened.

Veillantif pranced beneath Roland's firm grip.

"Upon my hands?" Roland replied grimly. "I've blood enough on my hands, but this shall not be a part of it. Release them or you will die!"

The officer laughed, but the sound held no humor. "You bring this on them!"

"Be their protection, O God," Roland whispered, his eyes never leaving his enemy's. "Forgive me for what I must do."

With a press of Roland's knees, Veillantif surged across the open ground into the captors and their human shields. The officer parted the woman's neck with a butcher's stroke then pushed her body from him. The little girl screamed and stumbled toward the twitching corpse only to be ridden down by the raider's counter charge. An old peasant woman in the group wailed after her, falling to her knees and scooping the child's broken body into her arms.

The two warriors collided with a crack that echoed through the nearby trees. Swords flashed, steel struck, and the combatants sought for advantage, each probing for vulnerable seams in armor while deflecting murderous cuts. The raider thrust at Roland, and the steel scraped across Durendal. The knight's gloved hand shot out and grabbed the man's elbow. Roland spurred Veillantif, pulling hard on him, and toppled the armored Saracen to the ground. Roland loosed his stirrups and leaped down after him. Before he could gain the advantage, the raider lunged at Roland, bearing the knight over with a thump while fumbling for his dagger. But before the raider's smile could fade, he gurgled blood when Durendal suddenly punched under his armpit to spring from his throat. Roland clambered to his feet and pulled the gory blade free.

Marcellus's company appeared then around the broken walls, hooves reverberating off the stonework, and the Frank troopers quickly encircled the ruins.

"Enough!" Roland shouted, wiping at the mud and sweat rolling down his forehead into his eyes. "You're prisoners of the emperor! Lay down your arms!"

One of the Saragossans rode forward a pace, his saber at the ready. He studied Roland's face then quickly scanned the Frank troopers who surrounded them. He spat. "We know how Christians treat their captives."

Roland extended his arm, Durendal's stained length pointed at the man's armored chest.

"You've seen how I treat my enemies," he growled.

The Saracen turned in the saddle and conferred in urgent Arabic with his comrades. There was a moment's hesitation. Then, as one, they sheathed their weapons.

Oliver rode to Veillantif, wandering loose, and grabbed the steed's reins.

The peasants gathered what remained of their loved ones into their arms and fled for the protective circle of Frank steel. The Saracens tossed their weapons to the ground, but that wasn't enough for one villager, who darted in close, reached up, and grabbed a dagger from the pile. He plunged the length of steel into one raider's gut, thrusting again and again all the while crying wordlessly. Roland grabbed the man's wrist and twisted the dagger loose from his hand.

"Enough!" the knight said firmly. "Hasn't there been enough blood today?"

The peasant broke into a sob, hanging his head and staring at the blood on his fingers. He wiped it in a red smudge across his rough-spun tunic then silently followed the rest of the villagers away.

Roland moved from one Saragossan horse to the next, his boots sucking in the muck, removing the stolen village loot from their saddlebags. Frank troopers followed behind, pulling the enemy from their mounts and one by one stripping them of their gear. A scuffle between a Frank trooper and one of the raiders gained his attention. A familiar symbol hung about the raider's neck. Roland stalked over and, ignoring the threat of being trampled by the raider's horse, reached up and grabbed the man harshly by the sleeve. He nearly unhorsed him when he snapped the silver ornament from his neck.

It was a crucifix.

"What's your name?" Roland demanded.

"It doesn't matter to you what my name is," the man spat back. "I'm still a dead man, is that not right?"

Roland rolled the cross around in his hand. On the reverse, he found Latin letters. He tossed it to Oliver.

His friend squinted at the engraving. "Alonzo."

"A Christian?" Roland demanded. "You're a Christian? And yet you attack your own brothers in the faith?"

Alonzo's face darkened. "Franks have no love for the Hill People. I owe you nothing."

"Yet you commit murder against women and children who hold your faith!"

Frank sergeants dragged him roughly from the saddle and bound his wrists. Alonzo only laughed, even through one of the troopers striking him with a mailed fist.

"In war," this time he spat blood with the words, "there are no innocents."

Roland closed his fist on Alonzo's crucifix. "As God is my witness," he said, "there will always be innocents. The wicked are those who make no distinction."

Troopers dragged Alonzo to his feet, but he focused on Roland with a palpable bitterness. "When you weep in the ashes of your own home and cry to the heavens for justice, then you will know the face of the wicked. I survive. I survive and I make no apologies!"

Roland tucked the crucifix into his belt. "Better to die with honor than to live in darkness."

He gestured for the soldiers to drag the man away with the others.

A partially burned shell rose above ruined huts, smoldering in the late-afternoon sun, crumbling walls all that remained of the small country church. The stones were scorched black, and the primitive mortar crumbled from the heat that had been unleashed there. The edifice itself wasn't large, but the rough-hewn stones and timbers had been a point of pride to those who had constructed it, laboring in devotion for a generation to be able to worship within its walls.

A straggling procession of villagers bearing the bodies of the fallen approached. They made their way up the few steps, through doors wedged open on twisted hinges, to crowd into the blackened interior. In the midst of the sorrow, Roland bore the shattered body of the trampled child. He laid her on the altar and then assisted the others who struggled under the weight of the other bodies, including that of the mother.

From the shadows emerged the hunched figure of the priest who served as vicar to these people. He hobbled through the fallen timbers with a crude crutch aiding his balance. One of his legs was a twisted red ruin, and an angry wound marred his balding scalp. He appeared to be a simple man, dressed in stained and threadbare garments. His face screwed up in pain when he raised his hands, waving at the people in frustration.

"Father," Roland said. "There will be a funeral mass for all who fell."

"I can't," the priest whined, tears streaming down his face. "There is none here but me."

"Father, I understand," Roland replied gently, "but each of us has our duties. Yours is to pray over these people, in life and death—to sing them into the eternities." He took a breath and looked sadly at the little girl's body. "And mine is to send them there."

The priest genuflected urgently as if warding off a demon. "You profane this house," he warned.

Roland held up both hands. "You're right, Father. I apologize. But, please—sing their passing. We will help as we can."

He fished in a pouch at his belt, produced a few coins, and tossed them to the altar next to the dead mother and daughter. The priest stared at the bits of metal and then at the torn bodies of his former parishioners.

"Honor the innocent," the knight continued. "As Christ honored the children."

The priest nodded, his face easing, though the pain clearly remained. He herded together some of the village boys and began searching through the wreckage for the items needed to perform a proper service. The townsfolk gathered about the altar, some of them pressing their hands against the torn bodies and garments lying on the bier. Roland stumbled from them, found a quiet corner, and sank to the floor, burying his head in his hands.

"I asked you to protect them, dear God," he choked, his voice a hushed whisper. "Please, take them into Thy bosom. And forgive me, Father. Forgive me, the cause of their death."

A O I

Roland led the Frank scouting party pounding up the muddy track toward the towers that rose ahead, the Saragossan prisoners mounted between them with their hands tied to their saddles and to each other. Marcellus's fortress squatted in the pastures surrounding it, old and stolid—the product of skilled Roman engineers that had been ancient when the Franks had first arrived in Francia nearly four hundred years before. As the party approached, guards rushed across the drawbridge to greet them and to take custody of the prisoners.

Marcellus, having returned while Roland tarried at the church, gamboled out on bowed legs to eye the new charges.

"My lord Marcellus," inquired a sergeant from the far reaches of the Breton March, "where will we be housing our guests?"

Roland eased Veillantif close to the rotund count and leaned over. "These men bear information on events across the mountains."

"Understood," the count rumbled through his beard. He pointed through the gate to a dark ironbound door set deeply into the inner courtyard wall.

Shouts of defiance mingled with terrified screams that echoed through the musty depths of the keep. Days had stretched into the better part of a week, yet the Frank jailer leaned once more over the smoldering brazier and thrust his instruments into the heat. At his back, bloodied tools lay scattered across a dark-stained wooden bench. A man lay strung out on a plank, stripped to the waist, his torso maimed and his face twisted in pain. His ankles and wrists were bound tight to keep him still, even under the terrible duress that kept his body twitching. Nearby, a dark-robed cleric mumbled in Latin, marking the points of the cross over his chest to ward off the effects of what he'd witnessed during the interrogation. Other prisoners strained against their bonds, only to have a guard prod them back against the wall with the butt of his spear, their chains clacking to keep time with the man's pained wails.

Roland stood nearby, stone-faced, watching the jailor ply his craft.

"Saragossa. The emir ..." frothed from the prisoner's lips in a rasp.

"And the caliph?" Roland demanded. "What's his part in this?"

"Please ..." the prisoner pleaded. "All I know are camp rumors."

The jailor held up a brightly glowing instrument, heat shimmering from the metal. A smudge of smoke rose from it, tainting the fetid air.

"When Barcelona's subdued," the man gibbered, "ships ... he'll land in Francia, north of Carcassonne, to support Saragossa. Some whispered a hundred thousand or more. It's Allah's will!"

Marcellus stepped from the shadows. His bushy eyebrows knit together, concern upon his round sweat-beaded face. "If this is true, all of southern Francia will be devastated."

Roland examined the man's tortured face.

"It is true," Roland said. "Cut him loose. And give them food and drink."

Roland turned and strode from the chamber, the shadows swirling in his wake nipping at the edge of his cloak.

CHAPTER 13

A HOUSE DIVIDED

Charles sat on his golden throne while the nobles of the realm crowded into the great hall. His ermine-trimmed cloak rested high on his shoulders, its particular purple hue the result of contention and negotiation with the Eastern Empire—for the Byzantines jealously guarded the color as a singular imperial prerogative.

As he watched the assembly jostle into the room and for position near the throne, his fingers drummed along the haft of a scepter of fine Byzantine craftsmanship topped by a gilded eagle with outstretched wings. He was restless to leave the machinations of the capital behind for a season—to breathe clean air free from platitudes and deceit. Behind him, Turpin and Naimon held places of honor as the king's advisers, Naimon serene as ever, the stalwart bishop fidgeting in his finest vestments.

Finally the room filled, chatter faded to a whisper, and Charles said, "It is time."

Naimon stepped forward, cleared his throat, then in a full voice declared, "Peers of the realm. I bid you welcome in the name of the king."

The remaining whispers died.

"Count Rene of Agincourt, if you please," Naimon continued. He then handed Charles a set of white calfskin gloves and an intricately carved staff, similar in style to the royal scepter.

The king stood when Rene emerged from the crowd, his peers

parting to let the tall veteran pass. The noble confidently strode the length of the room to halt before the throne with a martial flair and bend his knee to his monarch. Charles descended the two steps between them. With courtly solemnity, he placed the gloves and the staff into the count's outstretched hands.

"It shall fall upon my lord Agincourt to lead a contingent of my knights to the Saxon March. I bestow upon him all the rights and authority to act in my name in defense of the realm."

Agincourt raised his eyes and pressed the tokens against his chest.

"Saint Michael as my witness," he replied, his voice filling the room with a confident bellow, "the kingdom will be free from Saxon depredations in your absence, sire. This I swear!"

Charles nodded, gesturing for Agincourt to rise.

"I pray your words are prophetic, dear count."

Rene bowed deeply and returned to the front ranks of the nobles.

Charles scanned the assembly. "Noble Franks," he continued, "vassals, and friends. It is time to bid adieu to our loved ones. In a fortnight we journey to Spain. God save us all."

As one voice, the nobles echoed, "God save us all!"

Petras appeared at the door and watched for a moment while Ganelon directed the squires stowing gear for the long deployment to Spain. In his priest's rough and dark wool habit, he blended well with the shadows in the corridor. His serpent eyes quickly took in everything within the room.

A young ruffle-haired page of not more than ten years recklessly threw gear into a canvas bag. He yelped when Ganelon planted a boot in his backside.

"Everything has a place," the count growled. He sternly pushed the lad to the side. "Contents must fit in a certain way so everything can be stowed. A knight far afield cannot afford for precious gear to be left behind because a lazy squire took no thought to his task." He bent into the bag and began turning then fitting the pieces of gear. "Gloves fit inside the helmet. A spare pair of boots can be filled with garments and wedged back along the sides of the bag. Clothing is to be rolled tightly and stacked neatly." He grabbed each item from the child in turn, demonstrating as he reprimanded. "Everything must find a place. And when we decamp in Spain, you are charged with remembering where everything is, replacing it the same way. Whether the camp moves a hundred yards or fifteen leagues, it's all the same."

The lad sniffled. "Yes, my lord."

"Wipe those raindrops from your eyes," Ganelon said. "Or we'll put you to other assignments. You'll like them less, and your father will be months cleaning shite from your hair."

Petras entered the room. The lord of Tournai looked up at his steward.

"About time you graced me with your presence," he noted dryly.

He left the scurrying squires to their tasks and gestured for the priest to follow him into the foyer. The priest swept behind Ganelon like a shadow sewn to the heel of his boot.

In the next room, Ganelon halted before the stairs to his bedchamber.

"Between deployments in Spain and the Saxon March, the men of Tournai will be stretched thin," Ganelon hissed. "You must remain in Aachen to monitor my interests."

Petras scratched at his bare scalp. "My lord. Of course I shall do as you wish. But there remains much to attend to in Tournai. Many men shirk their duties as their lord and his heir both take up the sword."

"Yes, yes," Ganelon replied. "The absence of the whip lightens the yoke. But my lovely wife, the king's own sister, will need your wise counsel and, shall we say, oversight. You know her son will also be far away in the company of her husband. She will be distraught and vulnerable."

A thin smile twisted the corners of the priest's lips. "I shall remain at her side, my lord—to provide the guidance she will find necessary."

Ganelon slapped the priest on the shoulder, a rare sign of affection. "Of course. I'm sure she will be well cared for. A sharp eye can protect our much-loved wife from unintended conflict and tears."

"I shall be ever vigilant and include her in my prayers. She will be kept from harm."

"And from those who would use her," Ganelon added. "Her heart is much too kind."

At last Charles rode from the palace to the sprawling camp that lay outside the city walls. Behind him streamed ironclad horsemen in a grand procession, the flower of the kingdom's nobility off to war beneath rippling regal banners. As the train got under way, Ganelon inspected his horse for the journey, checking equipment with a meticulous eye. Gothard stood silently by the saddle with the stirrup in his hand. Finally and without a word, Ganelon finished obsessing, planted his foot in the metal footrest, and swung up onto the horse's back, prodding the beast toward the departing throng.

"Father," Gothard said, hustling to keep up with him. "I should be riding with you."

Ganelon's face remained a mask. "Such devotion," he observed flatly. "Your duty is with Rene in Saxony. Never fear, my son, there will be honor aplenty regardless of where you find yourself." He dug into the horse's flanks with his spurs, and the steed cantered across the courtyard to fall into formation with the other knights.

Gothard spat after him, kicking at the churned-up turf. He stepped aside as other knights clattered past, followed by a steady stream of motley-equipped Frank infantry.

"I know my duty," he growled at his father's distant back. "Standing at the river's edge watching sparrows and farmers. But there is no honor without war."

A Θ I

Far to the south, things were quite different.

Barcelona's walls groaned with the impact of stones hurled from Saragossa's patiently manned siege engines. Support timbers inside the stone fortifications cracked and bucked, causing defenders to scurry to brace up the walls with loads of dirt and grafted-in braces.

Outside those walls, Saragossa's formidable forces assembled beyond bowshot, preparing for what all—both within the city and without—expected to be the final assault. Bedecked in fine armor and silks, Marsilion watched the siegecraft from atop a fidgety white horse resplendent with tassels and gold braids along the fringes of its tack.

He signaled to Blancandrin, who called out commands from atop his armored steed. The general grimly watched the city begin to splinter.

"Have the sappers completed their work?" the emir queried.

The general nodded. "They prepare to take down the gate as we speak. Watch, my emir."

Marsilion returned his attention to the city. Blancandrin nodded to a messenger, who raised a bright red flag. A hundred yards away, the signal was taken up and repeated, passing from station to station down through the depths of the army to the front ranks.

There was a hushed pause as the entire force waited for what was coming.

Suddenly the city's great stone-framed portal groaned and erupted as if touched by the wrath of a petulant god. The gate's massive oaken timbers splintered, screaming with pulverized rock, and crumbled downward upon themselves.

"Very good," the emir sang out, clapping his hands. "Remember, Blancandrin, don't spare the brood of the traitor Sulayman."

"But, my emir, they are an honored family!" Blancandrin replied, aghast. "They've fought valiantly. Many would pay a handsome sum for their parole—even the caliph."

"They betrayed their people by allying with the infidels," Marsilion snapped. "Kill them all. I'll not have them at our back as we march into Francia!"

Blancandrin bowed respectfully in his saddle before flicking his spurs against his horse's hide, riding off to organize the final push.

The emir watched the swirls of dust rise. Through his well-groomed beard, he grinned with delight.

AOI

Marcellus's quarters within his stone keep were well appointed with tapestries, mosaics, and old furniture that bespoke his family's ancient ties to the land. With its venerable splendor, it was well suited as headquarters to the Frank vanguard preparing to cross the pass at Roncevaux to the Iberian Peninsula southward. The chamber Louis had selected for his war room was illuminated through tall, narrow windows. For this warm spring day the shutters had been flung open to catch a fresh breeze and chase out the last stale air of winter.

The prince hunched over a table scattered with maps and documents—lists of provisions, rosters of local levies, and assessments of the lands beyond the mountains. The only things missing were intelligence reports by the spies and scouts sent by Roland southward to glean information on Marsilion's movements.

There was a respectful knock at the door, and Roland himself entered the room.

"Highness," he said, bowing low. "You summoned? I came as quickly as I could."

Louis waved him to the table.

"Cousin, I need some advice."

"Of course," Roland replied.

Louis looked up from the maps then and smiled. "It's good to have you here. I've always been able to trust your judgment."

Roland smiled faintly, hiding conflicting feelings behind the circumspect expression—gratitude and pride on the one hand standing at the forefront of the expedition—and bitterness on the other over years lost twisting under Ganelon's thumb since the death of his father. But none of that was Louis's fault, and he nodded in acknowledgment of his cousin's compliment.

Louis continued. "Father will arrive soon, and we must know what we face across the mountains. What have you learned?"

Roland stepped close to the table and moved the clutter off the map. He traced his finger along the old shepherd's track that doubled as a trade route south through the pass.

"We've word that some of the Hill People could put up resistance where we mean to cross," he explained. "But to move further to the east or west will stretch our supply lines. I recommend that we cut through Roncevaux in force as planned then stage here, to the south."

Louis chewed his lip thoughtfully. "And Barcelona? Is he prepared to support us?"

Roland tapped the mark for the city of Charles's primary ally among the Saracen lands south of the Pyrenees. "We've sent men to scout the region," he said. "But I fear Saragossa has drawn the noose tight about the city with his siege, for none have actually entered its walls."

"And my father?" the prince asked. "What shall I advise him?"

"What intelligence we can gather suggests no changes to our plans," Roland said. "Charles must send a strong vanguard to provide a cover for the remainder of the army to cross. Then we strike, driving toward Barcelona to join forces with our allies. If we hit them hard, we can lift the siege and consolidate our forces for a push on Saragossa itself."

Louis steepled his fingers before his eyes and examined the map. "You believe this? We can break them?" he asked.

"I believe we can," Roland replied. "Granted, our last messenger reported Saragossa was entrenched about Barcelona's walls, and to succeed we must roll him back away from the city to his own lands. That will take effort, but the reward will be to ensure the caliph thinks twice about lending support."

Louis straightened and walked toward one of the sun-drenched windows, staring out over the courtyard and beyond at the growing camp of levies that continued to arrive from local districts.

"Then the van must be prepared to march south when Father arrives," the prince said.

Roland bowed. "Of course," he said.

ΑΘΙ

Aude stretched across her bed with sheets of vellum and a small inkpot for her letters home. Her room lay in the quarters her father kept in Aachen to house his family while at court. But it had been years since he had visited, suffering as he was from old age and what the physician called consumption. In her hand was a letter from her mother, written very neatly with the miniscule Latin letters fashionable among court scholars and those with interest in Charles's ongoing scholastic pursuits. Aude revered her mother's sharp curiosity—a woman who would rather pen letters than embroider scenes in tapestries.

A sudden knock on the door startled her. She set the letter down as another knock impatiently rattled the door.

"Coming!" she said, bouncing off the bed and hurrying across the room. She pulled the latch, cracking the door open. Outside stood Gisela, wrapped in a cloak against the chill night air that swirled through the corridors.

"Your servant let me in," she apologized. "I'm sorry to disturb you, my dear. But I must speak with you."

Aude pulled the door wide and gestured for her to enter. "What troubles you, my lady?"

Gisela pressed a small amber-colored bottle into Aude's hands. "Roland asked me to examine William's things. I found this. I'd never seen it before."

Aude pulled at the cork and wrinkled her nose. "What is it?"

"Careful," Gisela warned. "It has a nasty stink. Who knows, it could be a distillate of something useful. Lord knows when I was a child my own mother pried my mouth open to feed me nasty remedies."

Aude pressed the cork back into the bottle.

"I'll try to find out what it is."

"Thank you," Gisela said with a forced smile. "I prayed you would. Too many eyes watch my movements for me to carry this out quietly myself."

"Do you think—" Aude began, but Gisela raised a hand, cutting her off.

"I'm sorry, child," she whispered, patting Aude's hand and then reaching for the door. "I'd rather not think."

She hurried from the bedchamber with the rustle of her skirts the only sound of her passing.

Aude closed the door. She studied the innocuous vial in her hand. Stepping closer to the window, she held the bottle up to the light. The liquid was inky, and she could still feel the bite of it in her nostrils.

"Maybe it's really something helpful," she murmured hopefully.

Guttering candles kept the keep's small chapel dimly lit, the shadows relegated to the edges. But tonight that suited Louis, who was wont to pray when he could avoid the pomp and ceremony that normally accompanied a member of the royal family. The simple roughed-out room allowed him the private supplication his soul craved far from the prying eyes of sycophants who bent their knees alongside him only to use his pious inclinations to curry favor. He bowed his head and murmured a prayer. Even as he recited the words, he knew communion with God required a more focused devotion. Yet despite attempts to separate his thoughts from the world, he could hear the commotion from readying troops in the courtyard just outside. He tried to shut out those sounds too so that he could hear the whispers from the divine.

Shouting chased away the last of the prince's elusive reverie. He squeezed his eyes shut, but the shouts swelled to cheers that continued to gain volume. When the chapel door burst open and a tall figure strode into the sanctuary, Louis heaved a resigned sigh and rose, turning to meet the interloper—then broke into an excited smile. Charles still wore traveling clothes spattered with mud, but his face was fiercely alert, and the winter's pallor had been chased from his features by days in the sun. The king genuflected without breaking stride, each step clattering up the length of the chapel. He clasped his son in a firm embrace.

"Good to see you, Father!" Louis said. "We've carried out our charge—preparations for the campaign are well underway."

"Good, good! Come with me, son. Let us walk."

They walked together back into the nave, its rough walls covered in Roman-style tiles chronicling the lives and deaths of the apostles.

"You've done well," Charles observed. "We passed the main camp as we approached from the road. Everything looked in order. But what of local support?"

"Encamped to the east, toward the pass. Fifty-five thousand levies."

Charles paused, clapping his son affectionately on the shoulder. "Very good," he said. "And Roland? Is he ready to lead the army?"

Louis nodded. "Father, he is the hunter unleashed!"

The chapel door opened once more, and a woman slipped through the portal. She pulled back her traveling hood, revealing her face. Aldatrude smiled brightly at her brother and curtsied before she passed him, crossing herself respectfully before the altar in very precise motions.

"You didn't mention bringing her with you," Louis murmured.

"Your sister?" Charles responded. "I value her counsel, as I value yours. She's a good daughter, as you're a good son."

"Pah," Louis spat. "She's nothing like me."

Aldatrude batted her eyelashes. "I should hope not, dear brother," she purred.

Louis turned away to the chapel door and pulled it open to find Roland standing there.

"Seems we've a family reunion," he hissed.

Roland hurried in and fell to one knee before the king.

"Uncle, welcome," he said. Charles offered him a hand and drew him up, kissing him on both cheeks in greeting. "And welcome to you too, cousin," Roland said to Aldatrude. He took her hand in his and kissed it.

"Well, this is more like the welcome I imagined," she said cheerfully. "And welcome to you too, dear cousin."

"My son believes you are ready to lead the van across the mountains," Charles said. "Is that so?"

Roland bowed slightly. "I believe we've spent the time wisely, building our forces and capabilities," he responded. "I'm ready to lay siege to the gates of hell at your command, sire."

Charles considered Roland's words. "Consider the command given, Champion. Organize the vanguard and cross into Iberia. And I've heard there are prisoners already?"

"Yes," Roland said. "They await your judgment."

Charles glanced at the altar.

"Hang them along the road," he said. "A sign to the Saracens of our resolve."

That night, Count Marcellus hosted the royal party with a feast to celebrate both the ending of winter and the launching of the Iberian campaign. The kitchens turned out all manner of local meats dressed with the last of the stored vegetables, washed with abundant casks of dark southern wine sourced from local vineyards dotting the rich countryside. Roland sat next to Louis on Charles's right hand, a place of honor among a famished host who tore into Marcellus's generosity with great gusto. Serving women delivered heavy trays to the tables in a steady stream, dividing the men's attention between the steaming food and other hungers that required sustenance.

Roland's eyes explored the nobles, their interactions, and their strained relationships exposed through too much drink. At a nearby table, Ganelon ate in a muted hush with his bannermen from Tournai, most of whom Roland barely knew from a brief visit to the count's estates after his marriage to Gisela. Ganelon's eyes met his, and Roland responded with a tight smile. He raised his cup to his stepfather. Ganelon blew a bone through his pursed lips then returned to conversation with his men. There was no respect there, nor ever would there be.

After the festivities had worn beyond the twilight, Demetrius caught Roland's eye from his place further down the table. The diplomat nodded discreetly toward the door, then waited a few moments before politely excusing himself to make his way there, all the while laughing and bantering with friends and comrades from his many years' service for the emperor of the Romans among the Franks.

Roland drank another cup and listened to the count of Poitiers regale the group with stories of his most recent boar hunt—an encounter with a fearsome beast that had left a wicked tooth buried deep in the count's thigh. The man even stood and dropped his trousers to show one and all the puckered scar. Roland roared with laughter with the rest and congratulated him for his kill. Then he quietly made an excuse to the king and took his leave out a door opposite of the one Demetrius exited.

The revelry echoed in the surrounding corridor as Roland circled the hall until he reached the shadowed corner where Demetrius stood waiting. The two men clasped hands. There was a third person with him.

"This is the young man I told you about," Demetrius said, his voice low and deliberate. "His family is from near the Saxon March. Julian, this is Lord Roland."

Roland clasped the youth on the shoulder and, as was his habit, looked him in the eyes.

"This is dangerous business that you will be tasked to do," he warned.

Julian's brown eyes returned the look without faltering.

"Sir," Julian replied, "I've lived on the frontier my whole life. Each new day is greeted as a miracle in my house."

Roland nodded. "Very good. But this job will be subtle. Watchful."

"As it pleases you, my lord," the youth agreed.

Roland smiled, squeezing Julian's shoulder again.

"Yes, you'll do fine. Keep your wits about you. There's a noble who travels with the northern levies. I am to know everything he does, who he associates with, what he says. Understood?"

"Most clearly, my lord," the youth beamed.

AOI

The following morning, the column of steel-clad cavalry clattered from the keep's gates onto the muddy track and turned toward Roncevaux. Roland and Oliver rode at the head, followed by Otun, Turpin, and Demetrius. Above them, the rippling wolf banner of the champion marked the path for the following bandons where captains and sergeants ranged the ranks to maintain strict martial order. It was well known that Roland required precise discipline among his men, hearkening back to the days when Romans and Germans had served together in Rome's storied legions. Within the troop, the marchmen, headed by Kennick on his stocky steed, formed their own cohesive unit bolstered by the Danes and Saxons serving among them.

As the lead elements approached a curve in the road, they spied gnarled oak trees where the Saragossan raiders swung by their necks among the limbs. Crows danced and squawked in the branches, fighting over bits of flesh and gristle. Roland spurred Veillantif toward the bodies. Otun, riding up behind, scratched at his bristly red beard.

"Crows mark our path," he grumbled. "Odin has interest in our doings."

Turpin crossed himself with a dramatic flourish. "I for one don't want some pagan god's birdies along for this ride!"

Without a word, Roland cantered back to his place at the head of the vanguard that snaked under the frowning Pyrenees, making for the distant shadows of Roncevaux.

CHAPTER 14

CHASING SECRETS

The apothecary shop lay at the end of a dirty track that passed for a street in this poor section of Aachen, a neighborhood as far from the fineries of court as one could get. Merchants scurried along with one wary hand on their purses and the other on long knives at their belts. A few street vendors called out to the sparse pedestrians, pitching scrawny bits of hot meat and chunks of stale bread—all that could be spared in these lean times, for foodstuffs were diverted to support the troops both in the Saxon March and massing in southern Francia. Tattered homespun rags were the norm among those who scrounged through the goods for sale, some hoping to afford a scrap, others eager to pocket something without exchanging coin.

Aude walked quickly, lifting her skirts to her ankles to avoid the dark puddles while she scanned the signboards swinging idly overhead. A pace or two behind her shuffled her escort, Jerome, a kindly soul of sixty winters. His lean, craggy face surveyed their surroundings with cloudy eyes while his gnarled fingers nervously clenched a worn sword hilt tucked beneath his cloak. As a vale man, he was sworn to keep the lady safe, but it had been an age since he'd been tasked to use the weapon in anger.

A burly ruffian strode into Aude's path. Jerome closed the distance to shield her, but the man merely laughed and slurred, "Your search is over, lady! I've a satisfaction for you!"

Aude adroitly sidestepped him and kept walking. The brute stopped

143

and watched her pass then noticed Jerome eyeing him and made a rude gesture before stumbling on up the street. Jerome harrumphed at his back and turned to fall dutifully into step behind Aude, who already rushed up the apothecary's steps.

A small doorbell rang a cheerful peal that seemed out of place in the dark interior. Herbs hung from the rafters, making the shop appear lost in the undergrowth of a mossy forest. Fragrant smells twitched her nose. At the back of the shop was a large table covered with pestles of crushed leaves and braziers steaming with bubbling pots. Behind it sat a thin man with a bald head fringed by gray locks tumbling about his ears. He squinted over his work while his spidery hands deftly measured powders, mixed potions, and filled small bottles sitting in rows along the table's edge. As she approached, Aude noticed that each bottle bore a singular apothecary mark.

She stopped before the table and waited. The shopkeeper did not look up. She politely cleared her throat, folded her hands together, and waited yet a little more.

Sorting through a pile of diced herbs, he finally glanced up at her with an impatient tic in his left cheek.

"Yes, may I help you?" His Frankish bore a noticeable accent, like the priests from Italy in Charles's court.

"I didn't mean to disturb you," Aude began, a little tartly.

He waved a hand.

"No, no, you are not disturbing me," he said, but his eyes didn't seem to agree with his words. "What may I do for you?"

She pulled a folded cloth from her pocket, opening it to remove the bottle Gisela had entrusted to her.

"Would you be able to tell me what's in this?" she asked.

He pushed aside his handful of leaves, slipped on a calfskin glove, and took the vial from her.

"What was this used for?" He examined the contents against the dim light then scrutinized the mark on the roughcast glass.

"Oh, I can't say for sure," Aude replied. "It was found in the personal effects of a late friend."

He narrowed his eyelids, and his thin lips turned downward.

"Well, I've not sent something like this through my doors." He tapped the bottle, causing the liquid to dance inside. "The mark looks to have originated in Roma, or perhaps Constantinople. You'd do better searching those places to find who filled this. See the letter there?" He traced the mark. "I'm not a student of Greek. You need someone familiar with that language to learn about this little bottle." He twisted out the tiny stopper and sniffed at it judiciously. "Yes, this is something I've not seen in my work."

He handed it back and smiled.

Aude carefully folded the bottle in her kerchief and tucked it away again. "Thank you for your help, good sir."

"Of course, of course," he said, as if he had done her a favor. "And now, is there anything else I can do for you?" he asked with a more genuine smile. "A tincture for the moon, or maybe a potion for someone special?"

Back in the palace, Aude hurried alone to her chamber. Beneath the folds of her skirts, her boots were caked with the mud of Aachen's streets and left blotches trailing behind her on the stone floor. If she could just reach her room before being noticed, but a voice called her name and chilled her blood.

"Aude! Aude! Where have you been?"

She paused but for a moment to offer Berta the proper respect due to Charles's daughter. The princess smiled, puffing and waving her hands to accentuate the effort needed to catch up.

"I thought you'd been taken prisoner and spirited away from the palace!" The princess laughed, stretching on her tiptoes to give Aude a friendly embrace. She linked her arm in Aude's and pulled her down the hall, as if they had intended all along to meet up here and continue onward.

"Oh, no, no." Aude forced a friendly smile, feeling a bit guilty about being annoyed, for she truly had affection for Berta. "I can assure you that it was nothing more adventurous than seeking a trinket to send home to my mother. She has been shut in so awfully long with Father being sick, you know."

Berta flashed a radiant, childlike smile. "We should send your mother something more than a bauble. I'm sure there are wares coming in even as we speak from the Orient. Why, I saw some bracelets from Constantinople that are just to die for!"

Aude steered the bubbling princess around a court scholar who barely looked up from the stack of vellum in his hands.

"How thoughtful, my dear," Aude replied. "But my mother, well, she likes very simple things."

No sooner had the words escaped her lips than Berta began reciting the names of merchants, tradesmen, and small craftsmen who would be able to supply a wealth of simple things to inspect on a moment's demand. It was clear that all of Aachen could be at their disposal to find the right gift. And while they were at it, they could secure something for Berta's own dear father who was deeply missed at court.

Aude continued to smile, though the pleasantry did not extend to her eyes, for her mind was far from the conversation. Because of her love, Gisela's burden had become her own.

"… And we could take a coach to see Emile. You remember him, the Greek trader who ventures beyond the frigid north and brings back those fabulous stones that look like frozen drops of honey. As the tale goes, the ancient gods saw the honey trickle from their ladles while they brewed golden mead. They thought each drop so beautiful that they enchanted it to form amber. Oh, I am just so taken when I see those liquid stones …"

When the two young women swept down the hallway, a spidery figure appeared from behind a column, stopping to watch. Petras's bare head glistened in the light, and his hawkish nose lent a predatory air to his intense gaze. His eyes dropped to the mud track on the stone floor.

"And where have we been today, daughter of the Vale?" he whispered to himself.

CHAPTER 15

AMBUSH

Frank soldiers stretched through the pass, riding two abreast while their horses picked through the craggy reaches of the Pyrenees. Scouts ranged beyond the head of the column, scanning the trail for activity from the mountain denizens who eked out a meager existence squeezed between the caliphate to the south and the Franks to the north. Horns trilled from outlying positions, and Roland directed reinforcements forward. Soon the concussion of clattering arms echoed through the stony pass, quickly escalating to the human sounds of men locked in battle. Roland turned in the saddle and signaled to Kennick. That began a chain of orders shouted down the column of marchmen. Soldiers dismounted and readied weapons while Roland spurred Veillantif forward to take a position in the front ranks. Together they surged forward in a tight company, their footfalls echoing with a heavy solidity that drowned out the distant cries of men dying.

Karim and Saleem rode alongside Demetrius and watched the deployment with interest. After a long pause, they could hear the screams of hill folk who suddenly realized they no longer faced lightly armored scouts but rather the fully equipped and well-disciplined marchmen.

Saleem shook his head, concern on his face when he leaned over to Demetrius. "These Franks scurry about like ants. We waste time chasing shadows when we should be on to fighting Saragossa."

Demetrius smiled indulgently.

"But that's not the task for this company," he replied, waving his hand to indicate the vanguard as a body.

His answer piqued Karim's attention. "What do you mean, not the task?"

Demetrius laughed. "It's very simple, my friends," he said. "Roland is under orders to ensure the king's safe passage. He'll remove every threat to meet this obligation—including the mountains themselves."

Horns called again. Frank units rushed past the three men, this time with Bishop Turpin riding at their head.

"No time for chattering!" the cleric called out, a grin illuminating his face. He raised his hammer for the fight.

Demetrius drew his own long-bladed spatha, his genial smile becoming a mischievous grin that mirrored the bishop's, then hefted the weapon in his hand.

"My friends, that's why I love the Franks," he said. "Back in the empire, bureaucrats talk and talk until our enemies die of old age!"

He chased after Turpin to join in the skirmish with the mountain folk. Karim and Saleem shrugged at each other and spurred their mounts to catch up.

The sun fled to the west and cast hungry shadows along the foothills when Roland emerged from Roncevaux with the vanguard flooding out of the pass behind him. He surveyed the plain below, scattered with green from the early-spring rains. The air was crisp and cool. Soon enough Iberia would be gripped in summer heat sure to choke the Franks with dust in their preparations to grapple with Saragossa.

A Frank outrider carefully picked his way back up the rutted track toward them. Dirt clotted his horse's sweat-soaked hide.

"My lord Roland!" he shouted.

Roland wiped sweat from his brow and raised his hand in greeting. "You've news?"

"Yes." The rider pointed across the plain to a column of rising dust. "Barcelona lies yonder with his army."

Roland stood up in his stirrups for a better look, but the twilight was stretching into night. "How many men did he bring?"

The scout shook his head, disappointment displayed across his face. "His numbers ... well, they are not many, my lord."

"Show me," Roland ordered, waving his companions forward. They thundered down the slope in the scout's wake toward the dusty camp of Barcelona.

Guards, topped with conical helmets, stopped the Frank party with a challenge before identifying them and allowing them to ride on toward the camp's center. The place was a riot of soldiers, supplies, and wounded. Out of a large tent mobbed by bandaged wretches, a surgeon hauled a slopping bucket to tip crimson waste into a trench. He looked up at the passing Franks, his face a mask of exhaustion and his clothes covered in dark stains.

"Seems the siege of Barcelona is over and the war's begun without us," Oliver said.

"A fine observation," Turpin growled. "But rest assured, there's plenty of this war left for us."

Guards led them into the center to a large opulent tent and ducked inside while Roland and his comrades dismounted and waited. News of the Franks' arrival rippled through the camp, and Barcelona's men paused their half-hearted tasks to watch them with weary eyes.

The guards returned a moment later with a courtier dressed in a fine coat of exotic material. He stepped lightly through the blood and dust in calfskin boots then stopped before Roland and bowed politely.

"You've come from Charles?" he asked.

"Yes," Roland affirmed. "We're here to see the emir."

The man examined the Franks, scrunching his nose and squinting into the deepening dark, but upon recognizing Karim, his face brightened. "Please, please come this way!" he said. "You're a welcome sight!"

The guards deferentially pulled the tent flaps open to admit the delegation. Roland ducked his head beneath the fine canvas and stepped onto a thick rug that softened the ground beneath his feet. The appointments were exotic and finely crafted from the emir's own palace in Barcelona. The whole was scattered about with weapons that magnified the emir's martial status. A thin layer of dust from the flight across Iberia dulled the sheen of the precious metals—hands were too scarce in the chaos outside to spare for polishing and cleaning. The emir's servants scuttled about, some with bloodied surgical tools, others with buckets of fresh water or clean bandages that would be spent all too quickly trying to stem the loss of life and limb. A physician gestured for Roland to proceed through a silk divider at the far end of the tent.

He and the others ducked through once more and entered into the presence of the emir of Barcelona, who lay stretched across cushions, surrounded by physicians. Sulayman raised his hand weakly, though the spark in his observant eyes remained bright. He groaned when a physician pierced the flesh of his calf with a needle, pulling together the skin to seal up a wound with deft stitches. Another attendant poured wine over it and then bound the wound with fresh linen.

"My son!" Sulayman whispered, struggling to sit upright in the bed. "My heart is pleased to see you alive and well. And, my friends, welcome, welcome!"

Karim rushed past Roland to steady his father, gently pressing the emir back into the cushions.

"Allah be praised you live, Father!" he said. "But you should rest."

Sulayman nodded. "I fear I'm not myself at the moment."

"Emir," Roland said, "we bring you greetings from Charles. We are his vanguard."

The emir's face brightened, and he strained to sit up again. But Karim kept a gentle hand on his shoulder.

"Praise Allah," he whispered. "I feared my brother would be distracted by his Saxon problem for another season."

"As did he, my lord emir," Roland replied. "Yet here we are. I hesitate to ask—what of your city?"

Sulayman sank into the pillows. "We were driven from Barcelona after months of siege. We thought we could hold out until the eagle from the north arrived to our aid, but it was not to be. Even now the hounds nip at our heels."

"How far are they?" Roland pressed.

Sulayman waved his hand vaguely.

"A few miles to the east. We engaged them to cover the flight of my people—those who could escape the city, that is." His face clouded.

Roland turned to his companions. "Charles cannot be caught coming out of the pass. Saragossa would slaughter them before they maneuver into formation. It would endanger the entire campaign."

"Whatever you decide, we're with you," Oliver said.

Roland came to a decision. "Emir. Give me support, and we'll be upon them at dawn."

"Of course," Sulayman agreed. "We stand with you, my Frank brother. How many men do you bring to this engagement?"

"Nearly five hundred of my retainers for the vanguard," Roland replied. "Brave to a man."

Sulayman reached up and clenched Roland's hand in his own. "Saragossa will have his thousands, even tens of thousands."

"I know. Let them come. Now, Emir, if you will excuse us?" Roland left the emir with Karim and led his remaining companions out of the tent.

Outside, clear of the guards, he turned and clasped Oliver on the shoulder. "Move the men forward. No fires tonight. We sleep cold."

"The emir's men are spent. Will they fight with us?" Oliver asked in a low voice.

"Whether they do or not, we've no choice," Roland replied. "Pray to God we scatter them before they realize our numbers."

A O I

The Saragossan guards trekked about the camp at regular intervals, keeping a wary eye across the dusty fields that separated them from the smoldering campfires of Barcelona's depleted forces. Encircled by their course, men stirred in their tents and girded themselves for the battle to open the way through the mountains into southern Francia, where riches beyond imagination would be theirs for the taking.

A guard leaned on his spear and squinted into the morning gloom. There was movement within the distant enemy camp. He called to his comrades, who passed a signal along to Blancandrin's command tent. A short time later, the camp erupted into a milling engine of activity.

Marsilion stepped from his own opulent pavilion into a veritable stream of troops rushing past to their places in formation. Many who noticed the emir dropped into the dust out of respect, which added to the general confusion. Ja'qub, his court philosopher, scurried past Marsilion, his robes askew on his scarecrow frame, gray-shot beard in a riotous tangle, and rolls of documents bobbing under his arms. He jabbered pardons, but the emir snatched his flapping sleeve and brought him to a halt.

"My lord?" Ja'qub sputtered.

"What is all this?" Marsilion waved an arm toward the clamoring chaos of men readying for battle.

"The pretender!" Ja'qub huffed. "Barcelona! I believe he means to stand and fight!"

The emir's eyebrows rose.

"The fool," he muttered. He released Ja'qub and stalked toward the cavalry squadrons. Once before them, he shaded his eyes for a better view of Barcelona's troops, but the distance was too great. He snapped his fingers. Ja'qub, always close by, pressed the spyglass into his hand, a rare and treasured device made from two spherical glasses rolled in hardened leather and tied off with twisted metal and gold filigree. The emir raised it to his eye. The visibly enlarged enemy was even now forming up in a loose assembly, billowing banners marking the same units that Saragossa had crushed just days ago at the gates of Barcelona.

Blancandrin appeared at his side in his full war panoply.

"Have there been reinforcements to his ranks?" the emir queried.

"Our scouts reported none, though they have kept strong pickets out to keep us at a distance," Blancandrin said.

Marsilion chewed at the fringe of his mustache. "And now they stand to fight?"

Blancandrin shrugged, his mail coat glistening with an oiled sheen in the rising sun.

"We left many men to hold Barcelona, my lord," he reminded the emir. "We don't appear as numerous as when we last fought."

Marsilion considered his words and lowered the device from his eye. "But you confirmed that Sulayman is hurt, did you not?" he pressed.

Blancandrin nodded. "Sorely wounded. When they broke, he remained and fought in the center."

"So who leads them now?" Marsilion mused. "Surely they must know we will crush them against the very mountains. Why don't they just flee?"

Barcelona's troops gathered into ragged formations under the emir's defiant banners. Many of their weapons still bore the dark stains of their last engagement, and most of their armor had been repaired too hastily. Roland, dressed in native robes to obscure his Frank mail, rode among them with his hood pulled low over his features.

He guided Veillantif forward a few paces to better observe Marsilion's units. The sun continued to tick over the eastern horizon, yet they still did not launch their attack.

"They know they've the upper hand," he observed. "Yet they remain, vultures circling the carcass."

Sulayman sat nearby propped up on his steed, his wounds hidden beneath his exquisite armor. He grimaced. "He's ever wary, that one. Always has been."

Roland grinned, his features sharp and hawkish. "We'll have to coax the blackbird into the pie then, won't we?"

Marsilion stood before his tent, arms raised while his servants buckled and snapped him into his gear. First came the linen arming garments, then layers of mail and plate. As they worked, he watched Barcelona's lines with keen interest. A servant wrapped an ornate belt around his waist, cinching firmly a straight sword that had once belonged to his father. A stable boy brought up a beautiful black stallion with a flowing mane and tail woven with gold tassels. Once his gold-chased helmet was atop his head, two servants knelt before him on all fours. He adroitly stepped on their backs, placed his calfskin boots in the stirrups, settled into the saddle, and rode to the fore of his own formation.

A younger man, likewise clad in resplendent armor and mounted atop a matching horse, galloped from the ranks to his side. Marsilion raised a hand in greeting to his son, Farad, who impetuously grinned with a warrior's fierce delight, face framed by flashing conical helm and strands of deep black hair.

"Father!" he shouted excitedly. "Something is happening on their flank! Look!" He pointed to Barcelona's northern wing that stretched perilously thin toward the foothills.

Marsilion squinted through Ja'qub's spyglass in time to see riders race toward the mountains. He handed the device to Farad.

"Do they flee?" he asked for validation.

Farad's horse pranced beneath him, straining at the reins. Pride swelled Marsilion's breast with watching his son assess the enemy. The youth's energy was infectious.

"They're deserting, Father!" he said, his voice rising with excitement. "They flee for the pass. We must attack!"

Blancandrin watched the scattered horsemen beat into the foothills.

"Or they feint to draw us in," he observed evenly.

"Pah!" Farad spat. "You general like an old woman!"

Marsilion's heart soared seeing his son thirst for combat like a Rashidun falcon, eager to sink talons into the enemy. Then he saw a cloud of dust rising from their center across the plain. He snatched back the spyglass.

"What's this?" Men fought in a broiling clot around Sulayman's standard. He could barely believe his good fortune. "They fight among themselves! Sound the charge!"

Saragossa's battle horns blared, and the unleashed host leaped forward, multitudes of hooves churning up a choking dust.

Across the field, Barcelonan troopers rode in deliberate circles, kicking up an obscuring cloud of dust and banging sabers against shields in raucous metallic discord. Roland and his companions remained astride their steeds loosely clustered behind the circling lines, and they kept a close eye on the enemy's spirited charge.

"The blackbird leaps from his perch!" Sulayman cried, waving his saber above his head. Yet his excitement could not mask the pain he suffered from his fresh wounds.

"Keep it up!" Roland encouraged, banging on his own saddle with the flat of his hand. "He must fully commit!"

Karim rose in his stirrups to get a better look at Saragossa now closing the gap overshadowed by two massive clouds of dust.

"They are many!" he shouted. "They'll overwhelm us!"

Roland grinned wolfishly and drew Durendal. The blade flashed thirstily in the sunlight. He pressed the reliquary cross guard to his lips and shouted, "Now! Face them!"

To a man the playacting troops wheeled around, falling instantly into ranks.

Then the tide of steel and sinew broke upon them.

The torrent of horsemen crashed into Barcelona's troopers amid screaming edged weapons and torn flesh. Roland spurred Veillantif, driving the steed hard against the immense current. Durendal rose and fell in swift arcs, leaving Saragossans tumbling in bloody ruin from their saddles.

"The signal!" Roland shouted, rising up in his stirrups. "Now!"

The trumpeter brought a gold-chased ram's horn to his lips and let off a single peal before a Saragossan lance pierced him through the chest. Roland tossed off his disguise then, raising Durendal in the air, signaled to Barcelona's men.

"To me!" he roared above the din. "To me, men of Barcelona!"

He thrust at a Saragossan lancer, slicing through his armpit above the mail shirt in an eruption of blood. Veillantif lashed out and struck a foot soldier. The man staggered back and raised his hands to clutch protruding ribs but was trampled under by the armored horse.

Across the quickly developing sea of carnage, Farad fought with an abandon born of youthful immortality. Exuberance filled his breast with each enemy he faced, these men of Barcelona. When he spotted the wolf banner and saw the Frank champion fend off two horsemen, he let loose an exultant cry and spurred his mount through the chaos to meet the knight sword to sword.

The Frank parried Farad's attack and followed with a pommel strike to the prince's face, shattering teeth and bone. He drew back for another strike, Farad's blood dripping down his knuckles.

Not far away, alarmed by the youth's reckless charge, Blancandrin lowered his lance and drove through friend and foe alike after the emir's son.

The chaos washed past Saleem fighting in Sulayman's guard against men adorned with the painfully familiar liveries of noble houses of Saragossa. Lances crashed and blades flashed in the press of horses and steel, the spattering of blood, and the cries of the wounded and dying. Saleem twisted to dodge a lance and counterthrust until his saber blade ground against metal and bit into flesh. Grit stung his eyes, but he pressed on, unhorsing his quarry to be crushed under stamping steel-shod hooves.

Saleem paused long enough to catch his breath and scan the field for Roland's banner. A dozen yards to his right, the rampant wolf lunged over surging pointed helms. Only in the reach of the champion would he find the glory and renown that would keep him afloat once the intelligence of his father's revealed plans had run its course. He spurred his mount against another trooper, for an instant thinking there was recognition in the man's eyes. But he cut that short with a saber thrust under the man's chinstrap.

He rode hard against footmen that slowed his progress. The choking dust and clangor of weapons were thicker here, and there was less room to move. A bloodied trooper scrambled on all fours to get clear of Saleem, but the prince's horse leaped toward him and came down hard on the man's chest. Blood squirted through his mail coat. Saleem spurred his horse onward. He didn't have time or inclination to look back. There was a flash of familiar armor approaching from the left. Blancandrin shoved madly through his own men, making for the Frank champion. Saleem adjusted his track to intercept the general.

Blancandrin closed the last few yards, his lance slicing toward the champion's chest. Roland threw up his shield against the wicked iron tip. When the lance caught, wood splintered and shards flew into the air. His horse staggered from the shock, and the girth strap burst, tumbling rider and saddle to the ground. Farad turned on Blancandrin, wiping gore from his face and spitting more.

"Stop! He's mine!" he shouted then turned again to his prey.

The champion fought to regain his feet under Farad's renewed assault. The prince hammered down blow upon blow against his foe's ruined shield until he found a gap in the Frank's guard and his saber crunched against a mailed shoulder. Roland stumbled, and Farad drew back for a finishing thrust.

But it was a feint. The Frank lunged viciously under Farad's guard and punched his blade up into the youth's chin.

The bravado drained from Farad's face in a gush of blood. His body went slack, toppling from the saddle.

Blancandrin cried out, lowering his lance again and raking his horse with his spurs. The steed gathered itself and leaped, but horns sounded and a wedge of Frank horsemen crashed into the battle, pushing Blancandrin aside like so much flotsam. He fought to hold his ground, urging his horse forward, but the sheer weight of the Frank countercharge drove him relentlessly further from the champion.

He cast aside the lance then whipped his sword from its scabbard, striking in a torrent at the Franks and Barcelona men. But the die was cast; his own troopers began to flee even as he yelled for them to brace against the onslaught of Frank cavalry.

Saleem fought toward Blancandrin, but at that moment, the Franks charged with their massive thundering warhorses. He was carried away with the momentum. He struggled against the flow, screaming at his allies as their lines broke around him like a stream around a rock, until the line finally passed and he sat atop his horse for a moment in a sudden incongruous calm. Roland and Blancandrin were gone, lost in the seething mass of men, horses, and steel. Saleem suppressed the aggravation boiling in his breast and caught his breath sharply. He needed glory to survive in this barbaric world—glory that was being denied him by the fickle fates.

MICHAEL EGING AND STEVE ARNOLD

His eyes drifted across the fallen, their tangled bodies leaking fluids into the dry earth. There on the churned ground lay a familiar form—this one dressed in armor that, like Blancandrin's a moment ago, Saleem recognized from the parade grounds in Saragossa. This one, in those days, had strutted like a peacock with insufferable overconfidence. This one had been the root cause of a self-imposed exile amongst the unwashed Frank horde. This one, until now, who had been *the favored son.*

He rode closer.

Farad's broken body laid still, blood turning to gory mud in the dirt, glazed empty eyes regarding heavens that, in Saleem's opinion, the bastard did not deserve to reach.

Saleem spat on his brother's remains and turned back to the battle, his heart now soaring with sudden possibilities.

A pang of fear stole Blancandrin's breath. He tugged his horse around, searching for Marsilion. Amid the disintegrating Saragossan center, the emir fought encircled by his guard—his lips drawn back from his teeth in the snarl of a desert lion. Blancandrin spurred his steed once more, crying to Allah and the holy prophet. He raced through bloody dust-covered men to reach Marsilion's side and pushed through the guard of Saragossan troopers, grabbing the emir's arm.

"We must fall back!" Blancandrin cried over the desperate noise of battle. "My emir! We must fall back!"

Slowly the bloodlust washed from Marsilion's face. Then his eyes desperately searched the faces of the men around him.

"My son? Where's my son?" His eyes searched frantically beyond his guard to the men locked in combat with the enemy.

"Dead!" Blancandrin said with a quick finality.

Marsilion howled and madly spurred his horse to get back into the melee. Blancandrin leaned over, catching the emir's reins and dragging the steed to a skidding halt.

"We must regroup!" the general demanded. "If you fall, we will lose everything!"

Venom filled Marsilion's eyes and his breath rasping in ragged gasps. "Sound the retreat," he finally said with clipped words. "Identify the Frank who killed my son." He sucked a calming breath and exhaled. "And bring Farad's body to me."

Across the tumultuous field, Oliver's charge continued to grind against the Saragossan horsemen. The Frank heavy cavalry formed an iron wedge in the center of the field, fighting with a ferocious urgency. Roland ducked and dodged afoot through the deluge of horsemen toward his countrymen. With mounting losses, resistance buckled, and the enemy began to flee in a general rout. Frank and allied troopers spurred after them, stretching their lines recklessly thin across the Spanish countryside.

Roland sprinted to a Frank trumpeter.

"Order them to disengage!" he yelled. "Disengage, damn you!"

He seized the reins and pulled the steed to a halt. The man looked at the champion in disbelief.

"But, sir—" was all that escaped his lips. Roland ducked under the horse's head to snatch the horn from the trumpeter's saddlebow and blow a resounding staccato of notes.

Karim cantered to Roland. His face was flushed beneath the blood and grime.

"We have them!" he shouted. "Don't you see? We have them, and you're letting them go!"

"We have them for but a moment. Once they realize our numbers, they will swarm back across the field and overwhelm our men if we're strung out like this. My duty is to clear the way for Charles. That and that only!"

"But we have the serpent's head within reach!" Karim pressed. "We take the head, and the rest of the body falls!"

"Not today, Karim. I am sorry." He raised the horn to his lips and repeated the call to disengage. Across the field, Franks slowed their chase, closer men clutching at their fellows to turn them back to regroup.

Flushed, Karim booted his horse's flanks and rode back to the ranks.

Roland threw the horn back to the red-faced trumpeter.

Not far away, Sulayman sagged in his saddle, his own saber blade dipping limply in his hand, soldiers rushing to support him.

The Franks and the Barcelonans reformed their ranks while before them the enemy beat for the south in a cloud of dust. Elation marked the faces of most, though some resented being fettered when they sensed victory in their grasp. The marchmen once again demonstrated their iron-willed discipline in gathering up their allies and tending the wounded without further question.

His immediate task complete, Roland searched through the wreckage of battle until he found Veillantif lording it over a cluster of other riderless horses. The knight approached the sweat-drenched steed, holding out his hand. Veillantif pressed his soft muzzle to the open palm.

"You did well, my friend," Roland said. Across the carnage, a smudge rose into the sky, marking the passage of Marsilion's host through the dry terrain. "But we've a long way yet to go."

A Θ I

In the midst of the now-quiet battleground, a figure draped in a rippling cloak of heat-induced mirage stepped through the flapping and hopping crows. He stood, arms folded, amidst the dead—a silent sentinel awaiting the gruff call of sergeants bringing scurrying troopers to chase away the carrion and collect their comrades. William of the Breton March noted the stilled faces of those who had bled with him in battles long before and now had sacrificed one final time for his son.

The vigilant ravens edged closer, keeping wary eyes on the specter that living men were unable to see.

Seemingly satisfied, William turned and vanished. The crows took sudden wing, startling the less-seasoned warriors bending to their tasks. Some of the veterans could read the sign for what it was and crossed themselves reflexively.

The black birds lifted to the darkened sky and left the Frank dead to their own.

Barcelona's camp bustled with activity. Troops dug in against the hour when Saragossa would test them again. Blancandrin rode toward the camp flanked by a detachment of marchmen, his hands bearing a lance topped with a white flag. Sentries stopped the party. Upon proper exchange of passwords they were released to continue on. They rode toward the command tents, through air torn with the horrifying sounds of men who faced surgeon's tools. For these, the bone saw and subsequent infection were more feared than the lance.

They stopped in the circle of torches that surrounded Barcelona's tent. Amid the groans and screams, Blancandrin kept his eyes fixed on the man who emerged. But a youth, he seemed set apart from the olive-skinned denizens of Barcelona by his wild blond locks and fair complexion. On the knight's coat was embroidered a rampant wolf, which was also blazoned upon the standard that fluttered nearby. Yet this Frankish knight was no mere boy—his garments still bore more than a measure of blood from the recent engagement.

The leader of Blancandrin's escort, who had introduced himself as Kennick, raised a grizzled hand. "My lord. This man rode in under a flag of truce."

Blancandrin nudged his mount forward a pace.

The champion wiped his bloody hands on a cloth and sized up his visitor. "Your name, sir? And your purpose, if I may ask?"

"I am Blancandrin, general of the army of the emir of Saragossa. The emir has sent me on a sad errand." His command of the Frank language at least stood him in good stead here. "I beg your indulgence."

"Please continue."

"Today the emir of Saragossa lost his son. I am here to retrieve the body."

A man standing a few steps behind the champion laughed. "Better his body feed the worms."

Blancandrin fought to keep his emotions from his face, for he recognized the voice of Marsilion's own son Saleem.

The emir's son continued. "My lord, drive this man from your camp. He means you no good."

"Many sons were lost," the Frank said. "But this son of the emir, what does he look like?"

Blancandrin bowed in the saddle. "You would know, my lord. You wear his blood on your garments."

Recognition dawned in the Frank knight's eyes. "Yes. Yes, I do know." He waved Kennick and the guards off. "I'll accompany this man myself. General, come with me."

The two men warily crossed the battlefield, stepping between crushed bodies and broken weaponry. The cloud of crows circled overhead and discordantly protested the intrusion. They moved in a silence, but there were noises constantly about them. Frank and Barcelonan burial details plied the field, calling out to each other while they also searched among the dead for the wounded. The two, however, found Farad's body nearly obscured by the deepening shadows and freed the corpse from the debris. Farad's once-handsome face was smashed and grayed in death—caught in the moment that stripped him of youthful immortality. Blancandrin tenderly scooped the body into his arms, wet tracks tracing across the filth on his cheeks. He hefted the burden then placed it gingerly over his saddle and secured it for the trek back to the emir's camp.

Only when this task was done did he speak.

"Your name, Frank," he said, his voice low but firm. "What is your name?"

"I am named Roland, son of William, count of Breton March."

Blancandrin mounted the horse behind the body. "You've earned the enmity of the emir," he warned.

"This day I've earned the enmity of many fathers," Roland replied.

"Allah has a way of repaying Christian arrogance." The general balled up the reins in his fist as he tugged the horse toward Saragossa's lines.

CHAPTER 16

BARCELONA

The sun splashed fire across the mountains, a brilliant orange against the budding green clinging to the slopes. At their ancient feet, the pennants of Charles's northern lords waved bravely above companies and battalions spreading out from the mouth of Roncevaux in a glimmering tapestry of martial splendor. Roland rode out with his small band of companions to greet the royal party. Outriders had already alerted Charles to Roland's approach so that even before the champion could reach the clutch of bureaucrats enclosing him, the king cantered atop his finely groomed steed to greet him. As he drew close, he leaned from his saddle and clasped Roland's hand in his.

"It's good to see you, nephew," he said.

"And you," Roland replied with a wolfish grin. "We've supported Barcelona already against Saragossa."

"Very good," Charles beamed. "Very good indeed. Bring me your report."

By evening a light wind billowed the canvas of Charles's campaign headquarters, tugging the canvas while attendants set the last pegs in the shadow of the mountains. Even as the final support ropes stretched taut, couriers arrived from Francia with dispatches on everything from campaign supplies to holy festivals in Aachen to the spring tax collections. From just over the pass or from far-away Rome, all roads led to Charles's court.

Within the canvas confines, thick carpets from far-off Persia blanketed the ground, hushing the slippered feet of clerics and functionaries—though the thin walls did little to muffle the noises beyond of men settling into their campaign routines. Roland ducked into the tent to find a young page who met him with a respectful bow. The youth then led him through the gaggle of courtiers who kept the machinery of the kingdom ever grinding forward. At the far end, the page opened a flap, gesturing for the champion to enter.

Within this portion of the tent, Charles sat at a worktable. He drummed fingers stained black from signing documents on the desktop and gazed absently at the shadows of guards taking their stations outside the canvas partitions.

Roland cleared his throat and bowed.

"Oh, yes. Do come in," Charles said, his attention snapping back.

"Something bothers you, Uncle?"

"It's nothing," Charles shuffled through the papers on his desk. "Nothing at all."

"What is it?" Roland pressed. "You can tell me."

Charles studied him for a long moment then slumped back in his chair.

"I am wondering about the truth of dreams and visions. You know, I've heard of such things, but until now I thought they were only the purview of holy men," Charles whispered. "When kings have them— well, they don't always work out so well. Look at Pharaoh who sought out Joseph. The fatted cattle were consumed most ungraciously."

Roland grabbed a camp stool and pulled it up to the desk.

"Well, I've heard tell the pope anointed you emperor," he began. "God's servant on earth, giving you right to more than most kings. I suppose it wouldn't be unusual for God to want you to know something."

Charles smiled wanly at his nephew. "Yes, yes. Thank you, Roland. But I'd have told you anyway, without the reminder." He leaned forward conspiratorially. "Beware a priest bearing a crown. Well, where to begin? This dream—in it, I saw the gates of a fortified city and our men dying before them. And the heavens, they opened up fire and brimstone.

Suddenly I stood amidst the apocalypse, more horrific than anything written by John, beloved of Christ. What could it mean?"

Roland hesitated. He had only expected Charles to debate dreams in some general sense, not to actually tell him of a vision. "I'm sorry, Uncle," Roland hedged. "I'm a soldier who can barely read and write my own name. Such things as this, well, I am not the one to interpret them."

Charles nodded, tapping his fingers on the side of his chair.

"Neither am I, for such things must be of God," he mused. "And we need to talk of things that concern men."

Roland nodded. "Our scouts have reached Barcelona," he reported. "As we feared, the walls have been repaired."

"That will raise the price to take the city."

"It will unless we nullify that advantage," Roland agreed. "The emir's son Karim has been helpful. I've a way to enter the city."

Charles studied him carefully and reached out to pat Roland's hand. "Pray God brings success to your plan."

Roland's eyes glinted with confidence. "He will not abandon us."

Α Θ Ι

Over the next two weeks, the Franks marched westward along the southern verge of the Pyrenees in a determined reach for Sulayman's home enclave at Barcelona. Not only for shoring up the morale of their ally did they desire the city—it boasted a port capable of landing supplies from Massilia so vital in prosecuting the campaign to bring Saragossa to his knees. Minor skirmishes were all that marked that journey, raids by small scouting parties testing strengths and probing for weaknesses as Marsilion's army sought for advantage after their defeat on the plains. But these pinpricks did nothing to slow the inexorable advance of the Franks. Within days of their arrival about the city's walls, they entrenched firmly, just beyond bowshot of the Saragossan occupiers on the battlements. Troopers broke out rations and prepared for the call to the first assault.

The siege had begun.

Ganelon perched on a rock among the men of Tournai like a

predatory bird, his helmet, weapons, and shield stacked nearby. He tore into a stale biscuit and choked it down with a gulp from a water skin. His crag-faced uncle Guinemer hunched over his own kit, rubbing intently at a splotch of rust on the armor with oil and stone.

Not far away among the retainers, Julian cleaned and stacked weapons and armor, joking with his peers. Yet even focused on his tasks, he kept a half an eye on Ganelon and another out for Roland.

A knight in Charles's livery approached on horseback.

"Take your position!" he shouted. "Await the signal!"

Ganelon waved in affirmation, and the man rode on to the next unit down the line.

"So, Charles really does mean to lay siege to the city," Ganelon growled low enough for only his uncle to hear. "And the other half of our army sits on its arse in the Saxon March. The man's a damned fool."

Guinemer buckled his weapons about his waist and set his helmet onto his head. His gap-toothed mouth split into a wicked grin.

"Some say the vixen warming his bed has driven him mad," he spat. "Brought down a curse from God!"

"One well-placed stroke, Uncle, and the kingdom will fall. Then the madness will end. Only then."

Guinemer leaned in, lowering his voice even further. He glanced about for prying eyes—and ears.

"When is the time?"

Ganelon laughed and slapped his uncle on the back. "When is it ever the time to kill a king?" He scrambled from the rock, tossing his ration bag to a squire. "On your feet," he roared to the men. "We've the king's business to be about!"

Night lengthened the shadows that stretched across the earth from Barcelona's walls. Wearing the darkness like a shroud, Frank troopers hauled siege engines into place. Around those machines, companies of troopers scrambled forward to critical points in the ravaged remains of houses and shops surrounding the fortifications. Those men remained ever vigilant against defenders that might attempt to sally from their bastions to disrupt the tightening Frank cordon. From those emerging

Frank lines, two figures crept through the shadows and worked their way through the burned-out buildings. Close under the dizzying citadel wall, they entered a blackened building and scurried deep within to a staircase. Pressing against the fractured walls, they then navigated shattered steps upward to the skeletal rafters.

Roland tested the strength of one jutting timber. Satisfied it would hold, he skittered across to the tiled crenellations overlooking Barcelona behind her recently rebuilt walls. Karim followed along behind him.

From their perch in the building, they scanned the city's upper ramparts for movement.

"Saragossa has troops throughout the city," Roland observed. "You're certain your people will be able to deliver the signal?"

Karim chuckled. "Of course. I thought your book taught you to have faith, Christian."

"It does," the knight replied. "But how is it you speak of faith? You're an infidel."

"No, you're the infidel."

Both men laughed.

"We are a people of faith," Karim explained. "My friend, I believe in God as do you. Sons of Judah call him Elohim, and we know him as Allah. And Mohammed is his prophet. I've read your book, Christian— that and many others. We encourage education among my people. Better is the warrior who thinks beyond the battlefield."

"We've clergy who do the reading," Roland said after a moment's pause. "Soldiers do the work of war. That is the order of things ordained by God. Though one day I'll put my words on a page."

Karim feigned surprise.

"And what would you write?" he asked. "Of glorious battles and great heroes dying in far-off lands? Those tales have already been written, my friend!"

"Written words can speak of the heart," Roland said, averting his eyes to Barcelona's dark walls.

"Oh! You've a woman to send words to!" Karim appeared scandalized. His eyes crinkled with humor. "And here I thought you cared only for your men and that nag you call a horse! What would you write, soldier-bard?"

Roland jabbed him in the ribs. "Those words would be hers alone."

Just then a bucketful of smoldering embers dropped from the top of the wall. The cinders flared briefly as they struck the ground before going out in a feeble puff of smoke.

"Our signal?" asked Roland.

"Now, my friend," Karim replied, "is the changing of the guard. Hurry!"

They carefully navigated through the ruined attic and back to the ground. They rushed across the debris-strewn street, quickly pressing their bodies against the city wall by the ash pile. Karim patted at the stones until he felt a dark rope clinging to the heights above.

He tugged on it.

"After you, my Christian friend," he offered.

"I'm thinking," Roland observed, "that my face shouldn't be the first over the wall. Or you might find it greeting you on its way back down."

Karim knotted the rope around his hand.

"As you wish!" He laughed.

Agile as a squirrel, Karim crawled hand over hand up the wall. Roland jumped, catching the rope, and clambered up behind him, his boots slipping against the dusty stones. At the top, rough hands reached out to haul each of them in turn over the parapet to the catwalk where a silent clutch of partisans crowded in close, throwing robes and cloaks over them. In hushed tones, they urged the two toward a sliver of light shining from the door of a nearby tower. Once inside, they stepped over the torn bodies of Saragossan guards. The partisans whisked their charges down the stairs to the tower entrance where more bodies slouched inside the door to the street. There the entire group pulled their hoods over their heads.

"Move!" one of the partisans urged, pushing Roland to step more quickly. Above them, doors opened, and voices cried out as the relief guard discovered what had happened. Alarms rang out from the walls. Sentries' horns blared over the tiled roofs and echoed through the alleys.

The partisans hurried through back byways until they reached a building deep in a ramshackle district of the city far from the agitated city troops. They crowded through an open door into a small room lit only by the faintest of starlight filtering through a single shuttered window. Roland edged to one wall, stepping carefully to avoid stumbling over some scrap of junk and giving away their position.

The partisans sucking in stale air remained the only sound punctuating the darkness.

"We must keep moving," said a distinctly female voice.

"Praise Allah, Raisha," Karim said, throwing his arms around a slender figure. "I feared you were rotting in a dungeon, or worse!"

Raisha urgently gestured toward a darkened pool of a doorway. "Move! Or the morning will find us all a head shorter when Saragossa realizes we struck from within."

She wasted no more breath on words and guided the group down a series of crumbling steps to an ancient crypt beneath the city. At the bottom, she lit a torch from which the men brought a few more to oily, flickering life. Carved into the rock around them were egresses filled with moldering bones—Visigoths by the look of the rusty armor and Germanic blades.

"Sister," Karim whispered. "We must get to the North Gate."

Raisha's dark eyes narrowed, her features barely more visible in the guttering light.

"Are you daft? They'll cut us down before we cross the square! We'll discuss our strategy after we have had time to consolidate forces. We must wait for the right opportunity."

"That time is now," Roland interjected. "It must be tonight!"

"It must? And why should we believe you, Christian?" she asked, a dangerous edge rising in her voice.

"Sister, this is Roland." Karim took her by the hand. "He's driven Saragossa as chaff before the wind. He intends to restore our father to his city."

"The same Roland who slays any who refuse the Christian baptism?" she pressed. "Yes, we've heard the whispers from the occupiers."

"Sister," Karim said, "it's not true."

One of the men brushed Raisha aside and glared at Roland, the torches casting a red tinge on his bristly beard.

"Karim, we know you," he snarled. "But we will hear it from the mouth of the infidel."

Roland nodded his assurance to Karim then threw back his hood so all could see his face. The partisans crowded closer.

"Charles is here to protect his own kingdom from Marsilion," Roland declared. "That is all. As Saint Michael is my witness, we'll leave when this is done."

The partisans searched one another's eyes for assurance—these were men who risked their lives and homes for even speaking with Raisha, the daughter of the fallen, though much-loved, house of Barcelona. Yet now they were being asked to cooperate with the Christians who bristled with steel at the gates and prepared to inflict even more damage on their city.

Roland remained uncowed, looking each man in the face in turn. Many searched his gaze and after a moment returned it with a stalwart nod or smile of their own.

"Good!" declared Karim. "Now we must take the gate!"

In the deepening night, the men of Tournai tumbled into their place in the Frank line, pressing forward behind large oval shields. Arrows whistled at them from archers perched along the walls. Atop his armored horse, Ganelon sat tall and straight, his once-fine surcoat bearing the lily of his house patched and stained—yet his armor remained in good order even after the long march south, days of nipping at Saragossa's heels, and more days of digging in. Guinemer rode next to him, reviewing the preparations of the ladders and grappling hooks. The men loosed their weapons in their scabbards, knowing that scaling the walls would be a bloody affair that would exact a butcher's toll on the units selected to climb first.

"So what are our orders?" Guinemer asked, returning his attention to his nephew.

"We attack the west wall," Ganelon replied simply.

The older man adjusted his helmet, looking over the distance between the Frank pickets and the city looming before them. Already

Frank catapults discharged pitch pots in fiery streaks through the darkening sky, followed by the hulking whirling of solid stone shot. Between the Tournai men and the wall lay a cratered desolation of broken buildings that risked slowing the men who would race to lift the ladders against Barcelona's imposing fortifications and leave them exposed to the archers above.

"At night?" Guinemer asked. He winced at a *thwump* from a nearby catapult sending another deadly projectile into the sky.

"Aye," Ganelon replied. "We're to place ladders on the uppermost stones of the battlements."

"And nothing of Roland?" pressed his uncle. "Has he run off on some special assignment to miss our bloodletting?"

"Mark me," Ganelon hissed through gritted teeth. "After the noise of battle dies down, he'll appear in the dawn light and climb over our cold bodies to claim the victory."

Archers crept forward under the cover of the catapult volleys to positions among the ruined buildings. From there they popped up in ones and twos to fire arrows toward the upper crenellations. Enemy archers rushed for cover as the arrows scattered along the stone.

Ganelon waved his infantry forward under the ragged return volley that spattered among them. *An impressive force indeed,* he thought. The men trotted through the debris-choked street toward the wall—but he knew very few of them would survive to even place a hand on the upper battlement. Another angry swarm of arrows whistled through the air onto the warding Tournai shields. Three shafts lodged in Ganelon's saddle, and his horse bolted sideways. Men close to him rushed to calm the steed and attend to their lord. Ganelon waved them off with a laugh, snapped the arrow shafts, and tossed them to the ground.

"If Peter slams shut the gates of heaven," he roared, "then the fires of hell will keep me warm!"

His men let out a ragged cheer then surged into the killing zone, planted their ladders, and heaved them up to the parapets.

Across the city, the palace of Barcelona stood tall, its ramparts thick and well defended. Marsilion watched from a window high in an inner bastion. From that vantage point, his heart raced as the incoming projectiles crushed and burned indiscriminately.

Blancandrin rushed into the room, his features smudged with soot.

"My lord," he said, dropping to his knees before the emir. "The Franks send men to assault the outer walls."

"They'll break against those walls," Marsilion snorted. "Come morning the stones will be drenched in their blood."

"But, my lord," Blancandrin said, rising to his feet, "Charles would not spend his strength in vain. He must have something else afoot."

"Sappers?"

"We've no evidence. But there must be something. We must be vigilant."

A trooper, his mail coat shredded about the edges, urgently burst in and prostrated himself before the emir.

"What is it?" Marsilion demanded. "Quickly, man!"

Suddenly Blancandrin turned and bolted from the room without waiting for dismissal. Marsilion turned to look out the window and saw what his general had seen over his shoulder. Across the city's besieged silhouette, the North Gate began to billow smoke in thick columns that reflected the red light from the burning of the city.

The partisans fought with a hodgepodge of weapons, most of them pilfered from kitchens and butcher shops or rescued from the graves of moldering Visigoths beneath the city. Though poorly equipped, they fought tenaciously against the troops guarding the city's entrance until their blood began to pool among the rough cobbles of the square before the portals. What started as a skirmish quickly grew to an outright battle with combatants from both sides rushing into the fray.

Then clattering rose through the street, the harbinger of approaching cavalry—hooves striking the broken cobbles in a hammering staccato.

Blancandrin cantered along the thoroughfare with a squadron of elite lancers at his back. He stood in his stirrups to scan the carnage before the gate, marking the lightly armored Frank champion among the knot of partisans. With a growl in his breast, he dropped back into the saddle and drove his spurs into his horse's flanks.

"To the gate! Crush them!"

The order echoed through the squadron, and the lancers charged into the chaos, a wedge of armor driving toward the gate. Partisans fought tooth and nail against the weight of the new threat. They threw their bodies at the troopers. The horsemen discarded shattered lances and drew sabers for close-quarter fighting, swinging them down again and again until they dripped of blood and stained their garments in gore.

Blancandrin bore his straight Syrian sword, forged of the finest Damascus steel, to cut through sinew and bone until it wedged in the shoulder of a partisan who shrieked under the bite. Blancandrin kicked a foot out of his stirrup and planted it in the man's face. The doomed wretch clawed at the general's leg. He ripped the blade free then scanned the square.

The partisans were melting away into the alleys, and Roland was gone.

Deep in the darkness of one such alley, Karim and Raisha caught their breath. Around them the battered partisans choked down emotions while lancers continued to ride down stragglers in the open square. The armored cavalry had turned the tide on them.

"They're too many," Karim said, wiping grime from his face. "And more are coming. Can you hear them? How will we get through to open the gate?"

Roland craned his neck to get a better look through the billowing smoke from pitch-flamed buildings. Lancers continued to work their sabers, dropping partisans like so much wheat in a field, but the skilled horsemen pulled short of the narrow alleys where they could be overwhelmed in the tight quarters.

"I'll open the gate," he said finally. "Can you get your men over there?" He pointed to the far end of the square, where a building began to creak and groan as fire undermined its framing. "Anchor against that building and hit them hard in the flank."

Raisha rubbed at her face beneath her veil and readjusted her pillaged helmet.

"You're mad, Christian," she said, rolling her eyes. "You'll be exposed once you step into the square."

Karim clapped a hand on Roland's shoulder.

"You're a brave warrior," he said. "But you cannot do this alone."

Roland gripped Karim's shoulder in return. "Where's your faith, my friend?"

A dangerous grin broke across Karim's face.

"Allah have mercy on your infidel soul," he said.

Raisha and Karim passed back through the remaining partisans, whispering orders and pulling the men after them, and then together they slipped into back alleys. Within a few moments, Roland stood alone but for a few wounded stragglers. Durendal gleamed when he lifted the cruciform hilt to his eyes, the simple intersection lines of blade and cross guard momentarily becoming the focus of his attention.

"Dear God," he whispered, "give me strength to face this." He kissed the reliquary and balanced the sword in his hand, his fingers flexing around the hilt. But he did not have to wait long.

Shouts broke out a short distance down the street. The partisans assaulted the Saragossan flank with all manner of edged and blunt weaponry. Knives, rusted swords, clubs, and pitchforks tore at horses and men with ferocity born of desperation. Blancandrin bellowed orders, and his men wheeled about to engage the ragtag threat that erupted from the shadowed debris. Brave men and women would breathe their last tonight, bleeding out on the cobblestones under the hooves of the general's troopers.

Roland gauged the enemy movements, his muscles tense, until the last of the lancers finally turned and committed to the counterattack on the partisans. He sucked in a hot breath and sprinted across the corpse-littered square to the gatehouse. A brace of guards charged forward with a shout to meet him. But they were not prepared for the steel that greeted them. Durendal wove a web of death that drove them stumbling back. Roland thrust his shoulder into one man, knocking him into another who was attempting to sound a horn. The man lost his balance, and Roland plunged the sword into his throat to silence him for good.

Then the Frank knight lunged through the gatehouse door. Another guard charged, lowered his shoulder, and crushed Roland into the doorjamb. Roland drove his knee into the man's groin and yanked the guard's own poniard loose, driving it underneath his armpit. The guard struggled to keep Roland pinned against the building while his breathing became ragged. Roland twisted the blade and opened the wound further until the man crumpled at last. Roland shoved past him, racing up the stairs to the gate mechanism.

He reached the great winches on the upper level. Three guards rushed him, and a saber whistled through his light gambeson, slicing cloth and skin and flooding the garment with blood. But the cut continued wide, leaving the attacker open and his feet splayed. Roland smashed Durendal's pommel into his face with a crunch of metal on bone then wrapped his foot around the man's extended leg, toppling him down the stairwell even as the knight pivoted to deflect the second guard's saber cut with Durendal's flat. The third tried a flank attack, but Roland raked his poniard into the man's belly, and the man sank to his knees, blood and entrails spilling through fingers that tried to plug the murderous hole.

Roland crashed into the final man, flattening him against the gate's mechanism, and pounded his face over and over again. A crack of skull against the iron gear left blood and brains streaking downward when the guard sank to the floor.

Roland cast back the locking lever and gripped the lift chains. Gears clacked with each slow turn. He heaved, arms and shoulders cracking while blood dripped from his sleeve. The pawl clicked over the ratchet tick by tick, his neck muscles bulging with the effort and his breath coming in shortened gasps. The gate shuddered and groaned and slowly started to rise. Pain throbbed from his wounds but he ignored it and heaved harder, his body straining and cracking. Lights crackled in his vision, lungs burning. Finally with a resistant groan, the counterweights tipped and the gate started to rise on its own.

Roland staggered downstairs to slump in the doorway of the gatehouse, and Durendal slipped from his slackening fingers to clatter on the ground.

Frank horns sang out from the smoldering rubble outside the gate accompanied by armored knights thundering toward the open portal. From his position at the head of the charging column, Oliver yelled commands to engage the Saragossan horsemen and drive them back.

Behind the cavalry echoed the solid tromp of the marchmen's boots, led by Kennick, arrayed in tight formation with shields interlocked and spears bristling to engage Blancandrin's dismounted reinforcements.

Otun ranged on the edge of the formation where his ax spattered blood from Saragossans that dared to challenge the tight-knit wedge.

The tall Dane roared with pleasure, blue eyes delighted at the prospect of carnage. When he drew abreast of the gatehouse, the Dane spied Roland and, ignoring Kennick's yells, rushed through the melee to reach his master's side. He plucked Durendal from the ground and marked the flow of blood from the knight's fingers. Roland sagged into his arms. Otun wrapped one arm around his master and, brandishing his ax like a cleaver with the other, forced his way back to the marchmen. Troopers quickly parted ranks and then folded in again to enclose their champion in a shield of iron and bone, dragging him forward along with them.

The marchmen's progress behind Oliver could not be stopped. A rushing flow of men crowded through the gate, driving Blancandrin's lancers deep into the city.

Morning dawned with the sky obscured by a thick shroud of smoke. Allied Frank and Barcelonan forces had continued the fight against Saragossa through the night—driving the emir's men before them, building by building, street by street, in one bloody skirmish after another. Outside the palace, Saragossan troopers formed up into ranks. Their once-proud arms and armor were battered and stained with soot and gore. Tattered banners hung limply in the still morning air.

Marsilion shuffled from the palace to his waiting horse. The sound of hooves clattering up the main thoroughfare caught his attention—a messenger atop horse frothing in sweat.

"My lord!" he called to the emir. "A message from Blancandrin!"

Marsilion raised his hands to the silent sky. "Yes, yes?"

The man vaulted from the saddle, prostrating himself before the emir's slippered feet. He looked up from the dust, and Marsilion impatiently waved him to his feet. "The general bids you to heed his words. The city has fallen between the palace and the North Gate.

You must withdraw before the Franks can cordon off the southern thoroughfare."

Marsilion bristled, tugging impatiently at his jutting beard.

"No," he growled. He kicked at the messenger in frustration. "We must hold!"

"My lord," the man pleaded, "your men bleed to secure your passage from the city!"

Past the units assembled before him, Marsilion strained to see and hear the sounds of conflict in the streets beyond. Smoke hung thick and acrid over the city, marking the path of the most intense fighting. The nearby buildings cracked and crumbled from the bombardment.

Leaving galled Marsilion, but the tide was clearly against him. But even though they forced him from Barcelona, he suddenly thought, Sulayman would be burdened with nothing but a shell—the city was only a shadow of the metropolis the traitor had fled. That same ruined shell would be a millstone around Charles's war efforts. At least there was satisfaction in that.

"Very well," he conceded. "Tell the general we will withdraw."

Not long after, as he made his way in defeat out the South Gate, Marsilion heard the clear peal of a horn ring brightly off the walls of the city.

A Θ I

Barcelona's battered gates remained open for Sulayman's troops, who streamed into the city not so much in a victory parade as in a reunion of loved ones who had endured two sieges and the Saragossan occupation. The swarming populace choked the thoroughfares to greet their kinsmen, as well as the rumbling wagons behind them filled with tough field-baked bread and other foodstuffs. Once the crowds dispersed, the Frank army entered in a much more workmanlike fashion, carrying tools and materials to reset the gates and rebuild the fortifications.

Accompanied by a small party of his companions, Roland rode into the palace grounds, bypassing the celebrations erupting around them on the garden paths so recently vacated by Marsilion. In a small side courtyard, Karim met them with brief words of greeting and led them to a grim, squat building connected to the rear quarters of the emir's residence. Thick iron bars garnished its stark windows. A soldier awaited them with jangling keys, selected one for the outer portal, and turned the lock.

Roland crowded past him even though the door protested with a groan. Kennick, Oliver, and Otun followed him through, Otun ducking his head to avoid leaving his brains smeared on a rafter.

"This is the first we've been in here since cleaning out the Saragossan scum," Karim spat and stepped through after them.

A rushing stench from the darkness enveloped them, causing them to cover their noses with their sleeves. The soldier lit torches and handed them out before leading them further down into the pits beneath.

The main stairway was crude stone, the edges rounded and worn, creating a treacherous pathway into the pit. Roland and his companions cautiously followed the soldier deep into the earth where at the bottom a narrow corridor opened to a series of dark cells, many of the doors ajar. The search party spread out, calling for survivors. But rather than joyous responses, they found only brutalized, butchered bodies flung into the moldering straw inside the cells. After a thorough search of each cell, the men gathered near another door at the far end of the corridor. The soldier who accompanied them fumbled through the keys until he found one to spring the primitive lock.

Beyond lay another dark staircase descending into a pool of blackness, drips of water leaking in from the sewers and plumbing above. This time the steps were slick and narrow, and the men crept downward much more slowly before once more placing their feet on smooth flooring. Again they swept through empty cells where their guttering torches revealed only mildewed straw and scurrying rats. Roland scanned the cellblock, cursing that their search was in vain, when Kennick emerged from a rough-hewn doorway at the dark far end, covering his nose and mouth with his hand.

"More?" Roland asked.

Kennick nodded. "Slaughtered these too."

"Our sources said there were men here—live men," Roland said.

Otun tested a last closed door, but it wouldn't budge. He heaved his massive shoulder into it, causing the hinges to groan and the wood to crack. The Dane redoubled his effort, muscles straining and back leveraging against it. With a scream, the hinges burst apart, and Otun stumbled past the sagging door. He reappeared a moment later and waved to the jail master, pinching his nose against the reek. The guard handed him a smoky torch that the Dane waved in front of him before stepping into the moldy straw and whatever else lay beyond.

"Over here!" he called out. "Here! Two live!"

From the depths of the cell staggered two emaciated men, pale skin covering their bones nearly without the benefit of flesh. One of them, garments in rags, shuffled into the torchlight. His scraggly-bearded face was covered in fleabites and matted, lice-infested hair that was the same color as the darkness. The other crouched just outside the circle of light, skeletal hands thrown up to cover his eyes from the brightness. Roland handed off his torch and offered the first captive a hand. But instead of taking it, the man reached for the crucifix around the knight's neck.

"Christian men?" he croaked, his words heavily accented.

"Good God," Oliver whispered.

"Yes," Roland replied. "Men of Charles, king of Francia and emperor in Rome. You are Greeks?"

The man pressed the holy symbol firmly to his lips. After a moment, he said, "I am Leo. This is John. We served on a warship. Ambushed by pirates ..." His voice cracked from disuse. He cleared his throat with difficulty, and Oliver handed him a water flask. The man gulped some down, handed it off to his companion, and continued.

"After the battle, our ship sank near the Gates of Herakles. We were picked up by the caliph's men." He forced a smile, exposing shattered teeth. "You can imagine, he had a few questions for us to be sure. But in the end, he sent us along to Saragossa, fearing the empire would attempt our rescue."

"Why would the empire mount a rescue for just two men?" Roland pressed.

Leo helped John to stand, and the Franks saw for the first time the man's twisted fingers, a painful symbol of the Saragossans' questioning. In the wavering torchlight, a wicked glint reflected in John's eyes.

"Secrets," he said, placing a swollen finger to his mouth.

Where the original Roman walls of old Barcelona butted up against the palace, an ancient building still smoldered—the smoke but another smudge like so many that continued to rise above the city. Within, the ground was thick with broken rafters and ash. Soldiers diligently searched through the rubble alongside Sulayman's courtiers and Charles's friars. Charles and Sulayman stood nearby watching their progress, Aldatrude with them and dressed in filmy silk.

A courtier shouted from deep in the ruin, suddenly careless of the soot and grime streaking his expensive robes. He disappeared into a stack of stone and wood that teetered in delicate balance like a house of cards. A breathless moment later, the man struggled back into view, his arms wrapped tightly around a scorched bundle. In his excitement, he caught his foot on a broken rafter and spilled gracelessly into the ash. His comrades rushed to help gather his burden, but he righted himself, cheeks reddened beneath the soot smudges, and snatched back his prize. He skittered over the rubble to Sulayman and Charles, fell to one knee, and lifted his find for their examination.

Charles deferred to Sulayman to open the sooty canvas. The emir gingerly tugged the corners open, exposing a codex of bound vellum pages beneath his trembling fingers.

"What is it?" Charles asked, leaning over Sulayman's shoulder, the anticipation on his face growing.

Sulayman simply beamed with delight.

Aldatrude pushed a loose stand of hair from her face as she read the letters on the cover of the volume. "Father!" Aldatrude exclaimed. "It's the great scholar Aristotle!"

"You can read this?" Sulayman asked, clearly pleased.

"Oh, yes," she said, lowering her eyes demurely. "Father encouraged me to learn Latin and Greek. And this—this is *De Anima!* Scholars at Father's court believed no copies still existed."

"Indeed, I had feared this one lost as well after that bastard Marsilion had the run of the palace," Sulayman grumbled.

Charles took the document from Sulayman, opening the cover with reverent care and scanning an inner page.

"I wish to God I were better with my own letters," the king murmured, his eyes roving the page, intoxicated at each flourish, swoop, and curve of the Greek letters.

"My friend," said Sulayman, "let this be my gift to you. For my family, my people, and my city. I wish there were more we could do to show our gratitude."

Charles shook his head. "No." He took Sulayman's hand in his, placing it on the book. "This is a treasure for all our people. It's not something I can ask of you or take from your city." He swept the site with his eyes. "But we can recover these and set our scribes to copying that we might preserve them. We will learn together, my friend."

Sulayman embraced the Frank king. "Excellent! Then let us get started!"

CHAPTER 17

MANEUVERS

Far to the north, a warm damp wind rustled massive oaks and whispered of rain.

The great hall of Sigurd, king of the Saxons, was an oversized rough-hewn log house in the center of a motte-and-bailey fort surrounded by wood-framed walls filled with dirt. Along upper ramparts stood a palisade of sharpened stakes. Through the open gates rode a small party of mud-covered travelers, followed by a rumbling coach and wagon. Guards wearing heavy mail hauberks and bearing long spears stopped the strangers at the gatehouse. Passengers presented their bona fides with urgency, and after a cursory examination, the guards waved them through, directing them across the muddy yard to the hall. A runner sprinted ahead of them to seek out the king.

Inside the great hall, warriors lounged on long, split-timber benches while dogs snarled at their feet and wrestled over scraps of meat among the filthy rushes covering the earthen floor. Beyond the scampering serving girls and toppled cups of ale, King Sigurd slouched in a large, elaborately carved wooden chair. A bear of a man, he rubbed at his paunch that told of too many years feasting behind the Saxon shield wall and too few seasons in front of it. He stuffed a handful of berries into a maw framed by a dark beard stained with juice and littered with crumbs and bones from the feast. The arrival of the messenger elicited only an absent nod. Then the messenger whispered unwelcome tidings in his ear.

Guards tugged open the doors to admit a solitary figure. Honorius swept into the hall in his golden imperial armor, its rich crimson brocade cloak snapping from his shoulders over tall calfskin boots. In his hand he carried an ornate walking staff that thumped against the dirt in time with his paces. He kicked aside a hound and strode through the tables to stop before Sigurd's chair.

Sigurd braced himself against the arm of his chair and rose on unsteady legs.

"Horrid specter!" he roared, spittle and seeds flying from his lips. "Have you come to torment me with more promises? Your last assurances crumbled on the field when the Danes broke and left my men to be slaughtered!"

Over their cups, the Saxon warriors marked the unfriendly exchange between their king and this gilded emissary from beyond the Middle Sea with wary interest. Honorius signaled back to the open doors. Exotically dressed servants entered, bearing a heavy wooden chest between them. They halted before the king and, with a coordinated heave, dropped the chest to the floor. Sweeping his hand in an adroit flourish of a practiced showman, Honorius struck off the lock with his walking staff and threw open the lid, revealing a mound of gold imperial byzants.

"Sire, the great king of Miklagaard offers you assurances of his favor," Honorius purred, his voice dripping with diplomatic honey. "He knows you wish to relocate your people beyond the Rhine, safe from the depredations of the savage Avars. He desires to help."

Sigurd's eyes filled with the glint of the gold. He wiped at his mouth with the back of his hand, forgetting for a moment the berries smashed in his fingers. But then his eyes narrowed in suspicion. "This is a trick! A mad scheme for us to bleed doing Roman dirty work! The Franks lie in wait for us along the banks of the river, ready to attack if we but breathe!"

"There are some, this is true," Honorius conceded. "But nothing of worth can be had without sacrifice."

"Easy enough for you to say, Roman! But I lost many good men. Their widows and children still weep for them!"

"I have a secret for you, great king." Honorius grinned, eyes sweeping the flea-bitten rabble that gnawed at bones and swilled sour beer. "What you have seen beyond the river is not Charles's entire strength. Your brave warriors will easily overpower them."

"Still there are enough to slow us until the rest of his knights fall upon us!"

"Sire, you know as well as I that Charles's main forces are occupied far to the south with the Saracens."

Sigurd drew himself up and teetered forward to stand toe to toe with the Byzantine. "They will break the Saracens before the month is out, and then they shall be free. Free to come against us and destroy us as we lay stretched out on the far side of the river with women and children and nowhere to shelter!"

Honorius met Sigurd's glare with aplomb. "What if you had time to dig in?" He glanced around at the warriors representing a handful of Sigurd's many illegitimate sons. "Time to seek other allies for help?"

Sigurd snorted. "That would take a winter!"

"We could give you that."

"How? How will you keep Charles in Iberia for the rest of the season? He has only Saragossa left before him."

"We deal with many in the southern lands. Keeping Charles ensnared can be managed."

Sigurd studied Honorius carefully, but the Greek offered no other signs on his face.

"Managed? You gamble dangerously with my people's lives."

"Is it any less a gamble to leave them here, with the threat facing you from the east? How long before the Avars turn their horsemen on the Saxon people?"

Sigurd fumed and wavered. His eyes darted about the room to his vassals, who waited for his answer.

Honorius bowed slightly, placing his hand over his heart to soothe his words. "I swear, King. Charles won't have the strength to keep you from jumping a cow fence—or from taking leisure within the very gates of Aachen herself."

Sigurd searched for the deceit in Honorius's face. He looked then at the chest, spilling bright yellow light as if it shone of its own accord.

A wicked grin crept onto the Saxon king's pockmarked face, exposing feral, yellowed teeth.

A Θ I

The exhausted, rain-lashed Frank courier rode into Barcelona under a pale moon, barely able to keep astride his heaving mount. For seven days and nights he had ridden as hard, crossing fifty leagues of the eastern verge of the Pyrenees where their foothills reached down to the sea, stopping for nothing short of Armageddon.

He passed his missive onto the sentries at the gate and was led away to bed and drink.

The sentry sergeant read the dispatch and went pale. He stepped into a side chamber to wake the officer on duty.

"What is it, Sergeant?" the man asked groggily. He snapped fully awake a moment later.

"Carcassonne, sir. Saragossa has taken Carcassonne!"

CHAPTER 18

SECRETS

Carcassonne

The walled city was the southernmost Frank stronghold and last outpost before Saracen Iberia—founded by the Romans in the long-ago days of the Caesars. A bustling port despite being forty miles from the Middle Sea, it lay alongside the River Atax where rafts of goods from seaside Narbonne passed on through merchants to the interior of Francia in an endless stream. Silks, religious totems, spices, and displaced souls from the incessant wars in the east found a market in Carcassonne.

Carcassonne was lifeblood to Charles's southern vassals.

News of Marsilion's near-effortless occupation of the city sent shockwaves through Charles's armies. While they had busied themselves with refortifying Barcelona, the emir of Saragossa had managed to slip an army around them to secure the port. An impressive strategic move placed troops behind mighty walls on Frankish soil. Charles had been forced to pack up his armies and, with his champion in the lead, march north, spending precious weeks of the summer to prevent Marsilion from twisting the knife now thrust in his back.

And here they were, the bannermen of King Charles, camped once more against another set of walls, and things were not going well.

Carcassonne's dun-colored fortifications, ringed about with a deep moat and punctuated by massive towers, loomed over ironbound gates that defied Charles's advance yet another time. Soldiers straggled back to the lines, beaten, bruised, and broken.

Behind screens of brush and twigs, their comrades ventured forth to secure the wounded stragglers and the dead. Roland himself hefted a soldier, dripping gore across his shoulder. The blood ran down his surcoat to drip onto his feet while he trudged past catapults that bucked like the devil's own drumline, hurling massive stones against walls that only shrugged off the affront.

Demetrius ducked from one screen to the next, calling many of the soldiers by name. In these weeks in their company he had enjoyed more than a few friendly cups by their campfires while regaling them with wild stories of Eastern mystics who lived atop stone pillars in the desert, or of missionaries trekking the frozen north to bring the Gospel to distant heathens.

"Demetrius!" Roland deposited his wounded trooper at the surgeon's bustling tent and chased after the Greek.

The ambassador stopped and waited for him to catch up, a neutral look spreading across his usually congenial face.

"I'm sorry to keep asking, my friend," Roland said, wiping the sweat and blood from his face with the back of his hand. "But I must know—will they help us?"

Demetrius chewed his lip, averting his eyes toward the city that had defied wave after wave of assaults—a city that held no allies within it to throw open the gates. Most of those who would aid them lay smoldering in trenches inside the walls, the smoke still a smudge against the blue sky.

"You know I have no instructions from my government on this," he said. "John and Leo bear knowledge vital to the security of the empire. Our navies keep the sea-lanes free for Christian commerce, and the knowledge they possess is critical to that effort. It is the empire's single best advantage. If our enemies gained access to that secret— well, the commandeering of our trade routes could lead to the fall of Constantinople itself."

"Of course," Roland said. "I freely give you my word that the secret will remain their own. But as Saint Michael is my witness, it serves neither Francia nor Constantinople to see our armies broken before this city."

Demetrius rubbed at his chin and finally nodded. "Then I suggest you *ask* them to make the weapon, for they operate under neither your command nor mine."

A simple weathered canvas stretched between two poles constituted the tent billeting the Greek prisoners since their rescue. Roland opened the flap. Inside, Leo and John stretched across their blankets, devouring hard biscuits and tough chunks of meat. Occasionally they paused to converse softly in their native Greek.

"Oh, come in." Leo shifted to Latin, his words faltering but clear.

Roland threw the flap up over the roof and ducked inside. The sunlight streamed into the tent behind him, and the men threw pale hands before their faces.

"Hello, my lord Roland. How may we serve you?" Leo asked, peering through his fingers.

"I've come to ask the favor of you," Roland said, kneeling to meet the Greek's eyes.

"This yet again, my lord?"

"I need you. I need your skills."

Leo cringed and wrapped his arm protectively around his comrade, who continued stuffing his mouth with scraps. "I've not come to demand your services," Roland said, raising his hands. "It wouldn't be proper. You're guests among the Franks."

"But do you understand? We are sworn to secrecy!" Leo hissed. "They ..." He glanced in the direction of the city to indicate the enemy. "They cut us. They—they broke our bones. But we withstood them!"

"You did. You did well to keep your secrets."

"They could not break our spirits!"

"We honor you for that. You are brave men indeed."

But despite Roland's flattery, something in Leo seemed to give way, something that had made him cower for only God knew how long. He sat up straighter in the small tent. "Brave men? Sweet words, champion of Franks! We suffered for our secrets!" Leo struck his chest with his fist. "We faced death for our secrets! We longed for it! Should we give them up now to a silver-tongued patrician with an army at his back and a reputation to establish? Did we fight so hard to protect them in the dungeon only to exchange them now in the daylight for so little?" He met the champion eye to eye. "The empire trusts us. We made a covenant!"

Roland held Leo's gaze. "But that is not the only covenant you've made. You've sworn, as have I, to protect the Christian kingdom on earth—the greater Rome." As he spoke, outside the tent, men continued to return through the camp, bearing comrades to the surgeon. Over Roland's shoulder, the two Greeks could see the sawbones scurrying about, tossing aside body parts, vainly staunching spurting arteries, and searing gaping wounds. The stench of burnt meat stung their nostrils. Despite all that he must have experienced in those dark pits, John blanched.

"Good men die to keep Francia from falling beneath the Saracen sword," Roland continued. "Good men also died freeing you."

"But our secrets," John murmured from under Leo's protective wing, food dropping from his broken teeth. "Our secrets, our secrets ..."

Roland leaned forward, watched warily by Leo, and gathered John's crippled hand into his own.

"They remain your own," he said, looking directly into John's damaged eyes. "I swear this. But if you make the weapon for us, you will be striking a blow for the emperor in Constantinople as surely as for your Frank brothers."

Standing over them, Leo pressed his eyes closed to shut out the scene outside the tent, tears leaking from beneath his crooked fingers.

CHAPTER 19

ACROSS MILES OF DREAMS

A lone tree dominated the hillside overlooking Carcassonne.

The city was shrouded with a clinging haze from the pitch-pots bombarding the walls night and day. The shattered, once-elegant suburbs were littered with broken equipment, bodies, and rubble. The Franks continued with a determination to find a chink in the defenses, some point where the walls could either be scaled or brought down. But despite their best efforts, the city remained tantalizingly unattainable within its fortifications, topped with the interloping spears of Saragossa.

With the setting sun against his back, Roland knelt beneath the tree and observed the Frank pickets' movements between crumbling buildings. Sulayman's horsemen clattered through the streets to monitor the gates, assuring that the Saragossans remained caged within and unable to sally forth and wreak havoc among the Frank bivouacs. Roland tugged the wool cloak about his shoulders. The evening breeze held a chill.

He was troubled.

The siege threatened to sap momentum from the Franks' southern offensive. That Marsilion had been able to lead a sizable enough force around Barcelona was an embarrassment to the king, and his champion felt the barb acutely. Roland had heard the whispers among the campfires comparing the emir to legendary Hannibal—and he had been quick to point out to the gossipers how well soldiers can be motivated with a lash and harsh words. The champion promised them that that sort of fighting spirit usually evaporated in the thick of battle.

But for days the Franks had beat against Carcassonne, and to no avail.

Roland clenched his fist and scanned the walls yet again.

Nearby, a squad of troopers led a scraggly band of chained prisoners to priests waiting by a trickle of water to baptize them in the Latin rites. Haunting chants reached his ears as if on the wings of a dream, a dream of someone far away that deserved more of his thoughts than the war with Saragossa would allow. Alone, Roland assured her with words that were spoken only in his mind, carried on a whisper more sacred than prayer.

My love, I'd write if I could—if I knew how to make letters speak. He closed his eyes, allowing his mind to wander northward.

Aude strolled through the imperial garden at Aachen among waving flowers and ornamental trees. Deep inside her skirt pocket she bore the small bottle to remind her of a promise, even a duty, to her far-off husband. She had visited many shops since his departure, searching for the apothecary who originally mixed the toxic brew, but her efforts thus far had been fruitless. All around her, the women from court took leisure among the court's many fineries. She hardly noticed the warm summer days amid the chattering trivialities of the other women while minstrels strummed and sang of ancient heroes. Frankly their shallow preoccupations sickened her. As unpalatable as it was, though, she had to admit they were alike in at least one way—they were all lovers torn apart by wars and intrigue.

Aude thought of the dispatches that almost daily captured the attention of the court. She had been spending many hours with Gisela, poring over the letters for mentions of Roland, his skirmishes, his battles, and his efforts to cage the wily emir of Saragossa, and then she would wander through the garden with a smile that never quite reached her eyes to a bench beneath a tree. Today the sunlight filtered brightly through the foliage, making its worn surface slightly warm to the touch when she sat. She stretched her face up into a beam of sunlight, closing her eyes and half-speaking out loud to her knight so far away.

"What would you write, if you could, my love? Of daring knights and exotic cities, I'm sure—of places that smell of jasmine and other exotic perfumes. You must know that I would read your words over and over, a feast for my famished heart."

Roland shifted his repose and leaned back against the tree, recalling an ambush in a nameless village outside Carcassonne. Oliver had fought at his side, Halteclare glittering in the summer sun and spattering droplets of blood like rubies. The marchmen had formed up around them to fend off the arrows raining down from the edges of a ramshackle market square. In the midst of the ambush, unprotected civilians had screamed as the razor-sharp missiles sliced through them. But the volley did little harm to the heavily armored Franks. The marchmen had risen up as one, pushing aside the ravaged villagers to surge forward with swords like scythes reaping a harvest in Marsilion's archers. Arrows had hissed again, much more ragged this time, to be shrugged off by the marchmen's warding shields. Nevertheless, cowering men, women, and children had died with feathered shafts protruding from their bodies.

"I'd tell you all the happenings of this war," he mused. "How we fought through ankle-deep blood in the struggle to protect our kingdom."

After soaking up the light for a time, Aude stirred, rose, and completed her circuit of the garden. Then she wandered beyond the gardens to the palace, passing guards and courtiers alike, and took to the plaza beyond the main gate. Hawkers of food and trinkets crowded the plaza, which was rimmed with resplendent imperial buildings and monuments long dreamed of by holy men since the time of Augustine—a city upon a hill, bustling with new learning that many had thought dead with the final emperor to call Rome his home.

Aude passed merchant carts near the main thoroughfare and breathed the smells of fresh breads and smoked meats. Beyond the plaza, she came to the great cathedral rising high above the city, a place where she felt close both to God and her distant knight. Drifting toward the edifice, she noticed, with a slight catch in her breath, two lovers in the shadow of a house. The girl smiled and touched her full red lips to the boy's cheek gilded by barely noticeable blond down. They linked into a tender embrace. Aude lowered her eyes and hurried past, and within a few steps the imposing cathedral's sweeping buttresses drew her eyes heavenward.

How far away you must be, she thought. *I wonder if your words would bring you closer. Would each letter bear your face—each sentence speak in your voice? I fear some days the war will silence my knight. And I couldn't bear it if you were taken.*

The Saragossan cavalry rode hard, fleeing before the onslaught of the veteran marchmen. Roland stood at the edge of the village, Durendal still dripping in his hand, amidst the torn and still bodies of enemy troopers. Oliver clapped him on the back, and Kennick admonished Otun and the marchmen to remain in formation while in the growing distance the enemy scattered in a dusty cloud up the road.

"Many of their men fall to us," Roland murmured to his beloved. "Yet Carcassonne remains in their hands, taunting us with its high walls and thick gates."

Within the cathedral, Aude genuflected, her fingers reverently touching each point of the cross upon her breast, then silently made her way through the long nave. The sun sparkled through the windows high up in the clerestory and brilliantly illumined the checkered walls and columns. At the altar, she gathered her skirts and knelt to whisper a few words of prayer.

A cluster of women entered through the transept, the whole lot of them sobbing and wailing to the heavens. Their attire spoke of riches and station. The priest accompanying them tried to sooth their grief. Behind them followed a pair of altar boys who carried two battered shields, one blue and charged with a swallow, the other blazoned with checkered diamonds. They lay the warboards at the altar then scurried away.

And the fallen, Aude thought in concert with her prayers. Her eyes traced the chipped paint and torn leather covering the shields. *Their brave deeds must be enough to fill volumes in the greatest of the world's libraries. Minstrels already sing their timeless songs to comfort those left behind.*

In that tiny village, where the ambush killed so many, life had returned as the Franks and Barcelonans brought supplies and patrolled the dusty roads to protect against Saragossan reprisals. In a nearby field, peasants shed tears while lowering their dead into the ground. Roland, Oliver, and Saleem had taken some marchmen into the summer heat to deliver supplies to the mob assembling in the village square. The men had laughed and teased a gaggle of children who watched them as they tossed seemingly endless grain sacks into neat rows under the hot sun.

Then a shriek interrupted the rhythm of their labor. Grabbing weapons and racing across the square, the three men found a local merchant in the barest of homespun running out of a stable with tears streaming down his face. They followed his pointing finger inside where agitated animals stomped and snorted to the sound of rough demands and sobbing pleas. They searched quickly through the dusty light and found a stall on the far end where a Frank knight stood, trousers open, groping a young girl while another knight held her pinned and gagged. Discarded surcoats, one blue and charged with a swallow, the other blazoned with checkered diamonds, lay flung across a haystack.

Saleem guffawed at the sight as if the situation were remarkably funny, but Roland's fury burst forth, and Durendal dispensed swift justice at the champion's hand.

Roland shuddered at the memory of the blood of the condemned splattering across the girl's bare skin.

Saleem, standing near the champion in that dirty, small stall, had appeared truly dumbfounded.

Honor is a convenient garment for some, Roland mused on the memory, *for those without strength take it off at their leisure. Saint Michael as my witness, when we lose our honor, we are as bad as the heathen ...*

Aude, a world away from her knight, lifted her head from her contemplations. She pushed her flaxen hair from her face then stood and wrapped the women in her arms as they poured their souls out to the Virgin. She shed tears with them.

When the sobs subsided, she left them in the ethereal interior of the cathedral and emerged into the dying day.

Roland raised his eyes to the distant city. His duty remained before him. He scrambled to his knees, lifting his hands in supplication to God and to his love. *I plead with God,* he thought, *for the strength to remain true. Oh, Aude, if only I could write, you would know of my love for you. It's been so long, and God only knows when this will end.*

In the nearer distance, another Frank patrol thundered across the outskirts of Carcassonne, horses resplendent in gleaming armor and leather, riders tall and plumed with shimmering iron and steel. Roland hefted Durendal, buckled it to his hip, and walked back to the camp.

CHAPTER 20

Of Murder and Honor

The shop was little more than a mud hut sandwiched between two other shacks. That clutch of buildings comprised the whole center of what passed for a town on this rutted track through the Frank countryside.

Aude handed her horse's reins to Jerome, who stood patiently nearby rubbing at his baggy eyes. She carefully lifted her skirts above the muck and climbed the steps to the shop's front door. It opened with a creak, and she entered.

Darkness haunted the interior, for the only window was near the back, and it allowed only scant light to filter in. The smell of burnt oil and moldering herbs nipped at her nostrils. At a table under the grimy window, a man sat hunched over, intensely focused on his own gnarled hands that briskly sorted components into a small pestle. He was an ancient fellow, to be sure. The merchant who had directed her to this shop had whispered that this Gregory Apollonius could well be over a hundred years old, thanks to the Eastern potions and medicines he jealously guarded. Yet when Gregory's eyes met hers, he simply looked like someone's scholarly grandfather, his features wrapped in a white beard and wizened by a web of crinkles. He painfully straightened his hunched back as she drew close.

"I heard you enter, daughter," he said, a bland smile on his lips that did not extend to his eyes. "How may I help you?"

She fished in her pocket for the bottle and held it out to him. "What is this? Can you tell me?"

He took it and held it up to the feeble light, closely examining the markings through squinted eyes.

"I need to understand what's in the bottle," Aude continued. "I've searched high and low through Aachen for someone to help me." The old man appeared unmoved. She pointed at the sign painted on the glass. "Ethelbert of Tours visited the city two weeks ago and mentioned that you may use similar marks?" she prodded.

He rolled it between his fingers.

"Well," he observed, "the glass could be mine, but it could have been filled by someone else."

He found a clean cloth on the table, covered his fingers, and loosened the cork.

"I don't suppose this is a healing mixture?" he asked.

"I really don't know." Aude watched him with interest. "I was expecting you to tell me. This is your profession, after all, is it not?"

"No need to get cheeky, my lady." He sniffed the open bottle gingerly and ran his fingers through his beard. He wrinkled his nose thoughtfully as he considered the aroma. Then he swirled the bottle and eyed the motion of the liquid. "Aconitum, or wolfsbane, I should say. In certain circles in the East, the herb is used in minute doses as a tincture. But in larger draughts—well, it silences without a struggle." His hawkish eyes examined her closely. "Where did you get this?"

Aude felt color rush to her cheeks.

"Sir," she replied, keeping the timbre of her voice as firm as possible. "I serve the sister of the king." She pulled a ring from her finger, one that her mother had given her long ago, bearing the stag of the Vale. Her heart beat in her throat as she held her breath.

He glanced at the ring. "Of course you do." He pushed away from the table then shuffled to a desk where a vellum book lay open. Handwritten entries lay scrawled across the pages in blotted black ink. Ruffling page by page, he scanned lines until he found one in particular.

"Yes, here it is," he mumbled sullenly. "I've seen him a few times. I've not much call for this mixture."

"Can you tell me what he wanted it for?"

"I do not involve myself in the affairs of my customers, my lady. I merely inform them of the proper doses."

"As a tincture or as a silencer?"

He glared at her defensively. "One must know the dangers of an improper dose."

"Can you tell me anything about him, the one who ordered this?"

"Many of my clients depend on confidentiality."

She mustered her most imperious look.

He returned her stare but only for a moment before dropping his eyes, shoulders sagging ever so slightly. He pulled the ledger an inch closer.

"Let me see."

He lifted the book up to his nose, squinting. "I've a note here. A gentleman who made purchases with a scar over his left eye like so." He drew a line across his forehead. "I always observe those buying stronger brews." He seemed to be begging her confidence now. "And see here, this is the symbol I observed on his ring." He thumped the book defiantly down on the desk and pointed.

"He had a signet ring?" Aude leaned over the page, a chill running through her blood.

He reviewed his scribbles. "Yes. It looked—bit like a lily."

"A lily?"

"That's what I said, my lady." The irritation in his voice was just subdued enough to be decorous but not enough to be unnoticed. "Here."

Aude watched his finger trace the symbol. *According to legend,* she thought, *the lilies pointed the way across a river for King Clovis as he rode to battle. Charles's father, Pepin, struck the last of that line down years ago.*

She straightened as the realization struck her.

"I thank you," she whispered. She gathered her skirts and whisked from the shop.

A shadowy figure lingered in a nearby alley, watching Aude and Jerome ride hastily up the Aachen road. When she was out of sight, spider-veined hands pulled a finely made cowl over gaunt features, and Petras stepped out onto the track. He walked up the steps to the shop and pushed open the door.

Across the room, Gregory closed up the vellum book and shoved it to one side. He mumbled under his breath, turning to tend liquids bubbling in pots on oil braziers. The old apothecary paused when he heard Petras's footfall.

"Oh," he said, straightening and brushing thin strands of white hair from his eyes. "I didn't see you come in. How may I help you?"

Petras drew back his cowl, a friendly smile stretched across his lips. But his eyes remained coldly fixed on the old man's face.

"And how may I help you, Father?" Gregory said more respectfully, though this time a little more shortly.

Petras placed a hand flat on the book, his eyes still holding Gregory's.

"It appears that you've been visited just now by a lovely and inquisitive young woman," Petras said in a low voice.

Gregory paused, his eyes narrowing. "Why, yes. She was looking for an old family remedy. Something easily resolved."

"Oh? And how does one resolve issues of succession with a brew?" Petras hissed, a long-bladed seax appearing in his hand from the folds of his cloak. The single-edged knife gleamed wickedly in the dim light.

"I assure you," Gregory said, backing up a step or two, his feet painfully dragging the floor as he reached behind him, "I know nothing of succession or other things. I'm a simple apothecary."

"Yes, I suppose now you're just a simple apothecary," Petras noted. "As a man should be who concocted potions for the Empress Irene and was forced to flee the Eternal City when Nicephorus took the crown into his bloody hands."

"Sleeping philters are the norm of my trade, I assure you," Gregory countered. "What do you want? Speak, man, or leave my shop this instant!"

He backed into a jumbled table with deceptive clumsiness, but he was quick. He flung a bowl at Petras, spraying oily drops that ignited as they passed over the flaming braziers.

Petras threw his hands up. The burning droplets seared his face, smoking splotches scattered across his dark robes. He howled and leaped forward, quick as a cat, hurtling over the worktable to bury the long knife into Gregory's breast.

Blood spilled from the wound to the hard-packed earthen floor to sizzle among the flaming droplets of oil. The surprise and annoyance in Gregory's eyes faded for good. Tears streaming down his blistered skin, Petras straightened, pushing the body away in disgust. He plunged his face into a pail of tepid water by the back door and scrubbed at his flesh, leaving angry red welts across his pale features. Then he turned his attention to the documents scattered across the shop, and particularly on the vellum book upon the desk while flames began to lick the dried herbs on the shelves.

Moments later, his visit concluded, Petras drifted down the front steps of the shop and faded into the shadows of the encroaching evening. Behind him, smoke twisted out a window and then billowed out the open door. Flames spread through cracks in the walls and up to the moldy roof thatching. Villagers tumbled from their huts to combat the flames quickly consuming the shop and spewing glowing cinders into the air to threaten them all.

Petras dug his heels into the flanks of his mount and cantered at a breakneck pace toward Aachen.

Aude clung to the saddle pommel atop the lathered horse that clattered into the courtyard. She brought the steed to a hard stop and dismounted, thrusting the reins into Jerome's tired hands even before he could come to a stop behind her, then dashed up the steps of the palace.

In the adjoining garden, Gisela played with Baldwin. The young woman rushing across the tiled floor to the grand stairs caught Gisela's eye, and she gestured for a nursemaid to watch over the baby as she hurried after Aude.

At the top of the staircase, Aude's door was slightly ajar. Gisela knocked quietly and pushed it open to find Aude standing in the center of the room, wiping wet eyes.

When Aude caught sight of the older woman, she flung her arms around her.

"What is it, child?" Gisela brushed strands of hair from Aude's face. "What frightens you so?"

"Poison, my lady! A draught for a silent death!" Aude wiped her face with the back of her hand. "And the symbol of Ganelon's house? A white lily on a field of blue?"

"Yes. The sign of our Lady, the mother of God."

"As well as the symbol of deposed Childeric, exiled by your father, Pepin." She drew a shaky breath and plunged on. "The man who bought your potion bore the same symbol."

Gisela's hand trembled though her fingers continued to clench Aude's in hers. "As I had feared, but I was afraid to speak. So it was Ganelon?"

"No," Aude said. "The apothecary noted a scar above the eye."

"Gothard," Gisela breathed through her clenched teeth. "Oh, dear God, Roland was right. Charles must know."

Aude prepared for the journey south at a livery near the outskirts of the city, for the royal stables stood too close to the corridors of gossip in the palace. Besides herself and Jerome, only two retainers of unquestioned loyalty would be their entire strength. She opted for haste rather than building a cumbersome entourage that would not only slow each step but also draw attention to her movements. The older of her two retainers, Gregory, fretted over details much like he had in the years since being sidelined from service in the Vale's auxiliaries. In those days, he served as a supply sergeant, a man who knew everything from the daily price of meat in any local market to the weight of barley needed for soldiers' rations. And he knew how best to acquire such items, legitimately or otherwise.

Peonius, a tall, dark, younger man from the vale, augmented Gregory's obsessive focus with quiet strength and simple, honest humor. He checked gear and sorted supplies with nary a cross word or question. For the better part of two days, both men quietly vanished from their quarters early each morning, not returning again until just before the palace gates closed in the evening.

For her part, Aude sorted through the accumulation of things she'd collected while living in Aachen for the past three years. Most would remain behind, locked in her quarters to await her return. But she packed spare boots, a cloak, and trousers in her travel bag. She paused when she came to Roland's sparkling necklace. She pressed it to her lips, that magical night of their wedding now but a closely held memory. She thought she could still detect his lingering scent—

A young woman's voice said, "So it's true. You're leaving us."

"Oh," Aude said, a bit flustered.

Berta stood in the doorway, a frown upon her lips.

"My dear, you startled the life out of me."

Berta's good-natured soul never allowed her to long hold a frown. Still, Aude tended to tread lightly with all members of the royal family—a habit she'd acquired while dealing with Aldatrude's ever-changing moods.

"Imagine how I felt knowing you were leaving and hadn't told me," Berta said, pouting. "I thought I'd be the first to know such things!"

Aude put down her folded clothes.

"I'm sorry," she began, then launched into the excuse she'd worked up. "I've received word Father may not live through the autumn. I do want to stay, dear heart, but I must attend to him."

Berta rushed in and wrapped her arms around Aude, burying her head in her shoulder.

"I don't wish you to leave!" she blurted out. "There are so few to speak with, or even trust."

Aude returned her embrace. To her, the court nobility were just barely tolerable in their incessant jockeying for position—but there was a sweetness about Berta that Aude used for a refuge from the constant machinations at court.

"I shall miss you too," she whispered. "But it will be only for a short time. Before you know it, I'll return. Then we shall have tales to tell and confidences to exchange!"

Berta released her, and Aude brushed the tears from her eyes.

"Take me with you!" Berta pleaded. "Take me from this pit of vipers! Oh, I'm sure one or two mean well, but I've no one to confide in except old priests and the scholars with their fingers stained in ink. I'll be no trouble, I swear! And I'd love to see the Vale in the fall."

"I can't bring you," Aude said. "You're central to the kingdom, with your family campaigning in Spain and an army on the Saxon frontier. But I can bring you something, if you like. A gift from my home, perhaps."

Berta stomped her foot. "I knew you'd say that. I could have the guard hold you—keep you in the palace."

Aude smiled and brushed a stray lock of dark hair from Berta's face, tucking it gently behind her ear. "And then my father would die without his daughter at his side. I wouldn't be good conversation were that to happen."

Berta bit her lip. "No, I suppose that's true," she admitted. "You know I wouldn't do it anyway."

"Of course I do." Aude rummaged through her bag and withdrew a small silver-chased crucifix that had been given to her long ago. She held it up to Berta. "Here, sister. This was my mother's. Keep it safe for me."

Even with all the baubles provided by her station, Berta's eyes widened.

"You mean it?"

It was then that Aude realized that Berta had never been offered something so personal—a sort of acceptance into another's family and life.

"I do. Since I cannot take you with me, you must keep a piece of me with you."

Berta nodded, and Aude strung it about her throat.

"I swear to you, I will keep it safe," Berta whispered as she admired the delicate work, turning the crucifix gingerly in her fingers. Then she looked up, her eyes brimming once more. "Return to me, sister. Swear it!"

"I swear," Aude said, not knowing if she told the truth.

A O I

The pickets raised a noise along the river facing the Saxon frontier, startling the Frank camp from its fitful slumber. Shouted alarms passed from station to station. Soldiers tumbled from their sleeping bags, gathering weapons and armor as they stumbled into the gray dawn.

Gothard shrugged through his tent flaps, tugging a leather coat over his head. He craned his neck while he gathered his weapons and rushed toward the commotion. Soldiers jostled into hasty formation and armored knights thundered past atop their steeds. Gothard pushed through the ranks to the front, and what he saw arrayed across the field caused his breath to chill in his lungs. A vast Saxon army spread out in loose battle order along their side of the Rhine. Ten thousand enemy throats let out a raucous jeer as the Franks scampered into place, those with shields taking positions in the front ranks.

With no time to kit out his steed and locate the levies from Tournai, Gothard pulled on his mail coat and found a place among a group of peasant levies. Apprehension fluttered in his stomach. He shook his arms and legs to encourage circulation as a handful of Tournai men appeared at his side, having followed him from the tents. Gothard nodded to them wordlessly.

The Saxons stomped to within fifty yards and then with hardly a pause charged with a booming roar. The Franks drew their swords and braced themselves before the Saxons rushing across the field. With a metallic crunch, they drove into the front ranks and cut a swath with heavy blades that left the Franks struggling to fill the gaps of the fallen.

Gothard stepped over a peasant on his knees clutching at his ruptured bowels. He shouted encouragement at his struggling comrades to keep the heavily armored Saxons at bay, but the onslaught was unrelenting. The Saxons drove hard into the buckling center, cutting down the ill-equipped Frank irregulars with a bloody reaping that left the field sown in a torn and mangled human crop. As Tournai men fell around Gothard, even their bitter resolve began to melt. That melting became a stream and then a rush of men fleeing the field, leaving their comrades to struggle against the overwhelming Saxon tide.

A nearby youth dropped his weapon and turned to run.

"Stand and fight!" Gothard shouted raggedly. He deflected a wicked cut from a stout warrior and plunged his sword into the man's bearded face. The deserter hesitated as Gothard tugged his sword free—but only for a moment. He shook his head and turned to run. Gothard cut him down before he could take two more steps.

"Rally, men! Rally!" he yelled above the din.

A tall Saxon broke through the Frank shields, roaring at the top of his lungs and hacking through limbs with his broadsword. A spray of blood showered Gothard's eyes. Heedless, he stepped into the gap and took off the Saxon's head with a snapping cut.

Sudden pain shot through his own gut, and Gothard's body jerked. His heart seemed weighted by a stone. He looked down to see the tip of a rusty blade protruding from his belly through his mail coat. Blood exploded in a flood through his garments. He painfully turned to see who had stuck him, and his legs buckled, the ground rushing up to greet him.

The battle swirled and seethed around him but then passed him by. Retreating Franks were replaced by charging Saxons until only stragglers sprinting among the wounded to keep up with the fluid battle-line could be seen. Through blurring eyes, Gothard watched an old peasant sink down to embrace the body of the coward he had killed.

Gothard chuffed blood.

A passing Saxon swiped indiscriminately at the old man's neck. He clutched at a fountaining wound, sagging in a heap over the boy even as Gothard's own last breath choked through his teeth.

CHAPTER 21

FIRE FROM HEAVEN

Under the baking summer sun, Frank clerics herded an endless line of prisoners into the creek's sluggish flow. Dusty and dejected, prisoners went in on one side; muddy and defeated, they came out on the other. On the far bank, they sank to their knees before priests administering oaths, one of allegiance to the God of the Christians, and the other of fealty to Charles, before being led off to rough food and crude shelter.

But it was better than the alternative.

In the distance, something mechanical clattered and groaned beneath a thick cloud of smoke that rose from a mud-and-clapboard building. Even the Franks gave the place a wide berth. The prisoners whispered among themselves and speculated. Only a few ventured a guess as to what lay within, and those speculations lacked confidence, fueled only by rumors heard from drunken seamen relating frightened tales on stormy nights. A few murmured prayers to the god of their homeland, rather than to He whose water still dripped from their hair—secretly grateful that for them the war was finally over.

John, finally able to bear the sun once more, ventured out of the doorway of the smoky shack and shambled to the river with an empty bucket. Kennick stood at the water's edge, watching the Greek's progress and wrinkling his nose in disgust. Turpin stopped on his way to the baptisms and noted the look on the marchman's face.

"In all my days, Bishop," Kennick said, clearing his throat, "I've never smelled anything so vile." He spat as if it would help clear the stench away.

Turpin touched the four corners of the cross on his breast with a nod. "Rocks that stink this badly? Surely God meant this for the damned!"

Kennick grinned, his peppered beard bristling, and slapped Turpin on the back. "Something to look forward to!"

Inside the crude work shed, Roland spoke with Leo while the Greek shaped and bent copper tubes with curious tools. To Roland it looked like a senseless, twisted mass. Leo held the tangle before his eyes and squinted at it critically. With a satisfied grunt, he fitted it to a nipple on a cauldron burbling thick sulfurous smoke.

"The last shipment of oils arrived two days ago," Roland said. "And the smith finished the metalwork you required. When will the device be ready?"

Leo sat back on his heels and finally focused on the champion.

"We've not tested it," he replied. "It needs a trial run to ensure the entire apparatus is sound."

"But men are dying," Roland insisted. "We've no reinforcements coming to fill the ranks. We must make it ready before the caliph intervenes. If he succeeds in bringing shiploads of troops up the river, the siege will crumble."

John returned with the bucket. "It's a dangerous thing you require of us, my lord," he offered. "I see the men dying myself—every day I do—but many more would die, and even more if this explodes while pulling it through the camp."

Roland took the bucket from his hands and lifted it over the jumbled parts to set it next to the cauldron. "I understand that. But we must take the city. They continue to range from the northern gates and disrupt our supply lines. We must retake Carcassonne so we can move on to Saragossa."

Leo and John exchanged glances.

"We will prepare the weapon, my lord," Leo agreed, though John's face visibly tightened. Leo rose and crossed the workshop to a simple table littered with documents. He shuffled about until he found a sheaf of vellum sheets. "Here," he said, handing them to Roland. "This is the shell that will house the weapon, to keep it protected from missiles and the like. All the measurements are included."

Roland examined the document—the page covered with lines and numbers that frankly meant little to him. "We'll get men working on this immediately." He stepped out of the workshop eagerly.

"God protect us from our own handiwork," John muttered to Roland's retreating back.

Alans searched on foot through the forward units until he found the Tournai men laboring under Ganelon's supervision. With picks and shovels, the men strengthened the earthen fortifications that would eventually ring the city and plug the gaps in the Frank line. Between them and the city walls stood brush screens that obscured their activities from the archers stationed in the crenellations. Even so, an occasional random shaft whistled through the air, the missive of some bored bowman.

Alans waved to Ganelon, but the count frowned and gestured for his men to continue their work.

"What do you want?" Ganelon snapped. He grabbed a water skin and sloshed a swig around his mouth, spat it out, then took a longer pull. He wiped his mouth with the back of his hand and eyed Alans more closely. It was then he noticed a strangely humble look on the usually haughty face of the southern noble.

"I seek a man who's lost much in this debacle," Alans said.

Ganelon didn't try to stifle a mocking laugh. "Weren't you one of the loudest voices *for* this war?"

Alans shifted uncomfortably. "Do you remember long-ago days when we were young?" He stared past Ganelon to the distant wall. "We chased with Charles to Italy on his glorious mission to free the holy city. None of us imagined that Rome would throw open her gates in just a matter of days! Why, I remember the stink as the Romans thronged the streets to greet us."

Ganelon chewed the edge of his mustache. "The Saracens have more to lose than the Lombards, I suppose."

Unnoticed, the youth, Julian, found a task closer to the conversation.

He bent his back to drive the shovel blade into the summer-hardened earth.

Alans clenched his fists. "They force us to batter down every wall! We waste men in siege instead of using them to hold lands entitled to us by conquest! Surely Charles knows we're bleeding our strength in a wild goose chase!"

A sudden cry marked the luck of an enemy archer. Guinemer hopped into the ditch, pushing men aside to check the fallen soldier's wound.

"Look where he takes counsel," Ganelon mused, ignoring the moment's chaos. "From a general who washes the streets in our own blood, and the slut of his loins who warms his bed."

"Surely God has abandoned us." Alans genuflected to ward off evil.

"If He was ever with us," Ganelon hissed.

As night extended her shroud across the contested field before the city, a hush fell over the Frank army with the passing creak and groan of the massive contraption that crawled through their lines toward the gate—a large, bulbous wooden frame covered with stretched hides soaked in muddy creek water. At the forward end, a steel cover glinted in the red twilight, roughly worked into the shape of a frightful hell-beast with a gleaming maw jostling on its hinges. Smoke billowed and formed a dark smudge above the war machine, bolstering the impression that this fiery serpent crawled from the apocalyptic pit. Its wheels turned slowly with every heave from the men inside it, and with each measured step, the horrific creation inched forward.

Beneath the dripping hides, sweat-soaked men strained at push-bars extending from a cart beneath the Byzantine machine. Gritty cloths covered their faces to keep out the rank oily smell overlaid with choking dust and the stench of wet skins. Many glanced nervously with every whistle and pop at the winding copper tubes and kettles above them, fearful of the brew bubbling within the cauldron at the heart of the monstrosity. Further down the Frank lines, Charles rode with his entourage to the foremost trenches to gain a better view of the operation.

Shouts rang out from the city walls. Saragossans hastily repositioned on the imposing gate, a strong barrier bound in iron and topped with towers and murder holes steaming with vapors. From the battlements, arrows rained down on the machine's thick hide that bristled with the spent shafts. When it finally neared the gate, hot pitch spewed from the wall. Flame erupted, engulfing the shell. But the machine rolled onward.

The Frank army held its collective breath when the wagon butted with a muted thump against the gate.

Within the bowels of the monstrosity, Kennick and Otun grabbed the bellows' handles and bent their strong backs to the work. The entire contraption rocked with their effort, and the piping groaned with the increased strain.

"Keep going! More pressure!" Leo shouted over noise from the assault above them. He was covered in thick felt garments allowing only his eyes to show. Those eyes darted from the bellows to valves and to indicating glasses.

"Ready! Now!"

At the head of the machine, Roland and Oliver, similarly garbed, threw open the steel snout and lifted their shields overhead. Leo stepped under their protection holding a tube the size of a man's head connected by a stitched hose of leather and gut to the depths of the contraption. His eyes crinkling in what must have been a mad grin at his shield-bearers, Leo braced his feet widely and turned a brass lever atop the nozzle.

With a ghastly echoing roar, wet flames belched out, engulfing the gate in liquid hellfire that clung to the massive timbers. Sulfurous smoke billowed upward, blinding enemy soldiers who scrambled madly across the ramparts to escape the rising inferno. Leo angled the tube toward the heights and arced his stream of flaming death after them. Along the wall and across the top of the gate, even the slightest splattering turned men into human torches, many of whom desperately flung themselves from the heights to end their anguish, screaming until they hit the ground.

Charles gasped at the horrific vision before him. Just visible in the conflagration, a few defenders recklessly stood their ground, dumping water over the wall, but the flames roared upward without abatement until the gatehouse walls cracked. Heat rose in a rippling billow and obscured the horrible suffering on the battlements.

"I've seen this," Charles whispered, crossing his chest with sharp, quick motions. "It is my nightmare before my waking eyes. Dear God, forgive us for what we do."

Flames clawed from the gate to the battlements, and men continued to die. Stone blackened and cracked while iron fittings flared white-hot. Wooden catwalks shriveled and collapsed. Timbers and ash rained down on the shell as the pipes and the cauldron began to rattle and hum.

Leo nodded vigorously to Roland, all he could do in his thick garb to indicate his excitement. Moral regrets were apparently lost in the rushing power he wielded. He shifted his feet to strengthen his stance and gave the gate another blast.

Then a rivet burst, and Leo faltered. Within his heavy shroud, his eyes grew suddenly wide with fear.

Another rivet pinged into the flames.

"It's going to blow!" he shouted over the noise. He shut the valve, dropped the cherry-red nozzle on the ground, and lunged back to Kennick and Otun still pumping madly at the bellows.

Roland urgently waved the other men away. "Get out! Now! Get out!"

The crew spilled from beneath the covering and stumbled back to the Frank line. Half-hearted missiles from the farther walls whistled past them. Roland pushed Leo on ahead then turned to others who stumbled behind. Ignoring the sulfur stinging his eyes, he shouted at them to hurry along.

An explosion rocked the ground.

Brimstone hurled upward then plummeted back down in a fiery rain. A few steps behind the champion, a ball of flaming muck struck Kennick's shoulders and burst across his back. He stumbled, beating at the flames, angering them more. They spread to his sleeves and with a flare engulfed him in living fire. He shrieked.

Roland launched toward his friend, but Leo tripped him, throwing his body across the knight's. Roland spat a mouthful of dirt and wrestled out from under the Greek's scant frame while Kennick screamed and writhed.

Leo snatched at Roland's garments, tangling him up again. "You can't save him!"

"Let me go!" Roland hammered him with his fists. "God damn you, let go!"

Kennick slumped to the ground and twitched in a sickening display of agony.

"You cannot put it out!" Leo clung to Roland, gasping to continue. "He was dead when it touched him!"

Roland sobbed, the fiery air stinging his lungs and the stink of burnt flesh filling his nostrils. Balls of fire continued to strike the ground around them. Kennick's body lay where it fell, now nothing more than a pile of blackened ash.

The war carried on indifferent to the champion's grief.

The flames burned through the night, no longer needing the Greek fire to sustain them, and by dawn the city gates collapsed and took down the gatehouse wall.

The wails of the defenders rose above the roaring flames, and the Franks advanced.

Over the next days, bandons of soldiers entered the smoldering ruins, moving house-to-house and street-to-street in maneuvers perfected in alleys of Barcelona to root out remnants of Saragossa's demoralized forces. Those they found they dragged in chains to either the muddied streams for rites and peace oaths, or to the chopping block. Roland led heavily armored cavalry in pursuit of Marsilion's straggling lancers across ruined acres of wheat, cutting them down in relentless skirmishes to the very shadows of the Pyrenees.

Ahead of the chaos, Blancandrin directed a full-scale retreat, frantically driving his army around the mountains and across the summer-scorched peninsula toward Saragossa.

At his heels, the Oliphant sounded the victory yet again.

ΑΟΙ

CHAPTER 22

In God's Hands

Red-bellied clouds rolled slowly over the forest still shadowed with the dregs of night. From their lofty gossamer shreds, stray beams of promised sunrise bounced into deep recesses of dark boughs. In the shadows of the verdant canopy, edged steel glinted in the pale light.

A bow creaked. An eye sighted along the shaft and made contact with Aude's defiant gaze a score of yards away. She clutched Jerome with her good arm, her clothes warm from his blood.

Their desperate race to Charles had come to a grim halt.

And yet, not so many days before, Francia's northern forests had lain deep, verdant, and welcoming. Summer remained much the same as it had for hundreds of years. Farmers toiled against the hot sun and at times against the land itself. Motte-and-bailey forts rose from the forests, their walls of heaped earth and mossy timber battlements nearly indistinguishable from the surrounding verge. The old Roman road, upon which Aude's party traveled, intersected dusty cattle tracks leading to tiny settlements of mud-and-thatch huts alongside dilapidated Roman buildings, long since vacated by bureaucrats and now pressed into service as churches. Old and new existed side by side in the land of the Franks. Aude's own family attested to this—the line of Vale Runer stretched back in time not just to Germanic forebears but also to Gallic patricians who had considered themselves more Roman than the mobs of the Eternal City.

As the days stretched down the rutted roads, their flight became a trek—a slog of long hours in the saddle, avoiding unnecessary contact with other travelers. With only short breaks to enjoy a spot of shade and a clear draught from some small creek, they pressed on.

Aude pulled her hair back from her face with a silken band and remained atop her mount as it stretched its neck and drank from the stream. She waved a hand before her eyes to chase away a stray fly, watching the men feed their horses from scant pouches of grain.

Even though weeks had passed, she still felt a pang of guilt for misleading Berta. A necessary deception, for secrecy was paramount. And the daughter of the Vale realized she could trust no one until this mission was finished. Ganelon had spent his entire life in the orbit of the court and had acquired many friends who listened at corners and doorways. On the day they set out from Aachen, the narrow streets had still been dark with homes still shuttered. Yet the small band kept eyes fixed over their shoulders to double- and triple-check that no one followed while they chased toward Spain bearing accusations of treason and murder.

Her steed finally pulled its head up. Water drained from her bit like a fountain.

"This can't be good for my bones," Jerome muttered when he thought no one was listening. But listen she did—to him, to her mount, and to the land all around them. A strange sensation crept up the back of her neck, and every time they lingered too long at a stream or waited for beams of light to penetrate the leaves before stirring in the morning, she knew some nameless horror would be upon them. Her face reddened, and she turned her cheeks upward to the sky, hoping none of her companions noticed.

Oliver would likely laugh at her foolishness and remind her of the great care she had taken in keeping all a secret—even from Gisela. And she bore the message to Spain herself rather than trust it to another. The only loose end was Berta, who thought Aude flew to the Vale. She desperately hoped that false trail would send any pursuit days to the east and allow them to race south unhindered to the Spanish plain.

Yet the lurking fear remained, and she continued to watch and listen.

A few days later, Aude again turned her face to the sky, only this time cool drops pelted her skin. Gray enveloped the countryside with a storm that rolled into the region. She closed her eyes for a moment to shut out the swaying of her horse and the clopping hooves of her companions. The droplets ran down her face, around her lips and chin—a welcome respite from the summer sun that had accompanied them all the way through Neustria, in central Francia. She searched the sky and thought of the gray day of her wedding to Roland, and the light that had brought to the gloomy winter. Those precious moments in the champion's quarters seemed a world away now, and she desperately wanted to recapture them.

"Dear Mary, mother of God," she prayed in her heart and her mind, "please speed us to him. I beg you, keep him safe that I might see him again."

The crack of a branch snapped her eyes open, and she jerked upright in the saddle. The wind had picked up sharply, and her horse skittered to the side when the leafy appendage crashed across the road. Aude cooed to her steed while the men struggled to calm their own mounts. Jerome pressed his horse against hers.

"My lady!" he said against the sound of creaking timber and rising wind. "I'd advise shelter! This night will not be fit for man or beast!"

Aude brushed her dampening hair from her face and pulled up the hood of her cloak just as the rain began its assault in earnest. "If we pause, a messenger from the capital could reach the army before us! We must keep going!"

"My lady, if someone sent a message with official sanction, it will surely reach its intended before us anyway," Jerome replied with some urgency. "Messengers can ride alone and change out horses regularly." Jerome's horse pranced fitfully under his hand to the crackle of lightning and the delayed boom of thunder. "We must get off the road!"

Aude gauged clouds that appeared to stack up over their heads.

"You're right, of course. We must take what shelter we can find." She dug her heels into her horse and led them beneath the trees.

Not far ahead, a loud groan turned into a ripping crack as a limb broke loose, hurling impaling branches around them.

One of the men screamed, and Aude's steed bolted.

Branches and leaves whipped at her face, while beneath her the horse heaved with panic and galloped headlong back toward the road. She strained at the reins, but with the echoing booms of thunder, the horse was having none of it. The beast jumped a ditch, sliding through unexpected mud on the far side. Her companions shouted and struggled far behind her.

Aude leaned low and pressed herself against the saddle. A branch tore her cheek, flooding her skin with warmth. The horse leaped a fallen tree then slipped on slick muck to crash through sharp brambles. Hooves flew wildly when it lost its footing, and steed and rider tumbled hard into a crumpled, heaving heap as rain poured rampant from the turbulent sky.

The horse thrashed to its legs. Like a foal walking for the first time, it gathered its feet and stumbled a few steps.

Aude remained on the ground, staring up at the darkness, rain driving downward on her face. She gasped for breath. Sharp pains shot through her body.

"I'm sorry, my love," she choked. "I've failed you."

Her mind drifted while the storm gods danced across their high-vaulted halls in the heavens. She clung desperately to consciousness that she might remount her steed, find her companions, and continue on her desperate errand.

But pain and darkness overcame her.

Branches broke, and leaves rustled, letting in thin slivers of light.

"Here!" The voice caused her to stir. She choked out a breath.

Brush parted. Jerome, covered with grime and blood, thrust his face into view. He looked back over his shoulder. "She's here!"

Aude blinked against dappled sunbeams. "Where? Is anyone hurt?" Her throat was dry.

She tried pushing herself up, but grinding pain shot through her arm and shoulder and bound her tongue.

Jerome's face remained serious as he separated her clothes from debris. "My lady, we lost Gregory. He chased after you and cracked open his head against a tree limb."

"Oh, dear God, no ..." The words faded as she lost focus, struggling against the pain that clutched her lungs with each breath.

Peonius appeared above her and gently lifted her. She clutched at his collar.

"We cannot stop," she whispered through clenched teeth. "Please, my horse. Get my horse—we'll continue on."

But Jerome directed Peonius to set her down on a cleared patch of ground where he began examining her for injury. When his arthritic fingers probed her right shoulder and arm, Aude cried out.

"You're broken," he observed. He sat back on his heels and began tearing long strips from his sodden cloak. "We'll need to get you put back together before even trying to find aid." His hands, though swollen with age, worked with a tender skill as he probed her flesh to trace the broken bone.

Peonius cut a piece of wood, covered it in a leather strap, and then pushed it between her teeth. "Bite this. It will help," he urged.

Aude did as she was told, and Jerome wrenched the bones back into place. She ground the leather with her teeth. Sobs huffed through her nose, and tears streamed down her face.

Jerome wrapped her arm snugly into a trough of bark and slung it against her side. When he finished, Peonius stroked her jaw and eased the branch from her mouth. Teeth marks cut deep in the leather. He tossed it aside, then he and Jerome lifted Aude to her feet.

"My horse?" she croaked.

"You'll ride on mine, my lady," Peonius said simply.

Aude felt a cold tightness in her chest when she realized what that meant. An old man, an injured woman, and down two horses with half their journey yet ahead of them. She nodded, fighting the urge to cry out as the two men helped her onto Peonius's horse. She caught the pommel of the saddle and swung her leg over. For the first time, she looked about, ignoring the pain. The storm's fury left shattered branches jutting starkly against the gray sky as the last clouds scudded overhead on the tails of the wind.

Peonius clucked his tongue and led the horse to the road. Aude clung to the pommel, her face pale, cold sweat upon her brow. Yet she kept a brave face when Jerome swung his mount in beside her to set to a gentle pace.

The muddy track opened to a series of farmers' fields. Rows of turnips, wheat, and other greenery checkered the dark earth in shades of green. Her broken bones grated together, causing Aude to clench her teeth against the continued pain. She sought distraction amid the forests rimming the fields that passed slowly by to the measured plod of the horse's tread. She would pick some interesting tree ahead and trace its branches and study its roots until they drew abreast, then would find another further on and repeat the game.

Then, amid her desperate meditations, Aude saw leaves move against the breeze. Fever was her first thought. Many who lay at death's dark portal succumbed to strange visions while fever burned in their bodies. Suddenly feeling a bit unhinged with the constant assault of the pain, she slumped over the saddle. Jerome reached across between the two horses and kept her upright. Even so, her eyes remained on the woods, where the motion resolved into a shadowy figure.

"There. Who is that?" she whispered.

Jerome craned his neck. "I don't see anything, my lady."

Yet there was the figure of a man, she was certain, accompanied by the glint of steel. A cloak appeared to flutter like black raven's wings about broad shoulders. Martial echoes stirred in her mind. The figure raised an arm in what could be a greeting—or a warning. Overwhelmed by a sense that she knew who he was, her fingers stretched to touch him.

And then he was gone.

A breath of cool air on her cheek brought her back to herself. "He was there, Mary as my witness."

Jerome halted them and dismounted. "Of course he was. Of course."

He climbed up behind her to keep her steady and motioned for Peonius to mount his horse. With tired eyes, he scanned the wood line.

"What will we do?" Peonius asked.

"Ride on as fast as you can," Jerome said. "Find assistance."

To Peonius's credit, he hesitated only for a heartbeat then slapped the reins against his horse's flank.

Jerome clucked to Aude's mount, watching the forests warily as Peonius galloped down the muddy rutted road.

That night, Peonius led them to shelter in a small town, a simple room in a log-and-stone tavern, but it was dry and secure. While Peonius saw to the horses, Jerome found a graying woman who claimed knowledge of healing arts. In a back room, he watched her work, surprised by the deftness of her gnarled hands. She tugged rather brutally on Aude's shoulder until a *pop* and a *click* signaled the bones had moved back into place. The young woman, benumbed by strong wine, stifled a cry then sank back against the bed. The village matron wrapped Aude's arm with linens and wooden slats, immobilizing her arm to the wrist.

"Keep her still," she said with furrows deepening about her eyes. "She must rest."

Aude doggedly shook her head and struggled to rise. "No time. We must keep moving."

Jerome gently pressed Aude back down.

"No, my lady," he whispered to her. "We rest and keep counsel to ourselves."

Hours passed, and Aude drifted in and out of troubled slumber. When Jerome finally gently shook her, she stirred reluctantly, feeling exhaustion deep within her bones and torn muscles.

It was still dark outside the dirty, oiled parchment window.

"And now we must go," he said. "Peonius is bringing the horses around."

Aude tried with one hand to tie her tangled hair back from her face, but it was Jerome's fingers that finished the task.

"There were men here," he explained. "This evening, they stopped field hands returning home to ask about travelers on the road. We'd best put distance between us and the village before the morning."

Aude threw her good arm around Jerome's shoulder. Each step was a jarring effort. Yet they crept through the inn's common room to the kitchen and out a back door into the bracing chill of the night. Peonius lifted her into the saddle, and Jerome climbed up behind her once more.

They struck out across the nearby fields, picking up the road further south. Above them, clouds drifted across the face of the moon while the night wrapped them in her cool embrace. And then the moon, the sky, and the indifferent stars disappeared beyond the leaf-laden boughs of the forest when it closed overhead.

They rode silently, and for Aude painfully, for hours. Slowly the sky lightened, and the first birds began to sing.

Then Peonius tumbled from his saddle, a dark shaft sprouting from his chest. The air whistled, arrows speeding past Jerome and Aude. The old attendant buried his heels in the horse's ribs before Aude realized what had happened. Figures rushed through the brush after them. Steel flashed behind the trees. A man's voice shouted, and the horse shied. It threw its riders, and pain burst anew through Aude when she hit the ground. Jerome staggered to his feet, drawing a long knife from his belt.

There was a whistle, and an arrow pierced Jerome's throat. The old retainer fought to take a step, to protect his charge, but his legs crumpled. Aude cried out and dragged herself to him. Jerome sagged against her, gurgling his apologies through the blood gushing from his torn throat.

In the shadows of the verdant canopy, edged steel glinted in the pale light. A bow creaked. An eye sighted along the shaft and made contact with Aude's defiant gaze a score of yards away.

She clutched Jerome with her good arm, her clothes warm from his blood.

Out of the trees, a man stepped forward, chilling Aude's blood when she recognized the voice.

"Daughter, you've come so far," Petras hissed. "It's a shame the journey was for naught."

"You dare? You betray your king!"

"Betray my king?" the priest sneered. "Childeric is my king—dead these nearly fifty years. Yet his heir lives, and I shall see him returned to the throne!"

Aude straightened defiantly. "Then end this here. You've already spilled the blood of men more honorable than your master. What's a little more?"

Petras's smile stretched tightly across his lips, and he nodded to the archer.

An arrow hissed through the air, burying itself in flesh with authoritative finality. The archer crumpled, and chaos broke out among Petras's men. More arrows flew. Petras tried to rally his men, but more collapsed in cries of shock and spurts of blood. Petras turned to flee, but an arrow struck him in his back, followed quickly by a second. He stumbled only a few paces before falling to the ground in a dark spreading puddle.

Aude threw herself over Jerome's corpse, offering what scant protection she could from the soldiers breaking through undergrowth to cut down Petras's remaining men. She lifted her eyes and saw a cloaked figure step from the forest then rush to her with arms open.

"Sister!" Berta exclaimed. "Oh, my dear Aude!"

Tears streamed down both women's cheeks. Aude collapsed into Berta's arms.

"I knew you weren't going to the Vale," Berta whispered. "Do not worry, sister. Now you travel with me."

Aude wiped her eyes and for the first time noticed the colors on the soldiers' surcoats—brilliant red emblazoned with a royal golden Roman eagle.

CHAPTER 23

THE PRICE OF PEACE

Saragossa opened her tall gates to the flood of troopers streaming up the road. For miles beyond those gates, soldiers struggled for the city among the tide of peasants and merchants from the outlying countryside who also clogged the thoroughfares. All fled the Frank demon Roland and his hellish angel of fire that perched atop the smoldering bones of Carcassonne. The air reeked of fear. Refugees haggled alongside the soldiers for shelter, provisions, or simply for a place on the road to pass on to safer havens.

Near the city walls, chaos erupted at market squares as the mobs and residents jostled, contested, and then fought for scant supplies. Some merchants simply beat back the crowds and closed up their tents, choosing instead to keep what little they had for themselves. Others braved the assault, risking injury for coin, though each passing moment prices rose to meet the demand, and tempers mounted to match. Vigilant mothers shepherded their children through the influx of strangers and the ever-present ironfisted guards who strained to herd the refugees into some semblance of order.

Far above the Saragossa's streets, the emir's palace stood gleaming in the shimmering sun. Along the walls, banners snapped bravely in the warm summer wind. Within those walls, cool marble floors defied the heat and the sweaty smell wafting up from the city below.

Drumming his fingers on a drink chilled with ice brought from the mountains at great expense, Marsilion sat on the edge of his divan.

Intimates of his court surrounded him on thick cushions and argued over the disastrous progress of the war that would soon ensnare the city. The nobles' nervous faces examined the lines of the purposefully bland dispatches, hoping to read into them some glimmer of hope to stay the emir's fits of temper, which could only be reined in by Blancandrin's steadying hand.

"The entire extent of our lands—everything is in Charles's hands!" Marsilion slurped his drink. "His armies encamp within sight of our walls!"

Blancandrin leaned forward, his eyes intent. "My lord, without the caliph's aid, we're no match for the combined strength of the Franks and Barcelona. We must consider that he will use another machine such as at Carcassonne."

The doors behind them opened, admitting five figures dressed in plain dark robes. They padded across the tiled floor and bowed respectfully to the emir.

"Ah, what is this?" Marsilion asked. Blancandrin rose to his feet and placed a hand on the hilt of his sword.

One of them stepped forward, holding up both hands to the general.

"There is no need for concern with us, sir," he said, his voice low and coiled as an adder. "Emir, you sent to the Old Man of the Mountain for assistance. We are here to fulfill your request."

Blancandrin stepped between them and Marsilion. "My lord! These are killers of the night! You didn't?"

"Yes. Yes, I did," Marsilion said with a firmness that surprised all around him. A son was lost during the course of this war. Indeed he had lost entire cities. Now he was beyond honoring rules of engagement. "When the caliph couldn't send even a single horse and his fleet remains bottled up in Cadiz by pirates—well, we needed options."

The assassin smiled and gestured toward his silent colleagues. "We intend to provide you with those options, Emir."

A Θ I

Saleem rode with his retinue strung along with him through the captured village—a once-pleasant town that had been destined to pass to Farad until the Franks had taken it. The villagers bowed silently as the riders swept through their dusty street clad in resplendent chain mail under billowing cloaks of red and blue. Pointed helmets trimmed in gold stabbed at the sky atop their heads. A son of the emir was returned in cruel glory, but he remained too far from the seat of power yet inside Saragossa's strong walls. He rode past the prostrating peasants without a glance and drew up beside a wagon on the edge of town where five commoners bent their backs loading sacks of grain. Their threadbare garments spoke of a lifetime toiling to sustain a meager living. Saleem dismounted and strode to the wagon, inspecting both the men and the contents.

"Such provisions are rare during these times," he observed.

One of the men reached into the wagon and sliced open a sack with a slender knife. The grain spilled over to the ground, but the man ignored the loss and the hungry stares of incredulous villagers. He reached into the sack and pulled forth a silver-chased box. He opened it for Saleem with a deep bow. Inside, the velvet lining nestled a gold signet ring. Saleem took it and rolled it between his fingers.

It was his father's.

"Our benefactor promises you much more than this," the man hissed.

Saleem narrowed his eyes knowingly. "Oh, yes, he does. And he will make good on each and every promise? I assure you, I mourned with him when we lost my brother."

With a cold eye, he looked at the nearby peasants staring transfixed at the precious grain spilling to the mud.

"No one will speak of this." He raised a hand and pointed to one at random. "Kill that one, to be sure they learn the lesson."

His lieutenant cleared his throat. "But, my prince, no one would believe them anyway."

"I suppose you could join him."

The lieutenant blanched. He quickly nodded to two troopers, who dismounted, grabbed the condemned man, and forced him to the ground. A saber flashed, releasing a fountain of crimson to the parched ground.

Saleem slid the ring onto his finger. "It does look nice there," he observed. "Yes, my father has always been generous."

A Θ I

Ganelon's retainers huddled near their campfires, some scrubbing the day's dust from their gear and others quietly spooning up stew that steamed in their bowls. In the distance, sprawling settlements outside Saragossa's city walls were lit with roving torches while the populace continued crowding the towering citadel. Yet with victory in sight, a hush had encompassed the camp, for many troopers recalled the bitter street fighting of recent days and the toll it had taken on their army—too many of their brothers already lay in unmarked graves scratched from the baked Spanish soil.

Ganelon squatted at a cookfire with Guinemer and Alans hunched over their own bowls. Nearby, Julian dropped a bundle of wood onto a stack near the fire.

Ganelon lowered his spoon and glared into the faces of his compatriots.

"Our move comes soon," he said in a low voice. "Soon Charles will decide to return to Francia, and we must strike when he is most vulnerable."

Alans shook his head, grinding a piece of gristle between his teeth.

"But his war hound," he said. "We must separate the king from his champion."

"No easy task to cut the gristle from the bone," Guinemer observed.

Alans waved his spoon at Ganelon. "His power over Charles grows with each passing day. It must be soon."

Ganelon set his bowl down then warmed his hands before the flames.

"True," he agreed. "Roland must not return to Francia alive."

The two men grumbled in agreement.

Alans dropped his spoon into his bowl and wiped his mouth with the back of his hand. "Your men? They will follow you in this?"

"Of course." Ganelon laughed, surveying the Tournai men around them. "They've proved their mettle time and again—and their loyalty."

Alans reached down, grabbing his cup and lifting it to eye level.

"Then we are in this together," he toasted.

"Until death," Ganelon agreed, snatching up his own cup.

They drank long into the night while the fire burned into red smoldering embers.

And Julian watched.

Long after sunset, Frank guards leaned on their spears and squinted through the darkness. They straightened when a cart creaked toward them up the track. The duty sergeant rubbed his nose with his fist and narrowed his eyes. A single hunched figure, features lost in the folds of a deeply hooded cloak, held the reins of two slowly tromping oxen. The sergeant held up a hand and signaled to one of his troopers, who hefted his spear to arms and examined the vehicle in the gloom.

"There's no entry after sunset," the sergeant barked, holding his own spear at the ready while the other guards converged on the vehicle. "Turn your rig around. The quartermaster will see you in the morning."

The driver raised both hands.

"My apologies, eminent sir," he said, his Saracen accent quite apparent. "But we bring provisions that just reached port for Charles's own table—wine from Greece, dates from Palestine, and fish from Massilia. We don't want them spoiling while the king's own chef waits on them."

The guard warily held out a hand.

"Papers," he commanded.

The driver fished around under his seat then eventually produced a rolled sheaf. The guard snatched it and waved for a torch.

"Of course, we had trouble getting through," the driver continued. "Saragossa pillages wagons on the road. It made the trip quite dangerous."

While the man spoke, shadows crawled from beneath the wagon, mere whispers of black that moved with deadly precision. Barely a gurgle escaped the guards' throats when hands clamped over their mouths and sharp knives finished their grim work. Then the shadows dragged the twitching corpses to the back of the wagon.

After a moment, the driver tapped the oxen with his prod and continued into the camp.

Roland walked the picket lines in the darkness, accompanied by Karim and Oliver. Between the guard posts, Oliver and Karim debated.

"So you think Aristotle superior to even Plato?" Oliver asked.

"In the house of wisdom, Aristotle has no peer," Karim insisted.

"And our esteemed Augustine?"

"But a novice, my friend. A mere shadow of the original masters," Karim replied with a knowing air.

The grumble of wagon wheels on the track behind them caught Roland's attention.

"The last wagons already passed for the day, didn't they?" he asked his comrades.

The swaying wooden bulk of the wagon was just visible turning a corner toward the camp center.

"We cleared a whole line of wagons before sunset," Oliver replied.

"I remember," Roland agreed. "The guards better have a good reason for letting this one pass."

The wagon creaked toward a holding area where other shipments awaited inspection and disbursement through the rest of the camp. A guard stepped from the shadows to wave the driver down. When he got no response, he trotted to close with the wagon. There was no driver. He called out to his fellows, grabbing the dangling reins and pulling the beasts to a halt. Guards swarmed into the back of the wagon to find sealed barrels and crates. A squire was sent off for a crowbar.

The king's tent was quiet except for Aldatrude's purring breath drifting across the plush carpets from where she slept in a trundle bed at the foot of Charles's own grand canopied one, ornately carved by artisans in distant Francia as befitting the daughter of the king. In it she slept soundly, surrounded by an entire army—as soundly as if she remained in the great palace in Aachen.

A distant alarm rose near the edge of camp. Shadows danced on the canvas walls when soldiers outside the tent rushed to answer the call. Only a few silhouettes lingered, painted against the canvas, dutiful men holding their posts around the king's quarters. Then other shadows slipped in from the darkness and swallowed them up. One canvas panel went slack with a quiet *twang* as a tent peg was cut, and then a hand gripped the edge of the fabric and lifted. A shadow slipped inside, followed with nary a sound by four others.

Charles tossed restlessly beneath his blanket while the intruders closed on him. Aldatrude stirred awake. One man quickly pounced, drawing a knife across her throat and opening up a line welling across her slender neck. Though her drowning cry was muffled, Charles awoke with a start.

"What's this?" Charles demanded, voice groggy. "Who are you?" Then his eyes lit upon Aldatrude's body sprawled across her sheets, her limbs still twitching. "My daughter! Dear God!"

He lunged toward her, but an assassin blocked his path, a blade in his hands.

"Truly you are a great monarch, but you remain a threat to our people. Your deeds at Carcassonne destine you for hell. It is a great honor to send you there."

Roland, followed by Oliver and Karim, burst into the tent, tearing aside the canvas and crashing into furniture. The champion launched himself at the assassins, thrusting Durendal through one man's back to sprout out his chest. Oliver threw his arms around another and grappled the man to the floor, repeatedly smashing Halteclare's pommel into his face. Bones crunched, and the assassin's eyes rolled back. Blood flooded from his nostrils. His blade slipped from his fingers.

The lead assassin sprung for Charles, but the king grabbed his arm and deflected his strike. Then the man smashed the king across the face with his other fist. But Charles clung tenaciously to the man's dagger hand and threw his weight across Aldatrude's corpse, toppling the assassin over backward onto the carpeted floor. He punched the assassin in the throat. The man gasped for air, but Charles was relentless. He struck over and over again until bones and cartilage cracked under the assault, finally drawing a dagger from his own robes to thrust it into the man's belly. The man's eyes bulged, and then Charles gave the blade a wicked twist.

"Never lecture a king!" he spat in the man's face.

Karim struggled beneath the assault of another skilled killer. Straining arm to arm, the assassin's dagger scratched a line of red across his neck. Roland vaulted the bed and hit the assassin hard with Durendal's hilt, sending him sprawling. His knuckles pummeled the man's face.

"Stay down!" Roland growled.

Karim pulled himself to his feet and yanked back his attacker's hood as the hawk-nosed man struggled to free an arm. Roland reached out to stop him but was too late. The assassin's hand shot to his own shattered mouth, dropping in something that he quickly choked down with a chaser of blood. Karim tried forcing it back up, but the assassin only grimaced. Then a distant smile washed over his swollen face, a sigh rattled from his lips, and he too was dead.

For a brief moment, all was silent. Then the tent broke into pandemonium again when Frank soldiers rushed through the canvas with weapons drawn. But they were too late.

Oblivious to the disturbed chatter around him, Charles crawled to Aldatrude's pale, bloodied form and cradled her in his arms. He tenderly brushed her hair from her face, leaned down closer, and the king of the Franks and emperor of the Romans wept.

A O I

A Frank courier rode low in the saddle atop a sweat-drenched mount that pounded along the dusty track from the north. He glanced over his shoulder half-expecting demons to overtake him at any moment. When he topped a rise and at last caught sight of Charles's camp, he shouted with relief and raked his steed with his spurs. His mount blew hard, galloping for the Frank lines. Behind him rose a dust cloud obscuring the faint flash of arms—Saragossans racing to intercept him before he delivered his charge.

At the camp's boundary, the rider dragged the horse to a skidding halt. A sergeant strode across the defensive ditch that now extended from both sides of the road as part of growing earthworks threatening to surround the city. Recognizing the rider's livery, he whistled. Soldiers tumbled to the road, planting spears in the dusty ground in a wicked and deadly hedge line against the approaching enemy cavalry. The emir's troopers veered off through the dust and beat for the hills once more.

The sergeant turned back to the messenger and held up a mail-covered fist in both greeting and command.

"State your business," he growled.

"You're a sight for sore eyes," the rider began. He spat dust through his teeth. "I've dispatches from Saxony—from Count Rene. My charge isn't finished until they are in Charles's hands!"

At the sergeant's nod, two guards mounted their horses to provide the courier with an escort through the camp.

The sun relentlessly beat down on the canvas tarp stretched above the assembled nobles, providing only scant protection from the heat, dust, and flies. Sweat running down his creased brow, Charles stood at the head of his much-worn campaign table that remained, as always, covered in a jumble of maps and official documents. He raised his hands, signaling for quiet, and waited impatiently for the silence to ripple through his unruly nobles.

"Lords," he rumbled over them, his face stern. "I've grave news from Saxony. The enemy has routed our forces."

What subdued conversation that buzzed in the background was now completely quelled.

Charles's face was grimly set. "Even now they threaten to carve out the heart of Francia." He bent over the maps, his hands wide on the tabletop while considering his next words. The events of the past few days weighed heavily on his face. He pursed his lips, drew a deep breath, and continued. "It seems to me that we have a choice. Stand and fight to bring the emir of Saragossa to heel—or negotiate peace and return to our homeland to drive the Saxons back across the Rhine. My lords, I must have your advice and counsel."

Whispers broke out once more. Many nobles fidgeted, uncertainty rising in the stifling air. Whispers rose to babble, and fidgets became agitations.

Roland alone stepped forward to Charles's right hand.

"My king," he said, voice projecting to the rearmost fringes, "Saragossa lies within sight—within our grasp. If we leave now, eventually we will be forced to return. And on that day, we will bleed again to reach this same ground."

The nobles' chatter dropped to a hush, some of them clearly agreeing with his assessment. For who among them had not buried their dead in shallow interments that now littered the path to this city?

Ganelon, however, stood in a group of men who it seemed believed differently, for when he stepped forward, they urged their peers to silence so he could speak.

"Truly," he said, each word soaked with barely veiled venom, "on the battlefield, my stepson has no equal."

He gestured toward Alans and the other counts standing around him.

"But this is a decision for rational men—yes, men of reason," he continued. "We've stood with you, my king, we, your loyal counts of old. We've marched from the wilds of Saxony to the ruins of Rome! Hear us who love you! Rene's army flees before the Saxon onslaught, while we who could reinforce him sit on our heels before Saragossa. Quieting the emir through diplomacy may prevent greater tragedy at home. For if we weaken our forces in a lengthy siege—fighting not just Saragossa but also disease and hunger—we will not have the strength to face the Saxons, no matter the resolve and courage of our champion. Return home, great king. Return home now with honor and deal with the more immediate threat."

This time whispers erupted into catcalls between opposing advocates, rising to heated exchanges, which quickly broke into physical jostling that threatened blood. Charles pounded his hand down on the table, scattering the documents.

"Enough! Enough! Quiet, the lot of you!" The crowd settled into an uneasy calm. Charles pierced them with a critical eye. "Thank you, my lords," he growled. "I'll consider your counsel."

He turned and left the group without another word. Behind him, the peers of the realm trickled out of the shade, still arguing with one another in more quieted tones.

His bald head beaded with sweat, Naimon sought after Ganelon among the Tournai men and took him by the arm.

"A word with you, sir," he huffed, squinting in the sunlight.

"Of course," Ganelon replied, breaking off his conversation with Guinemer.

"I don't know any other way to tell you this," the king's counselor began. "The dispatches included notifications of the dead." He drew Ganelon to a halt. "Your son Gothard was among them."

There was an uncomfortable pause. Ganelon's face became a mask, impenetrable as stone, securing whatever turmoil he felt beneath an iron will.

"He did his duty, I am certain," the count said gruffly after a time. "If you will excuse me."

Naimon nodded. "Yes, of course. My condolences—"

But Ganelon had already turned his back and was stalking away.

A Θ I

Priests chanted a haunting Latin melody. Before them, knights clad in burnished mail and rich crimson-and-gold tabards carried the shrouded remains of Aldatrude to the grave that had been cut into the earth overlooking the city. Artisans had sweated and worked through the night to finish a monument befitting her noble heritage to stand at its head. There to keep her company in this distant land were rows of other more humble markers, remnants of other Frank dead who had fallen during the siege.

Roland stood on the right hand of Charles, whose body was rigid, his regal features looking past the preparations. The king's cheeks were wet from unacknowledged tears that strayed down his face to become lost in his wizened beard. Louis stood to the other side, face anguished by conflicting emotions.

The warriors bearing the young woman's body carefully lowered their burden into the hole while the faithful genuflected and bent their heads.

Charles knelt and picked up a handful of dry earth, touching the soil to his lips before scattering it across the shrouded corpse. Then he stood, turned, and stalked away before the priests could conclude the ceremony, leaving mourners free to crowd the graveside and toss in handfuls of dirt of their own.

Roland ran after the king. Upon catching him, the champion walked quietly at his elbow for a space. Charles stopped near his tent, looking past the canvas walls to the sky shimmering from the blistering heat.

"Uncle," Roland said. "I am sorry for the loss of Aldatrude."

His eyes moist, Charles glanced at his nephew. "She was my life, Roland. My joy."

"I know, Uncle. But please—and I am sorry to bring this up now, but—we must not abandon the campaign. We've paid too much precious blood for each step."

Charles narrowed his eyes, blinking the last tears dry. "Do not presume to lecture me on blood." His voice was cold and sharp. "We've all paid in blood. But each step the Saxons take in Francia is paid in the same coin. As king, I must think of the entire realm. I must see through the fog of emotions, like ... vengeance."

"Uncle, your daughter—" Roland started.

"Enough!" Charles snapped. "Unless the caliph intervenes, Marsilion remains trapped. This—" he waved back at the grave without looking "—was the act of a desperate man." He turned his gaze fully on Roland. "Nephew, what does your network of spies say of the caliph's intent?"

"Pirates have him bottled up in Cadiz, sire," Roland reported. "Take Saragossa and you end this war."

Charles ran his fingers through the white locks of his beard. "Leaving Saragossa is a risk. But after the thrashing we've given him, it will be years before he can rebuild and cross the mountains. By then we'll have dealt with the Saxons once and for all and be waiting for him."

"But we have the assets in place here—right now," Roland urged. "We can end this! Please, Uncle, we cannot dishonor the fallen."

Charles's eyes locked on Roland's.

"Burying Saragossa in ash won't bring the dead rest or ease the pain. For you, or for me." He placed a hand on Roland's shoulder. "You will have my decision in the morning, Champion. But for now, leave me to my thoughts."

The following dawn broke in a rosy smudge over the great plain beyond Saragossa. In that early light, the Franks assembled at the edge of their camp. Amidst the sea of men, Naimon stood near the king, bearing in his hands the gloves and staff, the tokens of royal authority. Before Charles, the tall and straight figures of Counts Basan and Basile remained at attention, dressed in their finest armor, coats, and boots. These two veterans of the Italian campaign had bled many times at the side of their long-dead champion, William, and had continued that tradition with William's son on the grinding campaign through Spain.

As one, they bent their knees and bowed their heads before the king.

"My dear Franks," Charles called over the assembled men, his voice clarion and clear. "We've all suffered loss in this important endeavor. But by the grace of God, I am your king. And I must put aside my own feelings to do my duty, as must all of you." He then spoke to Basan and Basile. "My lords, I hereby give you authority to speak in my name."

Naimon handed him the tokens. He presented Basan the staff and one glove and then gave the other glove to Basile.

"Thank you, sire," the men replied in unison.

"If the emir negotiates," Charles said, "then we end the siege. Dear God, I pray for your success."

"We shall not fail you," said Basan, his voice even and confident.

Charles rested a hand on his shoulder. "May Saint Michael grant you both a safe return."

The men rose, turned, and strode through the Franks to their saddled horses at the edge of the crowd. They mounted and, with a wave to their comrades, rode toward Saragossa.

Oliver and Roland walked through the camp as men continued the work of the siege, but already the talk had turned to Francia and the Saxons.

"Now isn't the time to pull back," Roland confided to Oliver. "Marsilion gains even though he's beaten!"

His friend smiled, eyes keen, for he too noticed the men's shifting attentions. "And yet friends and family are open to attack if Rene can't pull his forces together to halt the Saxon advance."

"True," Roland admitted. "But we've laid men to rest, warriors all, to reach these walls." He looked across the fields and suburbs at the city's imposing fortifications. "If we leave, their sacrifice was for naught."

"But," Oliver replied, "all that we have saved from Marsilion is now open to the Saxons for the taking."

A look of consternation crossed the champion's face.

"Oh, don't get me wrong," Oliver continued. "There can be no perfect solution. And you're correct—Marsilion will look at us suing for peace as a sign of weakness."

Battered and abused martial gear lay strewn all about the champion's tent—coats of mail, helmets, daggers, and chipped shields bearing the crimson wolf. A squire tried to sort through the collection while Roland examined each piece with a careful eye, discarding equipment beyond repair and oiling and packing the salvage into travel chests. He paused at his helmet, which still bore angry blue marks from the Greek fire at Carcassonne. He buffed on it once more with his sleeve, though it would do little good, as the blemish was burned into the steel. He tossed it back to the squire.

"Make sure there's a nice layer of oil on all this. Not too much, but if we are to head north, I'll not have my gear rusting."

The lad bowed and set to his task with a practiced purpose.

Roland stretched and left the tent. Outside, men rushed past him toward the edge of the camp.

"What's this?" He picked up his pace in their wake.

Atop a low hill overlooking the camp, Blancandrin orchestrated the proceedings atop a spirited steed wearing his most splendid armor. Seeing that he had the Franks' attention, he booted his horse into a stuttering trot toward them. Behind him, a detachment of soldiers dragged two men up the crest of the hill from the Saragossan side— Basan and Basile.

"Franks, hear me!" he shouted, his steed fidgety beneath him and straining at the rein. "I bear the words of Marsilion, emir of Saragossa! You have invaded our country, have put our brave sons to the sword, and have defiled our cities! For your crimes, these men will die!"

Charles's counts were forced to their knees.

At the edge of the camp, Roland clenched his fists. "My horse!" he ordered. "Hurry!"

Two tall Saragossan swordsmen stood behind the prostrate Frank nobles and drew curved blades that flashed savagely in the unrelenting glare of the sun. The steel blades blurred, and both men's heads fell from their shoulders, their bodies crumpling to the dusty ground like unstrung puppets.

Without another word, Blancandrin turned his steed toward the city. The Saragossan soldiers fell in behind him, leaving the dead where they lay.

Veillantif arrived, dragging the squires that held his reins, surrounded by Oliver, Otun, and a contingent of marchmen. Roland sprang into the saddle and pounded over the distance to the hill without waiting for the others.

He slid down to the ground at the blood-soaked scene and knelt next to the bodies, reverently touching each corpse's stilled chest with his fingers. He pulled his fingers away, sticky with gore.

"We will avenge you, my brothers," he vowed. "Blood will answer for blood."

CHAPTER 24

WHISPERERS

Multicolored birds from Africa and far-off Asia warbled in the carefully tended trees, flitting and fluttering about on clipped wings. Beneath their antics, women in veils and filmy silks chattered merrily. For all appearances, they were oblivious to the peril that amassed beyond Saragossa's walls—yet when left to themselves, their talk was infused with the latest news, rumors, and conjecture that was rampant within the elegant confines of Marsilion's private quarters and court.

Conversations died away when they caught sight of the emir hurrying past. His face was resolutely impassive. On his arm was the tall and fair Bramimunde, daughter of Visigoth kings who had once ruled the whole of Iberia—barbarians who had wrested it from the Romans only to fall to invading armies from North Africa. On his opposite hand, Blancandrin walked with head bowed, quietly relaying the latest intelligence on Frank activities. Behind them scurried Ja'qub, his slippered feet but a whisper on the tiles, robe fluttering about his scarecrow frame. Honorius, immaculate as always, rounded out the group—his Eastern lamellar armor exotic even in Marsilion's resplendent court.

Across the garden, the palace gates groaned open to admit a single horseman atop a heaving steed. The beast clattered into the garden sanctuary, causing a rippled hush through Marsilion's entourage. The messenger, covered in road dust from head to toe, slid from the saddle and fell to his belly before the emir.

Marsilion gestured with measured restraint for the man to rise.

"My lord," the messenger stammered breathlessly. "I bear word from the caliph! Emir, pirates have sacked Cadiz! He cannot send relief and advises you to negotiate peace with the Franks."

"What?" Marsilion snarled. The thin stoic veneer over his features melted away. "Is that all?"

The rider nervously bowed his head. "My lord, the caliph prays for your success."

Color rose in Marsilion's cheeks, beard bristling with boiling anger. "He prays for me?" He thrust his hands into the air and shouted, "While the Franks tear the city down about my ears? He prays for me as I administer justice to Frank envoys for crimes against my people? I need more than prayers!" He lashed out a foot at the messenger, who dodged deftly.

Bramimunde stroked his cheek with long, soft fingers.

"Don't negotiate with the Franks," she purred. "They cannot be trusted. They'll send their champion to burn us out like rats. Remember Carcassonne."

Marsilion pressed her fingers to his cheek. "What can I do? I can't break the noose strangling the city!"

Blancandrin lowered his eyes deferentially and cleared his throat.

"My lord, there is a way," he offered. "Take back the initiative by offering an olive branch of peace. If the offer alone isn't enough, clean out the treasury to pay Charles off. After prolonged sieges and loss of men, do what it takes to convince him it's time for the Franks to return to their homes. Surely he'll see the wisdom in your entreaty."

Honorius shook his head, offering Blancandrin a cloying smile. "Do you believe that is wise, gracious emir? The Franks are a vicious and unpredictable people."

Marsilion ignored the ambassador. "Continue," he said to Blancandrin.

Honorius bowed his head, wearing well his diplomatic mask, for no emotion showed at the rebuke.

Blancandrin went on, "My emir, tell Charles that once peace is concluded, you'll follow his armies to Aachen, and there swear fealty to him. If he desires hostages to secure the agreement, give them. Make him believe there's no more need for bloodshed."

Honorius's words were smooth as a garden serpent's. "You know it will not be enough. There's been too much blood on both sides. He'll demand a pound of flesh as well as coin."

"It will be enough!" Blancandrin shot back. His hands balled into fists at his side. "And if needs be, I'll offer up my own son as part of the price. It would be better to have hostages carted away to Francia and there lose their lives than to have Saragossa ripped from us. Without this city, we would be reduced to nothing more than beggars in our own land! If you do this, Emir, they'll go home. Their army will melt away to harvest crops and herd flocks before the first snow flies in the north."

A stern look and wave of the emir's hand stifled a retort on the ambassador's lips.

"Go on," Marsilion said. "There is more, yes? We don't just swear loyalty to these—these—brigands for nothing!"

Blancandrin bowed humbly, feeling the sting of Honorius's eyes upon him like so many biting ants. "At Michaelmas, as all know, Charles holds a great holiday celebration—days of drunken feasting. We'll be expected to arrive and in dramatic theater swear fealty to him before his assembled people. But we will not. We will remain here. For that, he will indeed have our hostages killed, and he will rage with anger at the heavens—but let him rage, I say! He won't dare come back here, knowing that we've prepared to hurl his armies into the pit!"

Marsilion grimaced but nodded thoughtfully. "Yes. Yes, we will let him rage."

A Θ I

The Tournai men continued to expand their earthen fortifications behind their screens while roving bands of Saragossan horsemen darted close to the lines and launched arrows at them, only to scatter before Frank cavalry could gallop in pursuit. Loads of dirt rose into earthen works, behind which men and equipment could move more freely to continue extending the fortifications around the city in a strangling noose. Amid that backbreaking work, Julian snatched up a water bucket then slipped away into the constantly moving mass of men. Once out of sight of the Tournai men, he hurried toward the finer accommodations in the center of the camp.

In a nearby pavilion, Guinemer directed a farrier tapping out a dent from a helmet. When he straightened to wipe sweat from his eyes, he also caught a glimpse of the youth moving through the crowds. His shaggy eyebrows furrowed together when Julian reached a gap in the traffic and cut a beeline toward Demetrius's tent.

Guinemer stepped out of the canvas shelter, covering his eyes with a hand against the sunlight, and watched the youth disappear inside.

Guards, who just a moment before sagged against their long spears, snapped to attention when Roland approached the sentry position. The champion acknowledged them then stepped across the defensive trench to stand alongside them and watch the horsemen kicking up dust from Saragossa. Blancandrin rode his familiar black steed, his long lance topped by a white flag tight in his grip. Behind him straggled an awkward party of timid, robed men that put Roland in mind of their own priests. A Frank outrider circled the plodding procession and then pounded across the parched ground to where he stopped before the champion.

"My lord, they've no weapons," he reported.

Blancandrin placed a hand over his heart then bowed slightly from the saddle.

"I bear greetings from the emir!" he called out. "He wishes to discuss peace with the Frank nation!"

"Peace is a convenient word, is it not?" Roland asked. He pointed to the white cloth on Blancandrin's lance. "You've killed our own under sign of truce. That also was a discussion of peace."

A thin-lipped grin touched Blancandrin's face.

"Blood has satisfied blood. Today is a new day, and perhaps further shedding of blood can be avoided."

"A new day, indeed." Roland slapped the shoulder of the sergeant standing at his elbow. "So what say you?" he asked the man. "A change of heart?"

A gap-toothed grin broke the sergeant's pockmarked face. He looked the Saragossans over with a critical eye, and his response was quick. "I wouldn't trust them, my lord."

"Agreed, I fear. But we must show decorum. We wouldn't want our guests to think us barbarians." He gestured for the guards to take positions surrounding the newcomers. Then he walked to the head of the party and led them toward the center of the camp.

Through the gawking Frank soldiers clustered along the way, Blancandrin rode bolt upright, his eyes unwavering in their focus on the large, multicolored canopy surrounded by fluttering eagle pennants and a cordon of stalwart Frank sergeants. At a respectful distance from the tent, the group stopped. Guards stationed there pulled back the enormous canvas flaps. A heartbeat later, Charles emerged, followed by Naimon and several other notables of the Frank court.

Blancandrin dismounted, handing off his lance to a scholar who fumbled it but at least kept it from landing in the dirt. The general took a few steps toward Charles before dropping to the ground to prostrate himself in the dust.

Charles folded his arms, a stern look upon his face. "A knee is all that's required here."

A low chuckle rippled through the assembled ranks. A curt look from the king silenced them.

The remainder of the Saragossans dismounted and, following their general's example, dropped to their knees.

Charles gestured for them to rise.

As protocol demanded, Naimon stepped forward.

"Speak your business," he commanded.

Blancandrin rose, reassuming the commanding air that he carried before the armies of the emir.

"Great king of the Franks and Romans! I bring you the greetings of all Saragossa and the words of Marsilion, its emir," he said in a crisp voice that rose through the ranks surrounding the audience. "Our scholars have studied the laws of the Franks regarding war and peace.

The emir graciously offers to satisfy them. Noble King, he shall pay you generously—enough to provide bonuses to your entire army. Then, during your holy days, my master swears to travel to Aachen where he will pledge you his service. All this he will do if you leave our lands in peace and return to your home beyond the mountains."

The nobles surrounding Charles broke out in surprised chatter. Yet the king remained silent, examining the general's face for a few heartbeats. "You are well spoken," he finally said. "But the emir is my enemy. He has shed the blood of my people and my own family. Why should I believe him now?"

Blancandrin bowed once more, his voice low and direct. "My master Marsilion has also lost family to this war. He desires nothing more than its end and peace between our peoples—so that generations of our nations live free from the shadow of war. To prove his words, he offers hostages as a guarantee of peace. Know this, great king, my own son will be among them."

"And I'm to value your son more than my own daughter?" Bitterness clipped Charles's words. "Naimon, have the men pitch a tent for our guests. Bring them food and drink. They will wait for my decision."

The champion's sun-bleached tent stood near the king's grand pavilion, the canvas sagging under the intense midday heat. Two of the walls were rolled up to take advantage of the barest breeze. Undaunted, Roland and Oliver stood within the scant shade, where they reviewed troop deployments and searched hastily sketched maps for holes in the enemy defenses.

Demetrius ducked under the canvas roof to hand Oliver a vellum document covered in miniscule script. Oliver began matching up the new intelligence with other documents.

Demetrius pulled up a chair and rubbed at his eyes.

"So what have you learned, my friend?" Roland asked.

"Of Ganelon? Not much, I'm afraid," the Greek replied with a frown. "He takes counsel with Alans, but our man cannot get close enough to gather details."

Roland leaned forward on his stool, an earnest set to his own features. "He must. I need proof, damn it!"

Oliver put the documents down.

"Ganelon is a wily one," he observed. "He's survived many years at court by distancing himself from controversy and leaving no loose ends scattered about. It is not a simple thing you ask."

"That's why it takes time to get close," Demetrius added. "It's a matter of trust."

Roland kicked at the stack of documents at his feet, scattering them in a flurry.

"Time is a luxury we don't have! We must get proof and finish this before the Tournai men get back over the mountains—back to Francia and those who sympathize with him!"

"Be assured," Demetrius said. "If a snake hides beneath the rock, we'll find it."

Squires scurried through the crowded conclave of nobles waiting outside the king's tent. Turpin, his tonsured head rosy beneath the morning sun, found Roland haggling with two northern counts, urging them to speak up and support his position. The men listened courteously, but Turpin could see in their eyes that they wanted no more of this war. Both men excused themselves when Charles stepped from the tent and into the sunlight with Louis at his side, dressed in their gold-trimmed royal finery. Turpin gave Roland an encouraging nod. The lobbying had worn down even the count of the Breton March's boundless energy. Regardless, Roland took his place on Charles's right hand, and Turpin muttered a prayer that the Lord would sort out the right of things and bless the Franks whatever the decision.

"My lords," Charles began, clearing his throat. "Marsilion offers us tribute and fealty in exchange for peace between our two nations. This is a weighty decision, my brothers. I ask you, do we accept?"

Bickering bubbled up as the counts jostled one another with opinions—never in short supply among an assemblage of Franks. Roland raised his voice to be heard above the cacophony.

"My king, we sent two of our finest to negotiate peace, and the emir brazenly violated a flag of truce. I say take Saragossa! End this war once and for all. Then we march to Francia and drive the Saxons into the sea!"

Many murmured in agreement with their champion. Ganelon gauged the response and then raised his hand for the floor. Silence took a few moments to take hold.

"Charles, great king," he began, irony in his voice. "Believe a fool—me or any other fool—and mark my word, we'll all pay dearly. Marsilion sues for peace! I wager he recognizes the wrong he has done to you, my lord. Thus he has offered up his coffers." He sauntered close, until he stood at Roland's elbow. "Anyone who opposes this offer doesn't really care for the lives of his comrades, either here or in Saxony." He did not look at his stepson. "I urge you to seek counsel with wise men that we might see beyond the clouds of passion and explore the offer based on its merits."

The council fractured, some cackling in agreement with the count of Tournai. But Ganelon's eyes never left Charles's, even when Naimon spoke.

"Count Ganelon's right on this, my king," the wizened counselor interjected, tugging uncomfortably at his beard with gnarled fingers. "Marsilion is effectively caged within Saragossa. If we continue this campaign against a beaten man, then we bear the burden of a greater sin."

Charles nodded tentatively in agreement.

"If we do this, then who do we send to negotiate on our behalf?" he asked.

"Of course, I will go," replied Naimon, straightening as best he could.

The king placed a hand on his old companion's bent shoulder. "No, old friend, remain at my side," he said. "I will have need of your wisdom before this is through."

Roland stepped before the king and bowed his head.

"I'll go, sire," he offered.

Oliver jostled to the fore, placing a hand over his heart.

"No, my king. Send me!"

Charles raised both hands. "This task requires tremendous

diplomacy." His eyes narrowed as they roved over the assembly. "Both of you are veterans of the battlefield—my best warriors. But you aren't seasoned for this task. My knights, choose someone to speak for me."

"Since you seek a man versed in peace, Uncle," Roland said, "why not send my stepfather? Marsilion will find great delight in his eloquence."

A ripple of agreement rustled through the nobles though Ganelon's face darkened and his eyebrows wrinkled together. He leaned over to Roland, his voice a dangerous whisper. "You had no right to name me."

"The king needs you," Roland breathed back. "If he commanded me, I'd take your place and spare you the danger of losing your head."

"Yes, it will be Ganelon," Charles commanded, either oblivious to the exchange or ignoring it.

Ganelon put on a fervent expression and spoke up for all to hear.

"Because Charles commands it, I shall do my duty!" A cheer rose from his supporters among the crowd.

"Very well," the king replied. "Ganelon, count of Tournai, we thank you for carrying our words to Saragossa. Come forward—receive the staff and glove."

Naimon passed the tokens, a matched set of those lost with Basile and Basan, into Charles's hands. Ganelon stepped forward and offered a precise bow, then took the glove from Charles's hand. The token slipped from his fingers and slapped on the ground.

The nobility gave a collective gasp.

Ignoring them, Ganelon scooped up the glove and straightened himself, gathering his dignity.

"Sire, since this matter requires urgency, I beg your leave."

Charles handed him the staff and a letter bearing the royal seal.

"Of course, dear count." He clasped a hand to Ganelon's shoulder. "God go with you and bring you success."

Ganelon bowed stiffly and then spun on his heel, striding through the parting sea of Frank lords without looking at them.

Turpin watched him go. To no one but himself he murmured, "God as my witness, nothing good will come of this."

Amid the tents of the Tournai men, a squire held the ornate bridle of a warhorse as Guinemer held the stirrup for Ganelon to mount. His retainers and common levies assembled to watch their master follow the footsteps of the first doomed envoys to the Saragossan court. Julian jostled among them for a better position where he could watch Ganelon more closely.

"God ride with you," Guinemer said.

Ganelon wrapped his hand in the reins then leaned down to his uncle's scarred face and spoke in a low voice.

"Uncle, ours is a mighty line," he whispered. "I swear it will not end here. I removed William. I will remove his king. The throne will be mine!"

He slipped Charles's letter into Guinemer's hand.

"Burn this."

His spurs bit the steed's hide, and it launched through the knot of Tournai men, who lifted their voices in bold cheers. With a slap of the reins, he continued on toward Blancandrin and the waiting Saragossan envoys. Julian watched until the commotion gave him cover to disengage from Ganelon's troops. Then he silently lost himself among the war host.

But as Guinemer tucked the king's letter into his sleeve, he spied the youth slinking into the throngs. The wily older man set his sights on Julian's back and fell into step a good distance behind.

Ganelon rode through the camp sharply cognizant of the thousands of eyes that followed him. Undoubtedly, he mused, many were wondering if this would prove his final ride. But the count of Tournai had weightier things on his mind, for seeds must be sown early if they are to bear fruit in season. Across the bustling camp, Breton marchmen drilled in a veil of dust. The wolf banner rippled and snapped defiantly. These were the very men who must be crushed to bring down the Crown—men who would rather die fighting for their usurping king than accept a legitimate heir with his bloodied hands clenched to the gilded arms of the throne. Ganelon chortled. He would crack them apart and break them down just like their own Germanic ancestors had broken the Romans.

At the edge of camp, Blancandrin and his company waited to escort him to the court of Saragossa.

Yes, the very instruments were near at hand to implement the plan formulating in his head.

Roland watched the horsemen depart from his position amid the marchmen's battle formation.

"Do you think it's to be peace then?" Oliver asked, huffing from the exertion.

Roland hefted Durendal in his hand, straightening his shield to cover the man on his left.

"What I think doesn't matter," he replied with a wan smile. "Marsilion may have been crushed on the battlefield. But he's achieved much more than a martial victory. He's destroyed Charles's spirit."

A Dane warrior jostled into Otun, and he roared in frustration.

"All right, lads!" Roland called out. "Let's work together!"

Otun grumbled with a mighty flexing of his arms. The other Danes laughed, but all once again fell into step, and the Breton March moved as a single unit—the tip of the Frank spear.

As they passed the last Frank sergeants at the outlying pickets, Ganelon rode next to Blancandrin. The Saracen general appeared much relieved by the growing distance between himself and the enemy. And yet there was something more in his tone of voice when he turned to the count of Tournai. "You know, your Charles is a mighty king. He leads powerful war hosts and has humbled many mighty nations. Peace will be a welcome season in this land."

"I suppose you're right," Ganelon replied, meeting the general's eyes. "But you should think on this—Roland, his nephew and champion, has far greater ambitions than even the king."

"Greater ambitions? What do you mean?"

"I have a tale to share, one not widely spoken of outside the circle of intimates surrounding the king and his family," Ganelon began. He glanced about conspiratorially to ensure no one else could hear his words. "Not many weeks ago, Charles sat beneath a tree to escape the miserable heat. Roland came to him, fresh from plundering near Carcassonne, his horse still covered in dirt and sweat. In his hand, he held the dripping head of the local sheikh. This he offered to Charles as a gift, saying, 'Dear uncle, take this—for it is the first of all the kingdoms of the earth with their thrones and riches, which I will seize for you.'"

"Surely you're joking," Blancandrin replied. "No man could be so consumed with bloodlust."

Ganelon smiled, a friendly but not altogether pleasing expression. "You've seen him in battle? You've seen him before the walls of a besieged city?"

"Of course," the general said. "He's a dangerous foe. I've played chess with him on the field and faced the edge of his blade in combat."

Ganelon tapped the side of his nose with his finger. "Then you have your answer. To achieve his ends, he would drench the earth in blood and cover what remains in ash."

Blancandrin swallowed hard. He remained silent while the company approached Saragossa's walls.

A Θ I

Marsilion fidgeted uncomfortably on his thick-cushioned throne while his court assembled around him in the expansive chamber. He flashed a painted-on smile at Honorius and Ja'qub when they took their accustomed places. Oh, how he hated these conclaves for their incessant chattering and second-guessing of his decisions—never mind that bringing his unruly nobles together bred sedition, if for no other reason than it was easier to speak against one's lord when surrounded by others who might do the same. And now this proud scion of desert lions faced not just his nobles but also an envoy from the Frank nation—the messenger from a proud and vengeful monarch. How he wished for a chilled drink, but then blaring trumpets announced Blancandrin's arrival. Palace guards threw open the great double doors and admitted the general with cluster of troopers flanking the solitary Frank. He was an older man who walked tall and straight, eyes boring straight ahead at the emir. Marsilion wrinkled his nose at the anticipated stench of this barbarian whose Frank finery was nothing more than rags and rusty bits compared to the Saragossan splendor arrayed about the chamber.

Blancandrin prostrated himself before his master. Marsilion waved for him to rise, but his eyes narrowed when he noted the Frank had failed to follow suit. Instead the man had only bowed slightly, a gesture that barely bordered on propriety. Guards' hands twitched on their spears, the men awaiting an angry outburst from the emir.

Blancandrin climbed to his feet then hurried to the throne.

"My lord, I delivered your petition to Charles. Praise Allah, the Frank king has sent this emissary to us!" He extended a hand to Ganelon. "May I present Ganelon, count of Tournai and brother-in-law to King Charles of the Franks."

Marsilion explored Ganelon's face through slitted eyes, his hand tugging at the end of his close-cropped beard. He nodded slightly, for this was an appropriate emissary to be sure—kin to the king. "Speak," he commanded. "We will hear you."

Ganelon stood planted where he had halted, his thumbs hooked in his broad leather belt and an arrogant grin on his face. "Emir, I bring to you the word of Charles, king of the Franks and Lombards, colleague to the emperor in the East, and servant of God." His words were stiff and formal, each syllable well rehearsed. "Before God and this court, I present terms satisfactory to the king. First, Charles requires you to be baptized, accepting the waters within the space of a day. Second, once you step on dry land, he shall return half your possessions. Third, you will swear fealty to him without condition. If you reject these terms, Saragossa will be destroyed."

Marsilion reeled in his chair. "Infidel!" he roared, his face throbbing deep red. "I shall never! Do you hear me? As Allah is my witness, I shall never accept those terms!" He vaulted from the throne and wrenched a spear from the nearest guard's hand. The emir rushed down the steps, the wicked point aimed straight for the Frank's gut.

The collective breath of all the spectators in the chamber stopped.

Blancandrin intervened, grabbing the haft and bringing Marsilion to a halt.

"Release me, mutinous cur!" the emir snarled, his words dripping with threats.

"Please, my lord," Blancandrin said, his voice low and even. "Listen to this man. Upon my honor, he, of all the Franks, means you no ill will."

"All the pain I've suffered, and yet you come to me with these harsh words?"

Marsilion spat at Ganelon's feet.

Ganelon raised his hands. "I am but the messenger. I swear to you the words are not my own."

"Please, Emir," Blancandrin said in a soothing tone. "Don't allow anger to cloud your judgment. Listen to him. Listen to what *he* has to say."

Marsilion stared at the Frank with loathing. Around him, he could fairly feel the stares of his vassals, ever watching with calculating eyes, trying to mark any weakness that could be exploited later. Then he looked beyond Ganelon to the windows and the smoke beyond them perpetually wafting over the city these last many days. He thrust the spear into Blancandrin's hands.

"Proceed," he growled, though his face remained darkened.

Ganelon bowed deeply, offering the emir a much more polite gesture than when he had entered.

"Emir, know also that the other half of your possessions will be given to Roland, the king's champion. If you reject these terms, Charles will order him to march on Saragossa and tear down her walls about your ears. Once the city is subdued, you'll be chained like an animal and dragged to Aachen where you'll be put to death in the cathedral square."

Marsilion charged the knight again, hands raised to claw at Ganelon's eyes. Ganelon raised his own hands in defense, but Blancandrin restrained the emir once more.

"Get out!" Marsilion wailed. "Get out before I have you torn apart and fed to the dogs! My own son got no better from you Franks!"

Ganelon cautiously lowered his hands.

"Emir, you are not the only father to lose a son to this needless war."

Marsilion sputtered while Ganelon's words sank in.

"You?" The emir then hissed, breathlessly sucking in air, straining against Blancandrin's iron grip. "Your son is dead as well?"

"Yes, in Saxony." He glanced at Honorius and then lowered his voice. "Abandoned on the frontier by his king."

"Tell me then," he said, taking Ganelon's cue and dropping his voice to a whisper, "what will entice Charles to give up this war and leave in peace?"

Ganelon leaned toward Marsilion. "With Roland as his champion and standing as his shield, Charles fears no man, not even the emperor in the East."

Honorius's eyes shot poisonous darts while he strained closer to hear their conversation.

Ganelon forged ahead. "This war will not—no, *cannot* end so long as Roland lives."

"But the caliph, our allies in Africa—with more troops, we can prevail," Marsilion said defiantly.

Ganelon shrugged. "Troops alone are not the answer. Do not forget, Emir, the walls of Carcassonne." Ganelon glanced again at Honorius, who had abandoned all decorum and stepped closer to them. He took the emir's elbow and bent close to his ear. "I have an idea. Listen quickly—with Roland gone, Charles and his usurping brood will be vulnerable, and I am the nearest heir to the true blood. Surely men such as ourselves could come to an accommodation."

A toothy grin broke across Marsilion's face, the fine seams around his eyes deepening with delight. He clasped the Frank on the back and waved his hands to the skies.

"I like this man!" he exclaimed. "Yes, we must talk, envoy of the Franks. Wine and food—bring us wine and food!"

CHAPTER 25

GANELON TRIUMPHANT

A dust cloud rose outside the city walls. Within its obscuring veil, a large party paraded from the suburbs of Saragossa toward the Frank pickets that strangled access to the roads. Scouts dispatched hurried messengers to the king when they spied Ganelon atop his sturdy warhorse at the head of the chaotic lot—a parade of mules, camels, warhorses, and struggling servants bearing heavy chests. Following them rumbled horse-drawn carriages loaded with other exotic treasures. The count of Tournai grinned at his countrymen's dumbfounded faces and, in faux annoyance, waved on the menagerie to keep up the pace. Rank-and-file soldiers scrambled out of the way, their eyes wide at the treasures spewing forth from Saragossa—at the flutter of colorful birds in cages, the mewling growl of a thick-maned lion that paced nervously in its cage, and many more wondrous sights.

Before the canvas chapel in the camp center, Ganelon signaled for his many charges to form a circle about the worshipers. He nodded to friends and winked at rivals with an air of showmanship. The triumph of Ganelon, envoy for the great king of the Franks, unfolded before both those who loved him and those who loathed him—he who had kept his head atop his shoulders yet again when others had failed.

"Charles, my king! May the Lord God save you!" he called when the king stepped out from the chapel with Turpin, Roland, and Naimon. "What a glorious day this is! Behold, my king, the riches of Saragossa laid before you!"

He waved to four tall Saragossan warriors, who advanced from the throng with a large chest slung on sagging poles. They set it heavily on the ground before Charles. One of them—a captain by the look of his polished chain mail and the colorful plumes rising from his helm—threw open the lid, spilling gold coins to the collective hush of the crowding nobles and soldiers. "Look for yourselves," Ganelon crowed. "The purest byzants from Constantinople! And many more silks and riches Saragossa offers to you!"

Naimon caught a glimpse of a group of frightened children, many in resplendent clothes, huddling together in fear from the battle-hardened Franks. "And these?" he asked, pointing to them.

"These?" Ganelon answered with a flourish. "Why, these are presents from the noblest of Saragossa's families! Hostages meant to guarantee the peace between our two peoples. Guard them well, sire. Guard them well!"

Charles allowed a hint of a smile to touch his lips, but Roland remained stoic.

"What are the terms, Count Ganelon?" Charles called.

Ganelon bowed respectfully in his saddle. "Marsilion has sworn to follow you to Aachen, where he has promised to swear fealty to you."

"God be praised," Charles shouted. "It is done. It is done!"

Ganelon slipped from his steed and strode to the king. He took a knee and bowed his head. "An honor to be your voice, sire."

Roland organized the last of his gear for stowage. All around him, squires and pages wiped equipment down with oiled cloths, leaving what gleam they could on the battered helmets, spears, and coats of scale mail. Roland looked up from his task when a squad of men approached carrying crowbars to pry up tent stakes.

Oliver threw open the canvas flaps.

"Your grand home-away-from-home is next to fall," his friend announced.

"Don't strike my colors yet. I want it to be the last thing they see retreat from the city wall."

Oliver laughed. "Well, that's more benevolent than sowing their bloody fields with salt, I suppose."

Roland flopped on his cot, snatched up Durendal, and drew it free of its battle-worn scabbard. He set to work on the brilliant steel blade with oil and stone, his keen eyes looking for even the slightest imperfection.

"I just never imagined we would fight to the brink of victory only to withdraw with the enemy laughing at our backs. Surely they'll be sharpening their claws for the next opportunity to set upon us."

"Maybe," Oliver said. "But the treasure the emir sent? Surely they must be paupers one and all within the walls."

"Ill-gotten gain his horde plundered from other cities before we intervened," Roland snarled. "I saw many pieces that surely came from Carcassonne." He looked down the bevel of the blade, slowly turning the sword so he could examine each angle. "Their assassins struck at the king's heart, and all the coin in the world means nothing compared to the loss of his daughter. Mark my words—good men will yet die before Marsilion is leashed. I feel it in my bones."

"Your bones have trooped too long at the head of the Frank nation," Oliver said. "All that jarring over rutted roads and wilderness tracks."

"Maybe so," Roland replied. But the look on his face should have told Oliver he was having none of the excuses that men were already weaving for exiting the field with the enemy behind them, intact and armed.

In time the Frank army set out northward, a great iron-and-steel serpent winding along the dusty roads bound for the mountains and pass that would lead them to the lush fields of home that lay beyond those towering peaks. Sergeants shouted commands to keep troops in ordered units within the tromping flow. Villagers and shepherds from miles around came to see the proud banners of King Charles and his brave bandons of knights. At the head of the martial spectacle, the royal eagle pennants of Charles's house rippled proudly, flanked by the wolf of Breton March on the right and the stag of Vale Runer on the left. The great houses of the Frank knights followed next atop thick, solid horses, clad in their finest armor to celebrate their triumphant return home. One and all looked north to Francia and prepared to face the resurgent Saxons who threatened their homes and loved ones. Lesser Frank infantry tromped just behind the Tournai knights, followed by miles of supply wagons.

Ganelon rode near his uncle, surrounded by Tournai men proudly marching under the white lily in their blue surcoats. Though he chose not to ride in the king's intimate company, he nevertheless could feel the full confidence of the nation.

"Say farewell to this godforsaken land," Guinemer crowed. "All this dirt and not a skin of wine to be found."

Ganelon wiped his cracked lips with the back of his hand. "Time enough for drinking upon our return, Uncle. We must remain vigilant. Opportunity is near at hand. On the other side of the mountains, the army will be strung out, and Charles will be deprived of his precious shield."

A wolfish grin stretched across Guinemer's lean, seamed face.

"God save the king," he snarled.

That evening the Franks encamped across a ridge in the foothills near Roncevaux pass, much as they had the night they had entered Spain. Campfires sprang up on the slopes, sprinkled points of light that chased back the night's chill. A merry spirit infected the Franks, celebrating one final time with the men from Barcelona. The conflict had begun with them as cautious allies, but now at the withdrawal from Spain, these Franks and Saracens found themselves to be blooded brothers in the struggle against a common foe. Germanic and Arabic voices mingled around many of the campfires in a dissonant melody of hard-fighting men who would recall this moment to their children and grandchildren for generations to come.

With the passing of the night, the fires burned to glowing embers, and the conversations faded. Karim gathered his men with Roland and his command at the edge of the camp, exchanging farewells, clasping hands and embracing one final time. Roland drew forth a dagger from his belt, a battle-worn length of steel that had accompanied him through every hard-fought step of the campaign. He pressed it into Karim's hands.

"Farewell, my friend," he said.

Karim examined the weapon then slipped it into his belt. He unclasped the curved saber at his side, a blade forged in distant Damascus that had carved a bloodied path to the west with Karim's forebears, and turned it over into Roland's fingers. It was a workman's weapon, and it had served the son of Sulayman well.

"It is not good-bye, my infidel brother," Karim replied. "Rather may the days be kind until we meet again."

Roland laughed. "Aye, that is a good way to part."

Karim mounted his sturdy desert steed, and his men did likewise. Roland watched them wheel about and melt into the shadows, their horses' hooves pounding into the night.

Movement caught at the corner of his eye. He turned and found Saleem standing beside him, also watching his countrymen leave.

"You aren't going with them?" Roland asked.

Saleem shook his head. "My path does not lie with theirs."

"So will you be coming with us?"

"No," Saleem replied.

"Then where are you bound?"

Saleem shrugged. "Who knows? Maybe I will set aside the world and make the pilgrimage to the homeland of my fathers in far-off Arabia."

"You are welcome among us," Roland reassured him.

"I thank you for the offer." He wrinkled his nose. "But your ways are not for me either." Saleem turned away into the darkness. "Farewell, champion of the Franks!" he called over his shoulder.

Roland stood alone staring into the darkness.

While the men caroused, Charles retired to his bed and an unsettled slumber. The king tossed and turned beneath the canvas tent. Though rest seldom came easily to the monarch, this night it stole upon him, spiriting him away atop a spectacular warhorse in a perpetual twilight. Across exotic battlefields he rode, the armies of his enemies falling before him in a bloody reaping. In his fist he gripped a long lance topped with a familiar rippling eagle pennant.

From mists drifting over a particularly ruinous salient, a lone rider charged him. As he closed, Charles could make out the lily of

Tournai emblazoned on his shield, Ganelon bearing down on him with a murderous force. Horses and riders collided, and the impact staggered Charles's doughty steed. Ganelon tore the lance from his hand, shattering it and sending splinters flying heavenward.

And then, as dreams oft will do, this vision whispered away as so much drifting smoke, and he was elsewhere.

The altar at Aachen rose before the supplicant king, who knelt with hands pressed together before him, whispering his prayers. Smoldering candles illuminated the vision of Christ hanging from the tree above. Something crashed across the long nave at the door of the cathedral. The deep, thundering boom echoed through the edifice, followed in quick succession by another and then another.

The hinges of the great portal shattered, and through it burst a gigantic wild boar. The beast's nostrils flared with a snort, and its small red eyes scanned the interior. Charles rose slowly, searching for a weapon. He grabbed a candelabrum and swung it, spilling wax to the floor. The boar shook its bristly mane and charged. Charles waved the guttering candles, but the beast was undeterred. Its massive muscles bunched, and it sprung at the king. A tusk slashed through Charles's sleeve, slicing skin and drawing blood.

Suddenly on his left, a deep, purring growl erupted into a blur of yellow and black and a leopard sprang from the shadows. Charles swept the candelabrum back, landing a glancing blow on the cat. But his desperate defense was not enough for both beasts, and they drove him back against the altar.

A wild howl caused the beasts to whirl in their tracks. A large, shaggy hound bounded through the broken doors and raced up the nave, leaping with slavering jaws into the fray. The other beasts attacked in a tumult of rending claws, teeth, and tusks. Then the hound found purchase on the boar's throat, bearing it to the ground. But the great feline raked the hound mercilessly with razor claws and spattered Charles in blood.

The hound's jaws remained clamped tightly onto the thrashing boar's throat in spite of the leopard's onslaught. It struggled valiantly, but the feral beasts bore the newcomer to the floor in a sloshing pool of red. Charles struck with the candelabrum, hitting the two monsters over and over, but was unable to drive them from the hound that thrashed beneath them.

Finally the hound ceased its struggles, choking with a ragged breath. The king kept pounding on its assailants until the hound breathed its last and finally released the boar's throat.

His heartbeat throbbing in his ears, Charles startled awake, drenched in sweat—the dream had been so vivid he could still hear the howls of the hound ringing through his head. He slid his feet to the floor and ran his fingers through tangled hair, gasping to catch his breath. He picked up a rumpled robe, tugging it about his body. Placing his bare feet on the floor, he stood and walked to the flap of his tent, pushing the canvas open to the night air. He nodded distractedly at the guard outside. The camp had quieted and lay still amid the cold of the night.

Roncevaux lay in the darkness beyond, a great cavernous maw filled with shadows like the deep gloom of an empty cathedral.

An oil light flickered in Ganelon's tent, and beneath its glow the count reviewed a stack of vellum sheaves. Each thick page accounted for his requisitions in gear, food, and monies won during the campaign—all to be loaded and carted back to his holdings in Tournai. The expedition, while costly in blood, would bring wealth to many hedge knights who would have otherwise been forced to scratch out a life in the fields alongside their own peasants. Ganelon chortled at the thought of conveniently removing a few during the trek home to retain their portions. He paused, holding up the gold byzant Charles had given him for a memento of his mission to Marsilion. He flipped the coin deftly between his fingers. It was a fortune for the lowliest stable hand but merely a tasty morsel for the right nobles, particularly with a kingdom at stake.

A scuffle outside the tent stole his attention. A young man stumbled through the entrance, falling to the ground, his face swollen. Guinemer stepped in after him.

"Here's a little one I caught snooping around, nephew."

Ganelon examined the youth more closely. Through the raging red welts and bruises, Ganelon recognized him—a stalwart young man who had been among the first with the ladders at Carcassonne.

The youth looked up at the count of Tournai's dark features. "I was just going to my guard post, my lord."

"Guard post?" Ganelon replied flatly. "Either you're late for your shift, or you intend to report very early."

Guinemer kicked the lad in the kidney, crumpling him in pain.

"I've seen him talking to Demetrius, the Greek," he spat. "He's Roland's creature."

"Really? Your name—Julian, right?" Suddenly Ganelon reached out and grabbed the lad by his shirt, dragging him to his feet and pulling him close. "So you spy for Roland? You've eaten my food! Bled with my own flesh! What have you told your master?"

"You are my master," Julian said, planting his feet and trying to straighten. "You are the one I serve, my lord."

Ganelon released him. "You know, the Lord himself said you cannot serve two. It just doesn't work that way."

Metal flashed as Ganelon slipped a long, slim dagger from the scabbard at his belt. He thrust it into Julian's belly. The lad's eyes widened in shock, but his cry choked when Guinemer clamped a meaty hand over his mouth. Ganelon twisted the blade, leaning in close to Julian's ear.

"Tell your master—I've killed wolves before. And I will have the eagle as well." He clenched Julian's chin in his hand, wrenching the young man's eyes back to his own. "Be sure he hears that."

Ganelon jerked the dagger free and wiped it on Julian's shirt.

"Wrap the wound," he ordered Guinemer. "Secure him in the supplies for the rearguard. Be sure to hide him well. By the time they find him, it'll be too late."

Guinemer opened the tent flap to drag the youth away.

Ganelon tossed the dagger back into his gear and continued counting coins.

A cool breeze stirred from the nearby pass, providing relief from the heat that chased them from the Spanish plain. Through that crisp morning air, trumpets sang out, their precise notes signaling the army's order of assembly. Franks tumbled from their tents, struck camp, and formed up in units for transit orders through the pass. As the final troops hurried into formation, Charles appeared atop his bedecked warhorse. A squire held the spirited animal's bridle while the monarch surveyed the host before him with eyes haunted by dark circles. After the men sorted themselves into order, the nobles fell into their places of honor at the king's right and left hand. Then the trumpets ceased, and a hush dropped over the assembly.

Since the earliest days of warfare, soldiers from all walks of life have constituted armies. Peasants in ill-fitting quilted linen armed with hand-me-down weapons lined up next to ranks of regular infantry stiffened by mail-clad sergeants. Hedge knights in their homespun tabards and trousers with patina-darkened helmets rubbed shoulders with stalwart landed warriors upon serviceable steeds—the very backbone of the heavy cavalry that had broken Saragossa over and over. And finally, proud beneath their gold-and-crimson pennants, Charles's own guard, those eminent nobles who had marched with their king from Saxony to Rome and now Spain, resplendent in ermine and brightly dyed fabrics over burnished steel plates. Many of these men traced their family heritage through the centuries to barbarians who had first threatened Rome and had carved out their kingdoms from under the noses of her legendary iron legions.

And then there were the men of the Breton March, who stood rank upon rank in trim and ordered rows. Charles's eyes lingered on the familiar faces of their brave columns, heartrendingly thinned by the brutal campaign. Those same indomitable men had campaigned under Roland's father, William. Now their legacy stood in disciplined order beneath the banners of the champion, the rampant wolf that led every charge, bled in every skirmish, and refused to bend in the face of adversity. Yet those same ranks would never appear undermanned so long as one of them remained. Charles cleared his throat, knowing that his nephew pulled his mount up at his right elbow. Even if not in agreement with his king, Charles knew his champion stood ready to drive back the Saxons without hesitation.

"My lords and dear men of Francia!" Charles raised his voice to carry across the massed formation. "In preparation for our withdrawal, we must appoint someone to command the rearguard."

With that cue, Naimon urged his light mount forward to Charles's side, holding the staff and glove of royal authority. A ripple of voices began in the marchmen, as if the formation would step forward as one to volunteer even without a noble sponsor.

"My king!" said Ganelon. The count nudged his mount forward from among the nobles. "Please, sire, I beg your indulgence. This has been a long campaign. All of us are ready to cross the mountains and kiss the sweet soil of home. But we know choosing the rearguard is an important decision. Our enemies must see strength even as we move northward. And who better to do this than my stepson, Roland? He's been a loyal and dutiful general. Giving him the rearguard will remind our enemies that betrayal is pointless."

Charles's white brows knit together. "And who will lead the van?"

"Why not Alans!" Guinemer shouted from further down the line of nobles. "Surely, sire, he's earned a place of honor among your peers!"

Roland jostled Veillantif closer to Ganelon. "If I'm given the rearguard, I swear before God that Charles will not lose a single man, horse, or mule in the crossing!"

Ganelon grinned in reply. "His Majesty should expect nothing less! And neither would I of my son."

Roland rode forward, turning his steed to face Charles. "Uncle, give me the staff and glove. I gladly offer to take the charge."

"Come and receive them then," Charles said.

Roland dismounted and stood before the king's steed. Naimon handed off the tokens to Charles, who leaned down close to Roland as he passed them in turn to the younger man.

"Half the army is yours if you ask it," Charles whispered, barely masking the apprehension that gripped his chest.

"If I had need, I would ask," Roland replied with a smile, tucking the glove into his belt and gripping the staff in his clenched fist. "I'll keep a thousand in my bandons, sire. The strength of the march is enough to do the job."

Before Roland could lead his horse back into the line, Charles tugged the Oliphant from his saddlebow, the cool metal shimmering in the morning light.

"Wait," he said, barely audible.

Roland paused, for now the king dismounted to stand with his champion before the army.

Charles thrust the horn into his hands. "If you've need, sound it," Charles commanded. "I promise I will return with all the fury of your brethren at my back."

"But the Oliphant has only been used to signal victory," Roland replied with concern. "I'll not have it used otherwise."

A smile spread across Charles's face, fine lines wrinkling into his beard. He clasped his nephew's shoulder firmly in his hand. "Take it nonetheless."

Roland solemnly accepted the horn, slinging it over his shoulder to rest at his hip opposite Durendal.

"I've spent my life striving to model Plato's philosopher king," Charles confided. "Yet in the end, I find myself just an old man. I am tired of loss. Don't dally on shepherds' paths through the mountains. Come home soon."

Roland clasped Charles's shoulder in return, a gesture that few would presume to make. "Safe journey, Uncle. I'll see you on the other side."

Charles released his grip, and Roland bowed smartly before remounting Veillantif. With a snap of the reins, the champion rode through the ranks of men. Oliver, Turpin, Otun, and the marchmen with their Danish brothers fell in behind to follow him through the ranks to the rear. Thousands of voices roared acclamation that echoed off the nearby mountains and into the distant reaches of the pass.

Once clear of the army's main body, the marchmen formed up into ranks. Outriders then galloped away from the pass to monitor the approaches, while the Frank army began filing homeward through Roncevaux's maw in columns of twos and threes.

Demetrius settled in next to Roland.

"Permission to ride with you, my lord?" he asked.

Roland laughed. "All this time, and I've never understood why you fight with us."

The Greek's lean face was almost feral when he grinned.

"It's an excuse that will declare me an eccentric rather than a bloodletting Frank warrior!"

"You're a craftsman with that fine weapon of yours," Roland noted. "How could I ever think less of you?"

"Well, truth be told," Demetrius continued, "as a lad, I listened to tales of Scipio Africanus who fought the Carthaginian elephants, of Belisarius who warred against the Goths, and of Heraclius who danced through the streets of Jerusalem before fragments of the One True Cross. I wasn't blessed to live in those magnificent times. But if I must live now, beneath the dome of the blessed Hagia Sophia, I have vowed before God to burn just as brightly."

Roland shook his head. "I never knew. You've the soul of a bard!"

ΑΟΙ

Far across the mountain heights and at the very doorstep of Marcellus's Gascon keep, a weary group of travelers beat down the rutted road, their mounts drenched in sweat and covered in mud. Guards stationed near the drawbridge stepped forward with their weapons at the ready, for these riders were not the usual day laborers or supply merchants with their slow wagons.

As the horses clattered to a halt, they lowered their hoods, revealing on the one hand a woman whose fair beauty shone through her mud-caked traveling garments. Even more startling to the guardsmen was the realization that her other arm was bound tightly to her body. The rider beside her was a younger woman, equally fetching, with raven hair and cheeks flushed with the autumn cold. Upon closer inspection, most of the party wore martial equipment bearing the royal eagle upon their crimson surcoats.

"Charles!" Aude said breathlessly. "Is he here?"

"You're from up north?" the sergeant questioned, looking from one to the other in confusion.

Berta's reply was sharp. "I'm daughter to the king! Now tell us where the royal court lies!"

The sergeant pulled suspiciously at his bushy mustache, his mailed hand jingling.

"They aren't here, are they?" Aude asked quickly before the soldier responded.

"No," the man admitted. "But we've had outriders from the army stop here over the past few weeks. They're likely crossing from Spain now, I reckon."

"Where?" Aude's voice rose. "Show me!"

The guard surveyed the mountains that extended above the forest as far as the eye could see. He jabbed a finger toward a distant gap, hooded with shadows from the rising sun.

"Roncevaux. About a day and a half ride," he said gruffly.

Aude already dragged her horse's head around, followed closely by Berta. The rest of the company wheeled behind as if they were pursued by the very demons of hell—or were determined to catch them.

CHAPTER 26

REVELATIONS

Oliver clambered over broken stones to stand atop an upthrust spar of rock. His breath streamed from his nostrils, nothing more than wisps of gray in the early-morning chill. The day since Charles had led the army into the mountains had passed uneventfully with the scouts patrolling their vantages over the nearby roads and reporting nothing. The count of the Vale stretched, continuing to scan the ridge and its scruffy trees. He took a deep breath of crisp air—a breath free from the dust churned by thousands of hooves and feet in the valley below.

We'll be in Francia soon, leaving this bad dream behind us.

Yet it was more than a bad dream, for the count's face bore scars from shattered metal and countless scrapes with Saragossans intent on burying him alongside so many of his comrades. More than that, horrid images haunted his memories of the men burned alive at Carcassonne, and though he wouldn't admit it, he was glad the Greek fire had not been needed at Saragossa.

Shading his eyes against the sunlight, he scrutinized the landscape more closely, starting in the east, beyond the scattered huts and pastures. The sleepy landscape was quiet enough to lull a seasoned scout. Oliver schooled himself to keep on task despite his mind attempting to wander back to the ancient forests surrounding the vale.

Unbidden or not, it was a welcome thought. His father's manor lay amid massive shady trees and broad fields of fertile land that yielded fruits and grain in abundance. *Home.* The word lingered like a prayer in his mind.

To the southwest, then south, he squinted above the scattered trees and meandering tracks. Nearby lowing of cattle added to the bucolic swelling that filled Oliver's chest with each breath. Autumn would soon arrive, and with it harvest festivals and then long winter nights beside a warm hearth. Many years had passed since he'd sat at his father's table before a roaring fire. Close friends ever surrounded his father's board, laughing amid steaming plates and flavorful wine—as all the while bards sang the latest melodies from Aquitaine and Gascony. He paused and blinked, thinking he'd gotten a smudge of dust in his eye. Then he refocused on the horizon to the southeast.

"What's this?" he murmured half-aloud.

Above the tops of trees and across the plain, a hint of dust rose. He glanced around for a higher perch. A gnarled tree topped another jutting rock not far off. The climb took but a moment, yet the added height provided a better view of dark specks that marked the land beneath the dust like a plague. He leaned out further and made out colored glints reflected from polished metal—snatches of contrast indicating armored men in formation under banners.

"Saint Michael's bones!" he growled. He swung down off the limb to the uneven ground. Thoughts of home fled in the face of what could only be Marsilion's armies moving like a roiling storm toward Roncevaux.

Roland warmed his hands at the smoldering coals of a fire. His fingers felt the bite of autumn even though the rising sun began warming his back. He raised his eyes at the sound of a squire skidding to a halt before him.

"Slow down there, lad." None of the squires assigned to him were fresh-faced anymore. Every one bore scars that marked them as veterans.

"We found a man, sir!" the squire blurted out, his cheeks flushed. "In the baggage train. He's dying—my lord, he calls your name!"

"Show me!"

The boy turned and ran. Roland raced with him through the still-stirring camp to the supply train, where even at this early hour men strained under the weight of equipment to be transferred back to Francia. The youth dashed through the rows, correcting his course until they approached what appeared as just another nondescript wagon on the fringe of the group.

"This is it, my lord." With waving hands, the squire parted the workers who were already crowding around.

Roland pulled himself up into the cart, peeling back the canvas covering to find a sergeant kneeling next to a pale form that had bled out into the sacks of grain around him.

It was Julian.

"There's not much more I can do," the grizzled sergeant said as he pressed a cloth to the wound in the man's midsection. "From the smell of things, it's sliced his bowel, and rot has set in."

"How is it no one found him earlier?" Roland demanded.

The sergeant held up a bloody rag in angry disgust. "They gagged him. We inspected the last wagons and only just found him."

"Get Demetrius!" Roland crept close to the young man.

Julian groped at his collar, hands unsteady as they tightened and pulled him close.

"Proof, my lord …" The words rattled in Julian's throat. His breath was acrid and the skin of his hands was hot and soaked with sweat where they brushed against Roland's chest.

"Not now," Roland said, pushing him back against the grain sacks. "We'll get someone to stitch you up. Lie still."

Julian groaned and shook his head. "I'm a dead man. Vengeance is for the living—Ganelon—he admitted. He killed your father. Oh, God!" Julian's face contorted with pain.

"I'll take care of him," Roland promised, patting his hand. "Once we cross the mountains, we will bring him his due."

But Julian heard nothing. Having held out to the last, his fevered body shuddered again. His eyes lost focus, and he ceased struggling for breath.

Roland gently disengaged the youth's hands from his shirt, pressing them back upon his own chest.

"Rest," Roland whispered. "Rest now, for you've done well. There will be payment for his crimes."

He stood and looked around at the men who crowded the wagon.

"Take him," he commanded. "Bury him overlooking the road to the pass, that he might always watch the way into his beloved Francia." He leaped out of the wagon back into the bustle of the supply train.

Toward the center of the camp, a bell began ringing madly. Further along the row of carts, he saw Oliver frantically scrambling toward him, shouting as he went. Roland waved him over, intent on sharing this grim news. But Oliver's breathless words sent a chill up his spine.

"Saragossa! Roland, we've been betrayed! There must be more than fifty thousand approaching from the southeast!"

Roland sucked in the chill air through clenched teeth, the report pushing aside any thoughts of righteous justice. He and Oliver raced for higher ground. Otun and Demetrius fell in with them at the hilltop. Oliver pointed out the host that darkened the fields below and swarmed through brush and trees.

Turpin huffed up the slope to join them. "We must warn Charles, Roland!"

"No one will get through the pass now that the army is gone on," Demetrius protested. "The Hill People have reclaimed the road. Even an entire squadron of cavalry will not deter them."

"And we don't have one to spare," Roland agreed.

Otun scratched a hand through his beard, surveying the outriders that extended from the mass of troops like fingers of doom.

"If we must fight," he observed, "we've got the good ground."

"Fight we must," Oliver said. "But how long can we be expected to hold alone?"

"We must hold until Charles's passage north is assured," Roland replied.

"But Marsilion—" Oliver pressed. "If we call Charles back, we can finish him once and for all! If we do not, and we cannot hold …"

Roland scanned the forces below. The banner men rallying to the emir of Saragossa were not yet visible, but the numbers darkened the plain beneath the foothills. Calculations of approaches and countermeasures laid out across that same landscape with each step he climbed higher on a nearby rock, but one thought threaded through them all, refusing to be ignored.

If I'm given the rearguard, I swear before God that Charles will not lose a single man, horse, or mule in the crossing.

"There is a great danger if Charles doubles back and the Saracens overrun our position," he observed with a coldly even voice. "The army could be slaughtered just as they emerge from the pass. We must hold on our own. I will not call Charles back."

Oliver's eyes narrowed. Roland met his gaze.

Turpin placed a fatherly hand on Oliver's shoulder. "Sound the horn, Roland. Let the Oliphant call Charles back."

Oliver shook his head and shrugged off Turpin's clasp. "No. Roland is right."

"And if they overrun us? They could take Charles from the rear!"

"On home ground," Oliver reassured Turpin. "And it will be the Saracens that are stretching supply lines through the Hill People."

Demetrius nodded in somber agreement.

Roland drew himself up to his full height there upon the rock, a confident smile spreading across his features. While this campaign had matured the champion of the Franks, some of the brawling young bravo remained. And he stood prepared to defend this ground for the sake of honor.

"We've beaten greater numbers before," Roland said, his voice carrying to the men who even now began to congregate around them. "We'll do it again. Assemble the men!"

Oliver saluted with a clenched fist over his breast, spun on his heels, and sprinted back to the camp.

Scant moments later, Frank war horns blared assembly, and the rearguard sprang into action. Men tumbled into motion, tugging on gambesons, mail shirts, and helms They buckled on swords and daggers, slid arms into shields, and mounted their Frank warhorses, those beasts that oft in the past had rolled back ranks of the foe before their terrible onslaught.

While Roland shrugged on his own armor, squires scurried about him buckling other accoutrements to his person. It was then he realized how scant his marchmen were in relation to the battalions that surged across the plain—a thousand against Marsilion's entire battled-hardened army. These were his men, veterans who had marched the length of Francia and Spain without complaint. They had survived to stand this day as the breaker against the surging tide of steel before them.

A squire led Veillantif, sleek and black, through the ranks, the horse clad from head to flank in steel and leather. Roland signaled for the youth to stand with the steed. Then he scrambled up the spar of rock that only a handful of minutes before he had used to survey Marsilion's forces.

"My brothers!" he shouted. A hush fell upon the ranks. "My brothers! We are betrayed, the peace broken, and the enemy numerous! But we are soldiers! We know our duty, for we are the iron fist that subdued Spain!" A raucous cheer echoed off the mountains and thundered across the fields between them and Marsilion's host. "If we call the king to our side now, our whole army will be destroyed, along with our brave bandons. Charles must not be slaughtered on these slopes! Like Gideon of ancient days, God even now embraces us in His strength!" Roland's voice rose over the acclimation of the rearguard. "We are His soldiers, and this is the test of our faith! We cannot fail. We must not fail. We will not fail!"

Turpin stepped forward, clad in his familiar white surcoat over his mail, arms outstretched toward the sky. His bald head glistened as if crowned by an angel's touch, his blue eyes filled with a martial holiness.

"Men of Francia!" he cried. "You've heard your champion. Now I speak as your priest! Confess your sins now. Pray to the Lord God for mercy!" He genuflected, touching each point of the cross on his breast, and bowed his head for a moment. Then he raised his eyes, extending his hand and tracing the points of the cross over the host. "I absolve every last one of you!"

The Frank rearguard knelt as one. Roland drew Durendal and followed suit on his perch above them, pressing his lips to the cross guard.

"Before Saint Michael," Turpin shouted, "there is but one

requirement of penance! Take up the sword and fight for Charles! And strike hard!"

The rearguard roared their approval, banging weapons on shields and multiplying their voices in another booming staccato that reverberated off the mountains.

"Dear God," Roland prayed, his words low and intended for God alone, "do not be silent this day. Speak through our deeds. And if we must die to fulfill our duty, take us into Your arms." He raised his eyes to the pass and the pathway north. "Aude," he continued, "forgive me, for my trial is at hand."

He jumped down from his perch and thrust Durendal into the air, the sun dancing across the surface of the blade. His voice rose to join the chorus of war.

CHAPTER 27

RONCEVAUX

The soldiers in the Frank column sang melodies punctuated with laughter with each step they marched north out of the Roncevaux pass into Francia. Brothers, cousins, and friends, they moved with a flowing martial order honed through hundreds of miles on the march and countless days in battle.

Charles and his retinue traveled among them. With the terminal end of the pass in sight, a weight fell upon the monarch's shoulders heavier than his shield and coat of mail—a burden that dragged on his bones and threatened to cave in his chest. Riding close behind, Naimon watched the king withdraw further and further into himself. He planted his heels in his horse's ribs to catch up.

"Something bothers you," he ventured.

Charles focused his eyes on his counselor as if emerging from a dream.

"I'm sorry, old friend," he said, his voice dry and cracked. "I slept poorly. Most likely badly digested beef."

Naimon offered Charles his water skin. The king took it and drank deeply before handing it back.

"Go on," Naimon urged. "Please, sire, go on."

"You know me too well, don't you? Am I but an open book?"

"Nothing so simple, my king," Naimon replied with a warm smile. "Not just a common book. Rather a richly illuminated manuscript colored by a master of ink."

Charles laughed, but the sound was anything but cheerful. "Simpler to read events on the page than to make sense of them as they happen. But such is the lot of man, is it not? A divine creature chained to the flesh and subject to the buffetings of mortality."

"True. And poets, philosophers, and clergy will debate interpretations of things until the final trump. And then the earth will be consumed anyway. But until then we must survive as best we can. I'm your friend and offer you an ear and my heart."

Charles nodded.

"Well then, that is what we must trust in," he said. "You see—I had a dream, and in that vision Ganelon charged me, ripping a lance from my hand and shattering it to splinters. Before I could ask him what he intended, I opened my eyes once more and knelt before the altar in Aachen. And as I prayed, a boar and a leopard leapt from the shadows to attack me. But a great hound burst through the cathedral doors. It fought bravely until the other two beasts bore it down in a pool of blood. Yet with its sacrifice, the noble creature saved me."

Naimon tugged at his beard, salt and pepper eyebrows knit together. "Well, I'm no soothsayer. But could the vision represent peace by shattering the lance of war? And the hound could represent all the brave men who died to secure that peace?"

The haunted shadow refused to lift from Charles's eyes. "What you say is possible," he said as he turned to look back at the mountains. "But the chill in my bones refuses to be warmed by it."

ΛΘΙ

The hillside was alive with activity as Oliver directed the cavalry to their positions on the wings of the battle line. The marchmen sat upright in their saddles, lances tall and straight, banners defiant in the scattered breeze. Otun strode toward Roland. At his back, a band of Dane archers were braced by a number of their brothers from the Frank infantry. The champion paused from surveying the foothills and pointed to a stone ridge to the left.

"Hide your men there among those rocks," he said. "That should give you a clear enfilade as they navigate the approach. Plenty of time to teach them their lessons this fine morning."

Otun bared his feral grin. "Lessons?"

"Yes," Roland replied. "Teach Saragossa to fear."

"I give you my word," Otun growled. "Fear shall sing them to hell. When all this is done, we'll see if it's Odin's maids or your God's angels who come for the dead!"

Across the hillside, Frank knights, sergeants, and infantry stood in formation, shields and banners bearing the symbols of noble houses—the stag and wolf foremost among them.

The Saragossan host crawled closer.

Marsilion's army advanced under rich silk banners of exotic houses rippling over warriors bearing weapons and armor of shimmering silver and gold. In the center of the host rose the scimitar-and-moon banner of the emir himself. Marsilion and Blancandrin rode together beneath that fluttering cloth, both clad in armor crafted in distant forges of the East.

The emir scanned the hillside, still partially obscured by shadows clinging to the base of the mountains.

Blancandrin leaned over in his saddle. "They're so few. Charles trusted the peace would hold."

"And you who brought this idea to our court!" Marsilion replied with a laugh. "Never fear, it will hold when Charles is deprived of his lance, his sword arm, and his very heart! Then we'll be in Francia before the spring blooms again, the whole land opened up to us!"

Blancandrin straightened in his saddle.

"Allah preserve us in our greed," he whispered beneath his breath. His own son traveled with the Franks and would be butchered for his father's part in the day's doings. He gauged the distance to the thin Frank line and marked an imaginary spot on the ground a few dozen yards nearer.

At last, when the Saracen line finally reached the mark, he raised his sword to signal the charge.

Saragossa's horns broke the morning air, and the cavalry lurched forward toward the lower slopes. Blancandrin gritted his teeth against the jarring of his horse's hooves upon the uneven ground. Around him, beasts heaved breath through flared nostrils as they labored to traverse the long yards to get at the Franks dug into the upper ridge. Too soon, he cursed himself. They could have waited another ten yards.

Then the sky blackened from shadows that reached out from an upper ridge and arrows shrieked down in a sluicing sheet of maim and ruin. Horses and men tumbled to the ground in deafening screams. The charge faltered.

"Keep moving!" Blancandrin harangued his men. "You must get through it to stop them!"

Survivors cantered over bristling bodies and under another shadow of pain and death that darkened the sky. Blancandrin's own horse reared. Behind him, Marsilion pulled up his mount, wavering among his own guard. With no time to brace the emir's resolve, the general turned his attention to the ridge.

Across the open ground ahead, a single horseman rode from the front ranks of the enemy. He sat astride his distinctive beast arrayed in scaled armor like a veritable juggernaut. Roland raised Durendal high overhead, the steel catching the sunlight brilliantly, and swept it forward in a gleaming arc.

From the ends of the Frank line, their massive cavalry erupted like a rolling iron wave to bear down mercilessly on the lightly clad Saracens.

Oliver led his horse soldiers over the crest in a thunderous tide, their long lances lowered to strike. With a deafening crash, the Franks collided into the floundering Saragossans and carried through them, trampling men and mounts like blades of field grass. The momentum of the surge drove the Frank cavalry deep toward Marsilion's pennants. Oliver shattered his lance against a Saragossan trooper and hauled Halteclare from its scabbard, and blade cleaved flesh from bone as the knight urged his steed deeper into the enemy's tens of thousands.

When the Frank attack finally stalled against the sheer numbers stacked against the ridge, Roland left his position in the center and plunged after his companion. With a primal cry, he cut a trooper from the saddle and parried another's thrust on the recovery. Veillantif struck a swift kick that crushed the knee of another's horse, driving the beast to the ground, its rider tumbling into the melee to be lost amid the crush. Saragossans dropped beneath Durendal's bite as the champion plowed toward Oliver, and the surging battle churned blood and dust into a sludge that clung to clothes and skin.

An impact jarred Roland hard when a rider drove a lance into his shield. But the saddle held, and Durendal sang in a wicked return arc, catching the trooper between hauberk collar and helmet, removing his head in a splash of blood.

The enemy parted before Roland's relentless assault. Once at Oliver's side, both men fought with devastating skill. They drove toward Marsilion's hard-pressed center where the banners now limply signaled lost momentum, carving a swath of broken bodies that caused enemy troopers to turn tail and collide with the ranks behind them. With the Saragossan resolve crumbling, Marsilion's personal guard rushed forward to fill the gaps with their shields high against the assault. Marchmen, close behind their champion, crashed into the guards and rolled them back.

Roland maneuvered Veillantif through the guards' desperate counterattack. Their sabers bit into his shield and skittered off his mail, but the undeterred hunter had his quarry in his sights. The emir shouted to rally his men, and Blancandrin advanced to fill the breach but to little avail. Roland charged through, turning the enemy general aside. Oliver rode but a few lengths behind and followed up with a spirited assault, forcing Blancandrin to defend his own life.

Veillantif launched through the gap even as Marsilion shrieked again for aid. The emir dragged his horse's reins around to flee but not fast enough. In Roland's hands, Durendal hissed through the air, cleaving the front of the emir's helm, clawing through his face, and cutting into his armored shoulder. Marsilion pitched back, streaming blood and flailing his arms to ward off further attack. At that instant, the momentum of the assault separated the champion from his prey.

Horns blared, and another wave of Franks rolled from the ridge upon the Saragossans, driving back rank upon jumbled rank and sowing disarray.

Blancandrin beat and stabbed through scattered and isolated Franks to reach Marsilion's mount. He grabbed the skittish horse's bridle then spurred for the rear echelons, the emir's guard straggling after their master's reeling form. With the turning away of Marsilion's proud banners, the rest of the army ebbed back down the ridge, and the marchmen cut them down as they ran.

Through the fleeing Saragossans, Roland spied Oliver weaving unsteadily in his saddle not far away. Roland spurred across the wreckage and snatched Oliver's reins. Bareheaded, face flooded with blood, Oliver lashed out with his sword and struck a solid blow to Roland's shoulder. The blade parted scales and bit into his flesh.

"Saint Michael!" Roland cried, jerking Oliver's horse around. "It's me! Oliver, it's Roland!"

"Who's that?" Oliver mopped the blood from his eyes.

Roland pressed Veillantif closer, clenching his fingers around Oliver's sword arm. "It's me, brother. I swear it!"

Oliver lowered his weapon. Around them now only Frank cavalry remained on the slopes amid the crying, wretched wounded and dying.

The Franks restrained themselves from chasing after the immense Saragossan army into the plains where their sheer numbers would surely swallow them up. Sergeants spilled over the ridge to pick among the fallen for wounded and dead comrades while Roland led Oliver's horse toward the ridge. Beneath the champion's battered helmet, tears tracked down his cheeks.

Across the carnage two horsemen made their way from the staging ground toward the bustle of a camp that too soon had prepared for victory over the Franks. Marsilion swooned in the saddle, and when Blancandrin braced him upright, the emir swam into lucidity, his remaining eye seizing upon his general.

"We have them! Do not fail me!" He clutched at Blancandrin's mail shirt to remain erect.

Guards rushed to assist their emir.

"We'll not fail, lord," Blancandrin replied firmly. "They'll be dead before nightfall. I swear it." He released the emir's horse to attendants and physicians who swarmed Marislion, hurrying him off to the large silk tent at the center of the camp.

He stared after their heedless devotion. "Allah have mercy on us all."

Blancandrin struggled to regain order on the plains while in the hills above the Franks adjusted their ranks, filling gaps in infantry and cavalry with a stoic professionalism. Otun and his Dane bowmen restocked quivers and hunkered down once more in the rocks just above the main body of marchmen but kept their axes and swords close at hand. The Saragossan charge had accomplished one thing—their ranks had been thinned, and for each one who fell there would be no reinforcements. The stolid men of the north were prepared to step into the ranks of the marchmen as their brothers in arms, and neither they nor the men of the march would give any quarter to an enemy who had betrayed them with trinkets and promises of peace delivered by one of their own. The betrayal was complete, and there would be no mercy on either side.

In the distance, the Saragossans advanced again.

Roland took a deep pull from a water skin, its stale liquid rolling over his tongue and down his parched throat. He wiped his face with the back of his gloved hand. Sweat and dust stung his eyes. Through the haze rising from the plain, he could see a mounted horseman clothed in shadows that defied the sun picking among the torn and broken dead. The rider became more discernible as he drew near.

William's shade once again rode the field of the dead.

"Father," Roland began, his voice a cracked whisper, a barely audible supplication, "I've so much to atone for."

Deep in the recesses of his mind, Roland could hear his father's voice bridge the distance. "My son, when you are the emperor's champion, you not only wield a sword in his name, you are indeed the sword of God. You do not just fulfill the requirements of honor. You breathe living steel, fearing no man and no weapon—not even the bottomless gates of hell. Only then do you find what you truly seek, my son—redemption."

Roland's heart beat in his throat when the Saragossan horns squealed. Veillantif stirred impatiently beneath him. He reached down and patted the steed on the neck. No further words came to his mind, for the Franks beat their weapons on their shields, and their voices raised in defiant martial harmony, "Roland! Roland! Roland!" Those words echoed across the hills as the Saragossans once again spurred their long-limbed steeds into the teeth of the Breton wolf.

An expansive shadow lofted high above the enemy, followed by Otun's oaths to pagan gods. Then a fury of fletched wood and steel howled from the sky to spill Saracen blood in relentless streams. Horses and men crumpled to the ground. Flight after flight of arrows rained upon them, exacting their frightful levy each time.

Yet the Saragossans continued on through the squall until they collided with the center of the Frank line.

"Hold!" Roland shouted. The Frank wall of iron and flesh braced against the tsunami of horses and lances. The front ranks strained, but those behind pressed forward to steady their comrades. Shield to shield, the line bent but did not break.

"Stand firm!"

With the closing of quarters, the Northmen tossed aside their bows and raced down from their vantage to shore up the center, tall figures with axes eager to part flesh and sinew in mighty strokes. Otun claimed a place at the fore as the Breton line sagged under the intense Saragossan momentum. Roland ordered the cavalry charge from the wings, rolling the Saragossan flanks into their own and intensifying the flow of men toward the harried Frank center.

From within those crushing masses, Blancandrin spied the giant red-haired Dane shouldering to the front of the marchmen line, roaring defiance at men and gods alike, hewing open a Saragossan horse and tumbling the luckless rider against the Frank spears. The general lowered his lance and, burying his spurs into his horse's flanks, vaulted across thrashing bodies. One of his own officers stumbled into his path, and he heedlessly beat the man aside as he thundered onward. The Dane turned, realizing the danger too late, and Blancandrin drove the cruel barbed lance into his chest with a shattering crunch of steel and bone. The impact threw him to the ground in an eruption of blood. Blancandrin released his grasp on the lance and tugged his saber from its scabbard at his side. The fallen Dane gasped raggedly, struggling to force his shattered body back into the battle line, but crimson spittle frothed his lips, and his eyes became unfocused. His last breath hissed from his torn lungs.

Roland's lance crashed with a bone-jarring violence against Blancandrin's shield, staggering both horse and rider in a flurry of splinters. Blancandrin slashed with his saber, but the cut went wide as his horse shuddered and righted itself. Roland cast his own shattered stub of a lance aside, drew Durendal, and spurred back around, raining blow after blow upon the general's shield until it cracked and split.

"Damned oath breaker!" The champion's words were stinging in their rebuke.

Saragossans rallied and drove against the marchmen to reach their general's side. But Roland's assault continued unabated, raining down blows that broke open seams in Blancandrin's mail. While the two fought, Oliver charged into the Saragossans and laid about him with Halteclare, and with a titanic will, the unbowed Franks began to push back the Saragossans, step by bloody step.

Blancandrin fended off another round of crushing blows, then shrugged aside his ruined shield and launched his own attack against the champion. Durendal deflected Blancandrin's curved steel in midair, and Roland pivoted the blade back around into a ringing blow across Blancandrin's helm. The general reeled as his horse staggered before Veillantif's own spirited assault. Vision blurred, he swung his blade once more to intercept a high cut, but Roland disrupted the parry with his cross guard and followed up with a mailed fist across Blancandrin's face. The clangor of battle faded, overwhelmed by his rasping breath. His heart throbbed in his throat.

Durendal struck him across the shoulder, biting raggedly into the links of his scale byrnie. Before he could turn in the saddle, the sword bit again, deeper, its ravenous hunger now tearing at his flesh. A wordless battle cry escaped his lips when Blancandrin swung his saber again, but rather than staving off the buffeting attacks, he only met jarring resistance from Roland's shield.

Durendal sliced under the exposed edge of his mail sleeve, cutting through muscle and bone. The general's senses exploded as his forearm dropped to the ground with the saber still tightly gripped in the fist. Only his years of warring made his left hand draw a long dagger to block Roland's pressing assault. The young Frank danced his mount around him, always just out of reach. Now Durendal bit at his hip, then at his chest, and finally across his back, stealing his breath. Blancandrin struggled to respond when Roland rammed Veillantif against him. The jarring collision caused him to slip off of his skittering horse.

He hit the ground hard beneath the dusty stomp of iron-shod hooves. His own horse reared to escape Veillantif's kick and came down to crush his ribs. Roland shouted wordlessly overhead then drove beyond, deeper into the Saragossans.

Blancandrin's last earthly vision was of Roland's sword rising again and again in a terrible reaping of the Saragossan ranks.

A squad of Saragossan horsemen charged like hounds upon the wolf to meet the challenge of the Frank champion. They drove him further from the marchmen ranks and deeper into the swirling horde. Blades and maces shattered his shield and tore at his mail coat, yet Roland continued his assault, and all about him dead horsemen tumbled from their saddles to be crushed beneath the press. Veillantif lashed out as well, shattering knees and churning more bodies into the ground. Yet still the Saragossans pressed the champion and his beleaguered mount until a trooper's barbed lance shot through Veillantif's eye.

The horse fell, pitching Roland to the ground. He scrambled to his feet before he could be trampled, to face an enemy rider thundering at him with saber gleaming in a downward arc. Roland danced aside and drove Durendal up into his torso. He grabbed at the saddle beneath the sagging rider and held tight, using the horse as a shield. The crazed mount bucked and kicked, chasing back those who attempted to close and finish the champion.

A wedge of marchmen, their long spears bristling, drove back the enemy horsemen. Roland jerked Durendal free of the corpse, released his hold on the horse, then dodged to the line where the veteran Franks closed their shields around him. As one, the marchmen drove ahead once more, pushing the Saragossans back upon themselves and down the slopes choked with the dead and the dying.

The leaderless Saragossans broke once more.

The rampant wolf still fluttered defiant over the killing fields, though fewer were the troopers now rallying around the tattered standard. Crows swirled overhead in a thick cloud, providing shade to the remaining Franks and Danes while they bound up wounds and traded out gear with the dead. For they knew beyond doubt that each wave of the Saragossan army, like storm surf, would eventually grind them as so much chaff. For them the outcome was not in question.

Roland searched the wreckage on the slope below their ranks, stepping over shattered limbs and broken weapons until he found Veillantif laying amid a pile of armored bodies, most of them Saragossan. He knelt down, sweeping away clouds of flies, and patted the horse's lifeless neck, covered with dirt and blood.

"It's been a long ride," he murmured as he undid Charles's silver horn from the saddle. "Rest now. Rest now, my friend."

He stood with the Oliphant, and his eyes swept the slope, which wept crimson. In the distance, Saragossa's still-massive army swirled, threatening to reform into another raging tide. Scattered troops coalesced into units that then merged into the main body. Roland turned away and trudged back up the grade.

Roland hefted the Oliphant in his hand—this very horn had hung at the king's own saddle in battle as well as in peace. It had passed through generations of Charles's house and had ridden to the ends of the Frank kingdom and beyond, on campaign even to Rome where the pope himself had crowned Charles emperor on a long-ago Christmas Day. Roland's fingers tightened about the smooth surface. His chest muscles constricted his heart, for he couldn't imagine his father standing in his place and considering his next action. Then again, the steel in his soul had been forged on different fires than that which had flowed through William. To be the sword of God, he must be willing to be the trump of the king.

He raised the horn, sucking in air that smelled of death. A shadow fell across him, and Oliver struck the horn away from his lips.

"Not now!" he said, anger bubbling up in his voice. "Not now! Why should you, after all this? What of your oath to protect Charles's withdrawal? Was that for nothing? Have our deaths meant so little that you call him back now?"

"This has not been for nothing. But, Oliver, please—"

"Look at you—look at us covered in blood! Saragossan blood! We've engaged the enemy and driven them back! We bought Charles the time he needed to exit the pass. It has been purchased with the final breaths of good men. Our men! Sounding the horn now will only bring us all shame. Sound the horn, and Charles will return—he has sworn to—and more men will die, and your oath, and the deaths of all these men will be meaningless!"

The horn slipped from Roland's grasp to dangle on the worn leather cord slung over his shoulder. He clasped Oliver's shoulders with both hands and stared at his friend's face, covered in blood, sweat, and dirt.

"My brother," he started. "Oh, God ..."

Oliver's eyes never wavered, crusted as they were with his and his enemies' blood. He embraced Roland without losing the sternness that clung to his eyes. "Oh, Roland, your prowess in battle—we've never seen its like before, and it will never be seen again! Through our lives, we've kept faith, you and I. We were companions, brothers. But everything we were ends today, cold and final on this field. No one will live to sing the tales of our deeds. Valor on this battlefield will be forgotten with the dawn. But if you sound the horn now, we *will* be remembered, as the ones who lost their courage in the final test!"

Turpin approached, chewing at the corner of his filthy mustache, thoughtfully listening to the exchange. His surcoat was stained and torn, his mail battered. Yet his fierce face was colored with emotion.

"Sounding the horn won't save us, Oliver, you are right," he growled. "We're all dead men regardless. But still, do it. Do it, Roland! Not to call back the army but because Charles must know we have breathed our last. And if he chooses to return—if he chooses—he will be forewarned. Then he can bear our bodies home with honor—and keep our bones from being picked over by the crows!"

The remaining marchmen, Demetrius in their midst, closed ranks before the gates of Roncevaux. Roland scanned their grim faces. Most he knew well, though here and there he found ones he had only seen in passing on this long slog through Spain. His gaze fell again on Oliver, whose fierce eyes never wavered.

He picked up the horn.

To you, Uncle, I leave my last report. Muscles straining with this simple effort, he raised the Oliphant to his lips and unleashed a long, hauntingly clear note, crisp and defiant. It echoed off the hills, seeming to gain strength with every reverberation, rushing northward to the ears of the king.

On the plain below, the Saracens regained their courage, found their places in line, and charged the slopes once more.

A Θ I

CHAPTER 28

THE SILVER HORN ECHOES

A day's ride to the north, Charles sat upon his regal steed inspecting the ranks of soldiers still streaming from the depths of Roncevaux. The men sat a little taller, and their horses stepped a little higher with the soft earth of Francia beneath them, as if the very strength of their native land rushed through their limbs.

Charles glanced back at the gloomy pass, obscured in shadow interlaced with stabbing shards of light.

"My king?" asked Naimon.

"What's that? What's that sound?" Charles gave his horse a boot, trotting a few steps toward the pass. "A horn? Or was it—?"

Ganelon rode forward, straining in his saddle and striving to appear vested in discerning fading strains on gentle breezes.

"Probably a herdsman trying to scare off a rabbit, sire," Ganelon mused. "Nothing to worry about, I would wager."

Charles nodded uncertainly before his eyes reverted back to the army that continued spilling into Francia.

AOI

The Saragossan battalions lost their discipline on the advance, mad with the smell of enemy blood finally within reach. The entire horde came en masse at the remaining Franks—a veritable flood of men and beasts, straight at their center. But the Franks stood firm with spears grounded

293

under their feet against the impact. Saragossan horses and riders alike impaled themselves on the shafts as lead elements slammed to a halt and were overrun by their own trailing echelons. The dead piled up, but the ones behind simply rode over them and continued on.

Turpin stepped into a gap in the line and lay about with his war hammer, crushing skulls with the heavy mallet and piercing flesh with the spiked butt. He grinned, gore covering his face, and croaked out a bawdy song. To his left, he lent a soldier the safety of his shield as the other fended off riders seeking to exploit the gap. The hammer caved in one rider's helm that leaned too far and toppled him to a crushed heap, and for good measure the bishop drove his shield down into the man's throat to smash his windpipe. At that moment, a Saragossan trooper drove his lance into Turpin's chest and threw the priest to the ground. He struggled to rise, a growl frothing through his lips, but the Saragossans pushed the gap wider and swarmed him down, plunging their curved blades into his body until he struggled no more. Demetrius spurred his horse through the chaos to the breach. An arrow to the chest staggered his steed. Its knees buckled, and it fell with a crushing clank of weapons and armor. The marchmen struggled to lock shields and regain their footing, but step by bloody step they were driven steadily back toward the gaping maw of the pass.

Across the field of death and mayhem, enemy horsemen surrounded Oliver and dragged him from his steed. But the count of the Vale twisted out of their grasp. He scrambled between their horses' hooves to pounce on a Saragossan infantryman. Halteclare's sharp edge bit through cloth, leather, and flesh, and he shouldered the man's carcass aside to lunge at a rider trying to reach in with his saber. Oliver thrust Halteclare up into the man's face and dropped him to the gory muck. As he tugged the blade free, he spied a figure watching him from atop a spirited horse, clad in dark, ornate armor with a visor pulled over his features, but before he could wonder at the apparition, the enemy troopers fell on him once more. Halteclare again wove an intricate pattern of death as Oliver punched and slashed from ward to ward, attack to attack, knocking aside weapons, shattering bones, and carving open flesh.

The dark figure beat back a Frank sergeant then dug his heels into the flanks of his energetic desert horse. The beast vaulted over broken bodies and found purchase in the ground made slick with blood. He charged. The wicked lance in the horseman's hand dropped into position and, with a grating of steel on wood, pounded against Oliver's shield, throwing the knight backward amid a shower of splinters. The horseman tossed aside the shattered lance while enemy troops swarmed the fallen knight.

Roland burst through them with a wordless cry. He was a specter of death, Durendal slaughtering any who hazarded to stand between him and Oliver, leaving a bloody path in his wake with rushing marchmen following close behind. They threw up their shields to create a perimeter around the stricken knight. Roland dropped to his knees and gathered him into his arms. Hot tears wetted his cheeks. Oliver raised his hands to Roland's face.

"There's no time—do not mourn!" Oliver choked on his own blood. "Strike. Strike hard!"

Roland nodded. "I will, my brother."

Oliver sagged against Roland, his breath rasping and ragged, while his life's fluids leaked from the seams of his mail coat. They left bright stains on Roland's torn and filthy garments. Roland brushed aside Oliver's matted hair as his tears purged the grime from his friend's pale skin.

Oliver drew a last rattling breath and was gone.

Roland roared over the din of battle, his anguished cry a paladin's wordless vow of retribution. He leapt to his feet and, with Durendal gripped tightly in his hands, plunged shoulder to shoulder into the line with the marchmen, the small wedge driving against the Saragossans, crowding them into the narrowing walls of Roncevaux.

Yet while the enemy continued to fall beneath the marchmen's boots and Roland's avenging blade, each comrade who fell left fewer to step forward to plug the gaps. Roland stood in the center of the line, cutting and thrusting at the endless enemies scrambling over the bodies of the fallen. Above their heads, Roland spied the dark horseman who had ridden Oliver down, hanging back from the fore, barking commands and urging his men forward.

Roland pummeled and carved a swath through the Saragossans toward him. This time the warrior raised his scimitar and charged. Roland dodged a stroke as the horseman passed and sliced at his saddle harness. The warrior savagely dragged his mount's head around for another pass. Roland crouched on the balls of his feet as they pounded closer. At the last instant, he lunged under a scything cut and plunged Durendal deep into the horse's belly. The horse careened past then collapsed to its knees, ripping Durendal from his hands. The horseman tumbled from the saddle, helmet flying but still clutching his saber.

"You?" Roland shouted. "You had a nation's trust!"

Saleem spat dust and brushed his tangled hair back from his face. "Now I've the renewed love of a father! What price could you place on that, Frank?"

Roland drew the long dagger from his belt then rushed to meet Saleem's charge. He caught the saber in midair on his blade, but Marsilion's son danced away. Without missing a beat, Roland sprang after him. Roland took an awkward cut on his mailed arm then thrust the dagger low into Saleem's groin, the blade parting flesh. Roland's mailed fist smashed his face, staggering him backward. Saleem clutched at the thigh wound and desperately waved his saber in circles above his head.

"Men of Saragossa!" he cried with fading strength. "To me! To me!"

But no one intervened. Those closest remained consumed by the raging battle, for the few remaining Franks were unleashing a berserker fury staining the earth in streams of red. Saleem limped to shake off the wound, raising his saber and daring Roland to strike once more. But the Frank silently circled him, waiting. Saleem thrust high, thrust low, but the champion continued around, his steps graceful and firm over the littered ground. Saleem licked the blood from his mouth. Armed with only the dagger, Roland didn't intend to close. The visibly weakening Saleem lunged, and once more Roland danced away.

"Stand, damn you! Stand and fight me!"

Raising his sword unsteadily over his head, Saleem lunged again at Roland, the saber whistling through the air. Roland stepped to the side enough to allow Saleem's artless downward cut to strike only a glancing blow on his mail shirt. He ignored the pain and the warmth spreading down his sleeve. He grabbed Saleem's arms, tripping his foe backward to the ground. Saleem struggled for advantage, but the wolf of Breton March prevailed, pounding Saleem's face with his mailed fist until the iron links tore Saleem's skin.

"Explain your faithless betrayal to God!" Roland drove the dagger up under Saleem's chin.

Blood erupted from the prince's mouth, his eyes widening one final time. Roland held Saleem's head firmly in place and forced him to look upon his executor until he finally gave up the ghost.

Roland staggered to his feet. All around him the Saragossans were losing their stomach to fight after beating themselves against the Frank wall of sinew and steel. A trickle of troopers turned and ran, and within moments those few grew into a flood of chaos. And with the martial ebb, the battle-madness in Roland's veins faded. He knew his few remaining comrades had borne their final wounds with honor, for once the immediate threat receded back down the slopes, the last of the Frank rearguard sank to the ground.

Roland, standing alone between the eternal columns of the mountains framing Roncevaux, raised the Oliphant to his bruised lips. With his hands shaking, he drew a deep breath then unleashed another note.

Impatient oxen with the smell of fresh pastures in their nostrils strained ponderously out of the pass dragging rumbling wagons behind them. The last of the baggage train had arrived. Charles prepared to dismiss his court for the evening but glanced over his shoulder back into the pass, hoping to spot some trace of the rearguard.

The ghostly trill drifted out of the gap again. "There! There it is again!" He looked around anxiously for agreement.

Ganelon coaxed his horse closer.

"Surely it's nothing to worry about, my king," he purred. "Wind upon the mountains."

Alans and the Tournai men murmured their agreement as they mingled with the king's guard.

The slopes before the narrow southern mouth of Roncevaux lay littered with broken men, horses, and equipment. Crows fluttered darkly from corpse to corpse while flies choked the lungs of the dying. Honorius covered his nostrils with a silk kerchief, picking through the carnage and ignoring the desperate pleas of the wounded. He continued until he came upon the familiar form of a man in Roman armor, his body broken and twisted.

Demetrius struggled to disengage himself from his dead horse's tangled harness. Honorius crouched next to him, lifting his head from the ground. A flicker of recognition touched Demetrius's eyes.

"Honorius?" he croaked through cracked lips.

"Yes, my friend," Honorius said. "It's been so long."

Demetrius reached up and clutched at Honorius's armor. "The emperor, did he send aid?"

Honorius smiled, wiping at crusted blood along Demetrius's brow. "Much has happened since that time we were together last. Remember that tavern on the Bosporus? The waves gently lapping the shore as we sipped the finest wine?"

"You treated with Saragossa and Cordova, didn't you?" Demetrius spat blood in Honorius's face.

"I did our emperor's bidding," Honorius said. "As did you."

Steel scraped as Honorius drew his dagger. Cradling the broken man close to his breast, he drove the blade into Demetrius's throat. Demetrius struggled as blood rushed to drown him, but Honorius continued to hold him tight until his body stilled.

He looked down then at Demetrius's slackened face.

"Sleep well, my brother," he whispered. "Your duty is at an end."

The sun was dying, the day's work haunted by shadows that could not mask the butcher's final bill. Roland found Saleem's horse and, placing a boot on its shoulder, heaved Durendal loose. His fingers gripped the familiar hilt. In his hands the weapon seemed possessed of its own life. He brought its comforting familiarity before his eyes—each line of the blade and facet of the cross guard by now was burned on his soul. When he lowered it again, he began to walk the ridgeline, alternately staggering and regaining his footing on the broken stone. Still he continued on, searching the lengthening shadows. A rock slipped beneath his boot, and he crashed to his knees in a shallow stream that trickled from the heights of the mountain before him—nature's own altar to the Almighty.

"You are truly a weapon of the ages—and I'm honored to have borne you," he whispered to the sword, his lips reverently touching the reliquary in the hilt. "But I'll not have you used against good Christian men. God will call you back, I've no doubt, when the kingdom again has need."

He cast about for a moment, finding what he sought a short distance away. A handful of ragged, splashing steps downstream brought him to the edge of a still, dark pool. He gazed into it, trying to judge its depth, but was unable to see the bottom and judged that to be sufficient confirmation. He brought the blade to a salute to the everlasting sky and then hurled it into the water, watching the last rays of the sun flutter off its bright surface until he lost sight of his father's weapon for good.

He sloshed weakly out of the pool and crested the bank.

Snorting horses and iron-shod hooves on rocks clattered nearby. Roland emerged into a company of Saragossans searching the slopes for Frank resistance. One of them cried out. Roland grabbed a shattered lance from the ground and charged afoot. With the length of wood, he gutted the closest one, unhorsing the rider in a crash. Then he jerked the tip free when another horseman charged, dragging his saber across Roland's shoulder.

Roland dropped to one side. By now the rest of the raiding party clattered closer, drawn to the noise of weapons. His attacker spun around and charged again. Roland slumped wearily to conserve his strength until the last instant before planting the end of the lance under his boot and impaling the man's chest on the second pass. Without pause he reached down to rip a saber from a dead hand and launched himself into the remaining horsemen. Roland lunged and thrust into men and beasts alike. Trooper after trooper fell to his onslaught, yet blood also dripped from the edges of his scale shirt, his breath rasping in painful gasps.

His ferocious attack chilled the bones of the men trying to kill him.

They slashed and stabbed, and though they wounded Roland over and over, he tore through them with savagery. Riderless horses trotted over the loose flinty stones back down the slopes toward Marsilion's camp. Finally the remaining troopers had a bellyful, and they broke, galloping away.

Roland chased them for a few steps, his vision and mind clouded by a veil of crimson that refused to be sated. He jabbed the curved weapon at the sky, Saint Michael's name upon his lips, but blood pooled deeper in his boots with each stride. The air was dry and fetid with death. Regardless, he hungrily sucked it into his lungs. His fevered eyes narrowed when he saw the Saragossans regroup and urge ranks to dare the slope once more.

He limped back up toward the choke point where the pass narrowed—to a place where he could stand against the emir's minions. At the narrowest point, he found a wind-wracked oak. He pressed his back against the gnarled trunk and braced his legs. His hand fell to his side, feeling the Oliphant's cool surface.

"Oh, Aude," he cried out. "Forgive me!" Clenching his teeth together, he pushed himself to full height and raised the horn to his lips.

As he drew breath, a Saragossan outrider rode into the pass, lance lowered.

Roland blew, and the note rang out once more, clean and pure.

The rider closed, and the cruelly barbed lance tip struck Roland in the chest. But the note soared crisp and true over the battlefield, echoing on through the pass as if lifted upon wings. A single brilliant beam of crimson light broke then across the rocks from the reaches of the dying sun, bathing Roland's eyes in its glow and holding at bay for the barest moment the encroaching shadows of everlasting night.

CHAPTER 29

RETRIBUTION

Charles waited, with Ganelon at his side, near the mouth of the pass until the day was nearly done before turning his horse's head toward the anxious members of his court. He started to raise a gloved hand to signify that the operation was, for now, complete enough to rest.

Abruptly he lowered his hand and strained about to look once more into the shadowed depths of Roncevaux. A long note, faint but clear, drifted down from the heights of the purple peaks and faded quickly.

"It's him!" he cried. "Good God, it's him!"

The words barely escaped his throat when a small group of horsemen pounded up the road, refusing to be challenged by guards and courtiers alike.

Aude rode bareheaded in the fore, horror crossing her face. She too heard the horn.

"My king!" she called. "You are betrayed!" She dragged the reins back on her steed, the lathered beast skidding to a halt before Charles. She jabbed a finger at Ganelon. "This traitor murdered William and even now plots against you!"

Like a coiled serpent, Ganelon and his band of conspirators sprung. Guinemer, Alans, and the Tournai troops turned upon their unwitting comrades. Charles reeled in his saddle to avoid a lashing cut from Ganelon. The blade's tip caught his cheek, drawing royal blood. Charles's steed danced back, but Ganelon struck again. This time Naimon pushed his mount between them, grabbing at Ganelon's extended arm. They

301

grappled, their horses stomping madly beneath them. Louis leaped from his saddle to seize Ganelon from behind and, with titanic effort, hurled him to the ground. They rolled around in a clatter until the prince pinned the grim-faced count with a dagger pressing his throat.

The fighting quickly died down when loyal troopers flooded through the wagons to the king's side. The conspirators, forced to show their hand before the army was strung out across the length of Francia, fought desperately until Alans and Guinemer were also beaten to the ground. Then, almost before the fight had really begun, the usurpers' men threw down their arms.

Charles spurred his horse toward the pass.

"Betrayed!" he shouted. "To me! We ride to relieve the rearguard!"

Hours passed until finally the night sky gave way to a sliver of light. A squad of mounted scouts stole warily from Roncevaux's darkness to the shattered southern hills, arms at the ready. Beneath the silent mountains, the broken bodies of friend and foe lay tangled together in heaps before them. Finding no adversary at hand, they reported back for the main body to advance.

Charles's red-rimmed eyes scanned past the hastily placed bandage on his face. He dismounted with a heavy heart. The entire company followed him to begin the long work of gathering the remains of the men, their brothers and cousins—they who until only days before had marched, laughed, and fought beside them. Charles stalked among the dead, a specter of his regal self, his pace quickening with the discovery of each familiar face found among the marchmen—Turpin, Demetrius, and Otun. Louis came upon Oliver and reverently gathered up Halteclare to be borne northward with honor.

Then, a short distance off, he spied Roland's lifeless body spiked to the ancient tree by the Saracen's lance. Charles cried out, hurrying to him across the loose stones. He sank to his knees next to the still form with sorrow washing through his body. Then he tenderly pried open Roland's fingers and lifted the battered Oliphant from the corpse's cold grip.

Charles's face streaked with tears that dripped on Roland's paled skin.

Naimon and Louis solemnly stepped forward to retrieve Roland's body, wrapping him in the king's cloak before laying him among his companions. A squire timidly handed Charles a torn length of soiled cloth. The king shook out the rampant wolf and laid it on Roland's chest.

"My boy," he whispered, "my champion, my nephew. Dreams are indeed the words of God. Even a king must listen to his counsel."

A Frank outrider spurred his horse up the hillside.

"My king! My king!" he shouted. "The army of Saragossa lies to the south!"

Charles stood and looked out across the plain.

"Again we've been betrayed. But this day I swear that Marsilion is a dead man!"

Charles handed the Oliphant to Louis. Behind them the column of Frank troopers continued to emerge from Roncevaux. Once along the ridge, Frank sergeants formed them into ranks, a veritable flood of ironclad men and beasts charged with lust for the blood of the faithless. They swelled to the edge of the hilltop—numbers building steadily as more and more marched through the pass. The morning sun had risen to near noonday before the last soldiers took their place in formation and stood glinting above the crest, away from the enemy's view. Louis rode before them with the king's silver horn raised above his head, eliciting a cheer from thousands of throats. He paused at the center of the formation.

The Frank battle line held its collective breath. Hands tightened on weapons. Heels poised over horses' flanks. Louis shouted a single word—

"Roland!"

He raised the Oliphant to his lips and let out a long, clear blast. The Frank battle cry broke like a raucous thunder over the plain, followed by the echo of their hooves as they flooded down onto the slopes.

The avalanche grew in momentum when the tents of Saragossa came into view. Enemy pickets unfortunate enough to be caught in the open were either crushed under hoof or fled before the seething Franks. At the outer edge, guards fell like reeds in a storm. Then the Franks were upon the heart of the camp, tearing through men with a rage that brooked no argument, deferred to no defense, and offered no mercy. Lances skewered the first of Marsilion's men, quickly followed by the butchering work of edged and blunt weapons. Saragossa's multicolored tents became a killing field, many buckling like so many maidens' kerchiefs in a gale of steel.

Marsilion stumbled from his palace of silk, his ruined face wrapped in bandages. In his hand was a sword that he swung with wild abandon. Frank troopers charged him, but they veered off, dancing out of reach. He swore at them. But when a single rider finally did bear down on him, the emir ran. Louis swept Halteclare like a farmer's scythe, and Marsilion's head leaped from his shoulders, his body stumbling several paces before it too finally dropped.

The fallen emir's great army broke, and the Franks cut them down, paving the road back to Saragossa with their bloodied carcasses.

AOI

CHAPTER 30

LOVE AND LOSS

The royal family's chapel in Aachen was not nearly as grand as the great cathedral; the smaller edifice was meant only for the intimate personal ministrations of Charles's family. Within the close fluted walls, two coffins rested before the altar, their plain wood covered with the torn banners that had led the marchmen and even the entire kingdom—the rampant wolf and the great stag.

The abbot knelt by a monk and offered prayers on behalf of the slain. Once finished, he then joined his companion in a hushed melody directed on high to saints and angels who surely must accompany such as these through the gates of heaven. With the sound of brushing skirts, he raised his eyes and glanced at the entrance. Aude stood in the doorway. She respectfully curtsied, hand touching the points of the cross on her breast, then stepped further in. The priests rose and stood to the side.

Aude paused at the first casket, her fingers tracing the golden stag of Vale Runer, its lines muddied and torn.

"Dear brother," she said. "I would once more see your sweet face. I would laugh with you. Cry for you."

The abbot raised a hand toward the image of *Christ upon the Tree* above the altar. "Lady, please come and share your grief with the Lord."

"For He will make your burden light," enjoined the monk.

A distant smile touched Aude's lips.

"Yes, I will lighten my burden and sink into blissful sleep."

MICHAEL EGING AND STEVE ARNOLD

She turned to Roland's coffin, splaying her hands over the pennant-covered surface as if placing her hands on her lover's chest.

"Be true to your purpose," she whispered. "Send me swiftly to my love."

The abbot's bushy eyebrows knit together. "What was that, child?"

But Aude no longer listened, consumed as she was with her beloved who lay beneath the coffin's lid. She leaned closer, her words meant for him alone, even if there were other ears nearby that might also hear.

"Your spirit cannot be contained by this pine box, nor by cold, dead flesh," she said urgently. "I'll follow you, my love, my husband—my champion! I pray your mortal deeds are sufficient to redeem me from this act, that I might be at your side in life and death, into the eternities—"

A spasm gripped her body. She gasped. The clerics rushed too late to her side as she slumped against the coffin lid—her body the final covering for her husband's remains.

As her breath stilled, her clenched fist relaxed, and a small amber bottle slipped from her fingers.

Courtiers, dressed in somber finery, stood in the palace courtyard, while around them crowded the populace of Aachen. Amid the trappings of power stood Charles, his gold-trimmed mantle heavy about his shoulders and his crown glimmering atop his white locks. But shadows clung to the fierce thick brows that obscured his eyes. Behind him stood Gisela, her infant son clutched tightly to breast. At the nearby gallows, two corpses swung by the neck, twisting slowly in the breeze—Alans and Guinemer, already sent to eternal justice.

In the center of the courtyard stood a lone defiant figure, bound and yet still erect. Ganelon—traitor, murderer, and stepfather of the slain champion—kept his eyes fixed on the face of the man he would have replaced on the throne.

"The evidence has been examined." Despite the exhaustion evident in his tones, Charles's voice carried above the noise of the gathering. Voices hushed, and the king continued. "Laws of God and man have

306

been broken. Ganelon, count of Tournai, husband to my sister, you stand condemned, and justice is demanded."

Ganelon spat on the ground before the king.

"What right do you have to judge me? Usurper!"

No emotion showed on Charles's face when he signaled to the guard. Armored sergeants advanced on the prisoner and wrestled him to the ground. Ganelon struggled, but the troopers continued and tied thick ropes to his wrists and ankles.

"This will not stand!" he shouted. "Pretender! I am the blood of Clovis, he who was anointed of God! You should honor me! Honor the family of your rightful king!"

"The four corners of Francia will know of your treachery!" Charles roared, causing many in the audience to shrink back at the unexpected outburst. "That will be your honor!"

Charles signaled again, and the guards stepped away. Gisela covered Baldwin's face.

A lash cracked and four horses launched in each direction of the compass. Ganelon shrieked in final agony as his limbs were torn from his body.

Hours passed before a solemn procession snaked up the boulevard from the palace to the great cathedral. Banners, pennants, kerchiefs, and streamers filled the air to proclaim the passing of the champion and his peers. Some in the crowd whispered while the coffins passed on their sable-draped wagons that Roland, Oliver, Turpin, and the rest were paladins, holy knights of God—even the once-heathen Dane Otun would be accepted into the Lord's rest, and none seemed inclined to dispute. Around the cathedral doors, the kingdom gathered to mourn with their king. The royal guard assembled, and when the wagons stopped, they stepped forward in a line and lifted the caskets to their shoulders. A moment later, many held their breath at the arrival of a single white cart but a few paces behind the others, bearing a gossamer-covered box. This catafalque was also lifted and borne up the steps into the nave behind the others. Within lay brave Aude, who had dared ride

307

the length of Francia to bring word to the king, and by grace of royal dispensation now followed her beloved through the veil.

Charles stood near Gisela on the steps to greet the champion and his dearest companions. As the procession passed, he heard the quiet sobs of a mother bereft. He turned and wrapped her in his arms.

"Your son saved us from certain destruction," he said, offering what comfort could be had. He brushed a tear from her face. "His sacrifice kept us from being consumed by Marsilion when all of us believed the olive branch of peace within our grasp. We owe a great debt to Roland and his brave men."

Gisela nodded, her lips trembling.

"And what of my remaining son?" she asked. "Ganelon's son?"

Charles thought for a moment, his eyes still following the champion's procession.

"He shall be as William's flesh," he proclaimed. "If you wish, heir to the march, and, in time, a peer of the realm. I pray, sister, that he walks in Roland's path."

Gisela allowed her moist eyes to drift back to the coffins that were slowly carried the length of the cathedral.

"Oh, William," she whispered. "This is all I have to offer."

She buried her head against Charles's shoulder.

"No," Charles said in her ear. "You've given us much more. Roland's deed, his song, will be sung through the ages. He will never be forgotten."

Gisela looked up past her brother, past the pomp and circumstance, to the clouds roiling in the sky overhead. A ray of light stabbed downward, and she felt the warmth upon her face. As she closed her eyes, the crisp note of a silver-chased horn echoed through the streets of Aachen, to the highest battlements of the city walls, and beyond.

A Kingdom Won

Southern Coast of Britain
October 1066

William, duke of Normandy, surveyed the wreckage of his battle against the stalwart Saxons. It had been hard going to defeat Harold—more so than he had expected. The enemy archers had very nearly driven his troops back and at the height of the combat he had been forced to ride the length of the field to prove to his men that he was, in fact, still alive. But in the end, his army had carried the day. He had feared he had taken a chance relating the story of Roland to them; the paladin had died in the end, after all—but the hero's fighting spirit had inspired them, and now Harold was dead and England lay before them.

Joachim sauntered up to William's side. "My lord! The day is yours!" He flashed a crooked smile. "The men have taken to calling you 'The Conqueror'!"

"Have they?" William snorted. He was almost disappointed. "The Bastard" had had a dangerous sound to which he'd become accustomed. "You had nothing to do with that, I venture?"

"The men will claim their own, my lord. I am merely their voice." He swept his cap off with a fool's flourish. "Good evening to you, sire, and may the morrow bring you greater victory in London!"

Joachim ambled away, ignoring William's gaze as it bored into his back.

William the Conqueror, the duke thought. *Indeed.* He couldn't deny them, though. They had fought hard and valiantly for him. God bless their hardheaded souls.

He turned, almost colliding with his squire who stood behind him with an oblong bundle.

"Gads, boy! You can move like a cat when it suits you, eh?" He motioned the lad forward, took the silk-wrapped parcel from him, and reverently folded back the wrappings.

Durendal had been lost centuries ago, somewhere on the Iberian plain never to be found. But the Oliphant had endured—indeed William was sure it had been the horn's ringing cry that had rallied his men at the end. He carefully exposed the glittering silver and ivory that gleamed as if still new. He knelt in the setting sun, bowing his head, and offered his thanks to Saint Michael for stalwart companions and noble heroes.

Victory was won. There was only one thing remaining.

He raised the horn to his lips and blew.

AOI

AUTHORS' NOTES

Roland and his exploits have been part of my life since I was very young. Some of the first stories I read as a child were from books of mythology that regaled me with the exploits of Roland and his peers. These tales then led me further to the chivalric deeds of Arthur and his Knights of the Round Table, *Men of Iron* by Howard Pyle, and the eternal *Ivanhoe* by Sir Walter Scott. Many a summer afternoon, after all the chores were done on our small Ohio farm, I spent curled up in the bole of a willow tree with some small volume smuggled from my parents' bookshelves transporting me to lands where brave knights faced insurmountable odds. The books in our home were plentiful, and when I ran out, my parents encouraged the use of my library card to seek out more. It was there that I discovered the feats of Byzantine emperors and generals, Charlemagne and his paladin knights, and many more historical tales. Unbeknownst to me at the time, my father was a kindred spirit who must have taken some pride in my interest in things medieval, and in particular a knight named Roland.

In 1987, while attending Brigham Young University, I had the good fortune to take a class on the early Middle Ages taught by Dr. Paul Pixton. Dr. Pixton, as part of the coursework, required us to read an English translation of *La Chanson de Roland*. Later, when I was his teaching assistant, we spoke about the poem, and he expressed the opinion that this would make for an epic movie. It was shortly afterward that I went with Michael Mitchell, who was also a teaching assistant in the History Department, to spend a short break between semesters camping in the Wasatch Mountains (with the indulgence of my patient wife, Lori). In the evenings, as the sun faded over the distant peaks, we huddled about a campfire to read aloud *The Song of Roland*. With each stanza one could hear the clatter of arms and the cries of the doomed as the brave words came alive. By the summer of 1988, I had outlined the first draft of a feature-length screenplay.

But life seemed to encroach upon my desire to write the script, and the outline remained untouched in a folder for a long time. However, Roland remained on my mind. My father had died of cancer during the autumn of 1986, and when I graduated from BYU, my mother presented to me a gift that he had selected prior to his death. From a long, slender box, with trembling fingers, I pulled out a replica of Charlemagne's sword. My father had found a way to touch my heart long after he was no longer physically with me.

Soon after I graduated, my boyhood friend and oft-times writing partner, Steve Arnold, and I plunged into writing *Annwyn's Blood*, which was based on a short story I had written in college. I always intended to come back to Roland and Roncevaux. But months slipped into years, and my children grew as I progressed in both my professional life, as well as in writing that I squeezed in around coaching soccer and running taxi duty for children's activities. As I neared my fortieth birthday, the realization hit me that if I didn't write down some of the stories swirling around in my mind and push them into view, no one would do it for me. With mounting urgency, I found the old outline and began work on the screenplay, at this point entitled *The Silver Horn Echoes: A Song of Roland*. The first draft was nearly two hundred pages long, and I had produced a piece of work with which I had no idea what to do. But I was driven to see this one across the proverbial finish line, even though film professionals I spoke with warned me that a historical epic as my first project would be a heavy lift.

And they were right.

Paul Young, a screenwriting guru, and William Nix, a film producer, both took interest in my progress and have become ongoing mentors and friends. Paul worked relentlessly with me to navigate the sometimes-treacherous passage between what I felt the story demanded and what would make for a compelling screenplay. But as I revised and redrafted what was now simply called *Song of Roland*, the screenplay evolved into a svelte one-hundred-page script that became my initial calling card to producers and production companies in Los Angeles.

During the summer of 2008, *Song of Roland* caught the attention of Alan Kaplan at Cine LA, who expressed excitement about packaging it for a feature film. Alan's enthusiasm for the material was infectious, and shortly after the option was negotiated, we launched into a familiar next step for a script in development—a rewrite. Working with Alan was a pleasure, and he always had broad insights into scenes that then allowed me to work through the mechanics. However, our collaboration was short-lived, and in December 2008 Alan died of cancer. Our vision for Roland was nipped in the bud, but I will always be grateful for the opportunity I had to work with him.

During the next few years, *Song of Roland* opened doors and started conversations that have continued to allow me to pursue other feature film concepts. However, I always knew that I hadn't finished with the story. In early 2013, I revisited Roland, Aude, Oliver, and the others as I began revising and drafting with the intention of writing a novel based on the screenplay, and Steve jumped in to help me bring the entire work across the finish line.

And now I come full circle with the story of Roland and his companions. My intent was to capture the spirit of the epic *Chanson de Roland*, and this telling, like the original, is not rigidly consistent with historical, or even geographical, reality. The goal was to provide a tale of intrigue and adventure set in a world very different from our own, and I hope you feel this has been accomplished.

In keeping with the spirit of the original poem, the anonymous author used a device that has never been fully explained. Inserted into the breaks in the stanzas are the letters AOI. We've sprinkled them into the story not only in honor of the poem but also to take the place of section breaks that would typically be placed within chapters at strategic locations.

Thank you to my wife and family, for this story is as much for my own children as it was for me so many years ago when I climbed the willow tree and lost myself in Dark Ages France. In addition, I owe much to Dr. Paul Pixton, who provided me with encouragement and threw me into a bygone age full of heroes, villains, and cataclysmic events that shaped our world today. Special thanks go to Steve Arnold, who bravely waded into a story that appeared fully baked, nevertheless always willing to collaborate and put his creative stamp on the material.

And finally, I wish to express my heartfelt love for my father, Clifford Eging. A hero from the greatest generation who served during World War Two in the very lands encompassed by much of this work. Dad, this is for you.

May the silver horn echo in your dreams,
Michael Eging
2017

When Mike asked me early in 2014 to help him with *A Silver Horn Echoes: The Song of Roland*, I have to admit I was a little surprised. Granted we had been writing stories together since our school years and already had collaborated on several projects, most notably *Annwyn's Blood*, which we had just published, but also the screenplay *Feast of St. Nicholas* (which was then going into fundraising and soon to be in the rewriting phase), and we were just getting started on *Shades of Knight*, the second volume in the *Paladin of Shadows Chronicles*. But I thought we had a pretty full slate as it was with these three—and that wasn't even counting several other books and scripts that were, and still are, waiting in the wings and being kicked around in small ways as inspirations strike and otherwise are waiting their turn on the docket. But when the ideas get in your head, there's little to do but get them onto paper, and like Mike said, if we didn't do it, no one else would. I knew he had been at the *Roland* epic for a long time as a script, and getting the bug to turn it into a book was a logical next step for him, but as far as I knew, it was a project he was trying to get finished on his own once we had completed the final draft on *Feast*. But then one day there was a message in my in-box with a large file attached. He needed a fresh set of eyes, and he wanted mine.

To be truthful, I hadn't had a lifelong passion for Roland like Mike. Arthur was always my exemplar, but that's probably because many generations ago my ancestors lived in southern Wales from where many of *The Once and Future King*'s legends originate. I was only very vaguely cognizant of Roland's story. I had read one of Mike's earlier screenplay drafts, but that had been some years ago, so when I opened the file, I was essentially diving in cold.

But as I worked my way through the manuscript, I found myself also drawn into this foreign world of eighth-century France, as Mike had been many years before. There was much I saw there that brought Arthur to mind—the struggle to maintain one's life in the face of foreign aggression, the treachery of ambitious family members, the tragic battle at the end—but with an entirely different flavor. Arthur's fall ushered in the depths of the Dark Ages, while Roland lived at a time lit by the faintest, earliest rays of the Renaissance. Despite his sacrifice, one walked away from it left with a sense of hope that the prices we pay for the things we value most are not vanity.

I thoroughly enjoyed the work done on Roland, and I am deeply grateful for Mike including me in bringing it to print. I think it's a story for our time and hope that its message of brighter dawns after the darkest nights will continue to inspire a new generation of readers.

With gratitude to Divine Providence for stalwart companions and noble heroes,
Steve Arnold
2017

ABOUT THE AUTHORS

Michael Eging is coauthor of *Annwyn's Blood*, as well as a screenwriter and partner at Filibuster Filmworks. He and his wife have five children and live in Virginia.

Steve Arnold lives in Ohio with his wife and kids. Besides coauthoring *Annwyn's Blood*, he has collaborated on everything from short stories to screenplays for Filibuster Filmworks.

CPSIA information can be obtained
at www.ICGtesting.com
Printed in the USA
LVOW11s1457041217
558579LV00001B/101/P

9 781532 020209